THE COLLECTED WORKS OF
LAURENS VAN DER POST

THE HUNTER AND THE WHALE

THE HUNTER AND THE WHALE

A Story

Laurens van der Post

Chatto & Windus

LONDON

This edition published in 1986 by
Chatto & Windus Ltd
40 William IV Street
London WC2N 4DF

First edition published in 1967 by
The Hogarth Press Ltd

British Library Cataloguing in Publication Data
Van der Post, Laurens
The hunter and the whale: a story.
I. Title
823[F]   PR6043.A378
ISBN 0 7011 3043 1

Printed in Great Britain by
Redwood Burn Ltd
Trowbridge, Wiltshire

Dedicated to
INGARET GIFFARD

CONTENTS

"Y sobre el mar la sangre se extendia
Como un manto de purpura flotante."
From *El Arponero*
by S. A. LILLO

"And on the sea the blood spreads out
Like a crimson mantle floating . . ."

CHAPTER ONE

A Matter of Luck

THERE was no one in the *Kurt Hansen* when I boarded her
that Saturday evening for my fourth season as a spotter
with the Norwegian whaling fleet based on Port Natal. As the
ship which had held the record the past three years for the
greatest number of catches, she occupied the obvious place of
honour: immediately alongside the quay and at the head of the
line of twenty-four whalers, moored three abreast in the crowded
harbour. Like the rest of the little ships, she appeared in that
restricted berth even smaller than usual.

Her crow's-nest, which, when I occupied it on watch at sea,
always seemed to me to stick out so far above the water, now
barely cleared the stern rail of the purple Royal Mail steamer
which had called in at dawn that morning, in a hurry as usual, and
now, with fires undrawn in her boilers, was lying almost against
the *Kurt Hansen*'s nose, trembling with impatience to be off again.

At the other end of the line of whalers rose the black bow,
tall saffron masts and long black funnel, topped off with two
thin bands of red, of the *Clan MacGillivray*, a bulky turret-
ship, whose Blue Peter, hoisted limp in the still air, signified that
she was about to resume her beat for freight around the world.
Beyond both mail ship and tramp rose the funnels and masts
of many other vessels, their flags flapping like household dusters
on the sky-line, and all anointed and shining with the yellow
of the sinking sun. As I knew, there was not a single hull in
this great concourse of shipping that did not exceed the combined tonnage of the fleet to which the *Kurt Hansen* belonged.
Indeed one could easily have had the impression of pigmies
huddled together for protection in the world of giants, were it
not for the way the whalers turned up their noses at the glittering pinnacles of glass and painted steel that surrounded them.
This air of self-assurance if not impudence seemed to me most

A*

marked in the *Kurt Hansen*, perhaps because after three seasons in her my senses were not free of bias.

For me the extraordinary thing about those remarkable little ships was that ultimately no two of them were alike. Built by the same people in the same yard to the same design, they were technically not just sister ships but twelve identical pairs of identical twins whose nurses, at sea, could never tell them apart without referring to the names inscribed on their sterns. Yet for us who sailed in them, there was always something, an oddity of mast, cat's-cradle of rigging, set of wheel house, mounting of harpoon gun, grip on water, or just subtle departure in general line which distinguished one ship from the others.

These differences, of course, manifested themselves also in their behaviour at sea, and I never ceased to marvel how members of the same united brood could differ so much in their performance. One would excel at pert answers to her helm, another rejoice in the roughest of storms, another make light of towing the heaviest of catches, and yet another out-distance all in the vital matter of sprinting from the drifting position with her engines stopped to full speed ahead where a vanished whale had suddenly re-appeared in an unpredicted quarter of the ocean. Or, to return to the ship which mattered most to me, to combine so many refinements of these qualities as to become the greatest all-rounder in the fleet.

I know there are people who, lacking direct experience of these ships, try to explain away these differences as consequences not of the individuality of ships themselves but of variations in the capacity of the crews who man them and, above all, the quality of the Captains who command them. Of course, no one could have served in these ships for long, particularly not in the *Kurt Hansen*, without appreciating the very great importance of the human element in these matters, but in the end the skill and devotion of sailors only mitigated and did not abolish the influence of the difficulties of which I have spoken. I sensed that there was only one element that could over-ride even the most formidable combinations of these differences, technical skills and human qualities, and that was the infinitely mysterious matter of luck.

A MATTER OF LUCK

Before I joined the *Kurt Hansen* for the first time as a boy of fourteen on long vacation from school up-country, I had never given this question of luck a thought. Since then we had rarely returned to land a catch at the slipway for the factory on shore without my respect for this awesome phenomenon being greatly enhanced. Indeed, it would have comforted my imagination even in those comparatively care-free days of my boyhood if I could have discovered some law which was in charge of the workings of luck in life and circumstance on earth, some calculation why, for instance, one ship and set of men should have so much of it, and others so little. It would have helped if I could have believed fully that luck could be earned and that we all, ships, men and stars, got the luck we deserved. But I soon discovered that this was only partially true and that, however wise it was to do all one could to draw luck one's own way, fortune was no mere extension of a system of human ethics, however exalted, nor just an instrument of some discernible principle of promoting life by injecting incentive of good and deterrents of bad into its processes. Where it appeared one day to coincide completely with the deserts of the recipients, the very next day it would shower good fortune on others who one would have thought utterly unworthy of such bounty.

We had, for example, one ship in our fleet which had been notoriously unlucky ever since the day of her launching fifteen years before. I am deliberately not mentioning her by name because of the belief held by all members of the *Kurt Hansen*'s crew that to do so would bring down on ourselves some of the unfortunate ship's capacity for mis-timing and mishap. I know that this will be dismissed as ridiculous superstition by most people on shore, where life in its metropolitan context wears such a plausible air of logic and security that they overlook what a fundamentally brief, brittle and insecure business it is, rather as persons who, shutting out the night by drawing the curtains and lighting a lamp in their locked rooms, no longer remember how great is the darkness and how remote the pin-prick of stars outside. But those of us who encounter life beyond the fortifications of towns and civilization, who still climb

mountains and experience their fall of cliff and avalanche, who till the land and endure the inconstancies of rain and harvest or sail the seas to hunt for whales, enter an uncircumscribed area of existence where all our brightest knowledge and deepest experience often fail and what is despised as foolish superstition becomes the best available answer to the onslaught of the great unknown in the mind and life of man.

Certainly the most successful whalers I had met in my short time at sea were those who combined a regard for efficiency and the disciplines of their calling with an almost religious observation of the rules prescribed by superstitions born long before their own day. Even my own Captain, who tended to be an exception in this regard and whose crew despite his great success and undoubted skill were worried by a suspicion of flippancy, if not cynicism, in his attitude towards their own deeply entrenched superstitiousness, would never let the name of this particular unlucky ship pass his lips. When he was forced to do so, I noticed that he never failed to spit after its utterance with the same lack of inhibition and no doubt the same instinctive purpose as the Amangtakwena, the Bantu people among whom we lived up-country who, whenever they caught the stink of a dead animal rotting on the veld, spat vigorously, convinced that thereby they ejected the spirit of evil which death symbolized and which had just tried to enter their person through their nostrils.

Now this unmentionable and unfortunate ship in the fleet could never do anything right. Some of the best crews and Captains had been assigned to her and had all been defeated in their turn, not one particular combination of men serving more than a couple of seasons in her. The representative of the owners, who lived in great luxury in a large house on the fashionable heights overlooking the city and bay of Port Natal and whom one would have thought safely padded against the pricks of superstition, had been so wounded by the ship's continued misfortune that he had already sanctioned three changes of her name because some of his more experienced skippers held that he might alter her luck thereby. Luck, however, is nothing if not a seaman too, and needed no names to tell one

ship from the others. For reasons strictly its own, it went on resolutely avoiding the wretched little ship. All in all, everything that was technically and humanly possible was tried to obtain better terms from fate for her, but up to this moment without marked effect.

I do not know whether they relished it, but in their plight, the ship and her changing crews should have had one great consolation: they were exceedingly popular in the fleet. One reason, of course, was that everybody felt free to be sorry for them and all the better in themselves for indulging their sense of commiseration. Another was that no one could possibly envy them as they envied the *Kurt Hansen*.

Just as the seasons behind me had been my kindergarten in the education of luck, so they were primary lessons for me in the radio-active fall-out of envy in the condition of men and their relationships. Our sister whalers may not have actually hated us, but there was not one among them, I am certain, who did not long for the *Kurt Hansen* to be reduced to their ranks with the same ration of success as they themselves received from the fates. It was as if in this regard they looked on luck as some kind of black marketeer of providence, and the *Kurt Hansen* its favourite spiv; whereas they valued our unfortunate sister ship as a kind of lightning conductor which would prevent the cumulative electricity of misfortune from being discharged through any single one of them. While this ship was there with them and continued to be so unlucky, they somehow assumed their own misfortune could never be too great.

And so I could go on multiplying examples, but I think this is enough to suggest how complex and pervasive this influence was in our minds and life at sea. I myself found some comfort in one thing only; a growing suspicion that luck, however much appearances were against it, was not capricious. I had a feeling that if we knew all now, in the beginning as at the end, we might see it woven into a surpassing pattern, an unbroken thread of such a multi-coloured brightness that we would find it difficult to forgive the limitations and blur of perishable senses which seemed to us so final and authoritative. I wondered more and more whether there could not be some vital

link between good and bad luck. Perhaps the only thing to do
was to trust one's bad as much as one's good fortune. Could
not what seemed to be so inexplicably bad today turn out years
later to have been a stroke of good fortune and both be part
of a meaningful whole amounting to something which was
greater even than the sum of their parts?

In fact I found it of help to admonish my own impatient
thinking by adapting a famous New Testament observation
and contemplating the probability that the children of this
world might well be luckier in their own generation than the
children of the light. Perhaps this is what we all unconsciously
implied when we said that so and so or such and such were
"lucky devils". Who, after all, had ever spoken of "lucky
angels"? The matter, I felt, could not be disposed of on all levels
until one had faced also the awful question: "Who was the
more fortunate, Barabbas or Christ?"

Now I have discussed all these differences and particularly
this matter of luck at such length because suddenly they were
very much on my mind that Saturday evening. I had no sooner
done with the water policeman on duty at the gates to the
docks and picked out the *Kurt Hansen* than these considerations
assailed me.

All these differences between our whalers that I have mentioned were somehow expressed in the paintwork of each ship.
It was as if the experience of each, though vanished behind
them, had left fingerprints in the varying patches of paint applied to repair the damage which sea, weather and time had
inflicted on them. At least so it had always struck me until this
particular evening when, for no known reason, at my first
glimpse of them in the last light of the sun, I seemed to be looking not at sets of fingerprints but into the hand of providence
itself. Proud, perhaps self-assured even to the point of arrogance
so tempting to the small, as the *Kurt Hansen* lay there, my delight at seeing her again was spoilt by an involuntary apprehension, and the valedictory light of the dying winter's day
seemed to enfold her like a mantle of fate. My uneasiness was
increased when next I hailed her and got no answer.

I quickly boarded her, opened the door at the head of the

14

companion-way leading down into the forecastle where someone on duty was most likely to be, called out loudly "Anyone
aboard?" but got no reply.

I tried the door to the saloon next with the same result. This
was so unusual, even for ships as notoriously informal as whalers,
that the more I thought on it, the more uncomfortable I became. We may never have considered it necessary to go to the
lengths of the great ships all around us who set continuous
watches night and day on their gangways but, as far as I knew,
it had always been a rule to have at least one man always on
duty in ships lying alongside the quay as was the *Kurt Hansen*.
However, telling myself not to be too fanciful and that a perfectly simple explanation for it all soon would be available, I
took my gear down into the saloon.

The air in this small triangular compartment was heavy
with the smell of the cigarillos the Captain incessantly smoked.
He anyway could not have been gone long. In fact a glass, which
I was certain had been emptied not long before, of a good measure of schnapps still stood by his place at the head of the small
table as if he had left in too great a hurry to put it away. Wide
open beside the glass lay the ship's big black Norwegian Bible.
This was even more astonishing.

The Captain, although a man of deep feelings, was not an
overtly religious person. In fact on Sunday, when most of his
colleagues and their crews were attending evening service at
the small Norwegian church close by the harbour gates, he
preferred to call on the owner's representative where after a
day of tennis there was always a lively assembly of people and
a great deal to drink. Now not one of the least of odd things
about it all was that the Bible was open at the 38th chapter of
the Book of Job. Since Job is perhaps the greatest text-book
available to any student of luck, I need not stress how the
sight of it stimulated the mood I had brought on board with
me.

I noticed that the Captain had underlined the sixteenth and
seventeenth verses, but as I read no Norwegian it was not
until I looked it up in the Authorized Version a week later that
I got its drift. I found then it consisted of some of those terrible

rhetorical questions that answer themselves only too convincingly and which the Almighty seemed to have used deliberately to increase the temptations of doubt and the feelings of helplessness in the heart of his good and faithful servant Job sitting there on his ash-heap already stricken so unfairly by any earthly measure of justice. "Hast thou entered into the springs of the sea?" Jehovah had thundered at Job, as if the answer were not self-evident. "Or hast thou walked in search of the depth? Have the gates of death been opened unto thee? Or hast thou seen the doors of the shadow of death?"

What on land or sea could have set the Captain reading Job all of a sudden? And why mark these particular lines which, considering the moment of the occasion, were so uncalled for in character? I turned over the pages and found the first sentence of the first verse of the 31st chapter similarly underlined. My immediate thought was that the Captain's reading had been as extensive as it had been out of character. Then I had no means of telling that it was this sentence which had fired his interest and made him probe backwards into this disturbing book. It was, of course, the famous question: "Canst thou draw out Leviathan with an hook?" I was not surprised to learn later that he had answered both the book and the man of whose visit there was at this time no sign with a triumphant: "A thousand times, yes," since by nature our Captain specialized in answers rather than questions.

I know that there are great scholars today who translate the original Aramaic word in this sentence not as "Leviathan" but as "crocodile". I do not think, however, that this is of any importance at all because all of us concerned in this story took "Leviathan" to stand for whale and "hook" for harpoon, and this fact, combined with its numerous references and profound feeling for the sea, drew me, for one, closer to that enigmatic Book.

As for myself at that moment my own questions had no answers but there did occur to me suddenly several remarks I had constantly overheard in the fleet which may have had some submerged connection with the matter since they occurred unbidden to me. "*That* Larsen's a lucky devil, he *sure*

16

is." Or another as common, but perhaps more disturbing was: "Larsen pushes his luck very hard and one of these days he is going to push it too far." And yet another uttered by the oldest skipper in the fleet at a farewell party given to him on his retirement by the owner's representative: "I have learnt not to call any sailor lucky until the end of his days at sea. Larsen has had three lucky seasons, the third luckiest of all. And third time lucky, we say. But I would not assume he can do it again. If he does . . ." The old sailor had shrugged his shoulders.

Finally, there was the remark that perhaps weighed most with me and was often reiterated by the ship's cook. He was an experienced sailor and had also all the instincts of a philosopher. He knew the seas from the black lava cliffs of Iceland to the white Antarctic fringe of the South Atlantic, and was perhaps the severest critic of the Captain. I had heard him say over and over again: "We take our luck in this ship too much for granted and no good will come of it in the end." And by "this ship" we knew, of course, that this proved and faithful servant of the sea really meant the Captain. Was not the fact that the ship had been left unguarded some evidence of the truth of the cook's observation?

I stood there with all this going through my mind, while my eyes looked over the tiny saloon, the tablecloth of a faded yellow plush with its fringe of tassels like mimosa blossom; the covers on the two built-in benches; the curtains which served as a door over the entrance to the Captain's cabin; and the small glass case, suspended in mid-air on brackets in the corner, which held the ship's manuals, Lloyd's register of shipping, pilot books and three fat manuals bound in brown morocco that looked like family portrait albums but were Larsen's "game books", since they contained the entries made in his sprawling hand, of all his catches, their time, place, duration of struggle at the end of the harpoon, their tonnage and finally the bonus paid on them by the owners to his ships. I might have been standing in a respectable Victorian deep-sea fisherman's parlour, and not the saloon of a modern whaler. Everything was as I had seen it last a year before, except for some things slightly out of position, like the dirty glass on the table, the

open Bible, and above it the dark gap it had left in the line of erect books on the shelf, as conspicuous as the space in a line of Guardsmen made by a soldier fallen out in a faint with the heat and stress of a Royal parade.

Were these inanimate things out of position signs that the *Kurt Hansen* had moved out of orbit, too? At seventeen, as I then was, a year feels far longer than it does at three score years and ten, and this year now became so crowded with possibilities that my imagination could readily conceive it long enough to have affected a radical alteration in any scheme of things. Life, after all, is nothing if not movement and change without cease, and it was change and movement that then seemed to give tongue in the long cello sound drawn from the *Kurt Hansen*'s mooring-ropes by the rise and fall of a sea which is never quite still, not even in so locked and so great a harbour. Also, whenever a lift of water more powerful than the rest gripped the little ship there was a squeak that came from the metal deep within her like that of a mouse suddenly gathered between the paws of a cat. I was half-inclined to climb back up the steep companion-way on deck in order to draw reassurance from the orderly and calm week-end scene outside in Port Natal. But the feeling seemed so irrelevant that I dismissed it.

I went through the plush curtains into the Captain's cabin. There were two bunks in it, and quickly I stowed my gear in the mahogany drawers underneath the one which had been allotted to me three years before. This unusual privilege was originally conferred on me because I was not a regular member of the crew. This ship, like all the rest, was manned largely by Norwegians brought out specially each year from Norway for the short whaling season in South African waters. One of the exceptions to this was our Zulu stoker 'Mlangeni, who had been with the fleet for many years. I was another exception, of course, and to the end remained the only amateur and outsider among them. In the tight establishment laid down for the little ships there was no room for someone exclusively occupied with the task of spotting whales, which was my task. In all the other ships, the deck hands each had their

turn of duty in the crow's nest to perform. The *Kurt Hansen* was the first and may well have been the last to depart from this procedure.

It all came about in a way which is worth recalling if only for the light it throws on our Captain's character.

CHAPTER TWO

Captain

THREE years before the opening of this story one of my school friends, Eric Watson, had brought me home with him for our long winter vacation, which coincided almost to a day with the whaling season. He was the son of the local representative of the whaling concern, Andrew Watson, who was also one of its main shareholders. We had hardly settled in for our holiday when at my urging, for I gathered he had done it before and did not like it over much for reasons that will soon be plain, he got permission from his father for us to spend some time with the whaling fleet. His father promised at once to speak to his most trusted captain, a man nearing retirement, the very next time his ship came into port. This experienced sailor, he thought, would be the ideal person to take charge of two high-spirited boys at sea. Yet in the end it was not this worthy man who was destined to take us whaling. On the Sunday evening after our arrival on holiday vacation when my host proposed arranging the matter with him, the captain had been unexpectedly detained in his ship. He arrived at the party too late for the purpose for which he had been invited.

However, Thor Larsen, to give our Captain his full name, was, of course, the first of the special guests to arrive. I say "of course", because I was to discover that he tended to be the first to arrive as well as the last to leave whether it was a matter of drinking with the owner's representative or quitting the whaling grounds because of a mounting gale.

I was still on the tennis court that Sunday when Thor Larsen joined the players sitting out, relaxed in their Madeira chairs on the lawn above, and watching the game.

It was almost as if time had recognized the significance of the occasion for me and used the winter evening to underline the moment. The scene, in fact, presented itself to me rather

like some painting by a "primitive", an African Douanier
Rousseau, wherein the detail was minutely charged with aboriginal wonder, and the encompassing vision, despite the apparent
sophistication of the matter, was innocent like that of man's
in the Garden before the Fall. The great spathodia trees around
the huge house, so mysterious in their immunity to winter,
presented a second manifestation of flower like a flicker of
pentecostal fire against the bright blue sky.

There was just enough of a shiver in the evening air to set
their leaves and petals trembling as if indeed some transcendental spirit were walking their perennial green. Beyond their
dark leaves and between their great trunks, I snatched at
glimpses of the ample house, first the outline of the old tiled
roof with an edge of gold to it from the westering sun and then,
since the building faced east, the white of the smooth walls
below it, ashen with shadow. As a result, the glass of the windows was secret and without lustre and the wide-open doorway
was re-sealed like a Nigerian tomb with the ebony of averted
light.

Below the broad terrace right to the edge of the tennis court
spread a lawn of Zulu grass in shrill barbaric green, each blade
keen as the head of an assegai. There, in the centre of a long
crescent of Madeira chairs, their wicker glowing with the sun
spilling over the leaves of the trees behind them, stood a long
table under a dazzling white cloth covered with crystal bowls,
cut-glass tumblers and decanters, all quick with light.

Beside the table stood the tall Zulu butler. When not serving
one of the flannelled men in the chairs, he stood massively
still as if fixed in one position by a great weight of undeclared
spirit within. He wore a long white coat of starched drill that
fell to his knees. From one shoulder a wide band of Prussian
blue velvet crossed his broad front to be gathered on his hip
into a long tassel of gold. The upper part of him looked splen-
didly ambassadorial, as if the great legendary African kingdom
of Monomotapo, which the valiant Portuguese discoverers who
had given the land its name had sought for so long in vain,
were indeed a reality and he its plenipotentiary. But when
one's eyes followed the stiff trousers beneath the coat down to

the ankles the impression was cancelled, for the man's broad feet were bare.

This may sound a small thing but the fact remains that it has persistently dogged me all my life, demanding evaluation from my imagination. All I knew as a boy was that where Europeans were in control this was the implacable custom not only in Port Natal but all over Africa. I knew several instances of white employers who had dismissed black domestic servants after years in their employ because they suddenly insisted on wearing shoes; and this was considered an outrage.

Today, perhaps, I can see further. Understandably, we like to think of ourselves as creatures of pure reason. But as I grow older I am struck by the power of something that is beyond reason and conduct and utterly non-rational in nature and intent. It appears that we are all subject to some dark symbolism that imposes on us patterns of behaviour which have to be obeyed. We can reject them in the light of reason and relieve them and ourselves of some of their and our own darkness in the process; but we cannot obliterate them. If they cannot have their way with us squarely and fairly, then they will do so violently and opaquely.

Today, this matter of the butler's bare feet is to me one clear image, among a host of others, of behaviour that we were darkly compelled to follow in Africa without really knowing what we were doing. The bare feet were, perhaps, a mark of the extent to which we exceeded our humanity in Africa and unwittingly assumed the role of gods, for certain forms of worship do demand that men remove their foot-wear before entering the temples. Anyhow, we are only now beginning to encounter, like the first faint ripples of a converging typhoon, the consequences of the equinoxial tensions we have set up both in the Africans and ourselves.

I suppose it is natural to tend to look towards established power, the commanding heights, the far horizons and the stars set in their Galileonian courses, for prescriptions of fate. But I think now that it is in the small and uncared for grains around our feet that the forces of change grow great and terrible.

That evening, I realized with the shock of hindsight that the

Zulu butler stood there not only as an image of some fateful contradiction in ourselves, but also as a warning predicting a dangerous decline invisible ahead. At the same time I found his incongruous state of apparel merely rather absurd and endearing. Whenever I had a chance to observe him it merely made me smile to see him standing there thus, looking so seriously over the men sprawled in the yellow chairs, their faces and necks pink with blood-pressure and exertion. And he continued to look with the utmost gravity out over the tennis court and the red roofs of the houses set in colonial fashion, in wide gardens full of native trees, their leaves a dark pagan green, lit here and there only by that quick spathodia flicker of which I have spoken, out over to the aspiring city, its glass glittering with the vivid sunset colour and beyond to the shining harbour and the blue Indian ocean as if at any moment there, on the faultless rim of the graphic winter's evening, would come a ship charged with a cargo of overwhelming import to him.

It was the first time I myself had ever seen the sea and I felt that perhaps just watching it could be a whole-time occupation. There was the great harbour, its open water shining like a speckled old mirror, framed in the archaic gilt of the sun. It was full of ships of all kinds, few of them flying the same flags or painted the same brilliant colours. There was something miraculous about having the ships themselves directly under my eyes to give living fullness to the paintings in museums and illustrations in books that I had seen. A ship which had just crossed the bar at the harbour mouth was swinging round north towards Mozambique. As she completed the movement she lay broadside on to us. Gathering way on her course, the muscular swell of the Indian Ocean, which here is never lean or feeble as it can be in other oceans, gripped her and pushed her slowly far over to her side. She went gracefully to starboard as if willing to be tumbled on her back, then righted herself and, coming back to give her port shoulder a turn too, caught the sun full on the windows of her bridge and wheelhouse to flash like a heliograph back to the land. I did not know her name or her destination but the flash was like a signal intended especially for me.

I turned my back on the sea to notice the butler giving me an oddly comradely look, as if he had read my reactions. That did not surprise me. The life that the black people of Africa led with us, who seldom spoke their language or knew their ways, forced them to rely on their intuitions and sharpened them to an extraordinary degree. Their awareness of what we were as human beings often was more accurate than our own judgements of one another despite our advantages of a common language and easy contacts. Or are these perhaps not advantages after all? Anyway it was not the first time that I had had to go to the rag-and-tatter Africans of my childhood to re-learn the importance of the look in the human eye. I got to know the butler better later but on this Sunday evening, though slightly astonished by the intensity of his regard, I was strangely pleased when he raised his hand above his shoulder to salute me and followed it up with a smile.

Presently I was on the court myself. My partner and I became hotly engaged; at last the match stood at 12–11 in our favour. The score was match point to our advantage when one of our opponents smashed a short lob from my partner at an acute angle down into my half of the court. Somehow I had anticipated his stroke, got to the ball and, as often happens when I have no time for deliberation, by sheer instinct I sent back a winner, a fast low back-hand stroke driving the ball just out of reach of the man at the net. For a moment it looked as if it were going out but a spurt of white chalk showed that I had just managed to find the far corner of the court.

The watchers in the chairs, who had stopped talking and followed the last two games closely, called out, "Well done, you two, well done!" and then immediately resumed talking and drinking, with the exception of one man, the only one of them not in flannels.

Rather apart, in a chair at the extreme left of the group, he went on clapping, calling out again and again in a loud voice: "Bravo! Bravo!" Indeed he kept it up so long that some of the spectators turned to stare at him.

If the man noticed it, he did not show it. Yet I doubt whether he did. Knowing him as I did afterwards, I do not think it

would ever have occurred to him that anybody would regard him as an inferior. Instead of returning their quick sharp regard, he kept his eyes on me even when he stopped applauding.

I had to walk close by his chair thereafter in order to reach my own, and as I did not know him and was in any case only a boy, would not have dreamt of speaking to him first. But it was he who stopped me and spoke.

Up to then I had always assumed that Scandinavians, particularly Norwegians, were all tall, fair and blue-eyed. Thor Larsen, for it was he, was the first of the exceptions I have since encountered. He did not stand, I believe, a fraction more than five foot seven inches in his shoes. He was broad-shouldered, unusually long-bodied, long-armed with a powerful chest, shortish neck and a face oddly Mongolian except that his slightly slanted eyes in the broad head above the high cheek bones and underneath black eyebrows and black hair were an intense and vivid grey. Yet there was nothing grey about the impression he made on me.

He struck me at once as a person strangely dark, like the midnight blue of the sea under a cloudless sky. It was a blackness, moreover, that owed nothing to colour of hair or skin. Thor Larsen's darkness was personal and part perhaps of his national character, for I have come to suspect that even the fairest of Scandinavians contain something of the darkness of their long Arctic winter in their spirit. Ibsen, Strindberg and even the fairy tales of Hans Andersen are charged for me with a frightening element of darkness. What light there is in them is, as it were, that of a sun low on the horizon, a native midnight sun of their spirit. But in Larsen's case it struck me there was a factor of choice—as if he turned to darkness freely as the element in which his self-assured spirit could shine to the greatest advantage.

As I walked past him, one broad hand left the empty glass he had been clasping in both, his long arm darted out and he seized mine in a firm grip.

"You play good, very good, not?" He addressed me in a deep voice, rasping and uninitiated in the subtleties of doubt.

His action was so unsuspected that I was startled by it, blushing at the ardent note of his praise.

25

Looking briefly into his intense eyes and down on a face that was marked almost as if by smallpox with long exposure to extremes of weather, I said diffidently: "Thanks. We were rather lucky to win."

"Nonsense!" he answered decisively. "You play good; your eye good, very good. Your reflexes quick, not?" Despite the clumsy accent and idiom, the phrases were fired rapidly at me. He paused briefly and then, showing that though English was a foreign language to him his ear was as ready as his tongue, he asked: "You're not English, not?"

"No," I said. "My people are Boers. I come from far up-country."

"Ha! A-ha! A Boer, a young Boer!"

Pronouncing "Boer" as "Bo-herr", he uttered the word as though it explained everything.

His father, he went on to say at some length, had fought for the Boers in the Boer War with a brigade of Scandinavian volunteers who had come out to help us against Milner's English, and his father had told him "Bo-herr" shot "damn much better" than anybody in the world.

"You too shoot good, not?" he concluded. "I think so, that's why you play tennis so good! Not?"

I was unable to admit that I did shoot rather well and that indeed I had quite a reputation as a quick and unusually accurate long-distance shot. I felt so embarrassed to be singled out and discussed so loudly in such a personal manner in front of people I had only just met that I tried to move on.

However, he held on to my arm and commanded: "I want to talk with you. You fetch a chair and you sit here!"

Much as I disliked the prospect, I could not refuse without being rude. I nodded, laid my racket on the grass by his chair and went to find one of my own.

Behind me I heard him shout "Jack!" and I saw the Zulu butler's monumental pose vanish into immediate action. Obviously knowing the precise import of the shout, he scooped up a tray with a decanter of gin and angustura on it, and carried it with long strides of massive grace to Larsen.

Chair in hand and thirsty myself, I went to wait at the table

for the butler's return. He was, as I had noticed since my arrival two days before, much older than he had appeared at a superficial glance. I watched him shake some drops of angustura into Larsen's glass, twirl it expertly round in his fingers and, like a born connoisseur, hold it up against the sunset to see that the bitters were spread evenly all over the glass. In that light his face was aubergine, the stained glass a brilliant transparent pink, and the half tumbler of gin he poured out flashed like melted platinum.

When he returned to the table, as this was the first moment I had had alone with him, I said to him in polite Sindakwena, the language of the Amangtakwena of Umangoni on whose frontiers we lived, "I see you, oh! my father: I see you."

His face glowed with pleasure, and from deep down, more from his stomach than his throat, he exclaimed "Auck! I greet you, 'Nkosan. Little Prince, I greet you."

"They call you Jack here," I went on, warmed by so chivalrous a greeting. "But what do they call you in your father's house?"

Well-intentioned as my host was, I suspected he would not have bothered to enquire after his butler's native name. Personal names among the Zulu are either so long or so difficult for European tongues that it had become a colonial habit to inflict on African servants simple European names like "Jack". My suspicion was confirmed when I noticed what warmth the question brought to the butler's eyes.

"My father has long since left me his kraals," he said, using the same idiom the Amangtakwena did to indicate that his father was dead. "But in my father's house I was called Nkomidhl'ilale."

Smiling to myself at the thought of what my host would have made of such a name, I took to it with relish. It meant literally "A steer that eats and lies down" and was, I knew, clearly intended to convey that he came of a family of substance and had been born into a state of plenty. I had all along assumed from the way he spoke that among his own people he must be a person of importance, for among them the three main marks of the gentleman were to be well-spoken, as he was,

27

fearless and intelligent. His name set assumption beyond doubt for me.

"Would you, Nkomi-dhl'ilale, please give me a glass of grinadella juice?" I asked.

"Auck!" he exclaimed once more with satisfaction, poured out a tumbler full to over-flowing of the thick green-yellow juice of the purple passion fruit of Africa, put it on a silver salver and handed it to me instead of giving me the glass direct.

"Auck!" he muttered, shaking his head and, putting the salver down, covered his mouth with his hands to laugh into them with happy surprise.

I wish I could convey how much that "Auck!" meant to me. Zulus have a whole range of exclamations which, like "Auck", are a direct musical abstraction of subtle shades of feeling and say, with one chord, what several sentences could not express.

The "Auck!" still alive in my ears, I was turning to join Thor Larsen when he whispered: "'Nkosan! 'Nkosan!"

"Yes, Nkomi-dhl'ilale," I responded, standing still and thinking I detected a note of urgency in his voice.

He did not reply at once and appeared to be pondering what to say. Finally he said slowly: "You are going back to the man whose place is on the great water?"

"Yes. Why?" I asked, receiving confirmation of what I had already assumed, namely that Larsen had something to do with whaling.

"He has the thirst of a chief of chiefs," the Zulu replied. After another pause to let this information bring its effect, he added: "And 'Nkosan, he has the eyes of an 'Nyanga—a witch-doctor."

His tone now indeed was urgent. Yet I felt he was not warning me so much as drawing my attention to facts of importance that he feared I might miss out of lack of experience. "It would be as well, 'Nkosan," he concluded, his tone low with the gravity of his exhortation, "not to forget to spit three times on leaving his presence."

I could not help smiling inwardly at the effect spitting even once would have had on that respectable colonial company. At the same time I was greatly touched that he should feel so

protective towards me. Thanking him for his advice, I felt bound to ask: "You do not like the man whose place is on the water?"

"Oh, no, 'Nkosan! It is not that," he remonstrated. "He is a chief among men, but he is a house visited by strange spirits."

I would have liked to have gone on talking to him. It was odd how much more at home I felt with him than the rest of the company, but Larsen was clearly getting more and more impatient for my return. The last thing I wanted just then was to be made conspicuous again by him bawling at me. I joined him not a moment too soon.

I had barely reached for my chair before he presented his first question like a pistol at my head.

"What did that black Jack say to you?"

The tone was suspicious, as if he had an inkling we had been discussing him. It was my first intimation of many that he possessed unusually sensitive antennae of spirit to reinforce his considerable powers of observation.

"I was asking him about his name in Zulu and so on."

"All that time just asking about a name!" The tone now was not suspicious so much as provisional and suspended between a statement and a question.

"It was a long name that needed explanation," I said.

"And what was this name?" he asked.

I told him, describing in full my interpretation of the meaning of Nkomi-dhl'ilale.

In the process he was to my relief overcome by a genuine interest. When I finished, he slapped his knee with satisfaction and exclaimed: "Just like the Vikings. Might be a good old Viking name almost, not!"

This apparently was a deeply entrenched scale of comparison of his for, noticing my surprise at the comment, he commanded me: "You look at the ricksha-boys, young Boher; they have horns on the head just like old Viking warriors. These peoples all the times make me think of Vikings even when I know not what for."

I knew then something of what he meant. I had already encountered the ricksha-pullers of Port Natal, those whom he

called "boys" in the accepted colonial manner, though they
were all grown men and many of them grey. In fact one could
not walk anywhere in Port Natal without numbers of these
black men in their colourful dress importuning one for the
privilege of being allowed, even on days paralysed with heat,
for a few pennies to pull one in their vehicles along the burning
streets and up the steep sides of the flashing city. They all wore
a head-dress with great horns at the side, just like the Vikings
depicted in my illustrated histories at home.

The comparison reinforced the sense of wonder the peoples
of Africa had evoked from childhood in me, and some of my
reserve towards Larsen diminished accordingly. When he started
to draw me out about my home and our life up-country,
apparently relishing the smallest detail of what he extracted
from me, this reserve vanished almost entirely. His imagination
indeed seemed as excited by the interior of our great land, into
whose great purple lap the day was beginning to settle, as was
my own imagination by his sea.

There was, however, a bias in his questions which I did not
understand at all. He was unusually interested in shooting
game and put me through a catechism of the animals I had
shot, starting characteristically with the biggest and conducting the whole examination of it in short rasping sentences.

"You shot the elephant, not?"

As I nodded, he immediately snapped: "How many?"

"Four," I answered.

His grey eyes went greyer with the light of a quickened interest. His look, as it took in my youth and size and set them
against the constant dream of elephant he had in mind, came
as near as it could to showing respect.

"Buffalo?" he asked.

"Six," I said.

"Lion?"

"Seven."

"Leopard?"

"Three."

I was not aware of it but the tone of my voice must have
changed. He was on to it at once.

"You do not like the leopard, not?" It was a statement as much as a question.

"No, I do not like hunting leopard," I amended, since I loved their starry look and easy eurhythmic movement.

"Why not?"

"We think they are very dangerous animals."

"More so than the elephant?"

"Many of us think so, but all do not agree."

"Nor do I, I think. I, Thor Larsen, disagree," he remarked thumping his chest with four fingers of his left hand, and undeterred by the fact that he was speaking outside his experience. "I think elephant must be far more dangerous."

That "must", and the emphasis he put on it, should have told me something of how deeply his imagination was concerned with the physical greatness of things. But it passed me by, particularly as I knew experienced hunters who thought as he did. Besides, he gave me no pause for any reflection, so anxious was he to continue his catechism.

So we completed a rapid run through in these stark terms of shooting of all the categories of game known to me. He readily absorbed my brief descriptions of the animals he had not heard of before. At the end I thought he might like to hear something about our birds as well since we have perhaps the most wonderful of all in Africa—even for those with a taste in outsizes, like the ostrich, Goliath heron, lamb-snatcher and giant bustard. However he was not interested in winged things and cut me short, his mind back on the elephant with which he had started.

"Me too!" he exclaimed laughing as if it were a rare joke. "Me too, am a hunter of elephants. I hunt the elephants of the sea."

Up to that moment I had known only by deduction that he must be one of my host's captains. Now I knew precisely that he was a whaling man and, judging by his presence among the celebrities gathered on the lawn of the owner's representative, one of the foremost captains in the fleet.

"And you, have you ever hunted whales, my young Boher?" he asked when he'd stopped laughing.

I shook my head, words failing me at the excitement set off by his question.

"Would you like to hunt whales?" It was only technically a question, for I am sure he knew the answer.

"Gosh!" I exclaimed; and, finding tongue, told him in a rush how much I wanted to, adding that already my friend and I had made his father promise to ask an experienced old Captain of his, on arrival at the party, to take us whaling with him.

Larsen and I both looked around us as I spoke to see whether the Captain had turned up yet, but we saw only men in flannels drinking and talking.

Larsen gave me a look, then stood up abruptly and exclaimed: "Much better you come with me!"

Without waiting for my answer, he marched with an odd balancing step as if the lawn were a deck heaving underneath his feet, across to where our host was talking. That, and the view from behind of his compact body, powerful shoulders, long arms and short legs, imparted something anthropoidal to his movement. Even his clothes, his best suit of a thick navy blue serge, were jungle dark in that gathering of flannels of cream, club blazers, white scarves and silk kerchiefs.

"Boss!" He interrupted his host, his voice audible all over the broad lawn. "Boss! I take your two boys whaling, not?"

The owner's representative, Andrew Watson, looked up as if a carefully cultivated urbanity would fail him. For a long moment I feared he would give the stocky captain a curt "No". But helped by the mellowing influence of his own gin, he checked the irritation that was in him.

"Have a chair and join us for a drink while we talk about it."

He gave Larsen a perfunctory smile, while indicating a chair, and beckoned unnecessarily to his butler who was already picking up his tray to come to them.

What precisely passed between them I could not tell but it didn't last long.

Larsen had no sooner swallowed his gin than he left as abruptly as he had arrived.

"That's settled!" he announced with gruff satisfaction, waving his hand imperiously. "Next Sunday evening you come to my ship and I show you the hunting of whales."

I was beginning to thank him when he shook a thick sallow finger at me and stopped me short.

"But I do not show you the hunting of whales without payment!" he remarked.

Consternation and confusion in me then was great and must have shown on my face. I came of a poor nation who seldom had enough money. We were rich in land. My own family owned hundreds of thousands of acres, thousands of sheep, much cattle and many horses. We never lacked food but we were a thousand miles from our nearest markets on the coast and often the rail charges were greater than the price fetched by our produce. Ready money, as our wool-brokers with unconscious irony called it, for I have never known a more unready substance, was difficult to come by. I had barely been able to raise my fare for my holiday by the sea. I could not possibly afford to pay Larsen anything.

Noticing my dismay, he reassured me at once: "Yes, you too must pay. Something for nothing is no good, not? For every whale I show you, you pay me one day, by showing me elephant. Next Sunday we open a whale–elephant account book, not? And no worry, I give you plenty credit."

He seized my arm in his broad hand, squeezed it, and a look came to his eye which, remembering the butler's description of it, might have been that of a sorcerer acknowledging a chosen apprentice, while he laughed as if it were all sheer fun. But I knew already in my blood and bones that he was being more serious than he had been over anything that had passed between us since we met.

In a state of wild excitement I excused myself and rushed to Eric with the news. He said in a voice that subdued me at once: "I don't think father would have liked that much."

"Why not?" I asked.

"He would have preferred us to go with his favourite captain. Besides, he's never told me, but I have a feeling, that he, that they all, find your friend Larsen a bit too strange for their liking."

He said all this in a way that made me feel responsible and I stammered: "Oh, I—I'm sorry."

B   33

"Oh, don't worry. You couldn't help it. After all, father could have said 'no' if he'd wanted to," he answered, more out of desire to reassure than out of conviction.

Fortunately I was too young and enthusiastic to let this cloud the prospect before us for long. Yet from that moment my host's attitude to me underwent a subtle change. The temperature and scale of the warm and expansive welcome with which he had received me contracted. It was, I think, a slight variation of the mechanism in the human spirit which in its extreme form once made an oriental potentate cut off the head of the messenger who had brought him bad news. It is as if none of us can quite rid our natures of the assumption that anyone involved in circumstances not to our liking cannot be wholly innocent himself. And our natures may be partially right. What we are in ourselves may well attract out of the infinite range of possibilities at the disposal of chance and circumstance those that correspond closest to it, just as a magnet will extract only one set of metals from among all other elements. Just as there are human beings who can communicate grave diseases to others by possessing it, although in a degree so small that they never succumb to it themselves, may there not also be human carriers in this matter of mischance?

However, in due course, we did go to sea with Thor Larsen, and so began the pattern of events with which I am concerned.

CHAPTER THREE

Port and People

O N   T H E   Sunday that we were to join the *Kurt Hansen* I decided to walk down early to the harbour three miles away. Eric was to follow later with our gear in one of his father's cars.

It was an evening just as beautiful as the Sunday that preceded it but for me even more exciting. It was the custom in the fashionable homes of Port Natal to release most of their Zulu servants from duty on Sunday afternoons, and they would all with rare exceptions make for the open spaces near the beaches where they congregated in hundreds to amuse themselves by talking, dancing, singing and playing their musical instruments.

On this particular evening there was an urgent feeling of release given out by the many black servants that I encountered on the steep slopes of the long hill above Port Natal, all going down towards the sea. I was young, and the history between us all was young, so there was still enough of the innocence of youth abroad to impart a brilliance to the moment.

The excitement for me was heightened by the music which accompanied me down the hill. Every black man walking the streets with me appeared to be a musician, some playing guitars slung minstrel-wise over their shoulders, others mouth-organs, or just modest Jew's harps. All were strumming away in the quiet air like the copper of telegraph wires in the wind, carrying from one man to another the urgent call to hasten from the heights to the meeting down by the sea.

Even I, though a young pale face, felt myself utterly belonging to it all. Every now and then the music was overwhelmed by outbursts of bells tolling in the towers of the great cathedral in the European quarter of the city. I do not know why, but as a young lad church bells always alarmed me a little. They seemed to speak mainly the language of climax, crisis and

challenge, and no matter how gay their peals, they always seemed to hold a profound warning in their summons. This evening was no exception. The cathedral bells seemed to flutter out wildly into the air as if the carved heraldic birds on their belfries had themselves been startled into taking wing to beat back this invasion of bright pagan music from the province of their holy church. Yet the moment the sound of bells returned to roost in the tall cathedral towers, then instantly, more vivid than ever, the gay, unrepentant native music swarmed in the vacated silences like fireflies in the hedges of the night.

The dress of these musicians too was as bright as their music. The Africans, when free to be themselves, dress for adornment with unashamed passion. There was one tall guitar player who impressed me in particular. He overtook me with a stride of incredible length and ease to pass me on the other side of the street. He had on a long white dress-shirt, the breast still stiff with starch, falling to his knees in front and to muscular calves behind. For a stud he had used a round brooch made of a bamboo frame and inlaid with vivid white, red, black and green beads. The ends of several bead necklaces formed a rainbow band round his throat. From each necklace hung a rectangular pendant also made of beads of fiery colours. Each pendant was of a different abstract design that had a definite meaning of its own in the tribal code. They were made for the wearers by the women whose fancy they had captured, and the number of pendants a man wore was testimony to the masculinity of his person. Below the lowest of the necklaces, flashing like crystal, hung a football referee's whistle, and below the whistle, flowing smooth as liquid in the rhythm of the guitar player's stride, emerged the unstarched ends of the shirt, the edges embroidered all along with beads of different colours. Copper anklets, burnished like new-strung telephone wire, shone on his feet; bracelets of elephant hair, locked with the metal of discarded paraffin tins silver with light, adorned his wrists; and from the lobes of his ears hung two large brass curtain rings. Everything about him flashed and jingled, and he passed me as a vision of such brilliance that both I and the few Europeans about seemed like ghosts trailing in his wake.

Just then a Zulu girl was entering the side gates of one of the larger houses. She was naked except for an apron of bright beads worked on ochre leather. Her dark skin had been polished with an ointment of hippopotamus lard so that it shone and added to the light of the anklets and bracelets of copper and metal as well as brooches and necklaces of beads smouldering on her person. She was tall, massive, strong, well-nourished, her body smooth and rounded as black polished marble and her breasts full and heavy. As she paused at the gate for a moment she threw a shy glance at the glittering minstrel striding down the hill. At the sight of her the Zulu minstrel abandoned even his music. He stopped playing, shouted aloud with joy and, as he did so, leapt with instant excitement into the air. "Oh you, you young woman there!" he called out. "I see you. I see the shadow you throw!"

She raised two long hands to hide the pleasure this recognition of her qualities brought burning to her face. Looking at him sideways over the tips of her fingers, her reply was made inaudible behind her broad hands.

At the shy response he laughed a laugh as bright and arrogant as a peacock's tail spread out before a hen. Far from intimidating her, his arrogance made her bolder, as if she knew that her hidden fire was mother of it all. She lowered her hands to rest them lightly above her breasts and looked at him more frankly.

"Mother-to-be of a nation," he called out again, "I see you have been waiting for me!"

"Oh you, you man!"

The response was in a low voice.

He answered with three chords plucked fiercely from his guitar, and picked up again his long resolute stride. At the sight of his tall shape swinging ahead, disappointment gripped her and she called out across the road; "But you! Where are you going in so great a hurry?"

"Not yet a wife but already an ipi-hamba* bush!" he

* Literally 'where-are-you-going', the name of a bush of dense, intricate, curved thorns which catch in the clothes of the careless walker and forces him to stop and disengage with difficulty. It is for this reason the Boer trekkers called it 'the-wait-a-little-bit' thorn.

answered, teasing her. Then added loftily: "I am just going."
Relenting, perhaps because the dazzle of the young woman
there at the gate behind him was still bright within him, he
condescended to explain, "My brothers are calling me and I
must go."

The girl stood staring after him striding purposively away,
listening not only to his music but to the words of his impro-
vised song which I can only render thus:

> "Yes! My brothers call me
> And I go. Look, how I go!
> Not the way of old women,
> The long path slow around the hill.
> But straight up the mountain,
> Steep down the side
> Like a lamb-snatcher striking
> Out of the sky.
> Yes! My brothers called me,
> And look! Oh look! How I go!"

Thinking back over the years, I can still remember that at
that moment the light of the late afternoon, turning everything
purple and gold in the fierce African sky, suddenly seemed old
and everlasting. Perhaps that native girl was getting her first
inkling of the part she would one day be compelled to play;
the constant Dido in woman staring at the ruin of her brief
encounter with the recurring Aeneas in man. Following the
minstrel, I passed close by the girl at the gate. And brushing
against her on the narrow pavement, I felt that I could hear the
congregation of her blood singing in the temple of her heart.

Once down on the flats between the height and the sea I had
to turn my back on such music and companionship. In an
open space hard by a golf-course, a long line of young black
men were doing a war dance. The light of the sun was on them
like limelight in a theatre. They had all locked arms around
one another's shoulders, except one man who was leaping and
whirling in front of them, chanting a theme of outraged honour
and heroic revenge known since childhood to them all. I saw
a silver whistle flashing between his teeth and heard a series

of blasts. As the blasts ended,abruptly a hundred or more black legs of the men behind him were lifted as one into the air and then brought down with such power that the earth seemed to shake like a drum with the dynamic reverberation.

Regretfully I left all that behind me because my way to the port led me through the Asiatic quarter of Port Natal. It was astonishing how the smell of the magenta earth of Africa raised by the pounding feet vanished as if it had never been. Here the air immediately was astringent with a compound of the spices of Zanzibar and Madras, Malacca and Malabar; cloves, curry, pepper, nutmeg, saffron, cinnamon and a whiff of burned-out sandalwood as well.

The streets were dark with shadow and yet alight with the colour of the clothes of the races of India and Malaya. At many a doorway of dark interiors in narrow streets women stood tall like candles, flickering with the incandescence of their saris or embroidered coats worn over silk trousers ending well above feet set in jewelled slippers with long upturned points like gondolas. Invariably these women were surrounded with clusters of chattering children.

The men, or the prosperous ones among them, sat in front of their houses and shuttered shops fat and silent, staring at the scene in the street, hands holding their ample fronts. The not so prosperous were thinner, their faces ascetic and surprisingly aristocratic.

They struck me as an unusually handsome people, doomed by their numbers to wither long before their natural time. The truly poor were fearfully thin, the men worn out with constant labour, the women by both child-bearing and work. They crowded the streets first thing in the morning, proudly carrying their produce, painfully extracted from the untamed earth of Africa, piled high in wide round wicker trays where they gleamed like Arabian treasure under the opal light above. Fine apples, persimmons, guavas, loquats and bananas, brignolles and grinadellas of amethyst, carrots and mangoes topaz among the green of papayas and lettuces lush as velvet. Even the scrubbed faces of their new young potatoes had a moonstone glow upon them.

But what struck me most perhaps was how crowded was this part of Port Natal considering that all Africa lay vacant about it. It was as if for the oriental there was no escape from the tyranny of his numbers even in this empty land of ours. The feeling that these people had renounced hope of bettering their human condition, and the acceptance that was implied thereby, was for me darker than the shadows in the streets through which I walked. Everyone around me seemed bowed down by the weight of too much and too long a history. It was a world of lost reflexes, and I just could not imagine the young men of this spiced and over-crowded quarter able to stamp out the defiant war dances that I had just left behind me.

After the Indian quarter, the European part of the city was strangely dull, and empty and silent except when a tram rattled by me. Lack of interest quickened my step along the pavements. At the entrances of many hotels, boarding houses and apartment blocks old Zulu watchmen, hair grey at the temples, armed with sticks and knobkerries, were already in position to guard the possessions and persons of their employers during the night. Occasionally they would call out to each other and, without moving, carry on long conversations right across the streets. I remember in particular one old man dressed in rags who looked as if he were old enough to have fought in the Zulu rebellion, the son of a father, perhaps, who served in Cetewayo's impis, and whose spirit doubtless had been nourished on legends of glory and of stories of powerful kings like Dingaan, Chaka and Dingiswayo. As he paced with a measured step up and down in front of the entrance to a jeweller's shop, its front stuffed with the artifice of London's gold- and silversmiths, Sheffield plate, Swiss watches and Japanese pearls, he carried the customary short knobkerrie with an abnormally big head that his people used for giving the *coup de grâce* to their enemies. Even then I wondered which was the stranger: the trust his employers confided in people like him, or the unerring loyalty with which they justified it?

I greeted him in his own tongue, calling him "my father". With a flare of emotion he replied in kind, calling me "his little chief". If so little produced so much, were there perhaps

no limits to what it would be possible for both sides to give,
and so induce a way of life for all that had never yet been seen?

The watchman's beat ended right on the edge of the city's
great square. I crossed it to where, beyond, stood Port Natal's
vast City Hall. Everything possible had been done to make it
look imposing. There was hardly a feature of European archi-
tecture that had not been mobilized to that end. On the remaining two sides of the square, merchants and planters had
piled their own offices high to match the pretensions of public
buildings, while in the centre of the square sat the great white
Queen Victoria, sealed in phantom marble, surveying the scene
like the midwife who had brought this hybrid brood of buildings into the world.

Had it not been for the fierce sunset fire in the sky, the tall
royal palms at the side of the war memorials, and the dark
pre-Christian green of the few Zulu trees (that had been allowed
to remain on the scene, perhaps, because they screened the
public lavatories from the eyes of the marble queen), it would
have been easy to forget that I was still in Africa, so uncom-
promisingly European was the fixed mask on the face of the
city. But now I was soon out of it, and at the bottom of a tawdry
little side street the bay of Port Natal lay spread out tranquil
and wide in the last of the day's sunlight.

I do not know if there is anything more beautiful than the
sight of a great natural harbour. I know for certain that then
no view had ever moved me as much as the sight of the sea
which travels so far and wide, coming home at last to the land.
It is a view with the natural image of the pattern of departure
and return which is the lot of all on earth. Something of this,
not as articulate thought but as a surge of emotion, made me
lean underneath a royal palm on green iron railings to look
over the embankment where sea and city met.

The tide was in, the water smooth and shining as glass, and
quickly around me the city of Port Natal lost its pomp and
confidence. I saw how the untamed land that contained both
it and the sea completely took over. This wide, wide land had
a rim of hills, covered with thick dark green bush, against
which the houses on their slopes seemed huddled together as

B*   41

if for protection. The crests of the hills themselves leapt livid with the colours of the sunset but their flanks already were blue with the ashes of the burned-out day. Only one great bluff of land to the south formed a tremendous natural break-water against the quarter from which came the most stormy weather.

The curled bush which covered the bluff was yellow with sunlight, and the lighthouse perched on the end of the cliff was as white and tall as a candle. Behind the lighthouse far above the narrow Port Natal harbour mouth stood the high white Signals mast. As I watched, a whole line of brightly coloured flags were run up to the mast-head. Something clearly was on the move in the harbour, and it made me move on as well.

At the harbour gates the officer on duty, his spirit crushed with the weight of the Protestant inertia of what Samuel Butler called "the great and terrible day of our Lord", hardly looked at me and just managed to raise a listless hand to wave me through. I found it incredible that anyone so dull could be employed in so exciting a place. I made straight for the quay-side and the first of the long line of ships moored to it.

I can even now recall the name of each ship, the port of registration painted underneath it on the stern, the colours it wore on hull, deckwork and funnel, the flags it flew and the condition of its paint, so great a marvel were they all to me. There was not one among them, not even the rusty, overloaded and ill-equipped Greek tramp *Leonidas*, that seemed ordinary. I think that is perhaps the most remarkable thing about the sea: its power to invest all that lives and moves upon it with a wonder that nothing on land can equal. Its authority over our imagination seems to me final, as if it is at our beginning as it will be at our end.

On this particular evening at the beginning of my lessons in the alphabet of the sea, the wonder of it all burned in me with such a blaze that the ships were not just travel-stained pedlars of commerce but instruments of a living mythology; members all of an eternal argosy seeking gold not in mines but in odd, dream-like glimpses which, as yet, have flickered only

on the far perimeter of the imagination; as the startling confrontation of Jason and the vision of the Fleece, or the flash of yellow on the bough which Aeneas plucked in the sacred wood for passport into the world below. I could not of course have put any of this into words at the time. But I know it was raw in the tooth-and-claw emotion of the moment, for I have only to think back, thus, for the same feelings to seize me again.

In this mood I strolled along the quayside, leaving the *Leonidas* of Piraeus for the Harrison freighter, *Spectator* from Liverpool, then on to another tramp, the *Yosukuni Maru* of Kobe, gleaming as if she like her crew had just emerged from the bath of purification preordained for all Japanese at the end of their day. The Swede *Gripsholm* of Gottenburg, decks stacked with neat standards of warm yellow wood; the *Adolph Woermann*, fat, prosperous and middleclass from Hamburg, a junior officer stiff with sense of duty at the head of the companionway; the British India, *Kandalla* from Bombay, the Blue Funnel *Nestor*, classical in shape as in name, with some deep scars in her paintwork from her passage through the Roaring Forties on her Homeric voyage from London to Fremantle; the P. & O. *Ballarat* of Greenock, a Blue Peter at her tapering mast-head and a long line of homesick emigrants from Britain staring out with set, white faces at the silent cranes and shut warehouses on the quay; the Red Star *Ceramic*, one of the longest ships of her day and the last steam-driven four-master in the world, giving all the flags in her signals locker an airing by dressing herself in their gipsy colours overall from her greyhound nose to her wind-swept stern.

Each of these struck great chords on my senses, ending with the mail-ship which had docked only that morning and was still breathing steam and smoke from her marathon run between the Needles and the Cape.

All her brass and metal had been polished, her decks washed and holystoned, and the glass of all the many windows of saloons, drawing-rooms, long-galleries and bridge as well as row upon row of portholes from water-line to snow-white deck, had been soaped and rubbed down with leather so that she shone and gleamed with self-respect and circumspection unequalled

even in the Dutch interiors of Vermeer. Even the gulls which were sailing high overhead looked newly-washed and continued for some time after the shadows of the evening had darkened the ship, to flash like snow in the slanted sunlight. Their cry, the long notes drawn up and down constantly from the mooring ropes by the high-spirited ship straining at them with the slightest movement from the sea, and the imperative blasts from a tug's whistle going at full speed to fetch in a new arrival at the roadstead before night should fall, combined to make a music full of nostalgia for me.

Finally, there hard by the mail-ship's bow, I found at last the whaling fleet moored in line three abreast, noses in the air sniffing at the smell of the open sea, which I could now hear plainly pounding on the breakwater built on the narrow spit of sand which formed the lower lip of the mouth of the harbour. The ships were so small that they could easily have been an anti-climax in their position at the head of the great progression of shipping behind them. But they were, after all, the hunters of the sea, and as the hunter preceded the tiller of soil on earth, as Cain came before Abel, so the first-born among sailors too was a hunter, not a merchantman. Lying there with no fat or pretension upon them but athletic and sturdy, they satisfied my imagination as much as the liners glittering behind them.

I made my way then to the head of this small line where Larsen had told me I would find the *Kurt Hansen*. He had not told me, however, that she would be lying farthest out of the leading three. As a result I took it for granted that the ship immediately alongside was his, confidently crossed the gangplank, and stepped on board. At first I thought there was no one in the ship and looked about me not knowing what to do. Then I saw the shoulder of a man protruding from behind the corner of the wheelhouse. I went up to him. To my amazement he was absorbed in knitting what looked like a broad scarf and did not hear me coming. Also his clothes were not at all what I had expected. No uniform. Only a thick brown woollen sweater with collar rolled back underneath his chin, a pair of heavy grey flannels and brown canvas shoes with rope soles.

44

"Excuse me. This is the *Kurt Hansen*, isn't it?" I asked diffidently.

Without dropping a stitch, pausing in his knitting, or looking up, he said in a gruff, indifferent voice with a marked accent:

"No. This is not *Kurt Hansen*. This is *Erik Hayerdahl*. That alongside *Harald Nielsen* is *Kurt Hansen*."

I stood for a moment irresolutely at his side, then I explained that I had been invited on board the *Kurt Hansen* by her Captain, Thor Larsen. Only then did he stop knitting to look me over from head to foot.

"So you want Larsen," he remarked while he stared at me obviously trying to puzzle out what Larsen's interest could be in someone like myself. The answer clearly evaded him and he soon dismissed the matter, muttering: "I think Larsen not back yet. But cook and stoker are there."

Once more he became absorbed in his knitting, so I left him to board the *Harald Nielsen*, walked across her without seeing any sign of life, and made my way to the gang-plank between her and the *Kurt Hansen*.

CHAPTER FOUR

The Crew

I WAS just about to cross over to the *Kurt Hansen* when from the companion-way opposite me appeared a handsome Zulu face, burned as black as the ship's Bible by sun and wind at sea. I was so astonished that I stopped to stare until the owner of the face had climbed out on deck and stood there in faded blue overalls, tall, broad, supple, feet planted firmly apart like an experienced sailor, looking at me with an enquiring boldness unusual among his countrymen on shore. Whatever my many associations with Amangtakwena and Zulus, they had not yet included the sea. Both races had, as far as I knew, traditionally a superstitious aversion to the sea. Neither, for instance, would eat its fish because they believed it would turn a warrior's heart to water. Indeed so out of the national element of his people did the big man in front of me appear to be that I was startled into speaking to him in English instead of Sindakwena as I would normally have done.

"This is the *Kurt Hansen*, isn't it?" I asked unnecessarily.

"This is *Kurt Hansen*," he answered in good English and a deep but surprisingly gentle voice for so powerful a man, adding with pride: "And I, I am the keeper of *Kurt Hansen*'s fire."

I was about to ask him for permission to board, when another voice with a Scandinavian accent and a rather precise, slightly schoolmasterish tone came up the hatch from below: "What's happening up there, 'Mlangeni?"

Before the black man could answer, a face appeared at the companion-way and the questioner himself stepped on deck.

"I see," he remarked at once. "I see, a visitor! Come on board, sir, come on board. I think I have been expecting you but I thought there would be two of you."

All this was uttered in the same manner that I have already

mentioned so that I had felt not unlike a new boy being welcomed by a pedantic housemaster to his future school.

The newcomer was almost as tall as 'Mlangeni, the Zulu sailor, but there the grounds for physical comparison ended. He was as slight as 'Mlangeni was massive, had long arms, long hands, and a long face under a broad forehead, which was made to look longer by a neatly trimmed brown beard. His eyes were hazel, with something sad or perhaps slightly weary in them, which belied his ready and incisive manner of speech. He was still dressed in his neat Sunday suit of coarse navy blue serge, white shirt, black tie and black leather boots. And as he raised his hand to wave me on board, I saw the wide band of a gold ring flashing on a second finger.

"Step on board, sir, please step on board," he urged me. "Which one of the two are you? The agent's son or his friend?"

I quickly explained who I was and what was happening.

"Ah, I see. Your gear is coming later. I will show you where you are to sleep."

Taking it for granted I would follow, he walked amidships and vanished through a doorway underneath the deck-house. I climbed aboard the *Kurt Hansen* at once, brushing by 'Mlangeni who had not moved and was watching all this with eyes brilliant against his dark skin. As I passed him, the smell of his African person came through clear and astringent. It was the ancient, unashamed smell of natural man, as welcome and as African to me as the smell of the red earth after the first rain to break after one of our long droughts, or the smoke of a wood fire at evening on the cow-dung floor of a bee-hive hut. The man's professional sailor's stance therefore seemed all the stranger.

Ducking through the doorway in my turn, I went down a narrow steep companion-way as I would down a ladder, my face to the rungs. My guide was waiting for me in the small saloon, his head nearly touching the metal of the ceiling, and everything was as it would be on that Saturday evening four seasons later that I have already described—except that now nothing was out of position and there was no smell of tobacco smoke.

"One of you to sleep there," he pointed to the plush-covered couch beside the triangular table, "and the other here . . ." He pushed through the heavy curtains over the entrance to the Captain's cabin as he spoke and I followed, to see him patting a bunk with the flat of his hand. "And here, you both put your clothes." He opened and shut two mahogany drawers underneath the bunk, before asking: "Where would you like to sleep?"

I said I thought I ought to take the couch in the saloon and let my friend share the cabin with the Captain.

He nodded and then asked: "You know Captain Larsen well?"

I shook my head and explained I had met Thor Larsen only once a week before.

"Ach! I see then. The agent arranged for him to take the two of you?" he asked.

"No," I said, and explained briefly how it had come about. Happily, that not only satisfied him but seemed to relieve him. I was to find that he, like everybody else who knew Larsen, had learnt from experience that most things imposed on Larsen by outside authority jarred so much that they could sour his mood for days. And the mood of so forceful a master in so small a ship was, to put it at its lowest, of the utmost practical consequence.

"Ach, good! Then he must have liked you very much."

He uttered this so confidently that I stammered, "Oh, no. It wasn't me. It was only because of the elephants."

"Elephants?" he said. "Elephants?" Far from being confused by the apparent irrelevance of such an explanation, he reiterated the word as if he understood it. Then, noticing my embarrassment, he dropped the subject to ask: "Would you like some tea?"

I explained that I had already eaten.

Well then, he said, would I like to join him on deck, where he was going to smoke a pipe before dark, and wait for Captain Larsen and my friend? He was certain they would not be long because he knew Larsen was putting out of harbour earlier than usual that night.

48

I could not help asking why.

He paused, his foot on the companion-way, shrugged his shoulders, and remarked with a forced laugh that came near to impatience, "Only Captain Larsen knows why. Captain Larsen does what he does."

On deck we found 'Mlangeni seated on the hatch cover, his great legs dangling over the edge, and his broad back and shoulders supported on his elbows, while he sang softly to himself a little song that reminded me of the music I had not long before encountered on the heights above the harbour. When my companion signalled to him to make room for us, he did so without interrupting his tune.

" 'Mlangeni is a great musician," my companion remarked, not without affection. "He sings to everything, even to the coal in the bunker and the fire in the boiler. Isn't that so, you great big stoker?"

'Mlangeni answered him with a flashing smile which, brilliant as it was, failed to stay his song.

We sat on, my companion smoking on my right, 'Mlangeni singing to himself on my left, the smell of Africa high and wide upon him,but added to it was another smell both unfamiliar and pervasive. It was, I knew without asking, the smell of the whale which is so adhesive that,although the little ships merely harpoon the fish and then transport the corpse lashed alongside to the shore, yet that brief contact was enough to make rigging, woodwork and forecastle perpetually reek of it. The smell made my senses reel with a kind of vertigo, as if it had brought them suddenly to the abyss of time out of which the whale, like a great Bedouin of the deep, trailed through the darkness over our beginnings.

Sitting there as interested in this smell of the whale as a puppy encountering a completely new scent, I took a large slab of fruit and nut chocolate out of my pocket. Dividing it into three equal parts, I offered one each to the two men at my side. 'Mlangeni stopped his singing, accepted his in two broad hands cupped together with an exclamation of gratitude. The Norwegian I think was about to refuse (like a confirmed smoker, he was not interested in sweet things), but fearing, I suspect, to

refuse one so young and eager to make friends as I was, he took his pipe out of his mouth and accepted the chocolate with a warm expression of thanks, at the same time asking: "Have you been in a whaler before?"

"No," I said. "I've never been to sea before. In fact . . ." I hesitated, embarrassed by confessing to such a woeful inadequacy in my experience. "This is the first time ever that I've even seen the sea."

'Mlangeni thought this funny enough to laugh.

But the Norwegian just asked, "How old are you?"

"Over fourteen," I answered, without mentioning that I had had a birthday just three weeks before.

"Fourteen! Well, you have plenty of time to see more than enough of it," the Norwegian commented. Then he added: "I went to sea at the age of eleven! There is not a day of my life in which I do not remember looking at the sea. But you know about elephants and I do not. I have not even seen one in a circus!"

"I know about elephants and about whales!" 'Mlangeni laughed.

"Now, 'Mlangeni, no boasting!" the Norwegian remarked good-naturedly. There was something about 'Mlangeni's laugh that made one feel good. "There is a lot you don't know about whales yet. God knows, there's a lot none of us knows or will ever know. I have been whaling for forty years now and every season I feel I know them less and less."

"Captain Larsen, surely," I interspersed, "must know a great deal about them?"

"Captain Larsen!" he commented again rather tartly. "Captain Larsen certainly knows a great deal about killing whales."

Abashed and somewhat amazed at the derogative qualification I asked: "You're not fond of whaling then?"

My amazement was spontaneous because I had been brought up in an environment where the hunter was one of the most important persons in the community and a number of the great ones were still figures of live and vivid romance on my native scene.

At once his precise mind picked on the word "fond". "Fond

of whaling? Almighty, no! I am not fond of whaling. I do not even like whaling."

"Why d'you do it then?"

The bald uncomprehending question was out before I knew it and I feared I might have gone too far.

The Norwegian merely shrugged. "A good question! One I have asked myself a thousand times. I can't answer it except by saying that I was taken fishing first as a young boy to help earn a poor family a living. Then I went whaling because it earned a better living. Then I woke up one day to find that whaling had become my life."

A few more questions from me and his whole story came out.

His name was Leif Fügelsang, his age sixty-one years. He was the eldest of seven children of a family farming on the edge of a fiord in northern Norway. His description of the fiord delivered with the light fading round us, the gulls overhead crying like a bosun's pipe summoning a night-watch on deck, the creaking of the ships all around, and the sound of the tremendous ocean pounding over the breakwaters and no doubt turning the level sand beyond into a mirror filled to its brim with emerging stars, made an awesome impression on me.

The steep cliffs at the back of the small and difficult family holding, Leif said, were black; the waters in front were as black as the cliffs and deep, fanatically still, so that they all welcomed any wind that drew a ripple of movement, or blew a fleck of kapok away from their glowering surface. Most sinister of all, they seemed blacker by sunlight than by night, in summer more so than in winter, which, thank God, brought some white to land and water. Living there, it was easy to believe the legend that the waters were full of trolls, the dark cliffs bedevilled with sprites. If ever there was a haunted moon-scape hostile to the sun, this was one.

The thin soil not surprisingly was no living in itself; the family had to fish as well as farm, and both pursuits brought in little enough. Born in every one of their people there was, Leif believed, an unacknowledged desire to escape, and the most cherished means of escape was education. But with such limited resources the advanced education necessary was possible only

for the younger ones, when the older children, and Leif was the eldest, could help the parents pay for it. Then his father, aged only forty, had died and Leif had become head of the family. "Which meant the end of education for me," he concluded. Later I was to see the photographs of his favourite sister and her son kept in two oval frames of embossed metal backed with red velvet. The photograph of the mother was altogether charming. She stood there, a young girl in national dress with two long thick plaits of shining hair over her shoulders, a sensitive, open face and large eyes, solemn with a sense of the occasion. The photograph was printed not in black and white, but brown and cream, which in some odd way seemed to be the tone of the young day in their lives when it was taken.

I found this sacrifice hard to stomach and asked Leif what he would have liked to do.

"Not farming," he replied after some hesitation. "Not fishing, certainly not whaling . . . I think . . ." He paused. "I'd have liked to be a librarian, to have looked after lots and lots of books . . ." He smiled at me. "You see, as you would say I'm *fond*, very *fond* of books. Only here I am, cook, house-keeper, part accountant even and a dozen other things in a whaler and no chance of ever being anything else." Perhaps he felt in danger of feeling sorry for himself, because he abruptly went on to dismiss the subject. "But there's nothing unusual about that. The world is full of seamen who would rather have been something else . . . What is strange, is 'Mlangeni's story. But he won't say much. Why not try to get it out of him?"

'Mlangeni had stopped singing, so I suspected he had heard and was prepared for questioning. When I did ask, his account began very much like the Norwegian's: too little money, too poor a land, and too many mouths to feed. He would have left it at that but, plausible as it all sounded, the Norwegian would not accept it.

"Yes, I know all that," he remarked impatiently. "You've told me that many times before. But what made you go to sea, 'Mlangeni? To sea? You are the only Zulu in the whole fleet?" He turned to me. "You see, he is working with a lot of strangers when the docks are full of men of his own kind earning regular

wages: and he could get a job among them tomorrow. How and why did he become a stoker?" He looked once more at 'Mlangeni with fierce curiosity.

'Mlangeni broke out laughing but I thought it went on too long to be altogether convincing.

"I 'Mlangeni, you see, I am fond of fire!" was all he said.

A moment of impasse had obviously been reached. Suddenly, almost without thought, I decided to try and break it. I interrupted his laughter and, speaking to him in his native tongue, Sindakwena, I asked him the name and place of his home town.

He was so astonished to be addressed thus that he leapt upright, looked down at me from his full height, shook his head at himself and me, and then remarked in tones of admiration: "'Nkosan, you are a great trickster. Your face is pale but you speak like the child of a black mother!"

"A trickster!" Leif exclaimed, when I translated the remark at his request.

I explained that the remark was intended as a compliment since a magical trickster was one of the best loved heroes of Zulu and 'Takwena imagination. Then I reminded 'Mlangeni that he had not answered my question yet.

Suddenly grave and once more seated on the hatch beside me, he told me he came from the place called Icoco, the Zulu name for the ring the wise men of the tribe wear on their heads. His home was so called because it lay against a great hill which carried a ring of smooth rock around its crown like a halo.

He was surprised I had not heard of it because the main wagon road from the capital into the interior wound round and over the shoulder of this hill. It was famous among all transport men because the road was so steep there that the oxen hauling their wagons had to strain at their yokes so much that the holes in their behinds yawned like old men fighting their sleep: hence it was also called 'Make-the-oxen's-arse-holes-yawn': but its real, its ancient name was Icoco.

'Mlangeni's homely phrase was so vivid that I burst out laughing, saying "Oh, man of Icoco, you have spoken!"

Leif, of course, immediately wanted to know what had made me laugh and, to my annoyance, I found myself hesitating. I knew from experience that a literal translation of African speech often shocked Europeans. Having lost their own innocence long since, they failed to recognise what innocence there was still left in the mind of Africans. Yet the Norwegian was so insistent that I had no option. My fears were partly justified. At first, Leif could hardly believe his ears; then, when he grasped the full picture, to my great relief he smiled at 'Mlangeni, who was looking at us, proud of this proof of his powers of speech, and said, "Surprised at you, 'Mlangeni! Thought you too civilised to speak like that!"

Again I was glad that 'Mlangeni did not know the word "civilised", for I am certain it would have hurt him, and as far as I was concerned, the process of making Africans as ashamed of their natural selves as we were of our own had already gone far enough. But well as 'Mlangeni spoke and understood English, the word "civilised" apparently had not yet come his way, for flushed by his success he started immediately to continue.

Unfortunately the first sentence was hardly out of his mouth when the sound of voices on the *Erik Hayerdahl* and the noise of someone clambering aboard stopped him. We all three looked up. We had not switched on our deck lights in *Kurt Hansen* yet but the *Erik Hayerdahl* had hers full on, so it was possible for us clearly to see a man crossing the gangplank on to the ship next to us and coming with a quick step across the deck.

'Mlangeni recognised him, leapt to his feet and, raising his right hand high above his head, gave him a loud histrionic version of his native salute for a king: "Bayede 'Nkosi! Gezizandhla, Bayede!"

"Cheers, Langenay," replied the newcomer, who unlike Leif could not pronounce 'Mlangeni's name properly. His voice somehow matched his quick step. I would say he both walked and talked with a slight lisp. I looked at him closely as he came on board not merely because he was a newcomer but because of the name 'Mlangeni had given him. Most Zulus ignore the names we give ourselves and give us a name of their own which somehow expresses our salient characteristics, and 'Mlangeni's

name for the newcomer meant literally 'One-who-is-always-washing-his-hands'.

As the newcomer stepped on board,'Mlangeni, still in his pose of exaggerated deference, pointed dramatically at the man, and said by way of introducing him to me: "'Nkosi Gorgeous! He was not born! He was belched up by a cow."

Gorgeous clearly had no idea of what 'Mlangeni had said. He thought merely that he was being teased and disliked it.

"I keep on telling you, 'Mlangeni, that my name is Georghius; Georghius . . ." he said in a rather vexed tone. Then noticing me he added, "Georghius is the Latin for George." Then once more addressing 'Mlangeni, he protested, "I won't have you calling me names in a language I can't understand. It isn't fair, is it, Leif?"

I had to struggle hard not to laugh. Georghius's appearance, for instance, was as over-fastidious as the Zulu nickname implied. He was a smallish man, fine-boned, narrow-hipped and yet oddly broad-shouldered. His face was round and smooth, and his eyes big and blue. His head was unusually well-shaped and covered with thick yellow hair of a wiry texture worn exceptionally long even for these days. On the second finger of his left hand he had a gold ring, with a big green-coloured semi-precious stone which completely covered the knuckle. He wore a pair of white shoes with toes of black patent leather, known popularly then as "co-respondent's shoes". His trousers were an exaggerated version of what was considered the height of fashion among young men at the time and were known far and wide as "Oxford Bags". For a year or more everyone at my school had coveted a pair but no one was allowed to wear them. A short double-breasted navy-blue coat had a pink silk kerchief in the breast pocket, a pink silk tie, and an immaculate stiff white collar with long tapering points. Starched white cuffs protruded well beyond the sleeves of the coat and were held together by a pair of ornate platinum and black stone links. The pink tie was held bulging to his shirt with a gold pin endorsed with the letters "G. Grieg."

I could well understand 'Mlangeni's admiration because among war-like Zulus such as the brave Amangtakwena

paradoxically it is the man not the woman who goes in for fine clothes and jewellery.

Mr. Grieg however, as I now took him to be, again repeated his question, "It isn't fair, is it, Leif?"

"I don't know," Leif replied, taking the pipe out of his mouth, and smiling gently. "We'd better ask our young friend here. He speaks the language."

I hesitated because I knew instinctively that the way I answered would determine my future relationship with 'Mlangeni. I did not want him to feel that I would ever use my knowledge of his language to spy on his mind. Much as I was drawn to Leif, I had experienced immediately a certain sense of kinship with 'Mlangeni, the kinship which comes alive in the children of Africa whatever their colour when they are among foreigners. I wanted him to know that I would both welcome and honour his confidence.

"Well then," I replied, " 'Mlangeni said merely that you were not born Mr. Grieg." I thought it best not to add he had "been belched up by a cow" as well. "He was paying you a great compliment. It is an expression his people use when they find someone unusually impressive. He's suggesting your arrival must have been almost miraculous."

"I say!" Grieg exclaimed both taken aback and appeased. "But that's going a bit far, isn't it? I wish it could have been explained to me before." He held out his hand to 'Mlangeni who took it shyly. "I wouldn't have been nearly so irritable with you all these years if I'd known what you meant."

Leif merely smiled enigmatically and then went on puffing at his pipe.

'Mlangeni, having dropped Grieg's hand, remarked to me in a way that made me feel I had passed the test: "You are indeed a trickster, 'Nkosi!"

"Well, I must be off," Grieg said before I could reply. "Got to change and wash." He looked straight at me. "Whaling's a dirty business."

Leif and 'Mlangeni just thought this highly amusing and grinned openly, Leif remarking:"Gorgeous comes from Bergen. His family was related to the composer Grieg."

Grieg heard him, and turned quickly. "Daddy was a fifth cousin. And the name is not Gorgeous but Georghius, the Latin for George."

With that he vanished into the forecastle.

"Odd thing about the people of Bergen," Leif went on, ignoring the interruption. "They tend to think they're superior to the rest of us. Take Grieg, there. He assumes that he is a kind of missionary bringing the light of culture to the dark souls in the whaling fleet. But he is a very nice man for all that; and first class at his job."

"And what is his job?" I asked.

"Helmsman. And by far the best in our fleet. Wait until you've seen him take the *Kurt Hansen* stalking a whale and you'll know what I mean. We like him, don't we, 'Mlangeni?"

'Mlangeni agreed with a nod of his great head.

"You'll find," Leif continued, "that Gorgeous will have been to the Sunday orchestral concert in the City Hall tonight. He goes there regularly. The rest of us poor dark souls merely go to church—that is, all of us except Captain Larsen, of course."

"He speaks jolly good English!" I remarked.

"His mother was English," Leif replied. "And he learnt his trade first in English ships. That's where the Gorgeous comes from. Oh, I know the sea looks vast. But the world of the sailor is very small and sooner or later all our secrets come out. With only one exception, this fellow here . . ." He pointed at 'Mlangeni.

I wanted there and then to ask 'Mlangeni to go on with his story, but at that moment the rough murmur of many male voices and the sound of many heavy footsteps reached us from the quay. The noise rapidly became louder and soon all round us we heard the other whalers hailing men on shore, followed by the sound of men clambering on board their ships.

"Church is over," Leif remarked, getting up. "I had better turn on the lights."

In the next few minutes I watched the remaining thirteen members of the crew board the *Kurt Hansen*. I do not propose describing them in detail, because they had no particular influence on me and none of them were with me in the *Kurt*

Hansen during all four of the seasons that I served in her. They were all men brought out on a four months' contract from Norway by mail steamer and at the end of the whaling season went back to their homes again. Some of them would reappear the following year but many would skip a season reappearing only the year after and then not necessarily in the ships they had left. Only a hard core remained regularly with their ships and an even smaller number would volunteer to go straight on for whaling in the Antarctic summer, as did about a quarter of the ships in the fleet, including the *Kurt Hansen*. I would only say this about the Norwegian crews, that they were an exceptionally decent and inoffensive lot of men. They were sober, thrifty, conscientious, hard-working and God-fearing, and they made whaling appear an oddly respectable affair. Certainly as they came on board this Sunday evening, every one of the thirteen dressed in a rough but neat suit of navy-blue serge, they looked the church-goers they had just been and not the 'catchers of Leviathan' that they were about to become. Among them only 'Mlangeni, Leif and Gorgeous served in *Kurt Hansen* all the time with me, and they were not of the regular pattern of behaviour and character in the fleet.

Anxious to change their clothes as soon as possible, the crew hardly seemed to notice me and hurried past the three of us, greeting Leif and 'Mlangeni with a brisk nod of their heads. I thought it merely a sign of their haste to get ready for sea, since Leif had told me we were putting out early. But I was to find it was just because they were men incapable of many words. In fact if ever they had a common issue that they wanted to take up with the Captain, they usually got Leif to do their speaking for them.

The last man had hardly vanished down the companion-way when Thor Larsen, followed at some distance by my friend and a Zulu chauffeur carrying our gear, appeared on board.

Larsen spotted me at once and, as always after a Sunday with the owner's representative, he was full of gin and high spirits, and bellowed: "Good, very good, there you are, my young Boher! You come below, we open at once the elephant–whale credit account! Not?"

58

Then his eyes fell on 'Mlangeni, and suspicion was immediately written large over his face. "What you doing here,
Langenay! I told engineer we putting out early. What about
your boilers? You're not to tell me you not ready yet, not?"

Without giving 'Mlangeni a chance to reply, he walked to the
hatch and roared down it: "Mr. Engineer!"

Almost at once a large plump man, without a coat but still
in Sunday trousers, black braces and white shirt, came up the
steep companion-way.

Larsen threw a series of vehement questions in Norwegian at
him. Fortunately the engineer's answers satisfied him, for soon
he dismissed him, came back to us and, ignoring Leif and
'Mlangeni, said in his hearty, rasping Sunday evening voice:
"Come on, my young Boher. Below, below! Down below!"

Leif and 'Mlangeni, no doubt used to their Captain's manner,
had remained unperturbed beside me.

"I'd better go, hadn't I?" I whispered to Leif.

"Yes. Of course, you must go," he answered. "Goodnight."

"Goodnight, Mr. Fügelsang," I said. "Goodnight,'Mlangeni."

'Mlangeni looked at me solemnly. He did not say goodnight but gave me that enigmatic parting utterance of Zulu and
Amangtakwena which can mean so many things. "Hamba
gahle!" Literally it means "May you go slowly," and somehow
I knew that 'Mlangeni was not only saying "goodnight" but
advising me to watch my step.

Meanwhile Eric, too, had come on board, got the chauffeur
to put our gear on deck, dismissed him and now stood watching
me. Aware of the fact that I had ignored him, I rushed up to
him, put my hand on his shoulder and said, "Oh, I'm jolly glad
you've come at last! We are going to have such fun. These
chaps . . ." I indicated 'Mlangeni and Leif, intending to introduce him to them.

He interrupted me rather brusquely. "Come on, pick up
your gear and let's get down below or Larsen'll be annoyed."

As he spoke he gathered up his own bag and walked by Leif
and 'Mlangeni without a glance.

Abashed, I picked up mine and, calling out "Goodnight" to
my new friends, I too went below.

"I see you've not lost any time making yourself at home," he remarked to me, not without a hint of sarcasm, when I joined him in the small saloon. "Who were those two?"

Somewhat dismayed, I explained. "The cook and the Zulu stoker."

"Lord!" exclaimed my friend with such scorn that I felt quite speechless.

He was immediately contrite. "Sorry. As a matter of fact I'm a bit rattled. Suppose I'm sea-sick again? Everyone says I'll have grown out of it now. But I wonder. If it hadn't been for you I wouldn't have come. . . . Besides, Dad's furious about us going with Larsen and not the other captain."

"Oh, gosh, how awful," I said. Then added impulsively: "Look, would you rather call the whole thing off and go back home? If you'd rather, I don't mind."

Had Eric taken me at my word I would have minded more than I can possibly say. But though the spoilt and only son of rich parents, he was generous enough at heart to say he wouldn't hear of it.

At that moment Larsen, full of energy, burst through the curtains over his cabin entrance like an anthropoid through a paper hoop in a circus.

"Ach, there you are, there you are!" he uttered with satisfaction. "At 2 a.m. I put to sea. If you like, you both come to wheelhouse with me. If not, you sleep till morning. Which would you like to do?"

"I'd love to come," I answered readily, and got a look of approval from Larsen.

"Thank you." My friend's response was far from clear to me, though Larsen appeared to understand. Slapping him on the shoulder with his broad hand, the Captain told him:

"Not to mind! To decide when time comes! Now I go to make ready for sea, and you, you two, you better go to sleep!"

CHAPTER FIVE

The Sea

THE clock in the saloon made it 8.45 p.m. when I switched off the light and lay down on the couch. It was long before my normal bedtime. I did my best to sleep and pretended to be deep in it when Larsen returned. But actually I was awake most of the time. Yet so great was my excitement and so much had the day given me to think about that sleeplessness did not bother me. It was only towards the end that I must have dozed off.

I was woken up by someone shaking me. The light was on and it was Larsen.

"You still wish come to wheelhouse?" Larsen asked in a whisper that could be heard all over the ship.

"Of course I do," I answered, getting up quickly, wide-awake at once.

"Good! Come you then. But your friend, I think him we leave asleep. Better. Not?"

Without waiting for an answer he went to the drawer underneath the couch opposite me, pulled a bottle of gin out of it, filled a tumbler to the brim and swallowed the liquid without pause.

"Warms the stomach," he said, smacking his lips. "No gripe. No inflammation of the lungs. You have small one, too: cold on deck, not?"

I shook my head.

"Perhaps you right," he commented. "Thor Larsen too, he never drink at sea. Whales and gin. No! They do not mix. You see, this Thor Larsen's last drink until he come back to port."

With that he went quickly on deck, and I hasten to add that in all the four seasons I served with Thor Larsen, much as he drank in port, I never saw him vary this rule. As a result, our

first day at sea would invariably be an unpleasant one because, as the effect of the final tumbler-full of gin wore off, he became more irritable and exacting, a state of mind which would vanish only when we harpooned our first quarry.

I had no time to think then, though I often thought about it later, how suddenly he had talked about himself in the third person as if he were, indeed, someone else.

I was up and dressing as quickly as I could, a yellow woollen shirt, thick grey woollen socks, an old pair of thick dark flannel bags and a polo sweater knitted for me by my mother in the dark-blue wool that was our school rugger colour. And finally a pair of tennis shoes.

Before going on deck, however, I tiptoed to the entrance of the Captain's cabin and, my ear to the curtains, listened carefully in case my friend, too, might be stirring. I could tell by his breathing that he was asleep, so I turned away.

I came on deck just as Thor Larsen rang for "Half speed astern" in the engine room. To my amazement the *Kurt Hansen*'s deck lights had all been switched off. There was no light even in the wheelhouse except two faint phosphorescent glows from the compass, which faced the man at the wheel, and the two dials of the signals box that connected the wheelhouse with the engine room. The other whalers, too, were in darkness but the light from the quay was just bright enough for me to see that our crew were all in position and had already cast off from the *Harald Nielsen*, for at that moment two of them, one fore and the other aft, jumped smartly from the whaler alongside, back on to the *Kurt Hansen*'s deck.

They were just in time, for as they jumped the propeller of the *Kurt Hansen* started thrashing and the deck began to vibrate underneath my feet. The spirited ship responded at once and, gathering way, began a rapid slide sideways into the main stream of the harbour. Had this movement been carried out by day, Larsen would have been compelled by the law of the sea to give three warning blasts on the ship's whistle for the benefit of the habitually dense traffic. But as we were the only ship moving in the harbour at that hour, he ignored regulations, whether out of consideration for the many sleeping craft around

us or just because it was unnecessary I could not tell for sure, although I myself suspect the latter of the two alternatives to have been his reason.

As we moved thus, steam hissed loudly in the safety valve alongside the tall funnel, out of which black smoke was bubbling so thick and fast that it looked as if it might burst its rivetted seams. The hissing of the steam, the deck trembling underneath my feet, the powerful thrust of the screw, the ease with which we glided backwards and the speed with which the gap between us and the rest of the fleet widened, made the most dynamic of impressions on me. I was not only elated by it but suddenly felt very proud of the *Kurt Hansen*, privileged to be in her, and, as I realised with amusement remembering my conversation with Leif and 'Mlangeni earlier on, already fond, very fond of her, indeed.

I gave one look at the still dark, shining water between us and the quay. The riding lights of the moored ships, the lamps blazing on the quay, lay trembling deep within the water side by side with quick, quivering stars, as if they, too, marked another great concourse of shipping just waiting for the dawn in order to cast off.

By the time I joined Thor Larsen in the wheelhouse my eyes had become sufficiently accustomed to the darkness to see him grasp the levers of the signals to the engine room and ring for full speed ahead. I heard him snap out in Norwegian to the man at the wheel the order "Amidships."

"Amidships, it is!" the man acknowledged.

I had no difficulty in recognising the voice of Gorgeous, who instantly bent down, came up and bent down again as he spun the wheel round deftly to bring the rudder amidships. Even in that half light he was a neat, incongruous and oddly elegant figure, a white kerchief visible in the left sleeve of a thick sailor's jersey reaching almost down to his knees.

"Good morning, Mr. Grieg. How are you?" I greeted him.

"Not to speak to the man at the wheel!" Thor Larsen intervened harshly before Gorgeous could think of answering. "Not to speak until I tell you. Not, not!"

Embarrassed, I retreated to stand discreetly against the back

63

of the wheelhouse while the Captain took up position at the port windows watching the quay intently.

I heard the propellers stop and a second later begin churning again more vigorously than ever before. The backward motion of the ship was quickly arrested. For a moment we lay with our nose directly opposite the stern of the mail steamer. Her decks were awash with lamp light although they were deserted except for her portly master-at-arms who was doing his round of inspection of the ship.

The sight annoyed Thor Larsen because he spat vigorously and muttered angrily at the ship, calling it, among several other names I could not catch, "Pig, you fat spoilt selfish pig, just like your owners! No consideration for others, blinding a sailor with your lights just when he needs his eyes most!"

This last remark partly explained the Captain's irritation with the mail ship. But I was to discover later that he disliked all merchantmen, particularly passenger ships, and most of all, the de luxe Union Castle ships. He disliked even warships, with the significant exceptions of destroyers and submarines, to which he always referred, with one of his grating laughs, as "naval whalers" and "whales". He really had no time for any kind of ship except his own whalers. Yet for me the mail ship had gained in beauty by the darkness. I felt even a little regretful that the *Kurt Hansen*, now getting into her full outward-bound strike, had to leave behind such a lovely pinnacle of light, shimmering with impatience at being bound to the immovable quay.

Soon we were entering the narrow channel between the breakwater and the steep narrow bluff that led to the open sea. The darkness there was great, except for the keen beam of the revolving light on the huge Roman nose of the bluff. The light was cutting deep swathes out of the night like a scythe in a field of opium-black poppies, and intermittently showing me the rigid back of the Captain standing, feet apart, to look straight ahead. Beside him stood Gorgeous, deceptively nonchalant, holding a spoke of the wheel as if it were no more than a cup of China tea.

I was to learn that Gorgeous's attitude was merely an instinctive effort at achieving balance of mind, as if the assumption

of a physical attitude of calm would counter the apprehensions of the highly sensitive and impressionable person that he was.

Considering his nature, he was perhaps the most gallant person in the ship, certainly, by my standards, more so even than the Captain, who had never known fear. I often wondered why, being what he was, Gorgeous never collapsed, and could only suspect that he, like Larsen, was fulfilling a pledge to the sea and whaling so profound that it had become a pre-condition of their being. However, I came to learn that, whenever Gorgeous's hand went to his hip and he adopted a nonchalant attitude, he was getting ready for something that would impose great strain on him. And in our way out of the harbour he had some cause for apprehension.

The narrow channel out of Port Natal was one of the trickiest in existence. As a result no ships of any size were allowed in it without a pilot. These pilots, each holding a master's ticket, had had years of service in one of the many tug-boats used to berth and unberth the ships in harbour, and were to steady them when some unsuspected condition of sea, current, wind or range of swell, swung them from their true course in the narrows. Whalers and a few fishing vessels, because of their small size and draught and long experience of the harbour, were the only exceptions.

So narrow was the channel now that the sound of the sea itself overcame the noise of the screw and engines of the *Kurt Hansen*. It was a wonderful Odyssean sound raised by those urgent white horses so sacred to Homer, as their great black hooves under their steaming luminous manes pounded the quaking shore. Sometimes, when a swell greater than the rest shattered itself on the breakwater, a dazzle of white streamed freely on the darkness, and consequently the disintegrated sea drifted like smoke on the air, penetrating the wheelhouse, where it overwhelmed even the smell of whale. Once a flash from the lighthouse coincided with a particularly heavy explosion of white sea water. The effect was so blinding that I half expected another outburst from the Captain. But none came, and soon we were so near to the bluff and so far below the light that it no longer directly reached us.

I heard Larsen grunt with satisfaction and saw him begin to pace the small deck within the wheelhouse, stopping at the end of each beat to peer fiercely into the night and,on resuming his beat, as he passed the wheel, often giving Gorgeous an order to correct or confirm course.

Ahead of us I could then make out the lights marking the harbour mouth, and knew that we were approaching the most difficult moment on our way out to sea. Winds, tides and currents worked incessantly to maintain a bar of sand across the entrance to the harbour. Although powerful dredgers were constantly used to reduce it, the bar still was much higher than the floor of the sea beyond. As a result,swell and sea making for the land would be forced to rise steeply and violently in order to cross it, and so tended to throw even the greatest and most powerful ships off their course. And the entrance was so narrow that the margin of safety was minute. All a pilot could do to counter the conflicting forces at work was to aim his ship truly and make it as responsive as possible to control from the helm by ensuring that it crossed the bar only at maximum speed.

Although we were still some cable lengths away from the entrance, the *Kurt Hansen*, now going all out, was already beginning to feel the range of the complex movement across the bar. At one moment I was admiring how the *Kurt Hansen*'s bow, darker than the night against the bright star sheen ahead, was pointed straight at the centre of the gap between the entrance lights; the next, it would begin to lift, and levelled first at one star and then at the other. As we approached the entrance the movement of the whaler became more and more violent, and the bow, to my alarm, began to waver like an alcoholic finger.

Once more the Captain went to take up position, legs wider apart than ever, beside Gorgeous who now had both hands firmly on the wheel and was constantly spinning it first one way and then the other. I was relieved then to notice that whenever the bow came down off centre, it would rise dead on the middle, or vice versa, and I began to have an inkling of what Leif had meant about Gorgeous's skill.

But perhaps the greatest tribute of all to Gorgeous was that the imperious Larsen, from the time we came within effective

range of the sea, gave him no further orders at all. He kept
silent even when we hit the sea right on the bar and the little
ship was suddenly lifted high into the night on the Himalayan
peak of one of those swells at which the Indian Ocean excels. She
was held briefly, shuddering, against the trembling stars before
she crashed back into what felt like an abyss, which she hit,
quivering, before rising higher than ever on the far side with a
feather of white sea snow in her cap.

I glanced quickly to port and starboard. Green and red
lights looked in at the wheelhouse windows, then fell away
below us before the *Kurt Hansen* was once more hurled aloft and
shaken out against the summit of the night, phosphorescent
water dripping like star-light from her being. When she came
crashing down again both port and starboard entrance lights
had vanished. We were safely over the bar, and the next swell
we met, though it lifted us high and put us down low, did it all
so smoothly that we shipped no water at all.

The *Kurt Hansen* at once picked up a regular rhythm and went
swinging out over the surging sea into the brilliant night with
a sailor's long rolling stride, across the unlocked ocean, leaving
the huge swells dissolving in classic thunder and fading away
far behind us.

"You hear, young Boher? I say, now you speak as much as
you like!" The Captain's voice brought me to myself.

Gorgeous, steadying the wheel against his knees, took out a
cigarette case, turned to hold it out to me, exclaiming with
obvious relief: "Phew, out of the garage, out of the street and
on the open road at last!"

"Thank you, Mr. Grieg, but I don't smoke."

"The name to you is Georghius." He answered affably, taking out a cigarette, snapping the case to, tapping the cigarette
end lightly on the case a number of times and then lighting it:
"Georghius, the Latin for George."

And from that moment on I became the only person in the
ship to take him at his word. For the Captain and the crew he
was always just plain Grieg except to Leif and 'Mlangeni, who
insisted when they were alone with him and me on calling him
Gorgeous.

"Are you fond of music?" he asked me now. But before I could answer, the door of the deck-house opened and Leif stepped in to ask something of the Captain in Norwegian.

"Chocolate! My God! You know damn better!" Larsen exclaimed fiercely. I suspect the only drink he could think of just then was gin, and Leif's question must have roused a diabolic challenge to his power of will. "But ask this young Boher and Grieg, they might."

"Would you two like a hot cup of chocolate?" Leif asked us, unperturbed.

"Ta!" Gorgeous replied.

"Yes, please," I said. Then, noticing that odd look of fatigue at the back of Leif's eyes, I added: "I'll come and fetch it."

"Good, very good! You go!" Larsen commanded.

I followed, or rather staggered, after Leif on to the deck and for the first time experienced the full effect of night, sky and open sea. Propped against the back of the wheelhouse with a solid roof overhead, I had not realized how high and how far the ship was being thrown by the sea. I had to feel for whatever support I could find, like someone in a game of blind man's bluff, and marvelled at the ease with which Leif walked ahead of me.

Steadying myself against the rail for a moment, I saw that the lights of Port Natal were a lovely diamond glitter behind us and, as we were already far from the land, the lighthouse was no longer a scythe cutting through the darkness but a large single eye of fire winking ceaselessly at us across the waves. The sky was deep and clear, the stars enormous and visible almost to the edge of the horizon. We were heading due east, so that I recognized Alpha Centauri, a bright gold just over the starboard horizon, then near it the Great Pointers, and hard by the Pointers the Southern Cross, its lack of symmetry giving the whole conception a strangely home-made quality and making it the most moving of all the combinations of stars in the sky. Just to the left were the Pleiades, then the Twins, Castor and Pollux. Everywhere I looked there were the stars either singly, or as great constellations, that I had known all my life since, with rare exceptions, I had always slept out in the open at six

thousand feet above sea-level under a sky seldom veiled with cloud. Yet I had rarely seen the stars bigger and so without impediment or distortion as now viewed from the deck of the darkened little ship shouldering the heavy night on a heaving sea. Wherever I turned to search the sky it seemed to me that I was not alone but had company.

On this occasion I felt this so strongly that I stood there for quite a while leaning against a stanchion, letting the feeling run through me like wine, and thinking I was linked, through such a night, with all the life there had been and ever would be. I knew that each of those stars, before their meaning was confined to what could be determined by telescope and spectrums, had had a personal significance for countless vanished peoples. I rejoiced, for instance, that the Pleiades of the Greeks could also be the Seven Kings to us, Seven White Heifers to the Amangtakwena, and the Digging-for-Stars to the Zulus. It was the Southern Cross to the Portuguese, a Sword to me, and the Giraffe to the Sutho peoples of Africa. The great black hole on the edge of the Milky Way, the Coal-Sack to some Europeans, the Entrance to Hell for us, the Cave of the Night to the Abwatetsi, and in Sindakwena The Great Bull-Elephant's Killing Place. Sirius The Great Scorcher, The Dog Star to the Greeks, Eye of the Night to the Amantakwena and the Great Grandmother of Plenty to the Bushman—indeed Mother of Plenty seemed the most appropriate because Sirius does not shine like other stars but seems to contain light so abundantly that often, lying on the veld, I had had the illusion of hearing it overflow like crystal water and drip on the earth beside my head. I recognised them all, saluted them in my heart and felt acknowledged in return.

The climax of this moment for me came when the *Kurt Hansen* suddenly altered course. For an instant our smoke was confused and spread itself streaming between me and the stars, like a Spanish mantilla glinting with sequins when caught in a swirl of wind. As the *Kurt Hansen* came down into the trough between swells, the sea countered with precious stones of phosphorous flashing on the velvet furrows of ploughed-up water vanishing sideways into the dark. Then the smoke took up its

proper station aloft like a pennant high over the stern, the sky emerged again unstained and intact, and I saw the whaler's perky nose pointing straight down a dazzling Milky Way. There the tip of our tall foremast was stirring the stars around, indeed was like a kind of magic ladle thrust deep into the night as into a great cauldron filled to the brim with the black brew of time, stirring and re-stirring it so that the imprisoned light within could break free in star-bubbles on the surface. So entranced was I by the experience that I might have stood there longer had not Leif come back to my side, asking: "Not feeling sea-sick, are you? You're all right, aren't you?"

I realised then, for the first time, that I had not suffered the slightest discomfort from the ship's lively movement and answered exultantly: "No! I'm all right. I've never felt better!"

He stood there peering through the darkness at me and then said casually: "Good. But of course, it's a very calm night."

"A calm night!" I exclaimed. "With the ship bounding about like a kitten of a wild cat and me not able to walk without support!"

He laughed at that and retorted: "All the same, it's exceptionally calm. This is only the regular swell. You wait until we get a swell with a gale-driven sea as well! Even so, you're doing very well for a landsman. But come along, Gorgeous will be wondering about his chocolate!"

I followed him down a companion-way.

After the dark the light below was dazzling; the heat coming up from the engine room after the winter air outside almost stifling. I stumbled down a short steel corridor and caught up with Leif standing beside the opening at the head of the steel ladder which led down to the engine room. Leif was pointing below. I looked through the entrance, saw first the broad, plump figure of the engineer in oil stained overalls still standing expressionless beside the wheel of his controls, and then 'Mlangeni, stripped to the waist, at work by the boiler.

He had just opened the door to the grate, and the vivid red glow from the fire leaping within shone on his broad chest and surrounded his great head with light. So organic, so volcanic in

quality was this glow that by comparison it made the electricity of the engine room look pale and clinical.

As I watched, 'Mlangeni turned his back on this living fire and plunged the shovel in his hand into the slope of a pile of coal which lay on the iron floor behind him and vanished at a steep angle into the gloom of the bunkers from which it came. The supple muscles of his arms and back stood out like those of a weight-lifter in a circus, and the sweat made satin of his smooth black skin.

"Listen!" Leif said.

But already I had heard above the regular clanking of the pistons, whirr of propeller-shaft and brushing of heavy water against the ship's side, the full round bass voice of 'Mlangeni singing loudly to himself in Zulu as he worked the long handle of the shovel to force it deeper into the coal:

> "Seed of the great mother,
> Black corn of the earth,
> Food of flame,
> The child is hungry,
> Come feed new fire:
> Yes, feed, feed this fire."

With that he would lift the shovel high out of the dark, swing round easily and with one thrust of his long arms pitch the coal cleanly through the open grate.

For a moment he would stand up with his hand lightly on the shovel at his side, his head bowed, looking down at the fire with the flames flickering over his face, and then would sing again as if to a person:

> "Red flame of the earth,
> Child of the sun.
> Look! Fear no water,
> Hunger no longer!
> Take food from the mother,
> Eat this black corn,
> Fill your belly.
> And grow, my little one,
> Yes! Grow strong and great."

71

Swinging round with his shovel, he would dig once more into the coal to begin his singing all over again.

It all had an extraordinary effect on me, as if I were watching the first man beside his first fire far back in time.

"Could you make out what all that was about?" Leif asked me when at last we reached his small neat galley.

I gave him a rough translation.

He shook his head in amazement and remarked: "Who would have thought that it is the savage among us who should be the poet and singer of songs? There's precious little music and only a living for most of us in it, except of course the Captain."

"Does the Captain sing?" I asked, surprised.

Leif quickly replied. "Good heavens, no! I merely meant whaling is something much more than just a living to him." Then his mind was back on 'Mlangeni. "I wish I understood him as much as I like him," he said. "But there's no end to him . . ."

"Does he go on for long, singing?" I asked.

"Oh, no," Leif answered. "He always starts out like that but before long the singing becomes a hum, the hum just a grunt with each shovel full of coal, and in the end not even a grunt."

And indeed, when we passed the engine room again on our way back to the wheelhouse, I heard no sound except the steady beat of the engines and the brushing of ploughed-up water against the ship's side.

On deck we found the *Kurt Hansen* had changed course again. Her nose was no longer pointing down the Milky Way but nearly a "quarter" off at a red unblinking star that I took to be the planet Mars.

Leif, of course, noticed it too. "Oh no!" he exclaimed. "It's not possible: he's swung away further than ever!"

"Swung away from what?" I asked.

"From where we broke off whaling on Saturday," he answered vehemently.

"But why?" I pressed him.

"Why?" He reiterated my question disdainfully. "I told you before there's no 'why' to what the Captain does. I can only tell you when we broke off whaling on Saturday with two big

blue whales lashed, one on the port, the other on the starboard side, the sea around us was still alive with whales. Surely the sensible thing to do would be to go back to where we were a bare forty hours ago? Instead we're heading as fast as we can in the opposite direction! There's no sense in it! And yet the chances are that the Captain will be right and that the whales will have changed their minds and suddenly turned back to south where we're heading. You'd think he was a whale himself from the way he seems to know what they are doing!"

He spoke with emotion and was compelled to raise the issue again with Gorgeous the moment he entered the wheelhouse. Noticing that the Captain was out on deck where we could see the tip of his cigarette moving like a firefly through the darkness, Leif handed Gorgeous his mug of chocolate, remarking: "I see he's done it again!"

He sounded as if he were making an accusation.

"Ta." Gorgeous thanked him before saying: "Yes, we've just changed course and are heading east-south-east."

"We!" Leif's tone was sarcastic but Gorgeous did not rise.

He took a sip of chocolate and commented: "You make the best chocolate in the world." Adding, "You know better than I do that he's hardly ever wrong about these things."

"You're right there," Leif replied. "I sometimes think it might be better for him if he were wrong more often. Anyway I leave you to him. I am going down to catch some sleep. What about you?" He turned to me. "We'll all have a long day tomorrow and nothing interesting is likely to happen for some hours yet."

For the first time I felt disappointed by Leif. As far as I was concerned, interesting things were happening all the time, and I was convinced that if I went below I would miss something of the greatest importance. I even judged it a flaw in Leif's character that he had ceased to find it all as absorbing as I did. I was at an age when I just couldn't understand why the whole process of getting older should be accompanied by a growing indifference, and I was quite resolved that, somehow, I would grow up differently. So, in answer to Leif's question, I gave an abrupt "No" which sounded almost disdainful.

Looking back I am certain the meaning of my tone was not lost on him, but far from offending him, it seemed to endear me to him. He patted me affectionately on the shoulder and said: "Thought as much. Enjoy yourself," and went below.

I was alone with Gorgeous and at once he repeated the question he had first asked of me before Leif and I went below for the chocolate: "Are you fond of music?"

I said "Yes", though I felt compelled to add that I knew little about it. We had no professional orchestras or organised music up-country, and I had only twice heard artists of distinction. Once when very young I was taken to hear Melba sing and on another occasion to hear Paderewski play Chopin on the piano.

"Melba! Paderewski!" Gorgeous exclaimed instantly: "I say, you're a lucky boy. I'd have given anything to have heard them."

He there and then concluded that my interest in music equalled his own and treated me to a long exegesis of his own tastes and musical experiences. I longed to change the subject. My mind was on more immediate things. I wanted to ask him about the sea, ships, whaling, Captain Larsen, Leif and so on. But there was no stopping him. He had on his voyages picked up the German word "fabelhaft" and I soon found that in the world of his choice the most "fabelhaft" were Beethoven and Wagner. He told me he had a great deal of Wagner on gramophone records below and promised to play them for me as soon as he had any leisure.

I must have listened to him for close on half-an-hour when the door to the wheelhouse opened abruptly and Larsen walked in. From the way he crashed it to behind him I gathered that the tension in him must have increased greatly since I had last seen him. Knowing his moods of old, Gorgeous instantly stopped talking, stiffened at the wheel and stared straight ahead.

Without a word Larsen in that heavy rolling gait of his went to the compass, bent down to peer at it as if prepared to find the ship off course. When he saw it was not, he merely growled. It was extraordinary what drama Larsen brought to everything and how his own inner atmosphere determined the climate for all around him.

Hard on the grunt came a curt order in Norwegian. I was soon to learn that in moments of compulsion and crisis Larsen spoke only his native tongue, in short, quick bursts and a tone more rasping than ever before.

The order made Gorgeous immediately step back and hand over the wheel to Larsen. That done, he turned away lightly, muttered an almost inaudible "Ta-Ta!" at me, and went out of the wheelhouse quickly, shutting the door behind him.

His going left me feeling acutely uncomfortable. The Captain so far had ignored me and looked as if he would continue to do so. All I could see of him was his square uncompromising back, rigid and black against the star sheen ahead like a silhouette in a shadow-show. I did not feel I could break the silence and yet did not see how I could go on cowering in the background indefinitely as if I were not there. And if I dared to speak, how could I begin and what should I say? So far the openings and the initiative had always been his.

I need not have worried for, once Larsen had got the feel of the helm and the response of the ship underneath him, without turning his head he rapped out the question, "And you, young Boher? What you wish now for to do? Go below and rest? Two more hours to daylight, not?"

Again I had no wish to go below. But neither did I feel like spending two hours in the company of a Captain who was as on edge as his manner and tone suggested.

"Please, sir," I said, as an inspiration came to me. "May I go out and watch on deck for a while?"

"You feel sea-sick." In his mood already fixed for the worst, instant suspicion made this harsh utterance an assertion of fact.

"Not at all, sir," I replied quickly. "I feel perfectly all right. I just thought I'd like some fresh air and watch from the deck."

"Good! Good! You go but to take care not to fall overboard, not?" For the first time he sounded almost pleased. I suppose because my words proved, as he thought, how right his first assessment of me had been.

I remained on deck until first light. Whenever I looked up at the wheelhouse it was to see the tip of the Captain's cigarette winking like a red star in the centre of the window above me.

His hands moved with the wheel but otherwise he never ceased standing there, feet planted firmly, staring straight ahead. It was extraordinary the effect that so small a thing had on me, conveying how fixedly and unalterably he was at the heart not only of the ship but also of all that was shaping ahead in the daylight to come.

The sky maintained its algebraic clarity, so that I was able to see the morning star rise in its entirety from the moment when it was just a quicksilver sliver in the narrow band of sea-moisture on the horizon, then a pin-prick of light and a darting spear-head of fire, swiftly followed by the shoulders and finally the whole brilliant body of Jupiter swinging clear of horizontal murk and vapour to drive the night authoritatively before it. At once the new starlight walked the water, leaving a footpath of silver to run between me and the east like a life-line through the multitudinous creases in the palm of the sea's black outstretched hand.

There is something most significant about the encounter of a human being in solitude with great abiding manifestations of nature. It is so intensely personal and specific that it demands some special recognition from one's imagination. That moment, indeed, grew great with natural divinity, and the vast uprush of light soaring after it with widespread wings became a miracle. I felt then as if I were witnessing the first day of Genesis and so near to some numinous presence stirring over the face of the waters that I had the impulse to pray in the ancient Amangtak-wena way. They greet the day by breathing into the palm of the right hand until it becomes damp and warm, holding it up to the dawn till the morning air has fanned it cool and dry, taking that as a sign that the breath of their lesser life has been made one with the breath of a greater. I had often when alone with them on the veld or in the bush found it perfectly natural to join in with them. But on this occasion something I was not aware of stopped me. I know now that it was a fear that Thor Larsen, up there at the wheel, would see me do it.

With the light, shape and colour in its purest and most limpid shades returned to the world. The swell which I had hitherto known only as ploughed-up water now claimed its full unbroken

stature. I was startled at first by the length and height of those seas rolling down on us and by the full extent of the ocean as now revealed to me. The *Kurt Hansen* looked really too small to fill so great a vacancy indefinitely. As the stars, one by one, vanished until Jupiter alone was left, the feelings of companionship I have mentioned before deserted me.

Happily these feelings did not last, for soon in our quick subtropical way there came the sun. It fell on my senses like the call of a trumpet. Immediately its colours were run up the mast of the sky and their reflection below turned the sea into the deepest of blues. At the same time the day went into action. Half-way between me and the port horizon a school of dolphins broke surface and went leaping northward, working a gun-metal shuttle of silver-blue stitches in and out of the yellow hem of the morning. Just ahead a purple porpoise arched its lazy back on the water so slowly that not a ripple troubled the glassy surface around it. Close to starboard the triangular fin of a great shark began to keep dark determined station on us.

The crew at the same time appeared on deck. No whistle or bell had summoned them. They all knew only too well from experience when they were needed and what each man had to do. In all the years I was in the *Kurt Hansen* I was never to hear a bosun's pipe or ship's whistle used to muster her men. Yet on this first morning when, without warning, I saw them turn up around me, I was certain that it was not habit but Larsen who, in the soundless way that he had of imposing his will on men, had brought them bubbling out of the hatch on deck. I had already seen enough of this kind of communication among gregarious animals and birds who could know what their leader wanted without any visible or audible signal from him, to think that human beings could not be denied a similar gift. Each man, the moment he stepped clear of the hatch, looked up at the wheelhouse where the face and shoulders of Larsen, the sun on them, were clearly visible. Even my own comparatively unenlisted eyes again and again turned to those set, determined features. It was most noticeable, too, how, having had their look at the Captain, the whole crew went to work with a will.

One man made straight for the foremast and began climbing

without a pause up to the crow's-nest. My excited eyes took in every refinement of his technique. The firm grip on the rope with the hands, one hand never relaxing its hold to reach upward until the other had consolidated its own clasp; one foot firmly pressed into the rope in the hollow between the ball and heel of the foot so that it could not slip before the other was raised for the next rung with the whole weight of the man pressing down and backward like a monkey on a stick, so that the knees could not get entangled with the ladder, and the rope of each rung was allowed to sag so it could bite more securely into the middle of the foot. My heart followed him with my eyes until he stood securely in the tub just underneath the top of the slender mast, the sky a great-coat about his shoulders and the light of the morning a halo round his head. I think I knew already that, of all places in the *Kurt Hansen*, that was where I would most like to be. Also there seemed a glorious natural rightness that, at the very moment when everything in the world was reaching upward, the sun into the sky, the dolphins into the air, the porpoise and even the shark and its midnight fin to the glassy surface of the sea, the first action of man, too, should be to rise.

Directly he was in position he gave a quick look round the whole horizon, then signalled with his arms that there was nothing to report. It seemed at best a highly provisional judgement for he had taken so little time to examine so great a view. The reason for his hurry, however, was plain when I noticed Larsen leaning well out in front of the wheel, his face near the window, staring upward at his look-out in the crow's-nest. The disbelief on his face at the negative signal and the distaste with which he stepped once more behind the wheel were most marked and filled me with some apprehension.

The next man, who happened to be mate and bosun combined, a huge, deeply religious, middle-aged father of seven, went right forward and climbed the platform in the bows on which the *Kurt Hansen*'s harpoon gun was mounted, securely swaddled in canvas against the damp like a Russian suckling against the Siberian cold.

At the same time one of the oldest members of the crew made for the wheelhouse. Now all our whalers, being designed to

work in Antarctic as well as sub-tropical waters, had two inter-dependent steering and navigating systems: the one housed for rough and cold weather in the wheelhouse we had used all night; the other was on a small open bridge above it. The man had hardly vanished into the wheelhouse when Larsen appeared in the long level light of the sun on the open bridge. He must have gone up the interconnecting ladder at the double and appeared to be in a hurry, for at once I saw the ash-blue canvas which covered compass and signals box, stripped off and being rolled up against his broad chest. A moment later he was at the signals box, pulling at the levers. Their bell rang out at once loud and clear, and seconds later an acknowledgement in kind came up from the engine room. Satisfied that his bridge-system was functioning properly, Larsen took to the wheel and a moment later he was joined by the man from the wheelhouse below. It was obvious that Larsen could hardly wait to abandon the wheel to the newcomer, for he vanished almost immediately from my view to come striding down to the main deck. There he made his longest scrutiny yet of the crow's-nest where the look-out was now methodically doing a steady detailed inspection of the entire horizon with German binoculars. Larsen, judging by the fierce expression that came to his face, found it more incredible than ever that the man still had nothing to report. In the end he went by me so angry that he didn't even see me, although I had jumped to my feet to wish him good morning, and joined his bosun in the bows.

The speed with which the two men stripped the canvas from the gun was impressive. While the mate stored the canvas, Larsen seized the stock of the gun and began to swing it about on its swivel aiming it at all possible angles at imaginary whales in the sea. I had seen many hunters, including some of the greatest in Africa, go through these motions with their own weapons before setting out into the bush, and I knew, of course, that this was a precaution that no hunter of big game could neglect except at his peril. One could tell, too, what kind of man and how expert he was, from the way the hunter examined the actions of his gun. Watching Thor Larsen at a similar ritual with his harpoon gun, I knew somehow he was to be counted

among the greatest. Nor did he stop with the gun. He paid as much attention to its charge as to the gun.

The harpoon with which it was loaded carried between folded flukes and sharp arrow point a war-head, a kind of grenade with a high degree of fragmentation. The grenade was designed to do two things: on explosion it spread the four folded flukes wide outward so that they gripped the flesh of the whale as firmly as ship's anchor does the bed of the sea. At the same time it drove tiny fragments of steel everywhere deep into the vital organs of the whale in order to try to hasten its end. The tough steel flukes of the harpoon were designed to hold the whale, whatever the strain, and the slot in the neck of the harpoon shaft was thin so that a wire strap could connect it with the end of a cable of the best manilla.

This cable was neatly coiled on the platform in front of the gun before being led on to the deck below to a block and tackle at the foot of the mast, and from there up to a pulley at the end of a derrick, and from the pulley to a drum on a steam-winch between mast and wheelhouse. The pulley was attached as well to a powerful spring which acted both as shock-absorber and brake when the harpooned whale dived in its mortal pain and quickly ran out the ration of free cable coiled in the bow. In fact the whole mechanism, from the moment the whale was harpooned, enabled the machinist at the winch to play the whale as an angler does a salmon with rod and reel.

Accompanied by the mate, Larsen examined his highly mechanised fishing tackle inch by inch from harpoon tip to the drum on the winch. By the time he got to the winch the mechanic was there, and from the steam smoking over the drum it was obvious that already he had made certain that the power was there to operate it instantly. Even so, Larsen made him start up his engine, winding the slack on his rope several times in and out to make certain the whole mechanism was properly interconnected. All the time he would stop at intervals to give the crow's-nest a fierce unbelieving look.

After one more look upwards Larsen suddenly stamped off back to the bridge with his resolute, rocking step. Once more the bells of the signals from the bridge to the engine room rang out

imperiously. A moment later the beat of the engines changed and the thrash of the propeller decreased noticeably. At the same time the ship's course altered, for I saw the *Kurt Hansen*'s impertinent nose slowly move slightly towards the east. Looking abaft at our milky wake, I noticed that we had begun a great wide circular sweep of the ocean at what I took to be at least half our former speed. Obviously the lack of positive news from the crow's-nest had not changed Larsen's conviction that there were whales in the vicinity.

When he came down on deck again a quarter of an hour later and there was still no sign of quarry, he looked baffled and for a moment rather irresolute and helpless as he stood there in the sun. I found myself feeling rather sorry for him. Then I saw him quickly square his shoulders, make for the companion-way to the saloon and vanish below without another glance at ship or crew.

I was not certain whether I should follow him or not. I felt that the moment had now come when I should go below and call my friend. Yet I was by now so under the domination of the Captain's mood that I felt almost incapable of doing anything except by his command. I stood there irresolute, the slight air of that clear winter's morning cool on my face, swaying as the great blue swell of the open sea rocked the *Kurt Hansen*, at one moment towering between it and the sun like a palace of glass and the next holding it up high on its shining ramparts. I had the feeling that I had become some kind of a puppet, and the ship indeed seemed just such another manipulated by an all-powerful sea.

Then Leif's face appeared at the head of the campanion-way. He beckoned to me and called out: "Breakfast!"

I realised then that without knowing it I had grown almost faint from hunger. With the appetite of a healthy boy I hastened down into the saloon. Larsen was already seated at the head of the small table. A large enamel can of coffee, steaming at the spout, three empty enamel mugs, a huge wooden board holding a great loaf of fresh rye-bread, a bowl of yellow butter, sugar, an immense round cheese, three plates and three knives were placed squarely in front of him.

As I came barging in, he looked up sharply. His intense, vivid grey eyes, the eyes of a born witch-doctor as my host's butler had described them a week before, looked up at me for a moment without really seeing me. If he were a house visited by strange spirits (as the butler had warned me and as I by now was inclined to believe), he was not being visited just then. His eyes appeared to see nothing. It was quite frightening, and the air in that little triangle of a saloon, though lit with the sun coming through the porthole, seemed dark around him. The sense of total obliteration within him made me think of a diver who, in the bed of a clear sea and at the point of snatching a pearl, found his light extinguished by a discharge of ink by the giant squid stalking strange game in the coral forests. The scraping of the sea against the ship's thin sides, louder than ever in my ears since the *Kurt Hansen*'s reduced speed, lent a startling validity to my unsought underwater association.

Nervously, I remarked loudly: "Good morning, sir. It's a lovely morning, isn't it?"

He went on looking at me as if from some remote dimension. Presently he growled, "Food. Eat. Call your friend, not?"

Relieved, I went directly through the curtains of his cabin, knelt by Eric's bunk, took him by the shoulder and said: "Wake up, little old one,* wake up! Time to get up and eat!"

Poor fellow, there was no need to wake him, for he groaned instantly at my touch exclaiming, "Oh, do leave me alone. Can't you see how awful I feel?"

"Oh, come on!" I remonstrated. "You'll feel better for some food and fresh air. It's a lovely day on deck!"

At that he did sit up. Unfortunately his gallant effort coincided with one of the greatest swells the *Kurt Hansen* had encountered yet. She climbed it swiftly, shuddering as if with ague, at so steep an angle that the curtains in the cabin vanished through the entrance into the saloon, leaving so wide a gap that I saw the Captain's chair at the head of the table and part of his motionless back. Then down she came again so quickly that the

---

* Literal translation of Afrikaans "Outie" much favoured in my youth as an affectionate form of address.

curtain came swinging again through the entrance until it nearly touched the opposite wall.

"Oh, God!" my friend exclaimed, sinking back into his bunk again. It says a great deal for his will that as he did so he apologized and added: "Please don't let me spoil the day for you. It's no use. I've been through all this before. If I can't take the movement lying down, I know I shan't be able to standing up."

"Coffee might help?" I suggested.

"Later. Just leave me alone, now, will you?" He answered with such vehemence that I left, promising to look in on him from time to time.

"I'm afraid he's not feeling at all well," I told the Captain back in the saloon.

He took the news without a word, just signalling to me with his hand to be seated and pushing the breakfast board towards me.

I thought it best to comply without a word, so I helped myself to a plate and knife, cut a thick crisp crust from the fresh rye loaf and a chunk of yellow Norwegian cheese, took a knob of butter and poured out a steaming mugful of coffee.

All the time Larsen had stared unseeingly before him but now suddenly he began to be interested in my presence. At first I did not like the new look at all. I felt he was not seeing me as I myself was, but as a character on the stage of his own internal drama. We are an Old Testament people in Africa and Africa is an Old Testament country, and this was an Old Testament moment at sea. I had been brought up to know the Old Testament almost by heart, and the look on Larsen's face made me think of Saul glowering at young David playing the harp just before hurling a spear at him. It so alarmed me that, as a natural act of appeasement, I stood up, took him the mug of coffee, put it down in front of him without speaking, returned to my own place trembling inwardly, and poured myself another cup and began my meal.

I have not since tasted any food I liked more than this simple meal. There was a wonderful ancient smell of fresh bread which came from the loaf once I had cut it. It was more astringent than

bread made from wheat and so therefore more appropriate since it countered the heavier, all pervasive smell of the whale. It joined with the smell of freshly made coffee, which is the one substance I know that smells even better than it tastes. I seldom get a whiff of coffee or a smell of new bread even today without remembering briefly the boy eating his first breakfast in the *Kurt Hansen*'s saloon.

Eating with such relish pushed my nervousness into the background, and soon I had the courage to look at the Captain again. He was still watching me but more closely.

As his eyes met mine, he exclaimed with satisfaction: "By God, you not sick! You damn hungry, not?"

I nodded emphatically, looking steadily at him over the rim of my mug of coffee. This seemed to have a soothing effect on him.

"You friend damn sick, not?" he said again, pausing before going on in a resentful voice far too loud for my liking because I was afraid my friend could not help hearing it. "He is sick because he's spoilt rich boy. His father spoilt rich merchant. All owners are spoilt. All peoples on land spoilt. Bah!"

His broad hand clenched and hit at the empty air, then he pushed his chair violently away, stood up, reached for my plate which was now empty, and said: "Now! I show you proper unspoilt whaler's breakfast!"

With that he cut me a slice twice as thick as the crust I had just eaten, spread it three times deeper in butter, cut a portion of cheese as thick as the slice of bread and, slapping the two together, pushed the plate at me, rasping out confidently, "You like that, not?"

"Thank you, sir," I said, and added: "Gosh, but it's a whale of a helping!"

"A whale of a helping!" he repeated deliberately after me.

I believe at another time and place he might have laughed. As it happened, it was a triumph that he was not displeased. He gave me a look of some approval, then dropped back into the bottom of the cleft mood in which I had found him. Snatching up his cap which lay on the floor beside him, he lumbered out of the saloon, leaving the mug of coffee I had poured out for him untouched on the table.

I was finishing my fourth slice of bread and cheese when Leif appeared.

Seeing the diminished loaf and lifting the can of coffee and finding it empty, he said, "Good! It looks as if the Captain's had something at last."

I flushed and then confessed that it was I who had done all the eating and drinking.

Leif shook his head wearily. "I might have known it! He never does the first morning out. So it's just to be another of those days . . ." He shrugged his shoulders and then added: "But I'm glad you ate well. There's a long day ahead. In fact, if you like, I'll make you some fresh coffee."

However, I had had enough, but I went on to tell him that I was concerned about my friend and wondered if there was anything I could do to help him?

Food to be sick on, fresh air and keeping on one's feet at all costs were the quickest cures, Leif assured me. In any case I was not to worry because sea-sickness was very good for the human system.

I had not much hope of success but felt compelled to try out Leif's advice on Eric.

"For God's sake, leave me alone, can't you?" was his only response.

After that I had no conscience in hastening away to go on deck. I went through the saloon from which Leif, together with all signs and smells of breakfast, had vanished. A ray of the sun shining through the porthole had found the bookcase in the corner and was moving across its contents like a finger, dipped in the ink of fate, once did over a Babylonian wall. It moved from "The Pilot's Manual", "Lloyd's Register of Shipping", the "Holy Bible", on towards Larsen's moroccan bound volumes of his kills and then back again, according to how the *Kurt Hansen* rolled and dipped to the beat of the Indian Ocean on her way out into that great, glossy, bland and blank winter's day.

CHAPTER SIX

'Tutuka! 'Nkosan, Tutuka!'

I WENT bobbing out on deck into the bright warm sun. The sudden brightness was too much for my eyes and I sneezed loudly.

I immediately heard 'Mlangeni's deep voice go up from behind the main hatch. "Tutuka,'Nkosan, Tutuka! Grow, little Prince, grow!"

His tone was warm with satisfaction,for among his people, as among my Amangtakwena, sneezing was regarded as a lucky sign showing that the spirits of a person's ancestors had entered him to protect him.

There were many ways of responding to the salutation I had just received from 'Mlangeni, so I did what custom demanded and called on all the spirits of his ancestors and mine, associating him with whatever good fortune the sneeze portended. "Bobaba, fathers, look upon us, and do not turn your backs on us."

"You will grow, 'Nkosan, do not trouble, you will grow," 'Mlangeni said approvingly as I made my way to join him.

He was seated on deck, his broad back against the sides of the forrard hatch, his long legs wide apart and stretched full out in front of him, and on the warm, golden wood between them were set a mug of steaming coffee and a platter piled high with slices of bread, butter and yellow cheese. He might have been sitting against the wall of his bee-hive hut in his own kraal at Icoco,so thoroughly at home did he look there in the sun. Not even those pinpointing eyes of Thor Larsen's constantly examining and reappraising the actions of all within sight could abolish the feeling of indigenous calm and contentment that 'Mlangeni gave out. For soon I noticed that, whenever he bothered to catch the Captain's eye directed at him like a demand for an immediate explanation of his presence on deck

when he should, perhaps, have been at his fire below, 'Mlangeni merely looked up at the safety valve beside the funnel implying that Larsen, too, might look for his answers there. And indeed, since the *Kurt Hansen* had reduced speed the excess steam in her boilers was so great that it was forcing its way into the air with a loud continuous hiss which would have made talk on deck inaudible had not the movement of the ship carried the noise abaft.

Clearly two could play at the game of wordless intercommunication. 'Mlangeni's response was, of course, a perfectly calm and just response to the Captain's unreason. But like most of us, the Captain would have found bias, particularly bias in his own favour, easier to endure than an absolutely impartial and just desert.

"Here, 'Nkosan," 'Mlangeni now said the moment I reached him, holding the plate of bread and cheese up to me with both hands. "Eat and grow." Native good manners demanded the gesture. I have never known Africans, no matter how poor, who do not offer to share their food even with strangers who happen to find them eating.

I was about to refuse and explain why when a gruff voice with a Norwegian accent broke in: "Say, what you two talk about?"

It was the man at the winch which was just forrard of the hatch. His name was Nils Ruud.

Gorgeous, who thought punning by no means the lowest form of wit, was later to say repeatedly of this man to me that he was a "Rude Ruud man, in manner and deed," but actually Nils Ruud's bark was much worse than his bite. His greatest defect was that he had no imagination and consequently was more literal, self-willed and opinionated than he should have been. At heart he was a decent enough fellow and, like the rest of the crew, always kind to me.

"What does he say?" he asked again as, taken by surprise at this interruption, I stared at him standing there, oil-can in a large red hand, his grease-stained overalls hanging on his burly frame and his small determined blue eyes bright with obstinate enquiry.

87

"Oh, we're just exchanging the time of day," I answered rather lamely.

"A long time and much words you take for your time of day," he repeated unbelievingly after me.

I said no more and he had to stoop, unanswered, towards his machine and resume making a show of oiling an engine that needed no oiling for the benefit of Thor Larsen, who never had his eyes off us for long.

I had not said more to Ruud because I had a hunch that the less I told the rest of the crew about my exchanges with 'Mlangeni the easier it would be for him to confide in me. Also how explain to a man like Nils Ruud what had just passed between the two of us? How make a regular church-goer like Nils understand that 'Mlangeni, ostensibly one of the benighted heathen, was more aware of the world of the spirit and its claims than most of us? To 'Mlangeni everything from a grain of sand to the fire underneath his boiler, from the movement of an ant to the lowing of cattle at night, even the sneeze of a boy, were all significant manifestations of meaning. What would Nils Ruud have said had I told him that 'Mlangeni was such a dedicated, accepting servant of the spirit that we, by comparison, became brutal materialists rejecting it?

Besides, it was even more complicated than that. For one thing, there was the fact that 'Mlangeni was black. I am not suggesting that the crew of the *Kurt Hansen* suffered from the kind of highly organised colour prejudice from which so many of my countrymen suffered. They were remarkably free of it and happily shared their quarters, ate at the same mess table with 'Mlangeni and shook hands with him as they did with one another. Yet his blackness did make a difference to them. Had he been white he would not, I am certain, have excited the constant curiosity that he did. Yet I had already learnt that there are many Europeans who are curious about primitive peoples not in order to understand them better, but just to laugh them out of the way. There had become something frightening to me about the European laughter over Africans and African practices. It was significant how, once the crew knew I spoke 'Mlangeni's language, they could never see the

two of us in conversation without being drawn to us, like iron
filings towards a magnet, to demand what we were discussing.

I suppose black is the natural colour of what is strange and
secret in the human spirit. It is the uniform of the unknown.
Somehow 'Mlangeni,through his blackness and his nearness to
nature, was a personification of those aspects of the *Kurt
Hansen*'s blond crew which were hidden, or estranged from
them; a living mirror wherein they saw the dark face of all that
was rejected and out of reach in them themselves.

Unfortunately, therefore, since the process of acquiring self-
knowledge is by no means painless or without humiliation,their
natural curiosity had an undertow of suspicion and apprehension. It seems an *a priori* condition of our so-called success in
civilising ourselves that what is to be rejected must in itself be
proved to be something discreditable. Consequently the crew
were both attracted and repulsed by 'Mlangeni. Not, I stress,
because of anything in his character but because unknowingly
they associated him with their own.

All this I was to learn much later; as also that it applied particularly to Thor Larsen. He did not even allow himself to be
curious about 'Mlangeni, just suspicious. Here in his own ship,
where everything exacted a Captain's commitments from him,
he was inclined to be subtly uncomfortable whenever he set
eyes on 'Mlangeni. And whatever caused discomfort to his
spirit was at once suspect or rejected.

I was to become aware later that, had 'Mlangeni not been so
outstandingly good at his job, Thor Larsen would have got rid
of him. But he was too good a seaman not to recognise 'Mlangeni's signal uses. His, for instance, was the only ship in the
fleet with just one full-time stoker. All the rest had two. Only a
person of 'Mlangeni's superb physique,and his pride in using it,
could have succeeded in so exacting a task. There were very few
occasions on which he was given help at his engineer's insistence
because we had been at sea overlong. That 'Mlangeni did all
this where no European could was, ironically, cause not for
gratitude but for more suspicion. Why did he do it, when no
one else did or could? What was he getting out of it?

That he was just an ignorant savage and knew no better

served as an answer for some, though it soon wore threadbare
in daily contact with 'Mlangeni. Even Leif at our first meeting
the evening before had implied how questions like these could
rankle with someone like himself who liked 'Mlangeni. They
troubled Larsen and his crew even more, and over the seasons I
was to see the suspicion grow that there had to be more to it
than the modest wages paid to 'Mlangeni. Similarly I in my
turn was neither quite as fair nor as aware as I might have been.

So, standing there on deck rather abashed by Nils Ruud's
obvious disbelief of my explanation, I was relieved to hear
'Mlangeni's round, unperturbed voice imply approval of my
behaviour; saying, "Do not trouble, 'Nkosan. He is a 'With-
ears-that-do-not-hear'* man. Come and eat."

I went and sat down beside him, thanking him and explain-
ing that I had already breakfasted.

I had hardly finished when Larsen hailed the crow's-nest. His
voice shattered the calm of the great glass-palace of a day like
a brick hurled through its roof and the splinters fell down into
my mind like hail.

Immediately we saw that another sailor was already hurrying
on his way up aloft.

Disconsolate, the look-out handed over his glasses to the newcomer, climbed out of the tub and back down to the deck where
he stood for a moment staring at the bridge. He then signalled
again "Nothing to report" emphatically with his arms as if in
outraged self-justification. Larsen ignored the man completely
who then turned about defiantly and ducked below.

After a while, when the new look-out also signalled "Nothing
to report", Larsen began to move, practically throwing himself
from side to side of his small bridge, barely three strides wide.
He made me think of a black bear I had once seen pacing to and
fro in a cage in Pretoria's zoo.

"Patience, 'Nkosan," between great uninhibited munches
and smacking his lips between each bite, 'Mlangeni let me know
what should be thought of the abrupt switching of look-outs in
particular, and the Captain's behaviour in general. "Patience

* Zulu idiom for a person without marked powers of understanding or inclination to listen to others.

is an egg that hatches great birds. Even the sun is such an egg."

He extended his right arm to trace the course of the sun from horizon to horizon with a long dark finger.

"And which came first, the egg or the bird?"

I couldn't resist teasing him with the question our agnostic science master at school had loved to inflict on his pupils.

"Auck, now you are a trickster again." 'Mlangeni grinned largely. "You should know that neither bird nor egg came first."

"Neither?" I questioned.

"Neither. Because patience came before everything!" Suddenly 'Mlangeni stopped me with an urgent: "Hush, 'Nkosan! Hush, and hasten. The little-killer-of-great-fish wants you!"

Disturbed by the tone of his voice, I looked instantly at the bridge.

Larsen was beckoning imperatively in our direction, but as there were several other people including Nils Ruud within the range of his gestures, how 'Mlangeni knew that I was the target, I could not tell.

I only knew that I believed him and got to my feet in such a hurry that it was not until the day was over that I realised 'Mlangeni had paid me the compliment of revealing to me his own favourite name for the Captain.

"Did you want me, sir?" I asked, as I popped out on the bridge, somewhat breathless from the speed with which I had come.

"Better you stay here." Larsen's tone implied a rebuke even though his actual choice of words did not. "Better for to see when the whale comes."

True as the explanation was, the real reason I suspected was different. The young are only inexperienced in terms of our brief and brittle concerns here. As far as the rest of life is concerned, they are as old as time. Some instinct told the fourteen-year-old boy I was then that the Captain got me away from 'Mlangeni because he was jealous of his stoker. Not because of me but because he saw in 'Mlangeni a kind of rival, another Captain in some right of his own in a dimension to which even Larsen's presumptuous brief did not run.

This was proved to me by the fact that, having once got me on the bridge, the Captain immediately lost interest in me, and resumed his preoccupations as if he had never relinquished them.

I longed to go back on deck to join 'Mlangeni and be free to scramble all over the ship among the many new and strange things so neatly laid out and arranged in the classical manner of the sea, and all transformed into treasure in my imagination by the lovely light of our sub-tropical winter's sun. Just the mere rope plaited and coiled beside the harpoon gun, behind the winch, the gleaming derricks, or the shining davits were all exceedingly beautiful to me. I longed to go and examine the ship more closely and discover the reasons and uses for everything. This longing was encouraged by the size of the *Kurt Hansen* herself. In comparison with the ships we had left crowded in Port Natal she looked not yet fully grown, and this morning her young proportions made her all the more appealing to a boy's imagination; as if she had been designed with the express purpose for young hearts to play with her.

But there I was, stuck on the small bridge, physically and mentally uncomfortable because I felt continually obliged not to encroach on such room as there was for the man at the wheel, the restless, driven Captain. As a result, despite my interest in the sea around us, there began one of the longest mornings I have ever known. But long as it was for me, I am sure it was far longer for the Captain.

I saw 'Mlangeni finish his breakfast and watched him sitting warm and content in the sun, his head slightly on one side rather like that of a hen brooding over her eggs. He looked indeed as if he were patience itself hatching one of those great birds of which he had spoken. Presently, without a sign or hint from anyone, he rose to his full height, stretched himself with hands and arms flung out straight and wide, then bent down to scoop up his breakfast things and went below. Clearly 'Mlangeni's fire was due for another feeding. But the deck looked bleaker for his going.

Thor Larsen, of course, did not fail to notice his stoker's departure. He snorted loudly.

'TUTUKA! 'NKOSAN, TUTUKA!'

The higher the slow sun climbed with the step of a somnambulist walking in a yellow poppy-drunk sleep, the bluer, the calmer, the blanker and the more reluctant the day seemed to become.

The early morning activity vanished. I no longer had any dolphins or porpoises to watch on a sea without ripple, only that dark dorsal sail of the shark's fin remained in station with us: and curiously it seemed to be the one thing that did not displease the Captain. He repeatedly turned to look behind to see if it were still there. Only once, speaking out of the middle of his preoccupation, he remarked: "It is there because it knows as I know."

Larsen had changed our first look-out at nine. He changed his successor at ten, and thereafter at every hour a replacement was sent up aloft to come down as unsuccessful as his predecessor.

Always the Captain made it clear without a word how deeply disappointed he was with us all; and the sense of failure among the men in the ship consequently became almost a tangible physical element. Men either stopped talking to one another, or did so in whispers, like persons in a deep Alpine valley afraid that the sound of the normal human voice would be enough to bring down an avalanche from snows piled on the steep heights above them.

Even Leif, when he appeared on the bridge at eleven with coffee, did not speak. The only bright sign was that the Captain drank two mugs of hot liquid quickly one after the other without waiting for it to cool.

By this time I was so uncomfortable that I seized the opportunity of this break in the Captain's concentration to ask him if I might slip down below to see my friend?

Thor Larsen glared at me over his mug of coffee as if amazed that I should continue to bother about such a triviality. But he nodded his head and as he handed his last mug to Leif, he ordered me bluntly: "But mind, not to interrupt that black stoker again, not? And you come back soon to see whales blow!"

Having delivered himself of this command, he gave the crow's-nest another fierce look, went silent, and resumed his bear-like movement from side to side on the bridge.

Close as I had been to him, even I had not realised what a potent weapon was this silence of the Captain's and how much it had affected the crew. Whenever two of them met they were now raising a different kind of mutter. I knew no Norwegian yet but the tone alone was enough to suggest they were beginning to resent this silence, were perfectly aware that it was being used against them as a weapon and thought it unfair. Steady, patient, phlegmatic as most of them were, they were beginning to criticise Thor Larsen openly in voices so low that only they could hear. I knew this simply because, as we passed the fore-mast, the last replaced look-out reached the deck and paused to speak to Leif.

"What did he say?" I couldn't resist asking.

Leif shrugged. "He said that it's unfair of the Captain not to speak his mind. He says it is not his fault there are no whales about."

Another man talking to Nils Ruud at the winch was even more downright. According to Leif he told Ruud: "By God, he's no right to behave as if *we* are in the wrong. It is *he* who's in the wrong. If he had gone back in the direction where we left the whales on Saturday, as the other ships will have done, we would have caught some by now."

I did not dare stay down below long. I made a perfunctory call on Eric and then tried to prolong my absence from the bridge by calling on Leif in his galley. But he, for once, would have none of me, although I believe he came very close to knowing how deeply uncomfortable the Captain and the atmosphere in the ship had begun to make someone as young as myself feel.

He tried to reassure me. "Look, don't worry. It's always like this the first day or two. No harm will come of it. Just you get back to the bridge as soon as you can and do what he wants you to do."

So I hastened back to the bridge. My prompt reappearance obviously pleased the Captain, though he still did not speak. But apart from this flicker of emotion, the atmosphere without and within was even tenser than before.

The day was at high noon now, and on the stroke of twelve

the Captain roared for his first spotter of the day to do another turn of duty aloft. The sound of his angular voice killed the silence.

I looked about and thought I had never seen so unresponsive and lifeless a scene as that buckled Indian Ocean, implacably lifting us up only to put us down again, like a deranged mind perpetually raising and re-raising the one thought it can neither penetrate nor escape. I have never seen a similar scene except, perhaps, at the height of summer in one of our terrible droughts on that wide plain deep in my native interior, which is called in Sindakwena the 'Where-even-courage-is-lost' plain.

I was jerked out of my contemplation of the sea by Thor Larsen suddenly bawling out to me.

"Ah! My young Boher! Your eyes damn good! Your reflex damn quick on tennis courts! You show me how good they are at sea, not?"

I turned about, afraid of what I would see on his face, but to my surprise he was looking rather pleased with himself.

"You get up there in the crow's-nest with Johansen quick and you spot me the whale damn quick, not?"

I didn't answer him. The moment I took in the import of Thor Larsen's command my heart started beating fast with excitement. I just made straight for the ladder, the first laugh of the day from the Captain grating out loudly behind me to encourage my eagerness to obey. I went down it in such a rush that I nearly fell and was at the foot of the port ladder to the crow's-nest almost as soon as Svend Johansen, the re-summoned first look-out of the day, reached the starboard one. Since there were to be two of us in the crow's-nest, we waited, our hands on the ropes, for the discredited look-out to descend. While he had a brief word with Johansen and handed over the glasses to him I beat the pistol as athletes say, and went up my side as fast as I could. Oddly enough, although I had never done anything of the sort and might have been expected to mount carefully if not apprehensively, the close attention I had paid since morning to the way the various look-outs went aloft gave me confidence and enabled me to climb the rope ladder itself without fear as if I had done it all my life. Leif told me afterwards that everyone

who saw my climb was convinced I had done it many times before.

But the fear I had then was of a totally different kind. I was terrified that I, too, would fail to spot a whale.

It seemed to me just then that suddenly everything had come to depend on me and that,if I failed,the consequences for us all, particularly the Captain, would be disastrous. I knew my eyesight to be unusually good,but except in illustrations in books in our school library I had never seen a whale blow, and these, I had already gathered from Leif, were totally unlike the real thing. So even if I saw a blow where Johansen did not,would I recognise it for what it was?

So great was my fear of failure and so intense my sense of the importance of what Thor Larsen had commanded me to do that I went up that ladder praying silently to myself "Dear God, please let me find a whale, and I will never do anything wrong again as long as I live."

So fast did I climb that I was in the crow's-nest before Svend Johansen. He came over the edge of his side slowly and lowered himself ponderously with a breathless grunt to the floor. He was to become one of my favourites in the ship but I was aware at that moment that he was not over-pleased to have me up there, not only because my presence in so tight a place, and the restlessness he expected from a boy might distract him; but also because he regarded me as a testimony of his Captain's lack of confidence in his powers of observation.

As a result, he gave me no welcome but just looked me straight in the eye and said in his frank way: "You keep still and just look. You see anything, you tell me first. You tell me before you shout, not?"

"Certainly, sir," I replied, looking him back in the eye.

He was,I should think,a man of about forty-five and there was just a suggestion of sadness around his honest blue eyes and a slight but distinct tensing of the muscles in their corners whenever he focused them on anything definite which made me suspect that, good as his eyesight might be, it had begun to decline, and that knowing it, he felt correspondingly insecure and vulnerable.

While he re-focused the glasses and began methodically to examine the sea ahead, I had my own look around. I looked quickly all over the sea first, saw nothing and then glanced below. It was amazing how the human face stands out from everything else when you look down on it from a height. All the faces below in the light of the sun were extraordinarily white, and every one of them, from Larsen's to Nils Ruud's, even that of the man at the wheel, was raised staring as if hypnotised at the crow's-nest. The other striking thing was how clearly and how deeply I saw into the shining blue sea-water. For instance, the shark still in station was no longer just a dorsal fin. I could see its full shape and every easy flicker of its tail sending it not moving so much as gliding lightly beside us.

It was an enormous fish. The time was to come when I would see men at Port Natal catch sharks weighing over a ton with mere line, hook and four-gallon petrol tins as floats. But this fellow below us I am certain was heavier. There was a terrible kind of perfection about his shape, as if he were the master model, the latest design, of an instrument intended solely for quick underwater battle and infallible destruction. Stranger still to me was the fact that the shark's shape did not look old like that of giant lobsters, octopus or squids, cunningly caught, as they seem to be, in the long tentacles of time. This shape was highly contemporary, even futuristic, as if the shark were the product not of Darwinian evolution but a conscious engineering feat accomplished from the blueprint of some avant-garde in the laboratory of life. I have lived to see missiles lifting themselves off the earth to enter outer space shaped not unlike that shark which was in orbit round the *Kurt Hansen* that high-noon day. But at that time the shark was, to me, the ultimate in the ballistics of disaster and death at sea.

All this took but a moment, and then my anxieties regarding my new task quickly compelled me to return to look at the water around. Svend Johansen was slowly and methodically examining the ocean ahead, first with naked eyes, and then through those wonderful German glasses that the *Kurt Hansen* provided. Although it may have seemed an unusual thing to do, my experience of tracking game (which was all I had to help

D   97

me at that moment), made me turn my back on the ship's bows and look astern to re-examine the way we had come. That was the inexorable rule for two alone in the bush: one took care of the front, the other of the rear in case, as often happened, the quarry they stalked was stalking them in turn.

The immensity of the view, the great blueness of sea and translucent swell making for the distant land impressed me profoundly. So clear was the day that to the north-west from behind a gleaming coil of horizon I could see a thick brown haze of smoke stand in the windless air like the tops of a grove of trees. Most exciting of all, between me and the smoke just on our side of the horizon, I saw in astonishing detail the purple Royal Mail steamer with her purple hull and scarlet funnels which we had left vibrating with impatience in the harbour the night before. Now she was going all out like a racehorse finding the straight on the track for the Cape of Good Hope to home. So clear were all the colours of sea, sky and ship, and so regular the rhythm of the swell, so symmetrical and formal everything in sight that it all looked like a conventional painted picture of the Seven Seas.

Loveliest of all, beyond the ship I saw the land of Africa which always rises steeply from the sea, first a wedding-ring on a finger of yellow sand, then a long band of blue, darker than the ocean but finally so illuminated with sunlight as it soared to the interior that it hung like a fall-out of volcanic ash on the air. It was all a great surprise to me because I had thought us far out of touch with land. But I expect the slow circle that Thor Larsen had set for our course had kept us closer to it than usual.

Looking at all this still entranced, for I had been barely five minutes in the fore-top, my eyes were suddenly diverted by a flicker of a something reaching them at an acute angle in their corners.

So slight was it that had I been a townsman I might have ignored it. But my boyhood in the bush with men of great experience in these matters had impressed on me that the greatest of events often showed themselves as the most subtle and apparently most illusory of movements.

Instinctively I turned towards it and there, away to the north-

west well beyond the murk of Port Natal, and about three of my fingers' width on the *Kurt Hansen*'s side of the horizon, I saw a little cloud of vapour spun as transparent silk form on the air and then suddenly vanish. I was still watching the spot not believing my eyes when suddenly there rose from the sea a jet of vapour to stand for a second on the blue water not like a palm so much but like one of the delicate silver poplars that I was to see later in the war all of a tremble on the rim of an oasis in Arabia.

I knew with certainty, as if I had been whaling all my life, that it was a whale; and also that it had to be a jolly big one to send up such a high secondary blow, to be seen so easily at so great a distance. My heart bounded like an Olympian hurdler and it was all I could do to prevent shouting. I just restrained myself, turned to seize Svend Johansen by the arm, jerked him about and pointed saying: "Look, a whale, way behind us!"

He came about as if having been stung, stared along my arm for a moment and then said sceptically: "I don't see a thing."

As he said it, the whale blew again, though not nearly as high as before but plainly enough to my eyes.

"My God!" I exclaimed. "There she blows again. Can't you see?"

He stared hard, shook his head and said lugubriously, "I wish for it to be so, but you mistaken."

It was too much for me. As I saw two more diminishing blows follow on one another and he still could not see them, I let my hand fall from his arm while I pointed with the other at the spot where I had seen the blows. In English, for I knew no Norwegian yet, and in the manner prescribed for these occasions in the books of adventure for boys in any library at school, I yelled as loudly as I could: "There! She blows!"

Poor old Svend gave me a look as if I had stabbed him in the back. Then instantly, feeling he could not afford to be neutral, put out his hand parallel with mine to repeat in his deep, manly voice in Norwegian: "Blåst! Blåst! Blåst!" Then, almost in a whisper, added ominously to me: "I hope before God you not make mistake!" And again urgently, as I was about to draw my

99

arm back to my side, he ordered: "Keep pointing, boy. Point! Point! Point at the right place!"

My voice, Leif said afterwards, was so clear, loud and urgent that he heard it below and it brought him on deck. Johansen's call following hard on mine, according to Gorgeous, made it all resound like the beginning of an Hallelujah chorus from Handel.

It was extraordinary how instantly not only the ship but also the whole day and sea came out of their trance. Even before Johansen's first cry of "Blāst!", I heard the signals to the engine room ring out loud and clear as Larsen pulled at the levers on the bridge in his quick imperious manner. Unlike Johansen, he instantly accepted my shout as valid.

Even in the crow's-nest we felt the quickening vibration as the engines were thrown over into full speed. Much as we were rocked from side to side at the end of the inverted pendulum of the mast whenever the swell from the Indian Ocean crossed us, now as the helm of the *Kurt Hansen* was thrown hard about and we turned fast around at the swiftly accelerating speed, we heeled so far over that I was almost afraid of falling out of the tub. I dropped my outstretched arm to grasp its edge.

"Point boy! Good God, point!" Johansen corrected me, his voice fierce with desperation, making me realise he had no real idea where the whale had blown.

It was not difficult for me to keep a finger on the exact spot because born on the wide, empty, almost featureless high veld, I had developed a lively sense of the importance of whatever slight variation there might be in the scene and always related my bearings automatically to them. Just above the place where the whale had blown there was a tiny pimple of yellow sand from a dune higher than the rest breaking the gleaming ripple of the horizon. I kept my finger firmly on it, and in the odd glances I stole at the deck below the real cause of Johansen's desperation became plain to me, for I could see Thor Larsen's head turning continually from his compass to the bows of the ship and then up to our outstretched arms in the crow's-nest and back again. The moment the bows had swung round white with sea foam he steadied the ship, and I was amazed at the speed with which the

'TUTUKA! 'NKOSAN, TUTUKA!'

Kurt Hansen leapt forward towards the place where I had seen the whale blow.

The moment he was certain that he had his ship on the true course, Larsen looked up and roared for Johansen to come down to him. I think Johansen had no special taste for the cross-examination he knew was to come, for, as he told me rather wearily, "Not necessary. Point now, boy", there was a despondent if not apprehensive expression at the back of his blue eyes.

He climbed slowly over the edge of the tub and went down backwards with reluctance. Leaning, with my arm tired from pointing on the crow's-nest, I resumed my watch ahead. I very nearly shouted once more out of sheer exultation, for almost in the same place I saw another blow followed by four more diminishing ones, and close by to their right came four others in the same descending order. I knew from what Leif had told me that they could not be from the same whale for, after blowing, the great fish invariably sounded—in other words, he vanished for anything from fifteen to thirty minutes or more according to size and species. There were, therefore, I concluded, at least three whales in the sea ahead of us.

I had hardly reached this conclusion when another bellow from the Captain made me look below. He was beckoning to me impatiently to come down. Apprehensive in my turn, I went down the ladder as fast as I could go, for I had never known any other way of dealing with my anxieties except by meeting them as quickly as I could before such courage as I had had left me.

I arrived on the bridge to see Gorgeous back at the wheel but this time with a brilliant light in his eyes that I had not observed before.

Larsen too was a totally different person. The look of "nothingness" had vanished. He looked unusually resolved and composed and quite indifferent to the fact that since the whales were behind us he had been right all along and that one or more of his look-outs must have slipped up badly not to spot them before. He not only made no reference to the fact but gave me the impression that victory had made him magnanimous, and I liked him the more for that.

"Johansen tells me," he said warmly, "that you saw the first blow."

Remembering the look of apprehension on Svend's face up in the crow's-nest and with a flush of respect for his honesty, I felt a need to shield him, and began, "Yes, sir, but only because as he was examining the sea ahead, I thought it best to look behind us. We do that when tracking elephant or other big game up-country. One man . . ."

"Yes, yes." He interrupted me impatiently. "You both did right. But what I want, my young Boher, is for you to tell about first blow and how far away, you think."

"I don't know distances at sea, sir. But the first blow I saw dissolved in a cloud of mist above the horizon. The second came out of the sea, as I measured it, three of my fingers held out at arm's length below the horizon."

"You see tail when fish sounded?" he asked almost before I had finished my answer.

"No, sir. Nothing at all except the blow," I replied.

"Good, good, you young Boher. Good! One damn big whale!" Thor Larsen exclaimed delighted. "Blue, female and fat and perhaps an hour's full steaming away. Now you two get back up top quick and watch damn well!"

Svend was already turning about to obey but I felt compelled to add: "That was not all, sir. While Mr. Johansen was below I saw two more whales blowing in the neighbourhood of the first."

I described what I had seen and added diffidently that since the blows did not seem so high as the first, I thought they might have been smaller whales.

Although this was final overwhelming proof of how right he had been all along, the Captain still remained utterly indifferent to the fact. He just seemed more delighted than ever, patted me affectionately on the shoulder and remarked, almost as a colleague, "Good! Good! You've done good. I, Thor Larsen, I thank you! And please now to get up top as soon as you can!"

We promptly did as ordered, but quick as we were I had time to notice how the whole mood of the ship had changed. Every-one stood alert at their stations, peering ahead with wide-open, bright eyes. Everyone moved at the double. One and all

appeared invested in a rediscovered sense of importance together with that ancient excitement of the hunter who has
found his quarry and has only one thought and that to kill as
quickly as possible.

I realised that the dark void in the day behind us was now
filled to overflowing with this ancient light blazing in all minds
and emotions. What else in life, I wondered (as I had often
done in the hunter's environment of my up-bringing), could
make men feel so important and full of purpose, as when they
were given a chance to kill?

The next blow was seen simultaneously by Svend and me.

Experienced whaier that he was, I found that in spite of his
scepticism he had looked immediately at his wrist-watch when
I had first shouted "There she blows!" Now it was exactly
twenty-seven minutes and fifteen seconds later. The blow came
out of the sea with such force that Svend estimated it to reach a
height of at least fifty feet. It stood there before our eyes for
perhaps five full seconds, a shining poplar of pearl in a mirage of
early afternoon flame before it lost its silver stem in the dark-
blue sea, to gather itself up swiftly into a cloud of mist and
dissolve with the same suddenness that it had come.

I thought it one of the most beautiful things I had ever seen:
it reminded me of Tennyson's description of the arm clothed
in white samite which came out of the black water of Avalon
to receive Arthur's great sword back into its waters, which
I had read two years before. Even today this whale spout holds
place in my heart with the manifestations of nature that I
treasure most—the sight of a shooting star, a comet before
dawn in Africa, the roar of a lion, the long lightning and the
sound of distant thunder up-country foretelling the break of a
great drought, and the mythological sunsets of my native high
veld. More, just as the return of the Excalibur of the dying
Arthur marked the end of an epoch, and the re-approach of
confusion and darkness in the spirit of man, I had a strange
feeling that the spout that Svend and I had seen so swift and
shining before our eyes also signified the end of a period for me,
as if I had just crossed a frontier and had ceased forever to be a
boy.

There was no need for me to shout or point this time. Svend did both immediately. The whale was a few points south-west of where I had first seen it blow and clearly it was cruising unalarmed and at leisure. I had been told that the species to which it belongs can be over ninety feet long and weigh more than a hundred and thirty tons, can swim without trouble for some hours at fifteen knots and in a crisis work up to sprints of twenty knots or even more. Clearly this fellow, had he been going at anything like fifteen knots, would have been far more to the south of our own course.

"Blahval. Blue whale!" Svend remarked to me, after his shout, as he pointed: "Very, very big. And cow not bull!" And then after a slight pause, he added something which endeared him to me for good: "Thank you, boy."

We watched four more blows following hard on the first, each less than its predecessors but all formidable enough to confirm that the whale was an unusually big one.

Gorgeous, under Thor Larsen's instant re-direction, deftly set the *Kurt Hansen* accurately on the whale's track.

Svend said the whale had been travelling on a slightly converging course to ours and had blown at the most five miles away.

The return of his confidence was so great that on this occasion he did not wait on the Captain to summon him. The moment Gorgeous had steadied the ship in the direction that he pointed, he left the crow's-nest and hastened to report all he had seen and deduced to the Captain on the bridge. He returned to the crow's-nest like someone released from a great burden. When I told him that I had again seen in his absence the other two whales blow somewhat to the north of the first, he patted me on the shoulder and said warmly: "You very, very good boy." Though grateful, I wished that he hadn't called me "boy" again. That, however, was soon to be put right.

The *Kurt Hansen*, Svend said, had never before steamed faster. He thought she was doing a full thirteen knots. I made a quick calculation, realizing that, provided Svend's calculation of our speed was right and the whale remained submerged again for another twenty-seven minutes and fifteen seconds, we would

at that rate overshoot by nearly a mile the spot where the whale had sounded at his estimated distance of five miles. The Captain obviously had made the same calculation. Instead of steering the *Kurt Hansen* as one would have expected him to do, straight at the place where the whale had vanished, Thor Larsen aimed his ship a little north-west of it. We were already in the realm of circumstances where skill, reason and powers of observation all would count for less than the hunches and luck of which I spoke at the beginning.

The manoeuvre did not pass unnoticed by Svend, for the moment the alteration showed in the graph of our milky wake he grunted to himself and shook his head disapprovingly. I happened to look down at the deck immediately afterwards and could somehow feel that everyone was taken aback by this enigmatic variation in our direction.

For twenty minutes we travelled this way at full speed. At the end of this time the Captain signalled his engineer to stop his engines. The signal and his acknowledgement rang out with astonishing force and clarity in the stillness of that placid afternoon.

For five minutes or more the *Kurt Hansen* glided forward with falling speed until it had movement enough left only for Gorgeous to keep its nose pointing the way the Captain wanted.

Two minutes later the whale broke surface a mile further to the north of where it had last sounded and farther away than even the Captain had anticipated. This time everyone saw it blow five times, the first rising magnificently, as Svend had estimated, a full fifty feet into the air. The elimination of doubt, however slight it may have been, has a positive effect on the human spirit out of all proportion to its substance. Captain, crew, bridge, deck, crow's-nest, ship and all became one dynamic entity at the visual confirmation of Larsen's anticipation, and that was as exciting a thing as I have ever experienced.

The whale sounded after its last blow, its dark back arched just visible above the sea but, in the manner of the blue whale, without showing its lovely fluked tail.

This time the Captain aimed his ship well to the south-west

of where it had vanished, and I knew there was not a man in the crew who was not at one with him on this occasion.

A mile further on this course, Larsen stopped the engines to let the *Kurt Hansen* drift. Over three full seasons, in the long moments of leisure between watches in the ship, I was to hear this kind of manoeuvre debated, with heat, again and again.

Some of the wisest of whaling men would have maintained that Larsen should have stopped his engines half a mile before he did. They would argue that whales, with their sensitive hearing under water, pick up the noise of screw and engines at great distances and when they hear it coming closer towards them they become alarmed, change direction, and make off at high speed. In their view the best course is to wait until the whale surfaces again, when its hearing, according to them, is least acute, and then charge down on it at full speed but stopping the engines to drift again the moment the whale sounds. In this way, the whalers work closer and closer, until at last the ship is near enough to fire a harpoon. The crew in the *Kurt Hansen* had a special word for this method. They called it "Luse Jag" and it was, as far as I could make it out, the equivalent of what we mean by stalking.

Others as experienced maintain that the only course is to make for the spot where the whale is expected to reappear, with utter disregard of the danger of alarming it. In fact some held that alarming it has its advantages because fear drives the whale to sound more quickly than it would normally have done, thus forcing it to take in less air than usual and so be compelled to re-surface sooner. I came to know gunners in our fleet who even fired their harpoon guns at whales when they had little chance of killing them in the belief that the boom of the gun would drive them under water all the quicker and so accelerate the process I have just described in which the whale at last rose comparatively helpless for want of air. Our crew again had their own word for that: they called this method "Pröyse Jag" or what I would in plain English have called "hunting them down".

I never saw Thor Larsen go so far as to waste a shot just to frighten a whale. But I was to see him use a combination of both

methods so effectively that he was by far the most versatile as well as successful hunter in the fleet.

The moment he stopped the engines, Larsen beckoned his bosun-mate to the bridge, left him there in charge, with Gorgeous at the wheel, came down the ladder with the cold deliberation that intense inner excitement produces in the natural man of action, and crossed the deck with a bearing suddenly so magisterial that his oddly anthropoidal walk could not mock it. He mounted the gun platform in the bows and stood with his hand on the slender pistol butt of the great gun, as immovable as a carved figure-head in the prow of a wooden ship, staring at the ocean ahead.

Simultaneously we all saw the next blow, for it shot up out of the sea less than half a mile dead ahead. Thor Larsen's signal to the bridge for full speed was unnecessary for as he raised his hand the bells in the engine room rang out like a summons for action-stations in a battleship. The *Kurt Hansen* bounded ahead in the manner for which she was famous.

The blow showed the whale to be going in the same direction as we were. The pressure in the *Kurt Hansen's* boilers now was so great, as a result of 'Mlangeni's stoking, that, despite our speed, there was an excess of steam escaping through the safety valves by the funnel.

This time we came near enough not to frighten the whale but to make it cautious. It blew four times only, the fourth being barely a puff of smoke on the sea, all because of its desire to take preventive action by getting away from whatever it was that the noise of the *Kurt Hansen's* screw and engines portended. But just for a moment before it sounded, there, in the shadow of a deep valley of two great swells and in the slanted sun, the great back of the whale stood out like an arch of triumph moulded in black marble.

We went at full speed through the slick hard on its sounding but, deeply as I could see into the water, the whale was out of sight. The great size of the slick in itself was a thing of wonder to me, the word perfectly describing the glossy and on this occasion long rectangular patch left on the water's surface where the whale had sounded. The older sailors in the ship

were convinced it was caused by a discharge of oil from the whale and took it as a sign that we were after rich quarry indeed. Later I was to argue the point because I had noticed often how the naked bodies of young boys, diving steeply into one of our river pools up-country, left a little slick of their own on the water which certainly could not have been oil.

But stranger still than the whale's slick was the column of smell that stood tall in the windless air above it. Thinking back, I am surprised that I was not overcome by disgust at this stink which stood there so solidly in the pure sea air. But this first encounter with the breath of the whale excited me even more than the first archaic smell of its body which was still clinging faintly to the *Kurt Hansen* when I had first boarded her in harbour. It made me feel strangely privileged, as if I really were sniffing the breath of the first life itself. I was even to remember this moment on my first battle-field smelling the human dead, and being moved by the element of strange sweetness in that last terrible scent of the human body. It was there in the compound of decay as if to remind us not only of the undying presence of the love we all feel but also of the compassion with which life gathers back into itself the humblest of its children whom the world betrays. But on this day at sea, on the tail of my first whale, it was the sense of the aboriginal commitment evoked by the smell in the air that stirred me so deeply.

We cut fast through swell and slick and went straight on for about a mile, turned sharply about and, pointing directly down our wake to where the whale had vanished, stopped our engines for nine minutes. Then at a signal from Thor Larsen we went back on our wake at full speed.

We made what was left of the slick about four minutes later, swung a few points to the north-east of the spot, and continued at full speed ahead. After about four minutes, two hundred yards to our starboard, I thought I saw nose-up an enormous torpedo body down in the placid water illuminated by the clear sun which was striking the ocean at a more and more obtuse angle from the west. As I saw it, it turned swiftly about and vanished in the direction from which we had come. Everyone in the ship later said it was a happy illusion.

I know Svend did not see it although my eyes were still on it.
But having more confidence in myself now, I yelled and pointed
without hesitation:"Ahoy! Ahoy! There she goes. Ahoy!"

Gorgeous, with his quick intuitive reactions that made him so
expert at the wheel when the hunt was full on, understood at
once. The bosun-mate in charge on the bridge was not at all
certain what my cry, lifted straight from a boy's book of adventure, meant and was looking to Larsen in the bows for a sign.
Larsen, who for once was not as quick to respond as usual, just
turned about at this unusual cry to stare up at me. His English
was not good enough, unlike that of Gorgeous's, to take in the
verbal import of my cry. But though the words puzzled him,
their meaning and the direction in which I was pointing made
immediate sense in the idiom of his own hunches. Even so, quick
as he was in matching the two things, by the time he was ready
to signal to the bridge, the *Kurt Hansen* was heeling hard over
with the speed at which Gorgeous was swinging her round. In
these moments, so close was the rapport between helmsman and
Captain that Thor Larsen merely signified his satisfaction and
then turned to brace himself, legs well apart, for a firm balance
behind the gun.

Watching it all from above, I saw in a flash the reason why
the Captain had kept his ship under weigh all this time, for at
full speed she was as manoeuvrable as a hare before a greyhound. All this raised the excitement in the ship to a brilliant
pitch.

It even brought my poor sick friend up from below, for as I
looked down I saw him, white-faced, helped and exhorted by
Leif, emerge on deck. He was an enthusiastic photographer and
had one of the most expensive German cameras hanging by a
strap round his neck. Once on deck he had barely taken two
paces across it, when he broke away from Leif, made for the side
of the ship and was violently sick. That, as Leif had predicted
earlier, clearly made him feel much better, for, after leaning
against a stanchion for a few seconds, he looked up at the crow's-
nest and waved feebly to me. I waved back, overjoyed, and
resumed my watch.

Quickly as all this happened, I was not a moment too soon.

Almost at once I saw the whale not far away swimming at a long angle towards the surface and a few points to starboard in a similar direction to our own.

Again Svend could not see it but Gorgeous responded at once to my cry and adjusted his helm to steer the ship to where I was pointing.

Some moments later, dead ahead, came the first great blow from the water. It came with such force through the whale's nostril that it screamed in my ears like more excess steam from the ship's safety valve. It lasted a full five seconds, showing how great was the whale's need of airing its lungs. A second and a third blow followed. I expected a fourth but it did not come.

Now thoroughly on the alert, the whale prepared to sound. A good fifty yards away its great back began to arch above the water. It was a chance at maximum range. Gunners in those days did not like taking on quarry at over forty yards. Aiming and firing the harpoon gun was a great art because the harpoon once launched travelled in a curve. It had to be aimed above the whale's back in order to hit —how far above depended on the gunner's estimate of the distance, force of wind, angle of platform on firing, and so on. There was no wind on this occasion but the distance was extreme and a swell was rolling the *Kurt Hansen* far over. Yet Thor Larsen, who had his gun following the whale from blow to blow, fired it the moment the steel-blue back first showed a sickle-edge above the water.

I thought he had aimed much too high. The harpoon at first seemed to travel so far above the whale with the attached line following after like a yellow cobra speeding to the attack that I was convinced it would overreach. But the harpoon quickly achieved the summit of its own curve and began to drop just as the back of the enormous whale rose high out of the water towards it. As the whale reached the peak of its own arc, ready to go over into its rounded slide back down into the depths of the sea, the harpoon struck it in the middle of its body well below the spine.

It was a wonderful shot at that distance and unfortunate only in that it did not hit the whale higher up. I was to learn later the ideal shot is to hit the whale high enough for the explosion

of the war-head of the harpoon to break its back. No one could hold it against Larsen that he failed at such a distance, since it was almost a miracle that he had hit the whale at all. None the less the results were distressing. As the harpoon struck there was an instant explosion. White spray and mist shot up from the water against its flank, followed by bits and pieces from the whale's inside, like lumps of clay thrown up by a mortar bomb exploding in damp earth.

Shattered as it was inside now, in great agony and terror the whale made a desperate effort to escape the death that was within it by dashing straight ahead. The slack on the harpoon line was soon exhausted and the spring to which it was attached by way of the pulley on the foremast, and which could take a strain of some twenty tons or more, was quickly stretched to breaking point.

Here the experience of the crew and the way Larsen had trained them was most impressive to watch. Each man did what was necessary, without a word of command or even a glance from the Captain. He had immediately re-loaded the gun with the help of a hand who sped on to the platform and was keeping his own eyes in the direction of his vanished quarry swimming with the speed and determination of life in a race against death. The mate on the bridge never took his eyes off the rope, pulley, spring and man at the winch. The moment the whale was hit he had reduced the speed of the *Kurt Hansen*. Now whenever the strain on the spring neared breaking point he increased the speed of the ship. At the same time Nils Ruud would release the brake on the drum of his winch and let the rope on it unwind bit by bit until more than half a mile of it had been run out. The ship indeed had become a mechanical rod and fishing line, and the technique used from now on was the same as that of the classical angler. Not a foot of extra rope or of forward speed from the *Kurt Hansen* was allowed the whale until absolutely necessary. Even so it was two hours before the *Kurt Hansen*, without any weigh on her and her whole bulk acting as a brake, achieved the moment when the whale could be reeled inwards fathom by fathom on Ruud's winch.

When this process started everyone in the ship, with the

exception of 'Mlangeni, was on deck to see what mystery the sea was about to yield. At the time I thought 'Mlangeni's absence below was due to the needs of his fire, but as, season after season, he never once appeared on these occasions, I began to wonder about it. On this evening, however, I was too involved in the excitement of the chase to take much notice.

Long as the fight had lasted and injured as the whale was, who can know with what agony, still fighting, it was drawn in towards the ship. Every now and then another violent impulse for freedom flared up in it and it would try to get away, even on one occasion towing the motionless ship after it.

I began to watch it all with increasing dismay and wondered in a way that was useless and perhaps irrelevant, if the old hand-harpooning method had not been kinder and the custom of following up the harpoon as soon as possible with a long lance, stabbing cleanly at the whale's vitals to kill it swiftly (as described in the books I had read), was not less cruel than this mechanical rod-and-reel game with an internally lacerated whale. Certainly the danger to the hand-harpooner as a person was greater. But here there was nothing of the element of fairness that danger introduced in the contest between man and animal. But what had fairness to do with it all? I had no answers then or, for that matter, no time to seek them.

These feelings reached a climax when within seventy yards of our bow the whale went into its "flurry", as whalers so aptly call the last heaving convulsions of the great mammal. It turned and twisted and rolled, everything about it shaking, quivering, trembling and rocking as a mountain of dark African soil caught in an earthquake. Where pearly vapour had recently spurted from its nose, now thick jets of blood, Indian ruby in the sun, burst into the air. Its fluked tail, those delicate, elegant products of the most experienced and loving technology of the Seven Seas, rose to smack the water as if knocking for shelter at the door of a home from which it was locked out.

Then suddenly it went still, turned over and lay on its back; the great yellow-white corrugated stomach, which had made the British whalers call the species "sulphur bottom", showed above the water, while at the same time the last of its warm blood,

crimson in the sun, spread itself shining like a mantle of silk far and wide around it. Already I saw the dorsal fin of the shark appear at the hem of the mantle and vanish as it dived underneath. The feeling of so much death was almost black in front of my eyes. I thought the whole lovely day would have been profoundly changed because of it. But the sun now was just a little lower in the sky, and the light more charged than ever with angelic gold. I had the oddest and most absurd of sensations that I had been there before at the same time and place. Or was it merely that some submerged element of inherited imagination had fore-suffered it all?

I looked at Svend. He indeed must have been through all this scores of times, yet there plainly was discomfort on his simple face and a look of conscience in his guileless eyes.

I think he knew what was passing through me, or perhaps it was merely to excuse himself, for he remarked as if replying to a question: "You see, boy, a catch like this one, so much big, help our people at home very much. And food now for many men."

I watched as the whale was then quickly pulled in alongside. The round shaft of the tail, just where the finely chiselled flukes joined it like the wings of a bird, was firmly caught in a noose of cable and drawn securely fast to the heavy chains of the two twin hawser pipes in the foreward bulwarks. All our catches were so equipped in order that they could easily tow at least two whales at a time. I saw the deck-hands plug with some sort of cotton waste the holes blown in the whale by the explosion of our war-head. Then with a long whaler's lancet they pierced a hole of their own straight down into the stomach of the dead whale, inserted a nozzle of the tube from one of our air-compressors, and pumped it up like a rugger football to keep it afloat. That done, they plugged the last hole most carefully of all.

They had hardly finished when I realised that, in the excitement, I and possibly all the others had forgotten about the two lesser whales we had seen blowing in the tracks of our dead quarry. I looked quickly about and there, about half a mile at right angles to our starboard stern, I saw another blow, smaller than that of the dead whale but big enough.

Suddenly I felt an old hand at all this. I did not wait for Svend. I just yelled: "There she blows!" and pointed.

Svend turned about to see two blows follow on the first one that I had seen before the whale sounded. We waited for the other whale to blow too, but nothing happened. Either it had done so before I spotted its companion, or had made off in another direction.

Svend thought this last was the real explanation, for as the whale sounded he remarked to me: "Young bull sounding, wondering what's happened to cow, staying near for to find out! Other one may be frightened away."

Meanwhile my shout had set everyone working as fast as they possibly could. Thor Larsen, for the first time since we had spotted our dead quarry, began shouting commands at his crew. He had rushed down on deck, saw that the whale was well and truly lashed alongside and, the moment he was satisfied, beckoned to the bridge to resume the hunt.

With luck there was just enough of the afternoon left to kill another whale. And luck we had to overflowing. Young and inexperienced, bewildered and naïve with profound anxiety over the disappearance of the great female he had obviously been courting, the bull was no match at all for the *Kurt Hansen* and her strange, intuitive Captain. Thor Larsen shot a harpoon into him when the sun had still a quarter of an hour's light left to give us, and this time so truly that the bull's spine was broken. There was hardly any struggle and the feeblest of "flurries" as a result. We had the whale alongside and securely lashed into the last red afterglow of the long day.

CHAPTER SEVEN

'Peter Bright-Eye'

SINCE there could be no question whatever of hunting any more that day, Svend and I both came down from the crow's-nest without waiting for Thor Larsen's permission. I watched the whole process of plugging, inflating and lashing the carcass from close by, Eric white of face but otherwise apparently recovered, photographing it all enthusiastically.

It made me happy to see him so active and alert, and I was taken aback therefore at what suddenly followed.

I had gone up to him, put my arm affectionately round his shoulder saying, "So glad you're up and about again." But as I touched his shoulder, I felt his whole body shrink from me. It is extraordinary how eloquent the movements of the human body can be. He was, the movement warned me, though I was not ready yet to read it for myself, profoundly estranged from me. However, there was no chance for self-examination just then, for as, dismayed, I let my arm drop from his shoulder, and before he could reply, I was hastily slapped on the shoulder and the Captain's loud voice burst in on us.

"Good, my young Boher, very, very good!" He said it loud enough for the whole ship to hear. Then turning to my friend, he remarked: "This boy has best eyes and reflexes, I, Thor Larsen, have ever seen!"

"I know!" Eric remarked with a stab of sarcasm that really hurt. "He's a regular Pieter Blinkoog. Didn't you know?"

At that he turned his back on the Captain with a rudeness I had never seen or suspected in him, and which I knew was only possible because he was the ship-owner's son.

I thought Larsen would explode in the rage that flashed through his quick nature.

"Pieter Blink-oog, sir," I told him quickly to forestall an explosion, "is the Afrikaans for Peter Bright-Eye. It's our name

up-country for a bird with particularly big, shining and observant eyes."

That mollified, indeed pleased him. He patted me on the
shoulder and laughingly announced for all to hear: "Peter
Bright-Eye, so you are, my young Boher, and Peter Bright-Eye
of my ship you shall be, not?"

There was no help for it. From that moment it became the
only name I was to have in the *Kurt Hansen*, except that the
crew, soon tiring of the full title, contracted it to Peter and
finally just to Pete.

Thor Larsen, however, as in everything else, had his own way
in the matter. He normally called me Peter but when he was
particularly happy he addressed me as Eyes, or at times even as
my Eyes.

While all this went on I could not help noticing the change
that had come over the Captain's expression since I had last
seen him. His face was now resolved and strangely innocent, as
if in killing the two whales he had done a penance laid upon
him by the gods themselves and had achieved absolution with
Heaven as well as his own conscience. Indeed the look on the
Captain's face was so naked and so brilliant that I was embarrassed by it. So I excused myself to go after Eric who was
back astern, hopefully trying to get a photograph in the colourful twilight of our last kill now alongside, still and cold as yellow
corrugated marble.

I spoke to him casually, but, without even turning to look at
me, he just said: "Can't you see I'm busy?"

Even so I was not prepared to leave him without making a
stand for the friendship that I now felt was at stake, though for
what reason I could not understand.

I waited for him on deck until he had finished. Then realising
I had not eaten or drunk anything since eleven in the morning
and feeling suddenly tired as well as very hungry, I went up to
him and said: "What about slipping down below and getting
Leif to give us some tea and some of that wonderful Norwegian
cake I know he's been baking?"

He stared hardly at me.

"Leif? The cook? Is he already Leif to you?" he remarked

with an edge to his voice I had never experienced before: "I must say, you've lost no time making yourself at home in this ship."

He meant to hurt me and succeeded. But suddenly perhaps my mention of food, or just the clumsy irregular way the *Kurt Hansen* was now moving with two unequal weights of whale lashed to its sides, brought the feeling of sickness back to him. He groaned, stumbled towards the hatch where I had sat with 'Mlangeni in the morning, and sank down on deck to lean against it.

And there he remained all night. Leif, I and even the Captain did all we could to persuade him to come below. He just claimed, with some justification, that the fresh air was best for him and more and more irritably refused to move. All we could do was to make him as comfortable there as possible, Leif bringing up a mass of blankets and pillows for the purpose.

Early in the night a cold breeze came down from the great mountains on land to meet us out over a sea warmed by a cloudless day. The wind was sharp and thin and smelt to me of snow and ice. I made a bed for myself next to Eric in case he should need help. It was as well I did so, for whenever he got up to be sick he would crawl back feebly to his blankets, each time more exhausted. If I hadn't been there to cover him over, I don't believe he'd have been capable of doing it for himself.

Truly tired as I now was, I lay beside him for long, wide awake, trying to explain to myself the change in him. I told myself that it was because he was sick. I thought also it could be because he was envious that I had proved myself in a sense to be the hero of the day in the ship while he himself had just been sick below. I could make my peace with all that. After all, perhaps he had brought me to his home with a natural longing also to impress me? But no matter how many questions I asked myself, I began to fear that the day's events had made him believe that, basically, we could never really agree, and had been held together only by the magnetism of a school hundreds of miles away in the interior. Between this fear and the recurring hope that perhaps it was just because he was sick, I found some uneasy rest beside him.

After his last, most prolonged and violent retching I had to help him back on his hands and knees towards his blankets. Sheer weakness sent him into a deep sleep then. He was still asleep when in an unusually cold dawn we neared Port Natal, the white lighthouse high on the bluff in the first light like a candle in the sky while it was still dark below on the sea.

As the day spread its wings I noticed my friend's face was no longer white but flushed. I put a hand on his forehead and was startled to find it hot and dry.

I had seen enough of fever in our malarial bushveld to know he was running a very high temperature. I went to fetch Leif who was already in his galley. He confirmed my fears and, since I was up, we piled my blankets too over my friend.

"Just let him be," Leif told me, "until he wakes. Then try and persuade him to have something hot to drink. I am afraid he's caught a very bad chill."

From that moment on I was so worried that I could not see or think of anything except my sick friend. I had no clear idea how we entered the harbour, an event to which I had looked forward keenly, nor how we dropped the whales at the slipway under the bluff from where they would be hauled for cutting up and rendering in the Company's factory.

For once I was indifferent even to the Captain's mood. He would have liked to return to the whaling grounds immediately from the slipway now that his hunter's instincts were well in command of his person. But Leif, more and more worried by my friend's condition, persuaded him it was his duty to put the owner's son ashore as soon as possible.

As a result, I think he would have been insufferable had it not been for two things. Neither in the approaches to the slipway nor in the harbour itself was there a sign of any other unit of the whaling fleet. The *Kurt Hansen* clearly had been the first to succeed that week, and the taste of such success was like schnapps to our Captain's system. He laughed with triumph at the sight of both approaches and harbour empty of whaler. Besides, docking now would give him an unexpected excuse to celebrate his success with gin.

Leif and I had agreed that as soon as we docked I would go

ashore to telephone to Eric's father. Permanently estranged from his wife who was often abroad, I knew that there would be now another dimension of feeling added to the normal one between father and son, and that he would take badly any news of his son's illness. I feared the moment also for another reason. I remembered the subtle contraction in his attitude to me ever since Larsen's invitation to take his son and me whaling.

Two hours later, as I stood disconsolate on the *Kurt Hansen*'s bridge watching her manoeuvring expertly towards her berth alongside the main quay, I saw Mr. Watson's car appear round a corner of the great Royal Mail shed. My pulse quickened. The moment was upon me. My relief when only the chauffeur appeared and saluted smartly was so great that it made me realise how deep in fact was my fear of meeting my host. Still, the mere fact that the car was there at all did not seem a good sign.

I was to find later that Eric's father had ordered both the staff at the slipway and the harbour signal station to keep a special look-out for the *Kurt Hansen* and report all her movements to him. When the signal station informed him that the *Kurt Hansen* was making for the whaling fleet's berth in the main harbour instead of turning immediately about to resume her hunt in the whaling grounds as all whalers normally did from Mondays to Saturdays, he at first concluded, knowing how poor a sailor his son was, that two nights and a full day whaling had been enough for us, and that Larsen had departed from the rule, to put the two of us ashore. But almost at once all the indefinable mistrust he had of the *Kurt Hansen*'s captain destroyed so reasonable and obvious a conclusion.

There and then, with the capacity for instant action on which he prided himself, he had reached for his telephone and ordered his car to meet the ship with a message for his son to get in touch with him at once.

But Eric was by then quite incapable of receiving his father's message, for he was half-delirious with fever. Leif and I had to carry him ashore, wrapped in blankets, and prop him up on pillows in the broad back seat of the huge car. I should perhaps

then have taken my host's message literally and gone at once to telephone to him but it seemed to me more important to get my friend home to bed as fast as possible.

As soon as we had settled him in the car, I begged Leif to fetch our gear while I went to thank and say goodbye to the Captain. I had no doubt in my own mind that the goodbye would be final. I was certain that this was the end of what we had planned as at least a week's whaling. Full of disappointment, sad at parting with the *Kurt Hansen*'s crew and Captain, I went back into the small saloon.

Thor Larsen was sitting at the head of the small triangular table. His latest game book was wide open in front of him; a great tantalus of red polished mahogany, holding three crystal ship's flasks of spirits which I had not seen before, stood sparkling on the centre of the table, and between it and the Captain a tumblerful of schnapps. So still was it in the saloon that I could hear the scraping of the pen as he laboriously entered with great deliberation the time, place and other details of his two latest catches, all except their length and tonnage which were to be reported to him as usual at the weekend by the factory superintendent.

So absorbed was he in his writing—I was to find he was almost entirely self-taught—that he did not hear me enter.

I called out: "Excuse me please, Captain, sir?"

He looked up as if prepared to be annoyed, saw me and at once laid down his pen carefully so that the broad relief nib protruded over the edge and the holder was securely in the fold right in the middle of his leather-bound book.

Smiling at me as he had done that day at tennis barely a week ago, but already almost a prehistoric moment to me, he called me by my new name for the first time as he exclaimed, "Ah! It is you, my Eyes."

Before I could say anything those intense grey eyes, brimful of satisfaction, looked down at his manual and he added: "That first whale, Eyes, you know, one, biggest I ever see. Everyone at slipway not believing their eyes. I think it is record and earn ship one hellish big bonus, thanks to you."

I was to learn that the big female was indeed a record for our

station at the time: ninety-two feet six inches long and one hundred and forty-three tons in weight.

I flushed and began to thank him but he waved for silence with his broad harpooner's hand.

"No! I, Thor Larsen, thank you. Now what you say? We put your sick friend ashore, about we turn quick and I take you place I know for to spot bigger whale!"

"That's just what I've come about, sir," I answered, "I fear this is the end for me."

I went on to explain how ill Leif and I feared Eric was, told him of his father's message and of my fears about the future, and my own regret at saying goodbye to the *Kurt Hansen*.

That made him rise abruptly out of his chair, pick up his tumbler of gin and swallow it without pausing for breath. As he raised it, I saw on the plush cloth behind it, what was apparently a paper-weight. It was a strange ivory-like tooth of sorts, just over two inches high with a band of gold round the base.

My eyes focused on it and remained fixed while he put his hand reassuringly on my shoulder and delivered himself of a statement which was perhaps the most elaborate effort he had made to enter into another human being's feelings for some time.

"Look you, my Eyes," he said. "Not to worry about your friend. He too rich to die. He too rich to be left sick for long. He be better soon and then you come back to *Kurt Hansen*. If not, I come fetch you myself." He laughed and his grip on my shoulder tightened as he went on to finish what was his idea of a comforting joke. "Not to forget you already in debt! You owe me two big elephants for two whales already. I, Thor Larsen, always must be paid!"

In a measure his rough exhortation did cheer me up and I held out my hand, but my eyes were still looking past him at that strange gold-bound tooth on the plush cloth of his saloon table.

"Ah!" he remarked. "You not my Eyes for nothing. You do well to look and look at that! Do you know what is?"

I shook my head.

"It's tooth of sperm whale!" he declared, a new excitement immediately showing in his tone. "Here!" He stretched out his

long arm, snatched up the tooth and put it in my hand. "Here, you feel that for some tooth, not?"

It must have weighed a good two and a half pounds, was strangely warm as if it were not dead but still alive. It felt oddly electric between my fingers and made my touch tense with premonition.

I gave it back to him quickly, saying almost with a gasp: "What an amazing thing!"

"You speak true, my Eyes," he replied not displeased with my answer. "You see, Eyes, the sperm may be not biggest of whales. But he is king of all whales. You not know hunting until you hunted sperm, and I know you will come back to spot sperm whales for me, many, many sperm. So not to worry, Eyes!" He filled his tumbler again with schnapps, raised it so that it gleamed bright in the dim light and, before drinking it down, said: "To our first sperm, Eyes!"

I said goodbye to him then, went up the steep ladder, out across the empty deck and down the gangway to the car, marvelling how the Captain, when one considered the size of his thirst, could be kept from drinking just by hunting whales.

Leif was standing beside the car waiting for me. I think he knew the many conflicting and forbidding things I was feeling, for as he said goodbye he added: "Take care of yourself, Peter, and come to see us again. Don't worry about your friend. He'll be all right. Only hurry to get him into a warm bed."

And hurry we did. Barely half an hour later I had him tucked into his bed at home. He rarely opened his eyes, but when he did so they were hot and red with fever.

I went to the telephone to ring up his father, but when his clipped, matter-of-fact voice answered my call I was not helped by his sharp response.

"Oh, it's you," was his unpromising acknowledgement. "Why isn't my son calling me?"

I began to explain when a loud "Christ!" broke from him and put an end to my explanation.

"Shall I call a doctor, sir, and if so . . ." I began again.

He interrupted, "I can do that for myself. I shall be at home within a quarter of an hour." He paused. "I look to you and

Jack to see that my son is kept in bed as warm as possible until I and the doctor arrive."

He was there within quarter of an hour accompanied by an old and reputable doctor who brought an air of well-being with him into that large and, for me, forbidding house. Moreover, he endeared himself to me by patting me on the shoulder and saying in a kind tone, "We'll have your friend well and about in a jiffy, don't you fret."

His presence and manner too had a soothing effect on Mr. Watson's mood, for he looked over his shoulder and said: "I don't expect you've had any elevenses yet. Tell Jack to give you some."

He was in an even better mood after the doctor's examination of his son for, as I heard the old physician repeat on the doorstep, the diagnosis was most favourable. "Remember it's only a chill, my dear fellow. The young run temperatures, high temperatures, quickly for the least of infections. Now if it were you or me . . ." He did not finish the sentence but only laughed and laughing got into his car.

But when he was recalled at midnight even he had an inkling of how wrong he'd been. My friend's temperature then was close on 105° and he was delirious, tossing and shouting out words many of which were the coarsest of swear words, together with a jumble of feverish sentences and obscenities, which deeply shocked his father as much as they surprised me.

An early morning visit from the old physician produced a confession that he feared there might be complications and that Eric must go to his nursing home as soon as possible. By the evening the news from the nursing home was that two specialists had confirmed that he had double pneumonia.

It was in the days when the dread of pneumonia haunted the Southern African scene of my youth. The present-day drugs had not been discovered. And by now I myself was so afraid that Eric would die that I not only prayed for him on going to bed at night and getting up in the morning but at all sorts of odd moments in the day. I had by then come to accept that, however unwittingly, I had been the cause of it all, for had it not been for me we would never have gone whaling. Had it not been for

the fact that it seemed a duty to my old friendship not to go away before I knew what was going to happen to Eric, I believe I would have taken the first train home.

By Saturday morning, however, the doctors were convinced that the climax in my friend's illness had been reached in the night. If he came through the next twenty-four hours, they predicted, he would begin to mend.

Meanwhile, I had never spent a more miserable time. My host, despite the fact that he was on the whole a fair man, continued to hold me responsible for the plight of his son. Serious for him too was the revelation of his son's secret mind which had come out of his delirium, which clearly must be the fault of wrong companionship, and for that, although he never actually said so, I sensed that he blamed our school and above all me.

Like all people in Port Natal in those days he had a poor opinion of the Boers of the interior, but he had thought it politic to cultivate a more tolerant attitude towards my people in order to counteract the anti-British and increasingly nationalistic spirit which was flaring up in our midst. But none of this was proof against prejudices conditioned by a history of antagonism of such long-standing between the races, particularly as he was now convinced also that I was a carrier of bad luck. For all this formidable compound of emotions, I was the recipient.

Apart from one dinner together, I had been left to myself in the house in a state of terrible conflict. Mr. Watson rose early, breakfasted on the verandah in front of his room in the morning sun and vanished from the house before I could meet him. He lunched and dined at his club, and I had to sit up late at night in order to waylay him to find out how his son was doing. When I once asked if I could visit Eric in the nursing home, I was told impatiently that he was much too ill for that.

My conflict and anxiety for my friend, my increasing remorse as my host's attitude daily heightened my own frantic feelings of guilt, were so acute that I had hardly ever thought even of our two great nights and one luminous day in the *Kurt Hansen*. When I did so, it was all I could do not to burst into tears.

My one source of comfort in those days was the butler, Jack, or Nkomi-dhl'ilale as I called him. No one could have been

more attentive, kinder and understanding. I followed him about the house like his shadow. In talking to him in his native tongue, listening to his stories and observing his natural reactions to all that went on around him, I found not only comfort but some honour again in my own natural self.

It was during one of these moments that I discovered 'Mlangeni was his "brother", as he put it. That meant not "brother" in our narrow European sense but, according to Zulu and Sindakwena usage, a blood member of the same clan. It was he who had helped 'Mlangeni to come to Port Natal and found him work in a whaler. But more of that later. What is of immediate concern was that even my association with Jack put me more in the wrong with my host.

On the afternoon of this Saturday when his son's illness had reached its climax, I had accompanied the butler during his rest hour to the servants' quarters, their kayas, at the bottom of the garden. These consisted of a single row of small rooms built in red brick with low walls and a flat roof of galvanised iron sheets. In summer the roof made the rooms as hot as a furnace. That was a matter of indifference to the employer because, like the rest of the European citizens of Port Natal, he assumed that it could never be hot enough for Africans. The fact that the same kind of roof made these small rooms as cold as an ice-box on a winter night was overlooked.

Most of the houses that I knew in Port Natal took care to hide their servants' kayas by placing them at the bottom of their gardens and screening them from civilised eyes with thick hedges of bougainvillea often supported, as in my host's large property, by spathodia, jacaranda, flamboyant frangipani and other sub-tropical growths. I am certain now that this was an unconscious defence to prevent odious comparisons between what they allowed themselves in their ample houses and the mean austerity exacted from their servants on the principle that what the eye did not see the heart could not grieve over. But what a different scene Africa would present today had we but had the merest suspicion in those young, young days that heart and mind had eyes of their own which no screen, however thick, could hide.

Yet this custom had its compensations, for it re-created at the bottom of each garden a tiny natural Africa with a nearness to the earth so dear to the native heart of men. Anyway I found it so on this Saturday afternoon and felt much more at home there than in the great house invisible beyond the hedges and great trees above us.

Full of a sense of rare belonging, I was sitting beside the butler in the sun by the door to his room, listening to the conversation between him and half a dozen other servants, the words humming between them as lively and natural as bees in summer, when suddenly a voice rang out: "Jack!"

The single shout was so charged with astonishment and accusation that we all jumped up like thieves caught in their act.

It came, of course, from my host, standing there on the fringe of bougainvillea, his round face still shaking with the force of his call. His servants were so overwhelmed that, instead of acknowledging his presence by the usual "Master", they instinctively called out their own "Nkosi!" (Chief).

He ignored them for the moment. All his emotion seemed focused on me and the fact that he had found me sitting there happily among his servants.

"And pray," he said, addressing me pompously. "What is the meaning of your presence here? My son, whom one thought your friend, is seriously ill. One could have assumed that you would have liked to stay near the telephone. But instead—" With an imperious gesture he ordered me back to the house.

I had, he told me a few minutes later, been nothing but a source of trouble since my arrival. He had borne it all because he knew it was unintentional, but what I had done this Saturday afternoon was more than he could ignore. I clearly had been a bad influence on his son and now I had started on his servants, inducing in them a contempt for white authority by gross familiarity.

On top of the anxiety and loneliness I had been suffering all the week, his words made me feel almost uncontrollably guilty, and I was about to break into tears from a mixture of helplessness and unfamiliar emotions of the most violent kind.

Then he made a remark that saved me. "The sooner," he said, "you get back to your backveld and your own uncivilised people, the better."

It is extraordinary how one can have courage on behalf of one's own people and country that one cannot summon in one's own cause. Anger so flamed in me that it dried my eyes at once.

"You leave my people out of it," I blurted out. "We may be poor but we'd never have treated a guest as you've treated me. I didn't ask to come and I shall be glad to leave at once."

I turned about and made for the stairs leading to my room but he called me back with that unfair authority that no young boy can disobey.

"There is no need," he reproved me, "for such a display of temper. As you say, you were invited here by my son and I'm responsible for you while you are under my roof. You'll stay here until I have made proper arrangements for your departure. Meanwhile, you leave the servants alone, understand?"

"No, I don't understand and I shan't stay!" I retorted and dashed up to my room to pack my bag. But at once I knew it would be impossible for me to leave. The first train to my home, two days and two nights journey away, did not leave until noon on Sunday. What was I to do until then? Where was I to go for the night, for instance? I had no friends and only a few shillings in pocket money, barely enough to buy me the simplest of food on the long journey home.

Suddenly I thought of the *Kurt Hansen*. It was Saturday and she was due in, like all the rest of the fleet, that evening for the weekend. Why should I not go down to the harbour and ask Thor Larsen to let me spend my last night in Port Natal in his ship? I somehow knew that I could not only take his consent for granted but count on a warm welcome as well.

The thought made me step out on the verandah in front of my room. Port Natal below me lay clear, full to the brim with light and lovely as ever. My eyes found the whalers' berth without difficulty and I counted twenty-three of them already secured alongside. That left only one missing and to my delight a glance at the silver, blue and gold roadstead revealed it making for the harbour mouth at the speed with which only the *Kurt Hansen*

was capable. That decided me. I hurriedly finished my packing. It took only a moment or two. Then I seized my bag and went down the stairs as quietly and as fast as I could, and slipped out of the front door without anyone seeing me. In a second I was round the bend of the circular drive, well hidden from the house by the beds of gardenias, hibiscus and magnolias that grew at its centre.

Out on the main street I was lucky enough to pick up a tram-car for the harbour almost at once. I boarded it and looked over my shoulder as if I still feared pursuit, but the street between me and the entrance to the great house was empty. When at last I found a seat right in front of the empty top deck of the tram, I was shaking so much with tension that I dropped the change the conductor gave me when I paid my fare, and had to pick it up, scarlet in the face at my nervousness.

The streets were almost empty and the tram passed stop after stop without halt, gathering speed until it seemed to be galloping like a runaway horse. It couldn't have gone fast enough for me, and it was with great relief that I left it at the main entrance to the docks and, suitcase in hand, made straight for the whaler's berth.

The *Kurt Hansen* was just coming alongside. Both Thor Larsen and Gorgeous were plainly visible to me on the bridge, intent as usual on their work. Larsen, I am certain, saw me and recognised me standing there on the quay but made no sign. That didn't worry me, so much was it in his character to concentrate his whole self on whatever he happened to be doing.

But on deck it was a different story. Almost the whole of the ship's crew, excited by their weekly reprieve from duty, was there to watch the manoeuvre. Among them I recognised both Leif and 'Mlangeni, side by side. Almost as soon as they saw me 'Mlangeni raised his hand in a royal salute high above his head and grinned. Leif waved too, but in manner both questioning and welcoming. No sooner was the vessel secured alongside than he and 'Mlangeni made their way across the two ships between the *Kurt Hansen* and the quay.

'Mlangeni just took my bag from me and turned back to the ship.

Leif took me by the arm and said: "Something's happened, Peter? Does this mean your friend's all right again?"

Before I could answer I heard the bells in the *Kurt Hansen's* engine room ring out their final dismissal of the engineer.

Hard on that came a shout from Thor Larsen that could be heard almost all over the harbour. "Eyes!"

Imperious as this summons was, there was no mistaking its rough welcome and the warmth.

Overwrought, I managed to give Leif an idea of why I was there before we climbed on board the *Kurt Hansen*. He said nothing except a grave "I see, Peter." But once on deck, seeing Thor Larsen was still occupied on the bridge, he took my bag from 'Mlangeni and remarked: "Come on. I'll come down below with you."

On our way to the saloon entrance I was heartened by the greetings I got from the crew on deck. I had the impression that they were all really rather pleased to see me again.

Once in the saloon, Leif, instead of leaving me there alone as he had done the first time I met him, sat down at the table with me. "I'll stay with you," he told me, "until the Captain's been."

He said it with a glint of resolution in his tired eyes of which I would not have thought him capable. I was soon to know why.

Meanwhile he changed the subject. "You know, Peter, we too have had a miserable week since you left us," he told me. "We have not caught a single whale since we put you ashore. The Captain's been in the blackest of moods and there is not a man in the ship who is not relieved to be free of him for a day or so. The only moment he came to life was when he saw you on the quay . . ." He paused, put his hand on my shoulder and remarked, "And not the Captain alone. Everyone in the ship is convinced you brought us good luck."

At that moment Larsen's quick, determined steps rang out on the companion-way and he walked into the saloon, throwing off his thick serge ocean-going jacket as he did so.

"Ah, there you are, Eyes," he rasped out with great satisfaction. "So you could not wait to come back to spot whales for me! Good! Good!"

As he spoke he made for the great mahogany tantalus where

E   129

he kept his spirits. But Leif stopped him and began speaking to him urgently in Norwegian.

At first I thought Larsen, interrupted in the process of reaching for a drink, would order Leif back to his galley. I think this might well have happened between Captain and cook in any other ship except a Norwegian one. But there was active in the *Kurt Hansen* between its unusually autocratic Captain and crew an underlying sense of being members of the same family so characteristic of the units of the whaling fleet. It was this which, in moments of stress, could eliminate privileges of rank.

As Leif spoke, at greater length than I had ever heard him, the Captain's impatience left him.

When Leif had finished, he just said reluctantly in English: "May be you damn well right."

Then he turned to look with fierce intentness at me.

"You would like to stay in *Kurt Hansen*, Eyes? Yes, not?" he asked.

"Yes, please sir," I replied.

"You would like to come spotting whales again? Not?"

"Yes, sir!"

My relief at the obvious trend of his questions was nearly too much for me. So too was another thought that brought me near to tears and made me add: "If only my friend does not die . . ."

He snarled at that, picked up his ocean-going jacket again, put it on awkwardly and said aloud, "I go to see about all that and every damn thing else."

As he disappeared up the companion-way Leif said, "I have persuaded him to telephone to Mr. Watson before he starts looking for you; and before our Captain starts celebrating as he will. Don't worry any more now. You'll be all right and I promise you, we'll all be glad to have you with us."

Reassured as I was by all this, the gravity with which Leif had treated the matter, the way he had stiffened his formidable Captain and forced a line of action which would not have occurred to Larsen on his own, made me realise what a serious thing I had done. It made me think for the first time, too, of its possible consequences for the Captain.

"Oh, Leif," I exclaimed. "I do hope I haven't put the

Captain in a jam? Won't he get into trouble with the owners now if he has someone like myself on board of whom their chief representative disapproves?"

Leif smiled, shook his head gently, and told me not to worry. Captains had great powers in their own ship, and were extremely jealous of interference from the outside. Unless they did something which gravely impaired the efficiency of their command, the owners would not dream of interfering. Besides, having whatever guests they liked in their ships was one of the captain's special privileges. There was not a captain in the fleet who would not feel affronted and threatened if one of their members was dictated to on that point. Besides, he added, Captain Larsen was far too efficient, important and industrious a captain for any sensible owner to want to offend him.

He had hardly finished reassuring me when Thor Larsen reappeared. This time, the moment he entered, Leif excused himself and left—an action which obviously pleased the Captain.

"There, Eyes!" Thor Larsen said with a rough note of triumph in his voice, throwing his jacket down and proceeding at once to haul up his tantalus of spirits on to the table. He unlocked it to get at his decanter of schnapps and poured out a tumblerful of it. "There! What did I tell you!"

He paused to swallow the liquid and fill the glass again, not noticing the anxiety with which I was waiting for him to complete his sentence.

My patience was nearly at an end when at last he concluded, "I told you your friend too rich to die. His father just told me on the telephone he much better this evening. All doctors now certain. So not to worry, Eyes."

"Oh, thank you, sir," I exclaimed. Then, as I saw him about to continue his drinking, I asked: "And what about me, sir? What did he say about me?"

The Captain made a disdainful gesture with his hand, as if that had all along been a foregone conclusion.

"Of course, you to stay." He paused in a way which suggested this conclusion between him and the owner had not been reached without argument.

"You stay," he repeated fiercely. "But tomorrow afternoon,

Eyes, you go back with me to say goodbye properly, understand, not?"

He glared at me as if he thought I might refuse. I suspect too that he would have liked to refuse on my behalf, had he not possessed for all his scorn of tact a certain deep-sea cunning.

However, much as I disliked the thought, I was too grateful and relieved to think of refusing. I just nodded, which made him grin and say, "You now to go to my cabin and unpack quick. Then come, for us to talk about elephants, not!"

So, the following evening, I accompanied Thor Larsen to the big house on the hill above the harbour. There was no tennis that afternoon, but the news from the hospital was so good that there were as many people assembled for tea and drinks on the lawn as on a normal Sunday. Mr. Watson greeted me smoothly, as if there had never been any quarrel between us, but it was most noticeable how quickly he separated me from Thor Larsen.

Once Larsen, amply supplied with gin, was seated in a comfortable Madeira chair, Eric's father took me over to another group of people. What bad luck on me and his son, he told them, that our holiday should have taken such an unfortunate turn. Fortunately, his son was much better, out of the wood in fact. But it would be a long time before he would be well enough to be up and about. In fact the doctors had all advised him to see that his son had a long and quiet convalescence. Meanwhile the problem had been what to do with me and the rest of my holiday . . .

He could not have sounded more considerate, thoughtful and selfless as he said all this, convincing everyone there of what a really "good sort" he was. Indeed, perhaps he was a better sort than I could admit to my own hurt self just then. But I saw nothing but hypocrisy in his behaviour, and a terrifying example of the grown-up capacity for pretence and calculation in what they think to be their best interests. Yes, he went on smoothly, his great problem had been to prevent my holiday from being the disaster that his son's had been. And he had hit on an almost ideal solution. At this he put a warm arm round my shoulder and, not waiting for my answer, hastened to say that I had

discovered such a liking for the whaling to which his son had introduced me, with such serious consequences to himself, that he had arranged for me to spend the rest of my vacation in one of their whalers. Hadn't that been a good idea?

Uncertain how much of this had been pretence, I ventured when saying "Goodbye" to ask if I could see Eric again before he left?

"I'm afraid that by the time you get back to Port again," he answered very coldly, "we shall be on our way to the Cape to join the mail steamer. But, of course, I'll explain it all to him."

It was the last time I was ever to try to see my friend. Indeed, we have not met since. But I was to see his father again, little as I wanted to. That afternoon, as I watched him switch from his cold dismissal of me to a great display of warmth in saying goodbye to his other guests, it all looked too smooth to be real. And I have always felt ashamed of the fact that, so intimidated was I by what had happened and was happening around me that I dared not openly say "goodbye" to Jack as he held the door for the departing guests. I just followed Thor Larsen, spluttering with good spirits, out into the crystal winter's night and so on to the harbour to begin my first season as a spotter in the *Kurt Hansen*.

CHAPTER EIGHT

The Fore-top

I HAD been deeply hurt by this incident but how deep the injury went even I myself did not realise at the time. There is a kind of natural anaesthesia in the human spirit which helps to absorb the shock of the operations which life performs on all who are its guinea-pigs. It is only over the years, as the anaesthesia wears off, that we are allowed to know how deep an incision was made in our being. It is only in the rediscovery of pain that one can know how severe was the injury.

It is, of course, a cherished conception of adults that the young quickly forget injury and recover easily from their unhappiness. Certainly the young have so urgent a thrust of life within them that it carries them quickly out of the technical area of their injury. But I believe that the young, perhaps because they care so much more and are so much more committed and helpless before hurt, can carry the injury itself, no matter how much overlaid by events, along with them. And because there is so much more life before the young, so the injury itself too has further to travel than with adults.

At this moment in my life I was just beginning my adolescence, and no human being is so completely helpless and lonely as at the moment of his adolescence. A baby an hour old is older, to me, than any adolescent. Babies seem to be born with all antiquity present and active in them. They breathe in a world that is rich, deep and meaningful with instincts, feelings, vast, simple appetites and an insatiable will to live, all tested, proved and hammered out by life, as it were, into patterns of gold in the smithy of time. Moreover they have an adult world which for some years continues to care for them on those terms, and only gradually converts the currency of their antiquity into the inflated coinage of the present until, by the time they reach adolescence, they find the values of their inborn antiquity

debased. They have come, as it were, to a market place where their ancient exchange is no longer valid.

This is the moment of their own private and personal birth, in which they face a distinctive future inwardly naked and curiously ashamed. All that seems left of their antiquity is a vast indefinable nostalgia. At all sorts of unbidden moments, when the wind gathers clouds for rain, or the lightning taps out thunder on the taut parchment of some drum of parched earth, or the red dawn fills the sky bringing light round the horn of the morning, they are reminded of what they have been deprived.

In addition, generally, there is the fact that there appears to be no reason or justification for the way things have happened. I was too young at this time to realise that tragedy is no tragedy if one finds reason or meaning in it. It becomes then, I was yet to learn, a darker form of this infinitely mysterious matter of luck. It is sheer tragedy only if it is without discernible sense or motivation.

Glad and grateful as I was to be back in the *Kurt Hansen*, once I lay alone in the dark in what had been my friend's bunk, listening to the Captain snoring with schnapps opposite me, all these considerations joined forces to attack my self-control and I began to cry. Afraid that I might wake up the Captain, who had set his alarm clock for two in the morning, I crept out of the cabin, out of the saloon and went to finish my crying on the empty deck.

It was the best thing I could have done, because the exhaustion from such an unaccustomed exercise, and the sight of the deep-sea sky of the African night breaking as if over a coral reef into the foam and spray of the Milky Way, calmed me so much that I was able to go back to my bunk and get some sleep before the Captain's alarm woke us.

As I watched him in the saloon tossing off his last drink of schnapps before setting out to sea, the surprising man suddenly announced: "Look, Eyes, you had bad night. Now why not sleep on until morning, not?"

Dumbfounded that he could possibly have known what a miserable night I had had, I just shook my head and said

perhaps over-enthusiastically: "I would not miss seeing you put to sea for anything in the world, sir."

My reply made him stare at me in silence, glass in hand, for a moment. Then he turned about to make for the companion-way but looked at me once more, struggling, I believe, with something unfamiliar in himself before he remarked with an odd kind of gentleness that I was never to see equalled in him again: "You're a good man, a damn good man, Eyes, not?"

As if shy of what he had said, he immediately swung his back on me and left the saloon.

It was the first time any grown-up person had ever called me "a man", and it was by far the most imaginative thing anybody could have done for me just then. I went after the Captain as fast as I could to start working. But I remembered the incident at all kinds of moments throughout the day and, for that matter, through the years that followed, with a reassuring warmth. I had also a growing conviction that Larsen had known exactly what had happened to me because he had been there himself before not once, but scores of times, exposed to inexplicable rejection and scorn to a far worse degree than I had ever imagined.

I say this with some confidence because of the difference I observed from now on in my own attitude to whaling compared with my reactions to my first experience of it. I have described the mixture of feelings of excitement, discomfort and even horror of that first occasion a week before. But on this very next Monday I found it was no longer so.

The moment the Captain and Gorgeous had taken the *Kurt Hansen* safely across the bar, I acted on a resolve I had made while standing silently in the background of the darkened bridge.

"If you please, sir," I said to him when I heard that wordless, oddly primitive sound of satisfaction which burst from him whenever he had put his ship's nose safely down on the way to the open sea, "would you allow me to take the first watch up top in the morning?"

He waited so long before answering that I thought I was in danger of being refused. But his reply which came in the form

of a question showed how his mind had merely been ranging beyond my simple question: "You like to do watch alone, Eyes?" he asked. "Or with Johansen as before?"

I longed to say I would like to do it alone, and I am certain, had I done so, the Captain would have given his consent. But at the mention of Johansen's name I remembered the suspected evidence of his failing sight. I remembered the great hunters among my own people talking of the tragedy of their kind when sight failed, and also a 'Takwena story of a great legendary hunter who had gone off alone into the bush to die when his eyes began to fail him. I remembered also that in a sense Johansen's failing sight had given me my chance to prove my own and that, together, we had brought the ship luck.

So I said: "With Mr. Johansen, if it's not too early for him, please, sir."

"Too early, Eyes?" Thor Larsen was deeply shocked by an idea so unfamiliar. "In the hunting of the whale, Eyes, there's no early or late. There's right moment and wrong moment, not? So you take first watch with Johansen at right moment, not?"

Pleased with a distinction as subtle, almost as metaphysical, as I ever heard him make, and still under the influence of his last drink, he laughed before leaving the bridge to smoke his cigarette out on deck and pace and peer alone all around his ship, into the sky, and the sea in the dark.

The observation, however, stayed with me for two reasons. One was the way it had referred to whales in the singular. I had noticed it before. Thor Larsen hardly ever referred to whales in the plural. It was nearly always "the whale", as if every whale we killed were a reincarnation of the ones that had gone before and, however cold it lay lashed to the ship's side, it would be resurrected for him on our next chase again. The other, of course, was that time, in the normal sense, did not enter into his considerations at all: it was just another dimension wherein one was either right or wrong.

So at the right moment, some hours later, I went aloft. It was a polished silver morning, for at the first assertion of light I was up the mast. When Svend Johansen came out of the hatch at sunrise I was already in position.

E*   137

I could tell from the way he stared up at me that he was astonished and might have continued staring had not Leif come up behind him, spoken to him and handed him a package, which he stuffed into the pockets of his wide reefer jacket.

I feared that he might be annoyed by my early start but when he climbed into the tub I knew at once he was glad to see me from the way he said: "Day, Peter."

"Good morning, Mr. Johansen," I answered, smiling with pleasure. "Lovely morning, isn't it?"

"Svend, is my name, Peter," he responded.

While I thanked him he took Leif's package out of his pocket, handed it to me, unslung his German glasses and began inspecting the sea ahead.

I undid the package quickly. Four sandwiches, thick bread with yellow butter and cheese and smelling as fresh as if they had just come out of churn and oven, lay inside it.

"I've had a good look round, Svend," I told him as, sandwich in hand, I too raised my head to re-examine the sea, "and I have seen nothing, so far."

I had hardly spoken the words when a great jet of vapour shot up out of the water not four miles away, between us and the sun.

"Oh, look, Svend! Look!" I pulled him half round and pointed. "A blow already, and what a blow!"

For once I could hardly believe my eyes and was too surprised to give the traditional shout.

As Svend swished about, a second blow almost as great as the first shot up. At that hour, against that clear sun of silver, the blow stood on the cobalt sea, a wheeling thing of pure spirit and fire, looking now as if it were coming not out of a living body so much as some pentecostal emanation.

To my great relief Svend, too, saw the blow at once. His experienced arm shot out, and his deep "Bla-à-ast! Bla-à-ast!" rang out, followed by my schoolboy yell of: "A blow! A blow! There she blows!"

It all happened so quickly that any other ship except the *Kurt Hansen* might not have been fully prepared, and have fluffed so early-morning an opportunity. But she did not.

By ten we had another great blue whale, pumped and securely lashed, sulphur bottom up, alongside. At two in the afternoon we had another and at sunset we dropped two great carcasses at the slipway to the factory. We were over the bar and out to sea again on our way to the whaling-ground before ten that night. And what is more we did not see another whaler on the way in or out. It is impossible to exaggerate the pleasure that gave our Captain.

It was after the killing of the second whale, when I came down to deck for the first time, that I was made to realise the change which had taken place in me.

Leif greeted me with a "Well, Peter, how does it feel now that you are one of us?"

Suddenly I was most uncomfortable and wanted to play for time. But I knew too well what he meant and liked him too much for such evasion.

I compromised by saying as casually as I could, "Oh, it feels all right!"

But it was more than just "all right". I knew that I had experienced a triumphant sense of accomplishment at the double killing. I had had a feeling of having got a little of my own back at life and was bent on having more of this repayment in kind. The eyes of Captain and Gorgeous, the helmsman, which had embarrassed me a week before, seemed not unnatural to me now.

No one can know what the feeling of belonging to a community means unless they have, as I had just done, come out of the cold of an impersonal metropolitan mould and found it, as I now did, in a small ship like the *Kurt Hansen* far out at sea.

Leif was the only person who in a sense spoilt it for me, not because he did not welcome me but because he cared more. It was this particular awareness, in the fastidious quality of his regard, that made his enigmatic responses to my success all the more troublesome to my peace of heart and mind.

On that very Monday evening, after my reply to his question, he rested his hand somewhat protectively on my shoulder to say: "Never mind, Peter. The Captain is more than delighted

with you. You could not be more of a regular member of his crew now than if you had signed the ship's papers."

"Never mind, Peter." I thought and re-thought of that phrase last thing that night before falling exhausted into a dreamless sleep. What on earth was it that I had overlooked "minding"?

Next day I was very busy. I spent the whole of all our days at sea now in the fore-top from dawn to sunset, or from dawn until we had killed enough for the day. I was young, physically mature for my age, and very strong. My eyes, used to the sunlight of Africa six thousand feet above sea-level, seemed immune to the glare at sea. The Norwegian look-outs would relieve one another at regular shifts, always bringing me my sandwiches and often flasks of coffee, cocoa or tea prepared for me by Leif, but I preferred to stay aloft until the day's work was done.

I soon saw that not only Svend but all the others liked having me with them. The Captain liked it too. In fact he had such confidence in me that,often when we were struggling with one catch in tow and trying in difficult weather to bag another, he would leave me on watch alone so that he had an extra hand to help below.

Whether I had brought them luck or not, as they all believed in the *Kurt Hansen*, I do not know. All I know was that the ship's luck had improved. That week alone we caught nine outsize whales—a record for the fleet. By the end of the season we had caught, as Larsen's sprawling hand recorded at the end of the season's entry in his moroccan leather game book, 34 per cent more whales than any other ship in the fleet, with a total tonnage $41\frac{1}{4}$ per cent greater than that of our runner-up.

Meanwhile, every day I had learned more about the appearance and external behaviour of whales. I could soon tell from the way they blowed, showed their backs above the water and sounded, to what species they belonged.

I had even the rare good fortune to see a pack of killer whales one fine day with their strange rather sharklike dorsal fins going hard by us, apparently making for some blue whale blows that my eyes had just picked up in the distance.

The whole crew stopped work to watch the killers, male and

female—you could easily tell the sex from the shape of the fin—
going by like torpedoes set for a certain hit. A strange quiet, a
kind of awe, possessed the ship as they passed us and vanished.
Even the little we had seen of the pack was enough to show us a
picture of the most uncompromising devotion to death and des-
struction that is possible on land or sea. Or perhaps our quiet
was not so strange. Was the cause more evident than we cared
to admit? Were not we, too, a unit of such a pack, sharing some
dark shadow of identification with the killers? Was that why
whaling men hated the killers—because they reminded them of
a self they ignored?

I saw more of the incident than most that day. I soon discovered there were three blows at which both the pack and we
were aiming. Two great jets and one tiny little one, clearly from
bull, cow and calf. Before we were within stalking range, I saw
a most inspiring sight. I saw one great jet and the tiny little one
so close together that they were difficult to separate with the
naked eye. Mother and child, aware of danger, had drawn closely
together. Then, way out between us and the blows, I saw an
enormous tail starting to twist, beat and thrash the water so
violently that the spray and foam flew up into the air. At times
the body itself was lifted well above the sea and the tail flew
into the air, curving like the lash of an ox-whip to come down
with a smack on the water that was audible in the fore-top. The
great bull had obviously gone out to meet the pack and taken it
by surprise before they could divide and attack the family of
three from different angles as they normally do with all the
cunning of a pride of lions or a posse of hunting dogs. Indeed, I
was told by Leif that one of their favourite manoeuvres was for
some to go for the head, or the lips and the tongue, while the
rest harried their victim in the rear. But for once, as a result
of his quick resolute counter-attack, the blue-whale bull had the
best of it and forced the pack to turn tail. A while later I saw the
trinity of jets sweetly at one again.

Considering the speed of the killer whale, his cunning in the
use of his numbers, and the fact that he has powerful jaws
armed with sharp pointed teeth, while the blue whale has no
teeth at all but merely the flat slats of pliable bony plate which,

effective as they might be in corsets, are no defence against such armament at sea, it had been a display of great courage.

Obsessed as I was that day with a fresh sense of purpose on duty, even I felt that the three now had earned the right to go peacefully on their way. But Thor Larsen thought differently. Before sundown father and mother were dead, lashed alongside, and as with the night about to fall I had my last look round that endless sea, I was dismayed to see the small baby whale still swimming beside its dead mother, while on the other side of the deck the great shark, our fatal satellite, kept on diving, turning easily on his side, and then tearing great chunks of flesh out of the carcass of the gallant father. I was not surprised to find the men all working rather silently together on deck when I came down among them. I was aloft again early the next morning and, though I looked everywhere, the baby whale was not to be seen.

There was however one flaw in our luck, mitigated only by the fact that that season none of the whalers was exempt from it. We did not kill a single sperm whale. This worried Thor Larsen a great deal. Though by no means the biggest of the whales, the sperm was still in those days the most valuable and for two reasons. It was the source of spermacetti, that mysterious substance taken from the cavities of the head of the whale, an oily liquid, colourless in the living animal but on extraction in the factory turning into a thin loose whitish sort of wax. I do not know what whalers do now but in those days, following centuries of tradition, spermacetti was still kept apart from the rest of the oil extracted from the whales and sold separately, fetching much higher prices than any other form of whale oil because it went into the best of soaps and oiled the finest of precision machines.

The second reason was ambergris. I have already mentioned it once as the precious substance sought by the makers of the finest scents of France. Its origin, function and presence in the sperm whale is even more mysterious than that of spermacetti. Usually it was taken from the intestines or rectum of the whale and is said to have at first the foulest of smells which it soon loses to acquire a smoky, Arabian-nights' musk-like scent. Sometimes it was found floating on the water and even washed up among

other flotsam and jetsam on the yellow beaches of my native land. But however or whenever found, it is treasure and to this day will fetch as much as £14 ($40) a pound on the markets of the world. There was even a whaler's golden age when ambergris sold at £17 ($85) an ounce.

Ambergris and spermacetti therefore made sperm whale the whalers' favourite quarry. Thor Larsen's disappointment obviously was influenced also by these considerations. But, remembering the paper weight down in his saloon and the way he had handled the tooth and spoken to me about the sperm, more and more was I to realise that the real causes of his chagrin at not killing any sperm that season went far deeper than matters of pay and bonus.

I should stress also that *Kurt Hansen*'s disappointment was all the greater because, by the law of averages, we should have killed any number of sperm, since for all its summer excursions to the Antarctic, and its love of travel, its home was in tropical and sub-tropical waters. The other species, like the blue whale, the greatest in size of them all, were only holiday-makers or tourists in our African waters. They lived, fed and grew great in the Antarctic but in winter followed the Polar currents up the coast of Africa to play, court, make love, marry, honeymoon and procreate off the shores of our fecund continent. Not the least of the many ironies of our whaling was that we chose this brief moment of their happiness to kill them with a ruthlessness and efficiency that every day grew more formidable. But more of this too later. I am concerned, for the moment, with the appearance and external behaviour of the whales as I observed them from the crow's-nest, and though we killed no sperm my first season, I was lucky enough to spot two. That we did not hunt them down then was due entirely to the weather.

Thor Larsen had a theory that sperm were found most frequently in the teeth of storms. He told me this over and over again. They liked to travel in schools, he stressed, but the greatest among them, the wise old bulls, preferred to hunt—for they were fundamentally hunters too—on their own. He knew that popular belief had it that they were alone because the young bulls had driven them off. But he, Thor Larsen, knew better.

He knew that it was they who had grown tired of the crowd and of collective pleasures, and had gone off to a free life on their own to do final battle against the greatest monsters in the deeps of the sea. He'd tell me more about that, he would add, when I had told him the secret of the African elephant's return to the great burial ground of his kind of which he had heard. He would always laugh at that, a laugh which came to him to disguise a deep, I am tempted to say deadly, seriousness always at his heart. Then he went on to say that the minds of all whalers had always been haunted by this phenomenon of the lone sperm. The old French whalers had a special name for him which showed the awe it inspired in their imagination. They called him 'l'Empereur'. He, Larsen said, preferred to call him 'Caesar', for he was the greatest Roman of all.

Well, in the van of two great storms, I was lucky enough to see two Caesars. Or were they really the same whale as Thor Larsen claimed? He deduced from my description, indeed, he was convinced beyond argument, that it was an 'old friend' who had evaded him before in these waters. I was the only one to see them clearly. The weather on both occasions was so bad that we were just keeping our nose discreetly into a sea of mountains.

It was a strange day with no wind. Our whaling grounds touched on the frontier of the cyclone zone which had its vortex over the sea round Mauritius, Reunion and parts of Madagascar. One of the most amazing things about the pattern of cyclones, typhoons or hurricanes is their high degree of organisation. However far and violently they travel they keep their shape, and they look like a rose of sulphur spinning and growing great out of a tormented sea. Time and again we were to come close to the outer packed leaves of a cyclone, our vision filled with its sulphur and in our ears the moan of the strain which it imposed on sea and air. Yet we would not feel a breath of its wind. Indeed so close could we be that we experienced all the travail of the sea caught in the system of wind itself. This is precisely what happened on the days that I saw Caesar.

Alone in the fore-top, I was waiting for a favourable variation in the pitch of the sea—you always get moments of calm in

the midst of the worst storms, as if the sea, like a tired soldier, were changing its step—to get out of the tub. I was aching all over from having swung about since dawn like the weight at the end of the pendulum of a manic grandfather clock. Suddenly I spotted the sperm.

I saw the blow first and, having been coached thoroughly by everyone as to how it would look, I recognised it at once. Unique in this as in everything else, the sperm's blow did not rise straight up into the air but shot out forward at an acute angle from its cut-away head. Whales in those days were roughly divided into three classes: right whales, rorquals and sperm. This blow alone showed how different sperm was from the other two and how much, indeed, it lived its life at an acute angle compared to that of the other great mammals of the oceans, for as it blew the sperm raised almost the whole of its body on to the water. It lay dark against a sky yellow with storm, right on top of the ridge of a range of brown water. It was the shape of a dreadnought, a geometrical body with a great battering head, equipped all over and armed for battle, much starker and more athletic than the arched and supple bodies of the whales I had known. It looked fit for inclusion in Jane's Fighting Ships. Moreover, when it had done its blowing and come to sound, it showed first a sharp, triangular hill-like piece of its back above the water and then the tail came right out of the water too. At that distance, seen in silhouette, the tail tip hovered for an instant like the wings of a great butterfly over the distraught surface of the sea. The angle of tail clearly suggested to me that the sperm was going straight down into the deeps as no whale I had yet seen. To this day I think of those flukes in the storm, like wings of the albatross, as one of the loveliest things I was ever to know at sea.

But what astonished me was how little the men who hunted whales knew about their nature. Perhaps this was not surprising because scientists even today know little enough about whales. The mystery has been dented here and there but it is still largely intact. I could have understood ignorance, but it was the lack of curiosity among the men with whom I sailed that I found hard to understand. The old hand-harpooners, I felt,

must have been different. Killing whales in our mechanised way, the modern whaler kills from a great distance, and this becomes a distance too between their own hearts, their imaginations and their kill.

Leif and Thor Larsen were two exceptions. Leif had read everything there was to be read about whales. Larsen had read little but he had experienced much, and picked up the gossip and patter all over the world since he went to sea when even younger than I was. Since then his imagination had been unable to leave whales, least of all the sperm, alone.

Meanwhile my ties with Leif, Gorgeous and 'Mlangeni had become closer. For all Leif's knack of disconcerting my youthful presumption, he did it with such a natural and delicate sympathy that I grew daily fonder of him. Gorgeous, despite the elements of incongruity and fantasy that he brought to the life of the ship, and his proficiency as a quartermaster, stirred an odd pity in me. Finally 'Mlangeni was a sure anchor for my new swinging, driving sea-self.

Not that I found him at all easy to understand. Why, for instance, was he never on deck to see a kill as all the others were? Why, when I had once to nip below between kills, did I find him coming from what looked suspiciously like the saloon? Clearly he did not always stay below because of his fire. He looked so disconcerted on this occasion that I couldn't help noticing it. Again, when I questioned 'Mlangeni about his "brother" Jack, my old host's butler, who had found him his job, I felt an instant restraint in him. The same restraint would show in some of his answers to my questions about his life at home. He was a great puzzle to me: so honest and frank at heart, understanding with great delicacy, yet often so easily evasive.

I was an inquisitive boy but not a suspicious one, and, with so much new to interest me, these questions soon vanished behind me. However, the day was to come when I would remember them again.

None of this however prevented 'Mlangeni becoming one of a close foursome with Leif, Gorgeous and myself. Some of my happiest moments were in the evenings when, with two great catches in tow and no hope of making Port Natal before

146

morning, we would sit against the hatch on deck talking, or listening to Gorgeous's gramophone.

I think a number of the crew were extremely envious of us because our differences of qualities, age, race and even colour were so complementary that they made us self-sufficient. Often too I saw Thor Larsen watching us. He still could not stomach seeing me alone with 'Mlangeni and would nearly always find a reason to get me away when he did so. I believed there were moments when he too would have liked to be able to sit down with us but the sense of being apart went too deep in him. Being apart and independent had become an heroic point of honour to him which alone gave his life such meaning as it possessed. In all the four seasons that I served with him he was to break in on us only once.

At these evening sessions of ours, the sun returning to its ample home in Africa, with the swish of the sea, an odd harp-like note plucked by some sudden stress from a taut ship's wire or bell-like clang from steel within the ship, the steady vibrations of the engines underneath us making the *Kurt Hansen* a thing of beating heart as well as floating iron, we would talk for hours.

Leif usually did most of the talking; I most of the questioning. He talked exceedingly well to such an audience at such a moment. I listened with a great hunger for the unknown world of his life and mind. One had only to listen to Leif once to know the truth of what everyone in the ship averred: that by his great self-education, experience and character, he could have commanded his own ship long since had he not deliberately chosen to be a cook. Why? The theories of the various crews I sailed with would fill a book. I, in time, came to my own answer.

At first, of course, I begged Leif to talk about whales. Did I realise, Leif would begin, that the blue whale was the largest animal life had ever produced? The greatest saurians of the prehistoric age did not approach them in size. As far as he knew, no reconstruction of the greatest prehistoric fossil so far discovered had been able to reach an animal of even forty tons—not a third of one of the blue whales that I had spotted on my first day.

One way to measure the whale's size was by its appetite, he would go on smilingly, as if he thought this scale would be more impressive to a boy like me than mere avoirdupois. In the Antarctic where the whales did most of their feeding, they found the krill, the shrimps that they loved above all else. He had been told that they would swim into layers of these creatures some thirty to forty fathoms below the surface, their mouths wide open, huge as garage doors, and with one gulp they could take in a ton of food at a time. Expelling the sea water through their whalebone mesh of teeth like liquid waste through a sieve, they would take the mightiest swallow of food possible by any animal in the universe.

In their short summer season in the Antarctic these whales would eat so much and put on such reserves of meat and fat that they had scarcely any need to waste their time eating again, when they came to play, court and honeymoon with uncompromising passion in these waters where now we were hunting them. In fact he had seen them go after food in these waters only once a year, and with luck we would see it too. He hoped so because it was an immense spectacle.

Sperm, however, were different. The sperm had teeth and a mobile lower jaw and was a hunter after different quarry. I should get the Captain to tell me about sperm, that was his speciality after all. Leif said this with an uncharacteristic edge to his voice before he added that, taken by and large, and considering their size, there had never been an animal so gentle, harmless or so deserving of man's respect if not love as the whale.

"I say, Leif!" Gorgeous obviously was uncomfortable at the thought that we should respect if not love the whale. "What about all those gulps and gulps of krill, a ton at a time. What d'you think the poor little krill must feel about the whale?"

Like man and all living things, the whale had a right to eat in order to live, Leif replied gravely. There was a dimension wherein the taking of life in order to live was understood and forgiven. Did we not realise that as we went about our daily life death was ceaselessly taking place within us in order to maintain life? Millions of corpuscles and cells were dying every second in our blood in order to defend us against the minute, swarming,

invisible enemies constantly invading us with deadly intent. Death in the service of life, dying to live, these were basic facts as good as they were true. But life in the service of death: this was his idea of evil. Killing disproportionately was the last unforgivable depravity.

Besides, Leif went on, the evolution of the whale was such a mystery. Scientists held that originally it had been a land animal. To this day it possessed physical characteristics useless for its life at sea, which were atrophied relics from the days when the whale had lived on land. But what had made it take to the sea? What had made it go back to the element from which, we were told, all life had originally come? Was there not perhaps some deep, living parable in the fact that,whereas the whale had been a relatively small animal on land, yet, by returning to the sea it had grown into the biggest living animal? Was there not, perhaps, here a demonstration that the deepest pattern in all life was one of departure and return? On the face of it, nothing at the beginning could have looked more impossible and absurd than for a land animal to go and try to make its home in the sea again. He looked at me. Think of the practical difficulties! Think of all the things the wise old land whales would have had to say to the first young whale who proposed such a thing!

At this 'Mlangeni began laughing uproariously.

I asked him what he thought so funny?

"I can see them all, 'Nkosan," he answered between more bursts of laughter. "I can see them all! Those old land whales sitting around on their tails like the old indunas* of Icoco, tapping their fingers on the metal rings round their heads as they speak to remind men how wise they are! I can hear them telling the young whale that never since the beginning of things, since Umkulunkulu, had such a foolish thought ever been thought. It was the foolish fancy of an idle young head and must be stopped at once! What was the world coming to when such madness could be uttered by the young?"

He laughed so much that,joining in, I said, "You speak as if you'd been there yourself, 'Man-in-the-Sun'!"

"I was there, 'Nkosan," 'Mlangeni said, still full of laughter,

* Counsellors.

"because the day I decided to become a whale myself and seek my living on the great water all the old men sat round me at Icoco and said just that to me!"

He laughed another great laugh.

Leif, reassured, went on to explain that nevertheless the land animal had grown to love his new element so much, and so prospered in it, that he apparently had no desire ever to leave it. Yet, fundamentally he remained true to all the best qualities of a land animal. For instance, he made love not like a fish but a mammal; he retained his warm blood; bore children the land-way at sea, fed them on warm milk, loved them individually with the passion of the earth for a flower, and re-adapted, with an efficiency no laboratory could equal, so that his land organisms could function at sea. The udder of the whale was a marvellous example. An old Portuguese whaler from the Azores, a hand-harpooner, had once seen a baby whale come to the surface of a flat sea, open its lips wide when the mother appeared, while she rolled on her side and from a distance of about ten feet squirted jet after jet of thick rich cream-yellow milk into the mouth of her beloved child!

How he wished he could have seen that! The same old whaler had told him there was no greater love between animals than that between whales. Their hearts matched their bulk. They were also believed to be monogamous, although they supposedly live to be a hundred and fifty years old. Yes, the great impersonal sea had changed the outward shape of the whale but at the same time it had confirmed and enlarged what was best in the spirit. It was as if the whale joined in one body the two opposites of life. Did we know that the ancient Chinese had a graphic symbol for what he was trying to say? They drew a circle as perfect as the sea horizon, which contained within it, in exactly the same proportions, a white whale with a black eye, curled up tightly against a black whale with a white eye.

I had not read "Moby Dick" and could not interrupt Leif by asking if there were white whales, though I was to learn later that Thor Larsen and several of our older men had seen some. I just listened entranced to Leif as he went on to say that the whale was the only living animal whose life went from Pole

to Pole, from the ice of one, through the equator and on into the ice of the other.

There was in all this, he suspected, a great moral for man himself, and wondering what it might be had kept his mind engaged for many years. All he knew was that he found it a source of infinite reassurance that the whale, in response to nothing but the urge of life within it, could accomplish with one great leap into the unknown the most remarkable technological revolution that the animal world had ever known. It reassured him in his daily contemplation of the spirit of destruction around about us all, seeming to demonstrate that life was always more than even the most inspired idea we could form about it: its blind urges were, ultimately, more visionary than our clearest vision or deepest insight. It was no accident to him that Jonah had had to become a whale for a while—for that was how he read the allegory of Jonah's sojourn in the great fish—before he could go forth and be a prophet among men.

Here Gorgeous protested, saying, "You forget there are whales who are killers too?"

Of course, Leif replied, all life had its cannibals. He, Leif, bitterly regretted that the killer whale was not a commercial proposition because then he would be hunted down and kept in check. As it was, he was allowed to travel the Seven Seas in packs, and the devastation he caused must be greater than that of any other animal except man. Gorgeous should not forget that the greatest killer of all was man. Had he forgotten the World War just behind us? Had he forgotten how we destroyed not only one another but animals of all kinds from the great elephant down to the vanished Dodo? And not animals alone, but plants and great forests? Did he know that the Sahara had been a land of water, milk, honey, thick woods, savannah and a rich wild life until man set foot in it? And what of the inanimate treasure of the earth which millions of years of minute forms of organic and plant life had perished in order to create?

He pointed towards Port Natal, rising out of a winter blue sea, glittering at that distance like a giant's castle in the valedictory sun. That, he said, was a monument to the greed and destructiveness of man. He had known it for twenty years

now and had seen the greed of speculators cut down the lovely
bush of Africa in a mad scramble to make money out of building houses and hotels. When he first knew it, it was so wild and
natural that monkeys and bush-babies played about in the trees
around the Post Office, and scarlet lorries flashed in and out of
the trees and the traffic. And where were they now? Killed by
the lack of awareness of the ultimate sanctity of life. What were
we ourselves at that moment but instruments of the same
greed and spirit of destruction?

Here Leif drew breath and then went on to say more quietly
that there was no longer the same need for whale-oil, just as
there was no need for whale-meat as food except, perhaps, in
Japan. The necessities which once justified the killing were
gone. There were mineral and oil substitutes in plenty that could
reprieve the whale. But whaling was an easy way of making
money and, through money, of getting power. Since 1868, when
the first world statistics were available, the number of whales
killed annually had risen from thirty to 28,240. And the figure
was going up by leaps and bounds.

Once, wherever a sailor looked on the sea he saw jets of pearl
rise up to redeem the vacant desert vision of the oceans. How
rare was it now! How great and mysterious a company had left
the round table of the sea! And because we had assumed the
role of gods we thought we could continue in this manner with
impunity. But tolerant as nature was of error, it must know
now that we had lost our innocence. We knew our own excesses
too well. The hall-mark of the modern spirit was that it was not
prepared to right what it knew to be wrong. And that was
something life would not forgive. Somewhere, he believed, it
was already preparing a terrible vengeance and was about to
call in that great healer, disaster, which alone could cure us of
our own wilful and narrow purposes.

I shall not soon forget the silence that would follow this
particular discourse of Leif's. Gorgeous would sit there baffled
and abashed, taking out his immaculate white handkerchief
from his sleeve and, folding and re-folding it, push it carefully
back into position.

'Mlangeni just shook his great head exclaiming "Auck",

and then silently watched the vast blue evening silhouette of Africa against the sunset.

But a vivid childhood memory came to me and I said: "You know, Leif, a great hunter once said to me: 'Little cousin, you know when the last man has disappeared from the earth there will not be an animal, bird, insect, plant or flower that will not breathe a sigh of relief.' "

Leif asked sharply: "Who was that man?"

I told him, adding perhaps tactlessly: "But he also taught me how to shoot."

"How did he do that?"

"He told me I was forcing the trigger," I replied. "He said: 'Little cousin, you must not pull the trigger yourself. Your job is to aim your gun, hold it straight and steady and then let the target press your trigger finger for you.' I didn't know exactly what he meant. But the strange thing is that now I hardly ever miss a thing."

"Did he kill a lot of animals?" Leif hesitated, then forced himself to continue. "Did he kill as Thor Larsen kills?"

"He hunted and killed for a living," I answered, "as everybody in our world did. But in his later life he shot only for the pot, though he spent almost all his days in the bush. In fact he died there."

"Ah!" exclaimed Leif. "Then there was another, perhaps, who had learnt that all life, all matter at heart, is sacred and allegorical . . . How lucky you were to have known such a man."

"He always said," I found myself repeating, "that Africa was the last country left with a soul of its own."

"And we, 'Nkosan, as children," 'Mlangeni broke in, "when the hunters came back with the kill from the hunt, were always taught to say 'thank you' to the animal for allowing itself to be killed."

"Oh, I say," Gorgeous spoke up uncomfortably. "That's going a bit too far, isn't it?"

And it was generally on a note of this sort that our great evenings on deck ended as the sun went down.

One Sunday morning in harbour Leif and I were alone on deck watching the quay crowded with curious visitors, as it

always was on Sundays. Much as they admired the great tramps and colourful passenger steamers, yet our little ships, so obviously scarred and stained with the dents and rust of blood in our war against the sea, the weather and our great mysterious quarry, excited them out of all proportion.

"You know, Pete," Leif said, "I've often wondered how well all these people would sleep if life had only given the whale a voice to match its size. Suppose he were capable of roaring out the agony of his slow death at the end of a harpoon? The sound would reach the town and I doubt if anybody would be able to endure it. I'm certain no whaling man could. It's the silence of the whale that is more than half his undoing."

I shook my inexperienced head and dared to argue with him, for I knew quite a bit about animals. I said that what had impressed me most about animals was their dignity in dying; the utter silence and lack of complaint with which they met their end—even when they had the voices to complain. They'd fight as long as a flicker of life was in them: but when the end came their acceptance of it was complete.

Again I mentioned my old friend, the hunter, who had told me that one of the reasons why nature, and animals in particular, were so important to us today was because they were a reminder that we could live life not according to our own will but to God's.

"I wish I'd known that man," Leif answered. "I hope you think of him sometimes when you are up there in the fore-top?"

Leif's remark instantly rankled, and I retaliated hotly, "If you dislike this business so much, why do you do it, Leif? Why not chuck it?"

"A fair question," he answered. "I suppose there are many reasons. I do it for a living. I do it because it's the only thing I know. But I daresay I could chuck it if these were the only considerations. But as I see it, Pete, everywhere there's something going on that is just as bad as whaling. If I waited on a perfect life, I'd wait for ever. All life is just an imperfect effort towards answering the perfect question. Besides, man is born part of a community. These whaling men are my people, my own people. The more they're in the wrong, the more I feel I must

draw close to them. There's no reason in it, it's an instinct. And I chose to do so not as one who hunts and kills but as the cook. I know it's what you'd call a compromise." He shrugged. "But I try, Pete, to do in the least destructive way possible what is nearest at hand and nearest in my nature. That is the only way that I can see that a person such as I can live."

He could easily, in the years that followed, have asked me why I myself came back to whaling year after year. The first season perhaps explained itself: I had been pitchforked into it by circumstances. But after that I came back by choice. Why? I wondered about it more and more as time went on. I would think of it particularly when we made harbour in the middle of the day, when I preferred to watch the sight from my position in the fore-top.

From there I would look through the ship's glasses at the bush as yet untouched on the long harbour bluff, swaying like sea-weed under clear water in that crystal sub-tropical light. I would be amazed at the monkeys and little bush-babies, active in the branches of the trembling trees; at the colour and flutter of innumerable birds; and occasionally, in the clearing at the foot of that tall white candle of a lighthouse, I could see a great black mamba, the long-feared serpent of Africa, curled in the sun and from time to time raising its head with a lift of light.

My answer to myself then was clear: it was for money. I received no pay, but the crew, with the first year's record bonus, unanimously agreed with Larsen's proposal that I should share it with them. It gave me as much pocket money as the richest boys at my school and with it a feeling of independence such as I had never had before. Yet I knew that there was more to it than money for me. I would have done it just for my keep if Thor Larsen had wished it so, because this life at sea gripped me as much as hunting in my beloved bushveld with the Amang-takwena. More, I would have done it just because of my pact with the Captain so gaily entered into by the tennis court on that Sunday evening.

Every season I asked Thor Larsen to come home with me so that I could take him hunting elephant. But so far he had had always a manifestly impressive reason why he could not come.

And until he came I felt obliged to return what I took to be his great kindness by staying on to be what he called "the best spotter of whales he had ever seen". In any case I was young and not given over too much to self-examination. And yet I couldn't take the whole process as much for granted as I would have liked to.

This was particularly so after some of our gramophone sessions on the hatch with Gorgeous. These often affected me profoundly, especially when he played Wagner. We would sit, the four of us, by and on the hatch with those great waves of sound like another ocean swimming around our senses. Even 'Mlangeni seemed to be impressed by this music which appeared to come straight out of the beginning of time, with some primeval dimension to it. And in the most marked way, the noise of the sea, the pitch of the waves, the movement of the ship, the colours of the setting sun, the first stars and the fall of the night, became an inseparable part of the music and us.

At the sunset hour Gorgeous had a preference for the "Götterdämmerung" which I understood, for how often had I not seen the sun walk over the veld onto the arch of the horizon like a god through a ring of fire into the Valhalla of our endless African beyond? Such music and such an hour matched each other. In particular, as the bright day burnt out and the night smothered the last glow among the ashes, Gorgeous seemed often to be playing the funeral march from the "Götterdämmerung".

Once I was amazed to see 'Mlangeni's shoulders shaking and, on looking more closely at him in the half-light, saw tears running down his cheeks.

Moved, I put my hand on his great fist and asked in Sindak-wena, "Oh, Man-in-the-Sun, why do you suddenly string the beads thus?* What is the matter, Man of Icoco?"

" 'Nkosan," he answered with difficulty. "A great king is slain and all his chiefs and indunas and greatest warriors are dead. The maimed and wounded are creeping back through the bush to nothing! There is no one left in the land to protect the young, and the cannibals are about to come down from the hills

* Beads: a Sindakwena simile for tears, and the whole phrase an idiom for great mourning.

to devour all! Oh, 'Nkosan, that music makes me a house full of dreams!''

Gorgeous and Leif of course wanted to know what he had said, and for once I translated it in full.

"But that all happened a long time ago in another country," Gorgeous said at once.

"Tell him," 'Mlangeni told me, though he could have done so in English himself. "Tell him that my head believes him when he says that it all happened far away and is behind us. But my heart tells me it all is still waiting in front of us, somewhere near."

Curiously enough, too, it was this very music which apparently caused the one and only interference with our group by Thor Larsen. The ship, of course, was so small that on a still evening you could not help hearing the music even on the open bridge.

One quiet evening, when Gorgeous started up the funeral march and the great pitch of death beat out as if the ponderous pulse of the whole universe had been slowed down to be attuned to it, Larsen's head and shoulders reappeared above the rail of the bridge. He listened, watched us, then vanished and reappeared on deck striding down on us.

"Grieg," he roared in English. "You stop that damn music, not! You stop at once, not! Always you play that God damn tune, until I'm sick of it. You not ever to play it in my ship again, not?"

Without waiting for an answer he swung about and went back to his bridge.

We had all leapt amazed to our feet. Gorgeous's eyes were bright with anger.

"H-he is the Captain," Gorgeous announced in so pronounced a rage that he stammered. "H-he can order me t-to do anything he wants in the ship and I'll do it. But I will not have him order my music about."

"I don't think the Captain meant to be unfair," Leif answered, "I think he was just upset by the music as 'Mlangeni was. It's a tribute to the power of the music really, Gorgeous."

Half mollified, Gorgeous just then saw the only other man on deck, Nils Ruud, standing with his back to the rail near us,

looking with a grin on his broad, insensitive face. He had clearly seen and heard it all.

That was more than Gorgeous could stand. He stepped over to Ruud and stood in front of him. "That's right, stare!" he yelled. "You'd never know any better."

I don't think Ruud half understood Gorgeous's machine-gun spurt of English but the tone was unmistakable. The grin left his face. He looked so shocked by Gorgeous, whom he had regarded as too emasculate ever to display such a fiery spirit, that no words came, and instantly a sense of victory appeased the last of Gorgeous's anger.

Soon after this I was lucky enough to see the only occasion, according to Leif, on which whales, other than sperm and killers, fed in our part of the ocean. It was when the sardines appeared.

This was an annual event. Once every year during the brief whaling season not shoals but a wide, deep, continuous river of billions of sardines came up the coast on the current from the south. The significant thing about this event was that it caused far greater excitement on land than it did among us at sea. Sardines or no sardines, our quarry was there. The whales, after all, were not there to feed but rather to graze in new sea-green pastures, to play, marry and give birth. We therefore had no overwhelming interest in the coming of the sardines. On land, however, the people of Port Natal seemed to go mad about the event.

The first glimpse of the head of this gulf stream of sequin fish life was flashed from far down the coast. Newspapers splashed it in large headlines on their front pages. Special correspondents were immediately despatched to keep visual contact with this flood of sardines pushing north.

As it came nearer the coast of southern Zululand and Port Natal, the excitement among people daily became greater. I do not know exactly why it was that in our part of the ocean sardines came so close to the land. Perhaps they found shallower waters there to escape the most voracious of their ocean enemies. Anyway the fact remains that here on the coast off Port Natal, and well within our whaling grounds, they came as near as

possible to the shore, drawing their high-sea enemies after them.
When that happened the population on land hastened to the
south coast either to fish themselves for fish that would not
otherwise come within hooking distance, or just to watch.
Special trains were run to deal with this rush from town, village
and hamlet. Thousands of men and women who never gave the
sea a thought wanted to participate in this event, and eager
landsmen spread along a hundred or more miles of the coast of
Africa either frenziedly fishing or watching others do so.

A friend of mine told me years later that the impression from
the shore was as paradoxical as it was astonishing. It was as if
neither the fishermen playing the great fish, nor the great fish
preying on the sardines, nor the crowds surging up and down
to watch the struggles were in command of the situation. Rather
it was as if fishermen, watchers and sea killers were being
hooked and played by an invisible angler who was using the
sardines as bait.

From the sea the sight was remarkable enough. It looked as
if every enemy that could possibly be mobilised against the
sardines was there. The ocean itself was a porridge of carnivor-
ous fish, sharks, porpoises, the lot, all gorging sardines until from
the fore-top I saw them swimming slowly away as if in disgust
from the scene.

Around the *Kurt Hansen* I had never seen so many whales.
They had also come to do their bit in this war of nature and
became so excited that they were blind to the fact that they
themselves were being hunted. All we had to do was to steam
among them and harpoon them at leisure. It was the only
occasion when I saw the whole of our fleet simultaneously
gathered in the same area. What was even more extraordinary
to me was the excitement communicated by the fish, in their
total abandonment to gorging and killing, to us. It was as if
death and destruction were a powerful archaic wine whose
taste had compelled these multitudinous diversities to unite in a
common celebration.

Even Leif's most gentle whales appeared drunk with the
endless opportunity for killing provided by this miracle of abundance of minute fish in the sea. One whale in its excitement

plunged so impetuously in among the sardines who were seeking safety ever closer and closer inshore, that it ran itself aground and perished there.

But even inshore the sardines could find no safety, for where the bigger fish had to break off pursuit, the birds took over. The sky was full of gulls of all kinds and gannets who, the moment they appeared over the scene, closed their wings and fell straight down exploding like mortar bombs on the blue water, gulped their sardine, then rose immediately to dive again for another. Where they went into action the sea was splashed with spray and foam as if with a regular bombardment from an army of gunners. I would watch one flight of gannets after the other quit so full of food that they could hardly fly; and as they left others appeared to take their place.

Yet, with all these forces mobilised against them, the sardines none the less survived. They lost their battles day after day, but they won the campaign, for we knew that the following year they would reappear undismayed in as great numbers as ever. I was to see this event four years running, and if anything it gained in importance and magnitude.

In this as in all else, Leif saw a lesson. Nature was all things, he said, a killer and creator, a builder and destroyer. He believed man's problem was to maintain the proportions, for life's deepest longing was to be rescued from these two terrible opposites. And surely at depth there was a point beyond which nature would take no more killing? Then its answer was to summon up its final and greatest weapon: the life of numbers. But this, of course, meant great sacrifices of complexity and quality in the system of life itself, for the bigger the number, the more inferior the quality. And the more the killer learnt to cope with the antidote of numbers, the quicker became the cycle of reproduction of the new inferior life mobilised against total destruction, until finally it would be so small that the most powerful electro-microscope could not observe it nor any scientific filter hold it. Nature had an infinite abundance to draw on for its ultimate purpose of promoting life. If necessary, if indeed it were the only weapon left against the heretical life which was denying life, it would not hesitate to summon up an

abundance of undetectable and unpredictable organisms to bring pest and plague back to discipline a world unaware of its own lust for killing.

In this and other ways my first season whaling came to an end. On the final day we were paid off and free to go home. Most of the Norwegians were being sent back to their country third class Royal Mail. Only three remained behind to sign on for another season in the Antarctic and to follow the whales almost immediately down to the far White South: Leif, Gorgeous, and, of course, Thor Larsen, who was taking the *Kurt Hansen*, now the champion of the fleet, to the Antarctic. I say of course, for Leif had already told me that the Captain had not been home for seven years. He just went, as Leif put it, straight from one season of killing to another. But the other two enrolments did surprise me.

Gorgeous had told me continually how this year, at last, he would be going to Europe just to do a round of concert halls and opera-houses until the following whaling season. Leif had warned me that Gorgeous said this every year, but when the moment came he never went but signed on again with Thor Larsen. He needed the money, Leif said. Had I any idea of how much Gorgeous spent on buying the latest gramophones and records? He'd even rented a small flat in Port Natal to house them in one of the most select apartment blocks. At weekends, he gave musical parties there. It seemed that all Gorgeous's talk of doing a grand musical tour of Europe was just another form of whistling to keep his courage up.

But Leif was the greatest surprise of all. I knew he hated going but he went, I suspected, because he needed more money for his responsibilities at home, the keeping of his sister and her son.

Nearly in tears, I said goodbye to them both, for they were my first, real, grown-up friends. I was sad also to leave Thor Larsen, though the strangeness of our farewell saved me from having too overwhelming a feeling about it.

It took place in the saloon. As usual he had his mahogany tantalus unlocked in front of him, his game book out and a tumbler by its side, but on this occasion he had not started to

F

drink or write. Instead he was sitting there fingering his paper-weight of sperm tooth, that far-away look in his eyes.

"Ah, it's you, Eyes," he said, coming out of his mediumistic stare. "I think, thanks to your eyes, we've had best season any whaler's ever had. But also I think it damn strange we get no sperm. Never before has it happened to me." The affliction in his voice was marked. "What happened to sperm?" he asked, eyes on the saloon ceiling. "Where has he been? You know, I think he been deeper down in the ocean hunting the greatest deep-sea monsters of all. I think somewhere terrible war between sperm and monsters that drew him all away. I tell you, Eyes, I, Thor Larsen, know there inside me, something very strange happening in the sea bottom this season, not?"

"But what monsters, sir?" I asked.

"Look, Eyes," he began, and forgetting all about his thirst and the schnapps there ready to satisfy it, he went on to tell me about the sperm at great length. Did I realise, he asked, that there were mountain ranges, with great cliffs, abysses and deep valleys in the sea and that these valleys were filled with jungles of sea-weed like tall Californian redwood trees and forests of giant coal fern and sea moss fathoms thick. No one knew what life, what monsters lived down there. But one great monster we did know about: the great squid, the giant "cephalopods", as that learned cook of his loved to call them.

He, Thor Larsen, had seen a freshly devoured squid that was forty feet long from beak to tip of tentacle which had been cut out of a sperm whale, and that squid he believed was but a baby of its kind. Yet what a battle there must have been between the two in the forests of the sea, and at what a depth it must have fought! Did I know that the sperm dived deeper than any other living animal, deeper than any human diver or submarine could go, to drag these evil monsters out of their caves and dens in the valleys of the sea? Did I know that off the South American coast a repair ship once found a sperm entangled in a broken cable 500 fathoms, 3,000 feet, below the surface where it had been hunting squid? Another repair ship elsewhere had found cables broken by sperm up to the depths of over 600 fathoms—3,600 feet.

There was no doubt that the sperm was the only true match for the hunter in man. Even if a diver could descend slowly to the depths that the sperm every day took in a flip or two of his tail, the diver would have to be brought to the surface slowly over days so that he did not get the "bends", that is, stifle from the bubbles of nitrogen released in his blood by the decrease in pressure. An ordinary submarine would crack like an egg-shell under the weight of water at these depths. Yet the sperm came and went in and out of that world at will. How? Some people said that the spermacetti found in the cavities round his head protected him. But he, Thor Larsen, had another idea.

What about the mysterious ambergris, this gold of the deep that the sperm mined and secreted in its system for man? Where did that come from? He, Thor Larsen, was sure it was manufactured together out of the squid and the greatest of pearl oysters and molluscs that the squid preyed on. He had often seen in ambergris fragments of molluscs and bits of the beak of the squid. If he were right, what other animal in the world could be compared to a single sperm whale that could perform all these functions? That was why he felt so dismayed that we had had no sperm for ourselves this season. He concluded: "You see that, Eyes, not?"

I nodded my head emphatically, still under the spell of this Grimm's fairy tale world of the sea that my strange, rough Captain had revealed to me.

Then I asked, for it was important to me, "When would you like to come home with me, sir, to hunt elephant?"

"Ah, elephant, Eyes!" he exclaimed, filling his glass with schnapps. "Perhaps next year when we have caught greatest sperm alive in waters? Sperm first, elephant next! And not to worry, Eyes, I keep careful account in this book here!" He grinned, tapped his game book first, took up his glass and swallowed his gin. "Not to mind. Only remember you come back to *Kurt Hansen* next year day whaling season begins. Not to mind, Eyes; until then, not?"

With that I shook him by his broad, rough, harpooner's hand, and left him filling his glass again and taking up his pen to write

laboriously a report for his owners on the *Kurt Hansen*'s achievement during the season behind us.

For some reason, whenever I thought of him like that in the following months, I felt deeply sorry for him.

CHAPTER NINE

Man-in-the-Sun

IT WAS right at the beginning of my second season with the
whaling fleet that I started the habit of getting up very early
on our Sundays in port and going for a day's outing by myself.
As yet I had made no friends ashore. Eric had never come back
from Europe, so that I could not have attempted to take up our
friendship again even had I wanted it.

I had gone ashore one day from the *Kurt Hansen*, for the first
time now at the head of our line, when Mr. Watson's car drew
up right in front of me.

I recognised it instantly of course, and straight away suffered
a turmoil of apprehension. But all that happened was that my
old host stepped out of it stiffly and slowly, while his black
chauffeur held the back door wide for him.

I was quite startled, even unbelieving, when he recognised me
even although I had quickened my step to get past unseen by him.

"One moment, young man!" he called out, and asked at
once, "What are you doing here?"

I felt like saying, "It's no business of yours," but I dared not
since he was the owner's chief representative. It might also
injure my Captain if I was rude to him.

So I answered merely: "Good morning, sir. Captain Larsen
has invited me to go whaling with him again."

"What?" he exclaimed. "He's done it again, after . . ."

He didn't finish his sentence but I had the feeling he was
trying to decide whether to warn me against the Captain or the
Captain against me. It must have rankled, too, knowing what
a great record Thor Larsen and his ship had established the year
before.

Suddenly he went off at a tangent. "You'll be glad to know,
I am certain," he told me, "that my son's completely recovered.
He's still in Europe but stronger than ever."

"I am very glad, sir," I replied politely, and could not resist asking, "When will he be coming back?"

"Not until he's through Oxford. He's at Eton right now and doing very well."

"I'm so glad, sir."

That was all I could summon up out of myself.

"I thought you would be," he answered not without sarcasm and then turning about to board the *Kurt Hansen*, he added: "However, I mustn't keep you. Good day and good luck."

I mention this mainly as an example of how right from the beginning of the second season I had not only had no new friends, but lost all chance of regaining those who once had been friends. I had to start by occupying my time as best I could. And soon my favourite way was to leave the ship at first light.

I was used to being out early and had developed a love of seeing the dawn and sunrise as much as the sunsets of Africa. Leif would give me a packet of sandwiches and a huge flask of coffee. He made the best sandwiches for a young taste that I ever ate, and always put some surprises into the packet as well; lovely dried Norwegian sausage, or a tin of Norwegian salmon, or sardines, and always a slice or two of his own cake. I would wrap these between my bathing trunks and towel, take a book from the supply I had brought with me, and well before sunrise would find myself on the far side of the long narrow point of land which ran parallel to the great bluff and formed one bank of the narrow channel from the sea into the harbour.

I would walk quickly along the artificial sea front and past its rows of hotels, windows on fire with the dawn. The front in those days ended abruptly against a long level beach of natural sand backed by great dunes covered with the thick indigenous trees and green-black bush of Zululand. I would quickly settle myself in there for the day under a cover of leaves and branches now black against the sky, so that I had shelter from the hot noonday sun to come, and also an unimpeded view of the sea and sunrise in front of me.

As I was alone, and silent, little apes and monkeys with coal-tar features, quick bright brown eyes, long delicate black

fingers, purple coats and fringes of silver hair around their heads and faces, would soon appear above me and all day long gossip and gesticulate to one another about me. But in front of me until about ten o'clock the beach would be deserted.

The beauty of those mornings and the feelings they evoked in me remain indescribable. I can only say that, after a week's hard work in the tight world of our little ship, it was sheer joy to be alone and free to absorb at leisure the miles of yellow sand and bush without house or man upon them. I could lie and watch the day flower, pure and single, like a lotus.

The eastern sky would turn into gold just before the sun strode over the rim of an horizon as faultless as if it were a ripple sent out by a pebble dropped in the centre of a round pond. Instantly the sea would become blue and silver, with the long Indian Ocean swell rolling towards the yellow sand shining like glass. The waves would mount, curving slowly to stand for a moment at their summit like great mother-of-pearl shells, before breaking in a brilliant foam of white over which hung a smoking rainbow segment, to roll hissing far up the long level gleaming sand. Still hissing, they would be sucked back into the shining sea, leaving miles of sand sparkling like a mirror with their quicksilver light.

Loveliest of all, perhaps, was the sound of their coming and their going. I would shut my eyes to hear it better and would sometimes feel as if I lay with my head on the breast of life itself, the thud of the surf its heart-beat, and the sound of the waves the steady breathing of the universe.

The first intrusions from the brash world of men, I had to admit, were lovely too. I would hear a sound that always lifts my heart: the quick sure hooves of horses on the earth. From where I lay they came so fast and urgently that they fell on the silence like a roll-call on drums. Sitting up, I would see the loveliest racehorses in Port Natal, the stable lads low on their bare backs like baby monkeys clinging to their mothers' necks, galloping across the firm wet sands.

Horses and their riders beside the sea are, at any time, enough to charge a dreaming mind. But at sunrise these horses, with the sun a halo around them, with their movement and the

beat of their battering feet like a quickened counterpoint to the great measured theme of the sea, were an enchantment. At the end of their run the riders never failed to walk their horses slowly into the ocean right up to their chests, and then stand them there facing the sun, the waves washing down their heaving flanks. Sometimes I could plainly hear the horses snorting with excitement as they stepped deeper and deeper into the sea, and the scene would take on the appearance of some ancient rite.

Later, when the horses had gone, would come the Indian fishermen in their black boats, riding expertly in on the surf. They would run their craft quickly up the sands so that they could man the ends of the long rafts of their drag nets, that they had dropped far out on the sea. Pulling their nets inshore,they always worked slowly, silently and rhythmically like the swell of the regular Sunday sea. I would see the flag which marked the centre of their net coming nearer, and in spite of the fact that I had had a week of killing at sea behind me, I found myself increasingly excited at the thought of what mystery the ocean was about to yield. Yet even when the white skirt of the silver sea was sparkling, flashing and darting with jewelled fish caught in the net, something held me back from going to watch yet another heavy harvest of doomed life. I would watch the men fill their boats with their catch, launch their craft against the will of the ocean they had just robbed,and then row as fast as they could towards their market point at the far end of the bay, their silhouettes black on the platinum water.

Then one morning there came a new intrusion, incredibly related to my life in the *Kurt Hansen*. I had settled down in a cleft further away than usual from the popular beaches. I had watched the scenes I have already described, and was about to undress and go for a swim in the burning sea when, from within the bush beyond the crest of the dune behind me, I heard a human voice. Someone with a deep round Zulu voice was addressing a group of people: every now and then a chorus of sonorous responses of wonder, gratitude, astonishment or agreement interrupted what he was saying. That there should be a gathering of people there at that hour was astonishing in

itself. But even more astonishing to me was what they were being told.

I heard the opening sentences clearly enough but unfortunately the thud of the surf and the hiss of the sea up the beach obliterated much that followed.

But the opening sentences struck a bugle note in my imagination. It began: "Oh, my brothers and my sisters, you who have come from our mother earth where the sun goes down, to be here to greet the sun beside the great father of the sea, I tell you today is today. Since the time of the first great spirit of our nation, Umkulunkulu, we have known our mother earth. We have kept close to our great mother and learnt her ways. But we have neglected and despised the great father the sea."

When next I heard the voice, it was telling the invisible audience that the sorrows and the ills, the defeat and subjugation, humiliation and incapacity of their peoples to rise again had come directly from this neglect of the sea, its secrets and its magic. It argued that the white man was powerful because he had mastered his fear of the sea, acquired its magic and knew where its roads divided on the trackless waters, even as they all themselves did in the land where the sun went down. He, the speaker, had been told by the voices of their ancestors, by Umkulunkulu himself, that it was time to renounce the ancient fear of the sea and lead his people back to the great water. This was the way to becoming great as they had been great in the days of Dinizulu and Chaka, when they were feared all over Africa. This was the way to add the white man's knowledge and magic to their own. And he himself would lead them to submit themselves to the great father the sea.

At this he broke into a song, the others immediately following, with such a variety of voices, all coordinated yet vibrating like a nerve, that I was deeply stirred. I was just thinking of hiding in the bush when I heard the music going by me on the far side of my cleft.

In a few moments I saw the strangest of processions making for the sea: at the head, carrying a high home-made cross of Zulu wood, walked a tall ambassadorial figure which I could not fail to recognize: it was Jack, the butler. He was dressed in a

F*   169

smock of blue cotton, cut like an old-fashioned night-gown with short sleeves. Sewn all over the dress were crosses made of strips of white cotton. Immediately behind him, similarly dressed, but carrying on his head an enormous empty glass jar of the kind used for transporting sulphuric acid in ships, came 'Mlangeni, 'Man-in-the-Sun', son of Icoco and my friend in the *Kurt Hansen*. Also dressed in the same way, though less elaborately and singing more and more ecstatically as they neared the sea, followed about seventy persons, male and female.

Without hesitation Jack walked up to his chest into the water, a yard or two from where the waves broke. There he turned about. The singing stopped and at once he spoke to his following. Unfortunately I could not hear a word because of the sea-sound but the reactions that followed for once spoke more loudly than the words.

First 'Mlangeni stepped out, took the great jar from his head and, with Jack to help him, held its open spout under the white, hissing surf around them. The moment it was full Jack helped 'Mlangeni to lift it on his head, and he stood there with this great jar transparent in the sun, flashing now like an immense opal on his head, steady as a rock and staring straight out to sea.

Only then did Jack beckon to his following. They came forward one by one humbly with expectation, their hands held out cupped in front of them. So near was I and so clear the morning that for the first time I noticed their hands were full of the magenta earth of Africa. Jack then made them kneel one by one in the water and with a humble gesture hold out their gift of mother earth to the sea, until their hands were washed clean.

That done, Jack waved his cross three times over their heads, went to each in turn, raised them with his left hand and led them deeper into the surf. Then as a newly-broken wave lifted the water to his shoulder level, he ducked them three times under the water.

Shouting the profound Zulu equivalent of Hallelujah after this strange baptism, they followed 'Mlangeni, carrying that jar of water on his head, back to the shore and so on to the place whence they had come.

Only Jack himself was left in the surf. He stood there for a moment facing the sun, raised his cross high three times to the blue sky, then shifted it to his left hand, spat into the palm of his right hand and held it high above his head to pray in the ancient 'Takwena way. Then immersing his own head three times in the water, he turned about slowly and came back to the land.

I was just wondering what to do next when from behind me I heard a clinking of bottles and 'Mlangeni's deep voice. I became so curious that carefully I crept up the side of the dune and looked down unobserved on the gathering. 'Mlangeni was filling chemists' bottles of all sorts and sizes with water from the jar. As he did so, the receivers were told the cost of each and given instructions how much liquid at a time was to be administered to the ailing when they reached their homes. There was no doubt that everyone present believed they were receiving mighty medicine, and I was astonished at the amount in sixpences, shillings, florins and half-crowns collected by Jack. When the blessed water was all dispersed, 'Mlangeni produced a small bundle made up in a bright cotton kerchief.

This was the greatest medicine of all, Jack announced, because their brother 'Mlangeni, who had been sent to learn the great magic that enabled the white man to know his way across the sea, had brought it back from the Paramount Chief of the ship he sailed in himself. It was the medicine that gave men power to defeat their enemies in life and overcome all their difficulties. He then dispersed some small things whose nature at that distance I could not determine. But small as they were they fetched the greatest of prices, one unknown item even being sold for a black and white stippled heifer to be delivered to the Icoco kraal itself. It was to be many months before I knew what these things were. But once all this was completed, the gathering dispersed solemnly to vanish into the bush and, no doubt, to change their clothes.

All this moved and disturbed me quite a bit. Nothing had ever shown me more clearly the confusion and tension that the European had inflicted on the spirit of Africa, and at the same

time demonstrated the dynamic urge in the indigenous heart of the land to resolve and transcend all and give to the men of Africa an answer of their own. Great beginnings tend to have the shape of the dwarf and the uniform of the clown. But looking back I have no doubt that I saw that morning a movement in the spirit of my native countrymen that would start processes that no human power could stop.

Though I was to witness this ceremony almost every other Sunday for several whaling seasons, and although it would take place within range of the sight of hundreds of Europeans who gathered further down on the beach, gay in their many-coloured bathing clothes and wraps under rainbow umbrellas, yet not one person among them was sufficiently curious to come and to see what this strange gathering was about. And had they come they would probably have dismissed it all as typical "Kaffir nonsense".

Even I could have found it easy to be cynical about all this had I not known the principals involved and the ways of these people. I had no doubt that they were sincere in what they were doing. Matter which is inanimate to us, is never mere matter to them but manifestations overflowing with the power of the spirit. Sickness is never just a physical infection but an invasion of the human spirit by another spirit of malign intent. I had no doubt therefore that Jack and 'Mlangeni believed that they had come on a cure for the ills of their nation, and that the weak and ailing after drinking the sea-water would absorb the strength and magic of the sea itself. I had no doubt they were a strangely dedicated couple, feeling convinced that they discharged a function of the utmost importance to their people and so were entitled to be rewarded for their services as were seers, prophets and witch-doctors.

What was of importance to me was that now I knew why 'Mlangeni had taken to the sea. Like so many of us he was in the ship for money, but for something else as well. The problem was whether I should let him know that I had discovered his secret or not?

Rightly or wrongly, I decided against it, thinking it best to wait until he himself felt like telling me about it. As far as I was

concerned, I didn't find it a difficult secret to keep because in a strange way this aspect of 'Mlangeni's life endeared him all the more to me. Clearly after his own fashion 'Mlangeni was a searcher.

CHAPTER TEN

The Stirrer-up-of-Strife

IT WAS half-way through my third season that a grave crisis flared up in the *Kurt Hansen* around 'Mlangeni.

We had started the season with a fresh crew, only myself, Leif, Gorgeous, the bosun, Nils Ruud and 'Mlangeni left of the old. Among the new members was a young Norwegian called Harald Foyn. He had done only one season whaling on our station before, consequently nobody among us knew anything about him. However, from the start it was clear that he had picked up both what was negative about life at sea and many of the prejudices that white people had against Africans.

I was the first to see him come on board, a duffle bag on his shoulder, our first Saturday evening of the season. Gorgeous, 'Mlangeni, Leif and I, who had just met after many months, had been exchanging news in our favourite place by the hatch in a lively manner. 'Mlangeni had just stood up and turned to go below when this youth came up the gang-plank from the quay. Seeing 'Mlangeni go down to the forecastle, he stood for a moment as if still with shock. He was tall, thin, with a long neck and a huge Adam's apple, and bits of thin pale yellow hair stuck out from under the brim of his hat.

He stood like that for a moment while we all stopped talking to give him a chance of announcing himself. But instead of doing that he merely hurled a question at us. "Was that a Kaffir who just went down the ladder?"

We were all three so amazed by his tone that we did not at once answer.

Instantly the youth dropped his duffle bag on deck and, legs apart, said aggressively: "If he's a member of the crew I tell you straight I won't stand for it."

"In that case," Leif answered him with quiet deliberation: "In that case you'd better start looking for another ship right

now. He is a respected member of this crew and his name is not 'Kaffir' but 'Mlangeni. If ever I hear you even refer to him as that 'Kaffir', I'll report you right away to the Captain."

Taken aback, the youth gulped hard, his Adam's apple going like a snooker ball up and down his throat.

"And who are you to tell me what to do?" he asked, at last getting over his surprise.

"Who I am is not the question," Leif said cool as ever. "This is our ship. The point is who are you to walk on board and start cross-examining us?"

That finally deflated him and he answered almost meekly: "I'm Harald Foyn, come to join the *Kurt Hansen*." He paused, looked round as if hoping he was in the wrong ship after all and asked, "This is the *Kurt Hansen*, isn't it?"

"Yes," Leif replied. "I've been expecting you. The Captain told me to look out for you. You follow me and I'll show you your bunk and the place to stow your gear."

As the two of them left I heard Leif break into Norwegian. Talking, he led the way down into the forecastle where 'Mlangeni was. I had enough of a smattering of Norwegian by then and knew Leif so well that I had no doubt the new-comer was being told in the most meticulous terms possible how he was expected to behave towards 'Mlangeni in future.

"You know, Pete," Gorgeous commented sententiously on what was clearly a disagreeable fact of life to him. "It takes all sorts to make a world. So I expect we've just got to endure that old 'Adam's apple'."

Despite my distaste for what had just happened, I couldn't help laughing. 'Mlangeni himself, whose people all have a genius for nicknaming, could not have done it better. From then on Harald Foyn was destined to be known among the four of us as 'Adam's apple'.

Harald Foyn, however, bad as his first impression on us had been, was not without a certain indefatigable cunning. From that moment, he was on his best behaviour. He was particularly nice to Leif, and the more influential the person in the ship, the more ingratiating he became. It made me feel quite embarrassed

to see how obsequious he was to the bosun and above all to the Captain. Hitherto, however moody, domineering and difficult our Captain, the exercise of authority and the hierarchy of discipline in our ship, as in all other Norwegian whalers, had had the feeling of being a kind of enlarged family system. Foyn's way was utterly different and so full of special design and secret calculation that he subtly spoilt the atmosphere in the ship. It is astonishing how one negative factor, even in so ungracious and obvious a form as that of Foyn, can have a good run in the small world of a ship before it is recognised for what it is.

Foyn soon was in the good books of most of the crew, particularly those of Nils Ruud. Ruud was not a bad fellow at all, merely rather unimaginative, insensitive and somewhat dim. On the whole he meant well, but he was the perfect prey for a person like Foyn. I had seen this kind of alliance of cunning and simplicity so often at school that I could not fail to recognise it at once for what it was. It all started, of course, when Foyn discovered how curious if not suspicious Ruud was of 'Mlangeni, as well as jealous of his relationship with the three of us. From that moment he flattered Ruud and paid so much attention to him that they were soon fast friends. Since Ruud, if not the most popular, was regarded as one of the steadiest members of the crew, the ship was inclined to take it for granted that the newcomer must be a good man too.

The one thing that comforted me as I watched Foyn enlarge his establishment in the opinion of the ship was that the Captain clearly could hardly stand the sight of him. The more he fawned and jumped to the Captain's orders, the more Thor Larsen seemed to be put off by him. Cunning as he was, Foyn was not intelligent enough to change his tactics. His lack of success made him re-double his efforts until it was quite painful to watch.

One evening we saw Larsen abruptly and pointedly turn his back on Foyn who had jumped forward to offer him some matches the moment the Captain took out his cigarette case.

"That's quite something for even 'Adam's apple' to swallow," said Gorgeous quietly.

"He'll swallow it and more," Leif told him.

The way Leif had spoken sounded rather ominous, so I asked: "What d'you think of him really, Leif?"

"I wouldn't underrate him," Leif replied obliquely. "Ruud seems to like him, too."

Gorgeous had strong feelings about Ruud. "No accounting for tastes," he shrugged. "As the Frenchies say, everyone to his own taste."

"Well, don't underrate the Foyn-Ruud combination," Leif replied quietly.

"We've nothing to fear from them," I interrupted. "What could they possibly do to us?"

"Not us perhaps—" Leif began.

He stopped at the sight of 'Mlangeni stepping out on deck and stretching himself in the evening sun before coming to join us. With a sickening realisation I knew then what Leif meant. I also knew better than any of them what the Captain felt in his secret heart about his Zulu stoker. I resolved there and then that I would watch Foyn with all possible vigilance, for I recognised that, with the strange cunning of an obsessional character, he had fixed on the one combination of persons and purpose that could prosper.

"When Idungandhlu joins with 'ndhlebe-ka-zizua," 'Mlangeni said to me in Zulu as he sat down just as Ruud and Foyn went by, "it is time to stand guard on the cattle even in the kraal."

"What did he say?" both Leif and Gorgeous asked.

I looked at 'Mlangeni first before replying. "He called Foyn a name meaning 'a stirrer-up-of-strife-in-the-house'," I replied, "and said that one should be on one's guard all the time."

Leif and Gorgeous exchanged glances and then Leif gave 'Mlangeni a warm glance of respect for this evidence of natural intelligence.

Patting the empty space beside him, he said: "Come and join us, 'Mlangeni. I'm certain Gorgeous would love you to smoke one of his cigarettes with him."

As regards Foyn, he never again to my knowledge called 'Mlangeni "Kaffir". But neither did he ever use his name as everyone else did. 'Mlangeni, of course, did not fail to notice

this, though he was too proud to mention it, and in any case he was so disdainful of what his instinctive appraisal told him of Foyn's character that he would not let it trouble him.

Once, as we watched Foyn and Ruud leaning close in conversation over the rail opposite us, he said: "You know, 'Nkosan, the 'stirrer-up-of-strife-in-the-house' is a man whose shadow has left him."

In Sindakwena it was a great compliment to say of someone that he "threw a shadow": to say of someone that his "shadow had left him" meant either that he was dead, or else so unreal that he might as well have been.

But why Leif's warning and this nickname of 'stirrer-up-of-strife' for Foyn? This was the question that was increasingly on my mind.

Often as I came down from my position in the fore-top to see 'Mlangeni come on deck to eat his breakfast, propped against the hatch in the morning sun, his legs well apart and munching his food with relish, a vague though vivid apprehension would seize me. Yet what could anyone have against that warm-hearted person, that great, natural being, so good at his work and so loyal and entertaining a friend? Yet there was not just a person, but a movement, on foot against 'Mlangeni in the ship. The attitude of the whole crew had subtly changed towards him; they were not as natural and free with him as they themselves had been in the beginning.

Apparently, he himself was unaware of the change and of any possibility of threat or danger against him. Often he looked so vulnerable that I wanted to go and sit beside him to show him that at least I had not changed and still enjoyed the warmth of the ancient fire of life burning so vividly in him. But my duties as look-out stopped me. Angry, resentful, puzzled over it all, I just had to go on searching the Indian Ocean for whales.

I had no doubt that it all had something to do with 'Mlangeni's blackness. I have already described how his colour affected all crews, even Thor Larsen. But what on this occasion had made this reaction so negative if not downright hostile?

I was soon to know.

One Sunday evening when I boarded the *Kurt Hansen* after

one of the loveliest days I had ever spent beside the sea, I found Leif alone pacing the deck in an oddly restless manner.

"Hallo, Pete," he exclaimed. "Glad you've come. I've been wanting a word with you all day!"

There and then he told me with unusual haste what was on his mind.

I probably didn't know, he said, but recently every week-end when the crew returned to port they'd found on fetching their money to go ashore that some of it was missing. The missing sums were never large, but added together these bits and pieces amounted to quite a tidy bit of spending money ashore. Indeed the sums at first had been so small that the men thought they themselves had made a mistake. But then one mentioned his suspicion of loss to another and soon it became quite clear that there was a petty thief at work in the ship.

My heart went cold at the news. Of all crimes, petty thieving at sea was one of the worst, since in those days sailors had no defence against it. Living as they did all together without keys or lockers, they were forced to trust one another if only because the opportunities for stealing from one another were endless and easy. Our Norwegians were a self-respecting crew to an exceptional degree, and this discovery was provoking the most violent reactions.

"But, Leif," I exclaimed, distressed, "who'd do such a thing?"

He looked at me before answering and then said in his measured, precise way: "I don't know for certain. But I know who is coming more and more under suspicion."

"Who?"

" 'Mlangeni," he replied, watching me intently.

" 'Mlangeni!" I exclaimed, jumping up enraged. "What nonsense! It's not true. 'Mlangeni could murder, yes, but steal from anybody, no, never!"

Passionately I went on to tell Leif how both Amangtakwena and Zulu deeply were men of honour and would rather die than steal from those to whom they had pledged themselves, as 'Mlangeni had pledged himself to the *Kurt Hansen*.

Leif stopped me saying gently: "Look, Pete, I know it's not

179

'Mlangeni. But unfortunately there's some evidence that it could have been him."

"What?" I asked disdainfully.

"Well," Leif answered, "he never comes on deck as we all do when there's a kill. And several times now when the whole crew's been absorbed on deck he's been seen away from his fire, prowling round the ship."

At that my heart sank, for had not I myself once encountered 'Mlangeni away from his fire, coming from the direction of the saloon and being curiously evasive?

I observed aggressively: "Someone else can't have been too absorbed either, to be able to spy on 'Mlangeni at such a time. Who was it, in any case, who started this rumour?" Then in a flash I knew. I burst out: "It was Harald Foyn, I bet!"

"Possibly, originally," Leif answered quietly, hoping to calm me by example. But it's not as simple as all that. The person who has been most active rousing suspicion against 'Mlangeni is our old friend Ruud. He first hinted it could be 'Mlangeni and then revealed that it was Foyn who had found 'Mlangeni prowling around below."

"And what was Foyn doing below when he should've been on deck doing a job of work?" I asked angrily.

"Going to the head—or so he says."

Leif's tone was ironical and for the first time I felt reassured.

"But, Leif," I went on, "isn't it strange that Foyn has to go to the head every time we strike a whale?"

"It takes some of us like that," said Leif gravely, "including 'Papa' bosun."

"So it's gone to the bosun already," I remarked soberly, realising from that how grave the situation had become. "And what was the explanation?"

"Ruud said," Leif replied, "Foyn had done it on his insistence, once the first thefts were discovered. Ruud said 'Mlangeni had never been seen in the act but time and again was observed near places where he should not have been. Moreover, Ruud pointed out, 'Mlangeni, so far, was the only member of the crew who had not complained of being robbed. All this has come from Ruud. But I am sure Ruud is too stupid and

lethargic a fellow to have worked up such an atmosphere by himself. I'm certain Foyn's prompting him."

"But what are we to do?" I asked.

Leif paused. "First I want you to talk to 'Mlangeni and warn him what's afoot."

"Warn him?" I exclaimed aghast. "Do you realise he'll want to murder anyone who could insult him with such suspicions?"

"There must be a way in which it can be done without hurting him," Leif insisted confidently. "But only you can know it. There's no time to be lost either, because I am certain 'Papa' bosun won't be long now before he goes to the Captain."

That decided the issue for me and I promised to speak to 'Mlangeni at once.

I had my opportunity that very evening, for Leif saw to it that he and Gorgeous left the two of us alone.

" 'Mlangeni, you've been like a brother to me since I came into this ship as a boy three seasons ago and I thank you," I told him as I took him by the arm and walked him to the stern of the *Kurt Hansen* where I knew we would not be interrupted.

We leant side by side over and looked deep into the darkened water, before I went on. "I want to ask you something tonight like a brother: and you must answer like a brother. Why do you never come on deck as all the others do when we kill?"

My tone had alarmed him but my question relieved him, for he laughed and said: "Auck, 'Nkosan, when you have been as long at sea as I have been, you too will lose interest in watching the killing. They are all the same. Beside, 'Nkosan, I have a hungry fire to feed. That fire of mine . . ."

"No, 'Mlangeni," I told him quietly. "It is not your fire. Remember one day when the killing was on I found you below far away from your fire? I asked you then and you avoided answering me. You are not answering me like a brother. Where were you coming from that day?"

A look of extreme wariness if not apprehension was visible in the starlight on his massive face.

"Why do you want to know, 'Nkosan?" he asked.

There was no more room for manoeuvre. Although I knew that with 'Takwena and Zulu the indirect way was always the

shortest way to arrive at a fruitful conclusion, I had already reached the end of my zig-zag course.

So I just said: "Look, 'Mlangeni, in the past few weeks every time there's been a killing, the crew have gone back afterwards to find some of their money missing. For the first time in the ship there is a thief at work and I want you to help me find him."

"You mean, 'Nkosan," he said, drawing himself up to his full height and his voice leaden with the weight of emotion, "there are men in the ship who think I might be the thief?"

"No," I lied, perhaps too quickly to be altogether convincing. "But Leif, Gorgeous and I want to work together in this with you to find out who it can be. And first we must know what we all do at the time when the thieving is supposed to take place."

He did not altogether believe my answer, and the fact that he could even be remotely connected with suspicion of this kind rankled profoundly. The only thing that prevented him from walking away in great anger was that he liked and trusted me in all else. He stood there as still as a monument of black marble beside me, with the nostalgic harbour and sea sounds around us, and at last he spoke.

" 'Nkosan, if I tell you what I was doing that day, you give me your word you will mention it to no one, not even Leif. You know our ways. Leif and the others do not."

"I promise, 'Mlangeni," I answered.

"Well, 'Nkosan," he went on, his voice low and full of apprehension, "I was coming from the saloon."

"But why the saloon?" I asked amazed.

"Please come with me quickly, 'Nkosan, before the others come on board," was his strange reply as he swung about and made for the forecastle.

I followed him below to find he already had a small tin trunk, brightly painted with a tribal design on his bunk and was opening it. Quickly he took out a bundle in a cloth I recognised as similar to the ones I had often seen him undo before those strange congregations on so many Sunday mornings by the sea.

He undid it and, pointing to the contents, said: "I went to gather that, 'Nkosan. Surely there was no harm?"

Understanding came to me with such a rush that I almost

laughed with relief. The bundle contained nothing but nail clippings, hair from the Captain's brushes and combs, discarded buttons and bits of string and clothing of no practical use, even down to cigarette ends. Anything Thor Larsen had handled personally was of value.

"I see and I understand, 'Mlangeni," I told him. "Body-matter! Matter for the medicine you and Nkomi-dhl'ilale sell on Sundays by the sea!"

Surprise made 'Mlangeni exclaim in his old spontaneous way. "So! You know even that, 'Nkosan! I always knew you were a great trickster but you are even greater than I knew!"

Understanding was not difficult for me because I had been brought up among the Amangtakwena, so close in language, history and custom to the Zulus. I knew their implicit faith that in possessing the body-matter, or personal belongings, of the powerful, they could make mighty magic for themselves to use against their own difficulties which, of course, is precisely what 'Mlangeni and Jack wanted for their people. Since Thor Larsen was not only the most powerful personality in the ship, but also the most successful in the fleet, and on any count a most unusual and forceful character in his own right, he was for a person like 'Mlangeni the obvious source of supply of magic material of the highest potential.

"Yes, I understand, 'Mlangeni," I repeated, certain I knew the whole truth now, and in my youth confident that armed with the truth I could defeat anything. "But you must promise me that you'll never leave your fire again while a killing takes place. And I promise you I'll gather for you every day all the body-matter in the Captain's cabin and saloon and give it to you each week in port."

"You'll do that for me?" 'Mlangeni answered, overjoyed. "'Nkosan, you will never see me away from my fire again!"

It all went off thus far more easily and naturally than I had ever expected, though I feared the dangerous resentment that might return to 'Mlangeni on reflection. On reflection he would not fail to realise the general suspicion which must have provoked my request. We must, therefore, uncover the thief

soon, as I told Leif that night when I reported 'Mlangeni's promise to me. The matter of culling the body-matter from the Captain's quarters I kept to myself.

"If 'Mlangeni keeps faith," Leif answered, "we should know within a week."

"He'll keep faith all right," I replied confidently.

However, the very next Monday night something happened to alarm me and to test my faith in 'Mlangeni as it had not been tested yet.

We had had a good day behind us, having killed two enormous sperm whales, and were making for the harbour with Thor Larsen and the crew all in great good humour. When I went below early to go to bed, as I often did on Mondays because we always left harbour in the night after the weekend and I would be tired for lack of sleep, I found Thor Larsen already in the saloon. He was obviously impatient, looking for something, picking up the few cushions, looking underneath them, throwing them down, feeling in all the crevices and was about to go down on his hands and knees on the floor when he heard me come in, straightened, and turned about.

"Ah, it's you, Eyes," he said curtly. "Have you seen my sperm tooth? I look everywhere and not find him."

"No, sir," I answered. "But I expect it's somewhere here. Let me look."

Without waiting for his answer, I went down on my hands and knees to search for the missing paper-weight. I found nothing. I went all over the ground the Captain had covered. I even took the manuals, Bibles and other books out of their case to look behind them. It was all in vain; the tooth had vanished. I had no need to look at the Captain's grim face to realise how badly he took the loss.

"It's one god-damn funny thing," he exclaimed out of his odd intuitive self. "Last night before we sail, the tooth he was there at the head of the table. Tonight he is gone. Something god-damn strange is happening in my ship."

"It can't be gone, sir," I pleaded. "I'll look again in the morning and we'll find it for you."

"No. Eyes," he answered grimly. "You the best eyes I know,

but not even you will find him. That tooth, he won't walk by himself. Somebody's took him for a walk, not?"

And there it was in my mind too: suspicion that 'Mlangeni had found too much the temptation to take what clearly would be for him the mightiest of the Captain's charms to add to his collection of body-matter. I found the feeling so intolerable that I just had to go and find him and speak to him.

He was alone in the engine room, the pistons clanking at half speed around him, standing there crooning to his fire. He looked so innocent that I was ashamed of my suspicion, yet it was nagging at my heart.

" 'Mlangeni," I said. "You did stay by your fire today when the killing was on?"

"Indeed I did, my 'Nkosan," he replied with an affectionate laugh. "I never left the engine room all the time. But why do you ask, when I promised."

"No reason at all, 'Mlangeni," I told him. Then on sudden inspiration I added, "I really came to ask you to let me have your bundle of body-matter to keep until the weekend. I have a feeling that the forecastle might be searched sometime and you'd rather no one else find those things with you, wouldn't you?"

"Indeed, 'Nkosan," he replied quietly, realising from my request that the weight of suspicion was still in the ship.

"Could you fetch it now and give it to me?"

Without a word he left me and a few minutes later brought me his bundle.

"Did anybody see you?" I asked anxiously as I took it.

"No," he said. "They all asleep like young children below and I make no sound to wake them."

"I'll take good care of this, 'Mlangeni," I told him, "but you must promise me you'll never leave your fire for the saloon again."

"I promise already," he corrected me and resumed his position by the fire.

I went down to my own bunk. The Captain was already in his, but instead of being asleep as he normally was after such a day of kills, I could tell from his restlessness that he was wide awake, his mind no doubt obsessed with the disappearance of

his whale's tooth. Hours later, after I had at last fallen asleep, I woke for a moment to hear him dress and go on deck, where he stayed all night.

I was about to leave the saloon myself early the next morning when Leif came in, sat down and broke the bad news to me.

Apparently in the night the Captain, relieving his bosun-mate, had told him of the vanished paper-weight. The bosun then felt in duty bound to tell the Captain about the petty thieving since he felt the two things might not be unconnected. More, he told the Captain of the crew's suspicions about 'Mlangeni. "By God," Thor Larsen had exclaimed, "I always thought something strange about that black stoker!"

The Captain had paused then for quite a while before uttering, as if the matter was already decided in his quick resolute mind. "It's a pity because he was best-damn stoker in fleet!"

"You notice the *was*," Leif pointed out, unnecessarily, to me.

"Oh, Leif, what can we do?" I blurted out.

"Persuade the Captain not to act or say anything until the weekend," Leif answered. "We must concentrate all we've got to that end. But careful, here he comes."

At that, Larsen, as tense as I had ever seen him, walked in.

"Ah, Fügelsang!" he exclaimed. "My breakfast quick! We'll be at harbour entrance within hour, not?"

"Yes, Captain," Leif answered, vanished and in a few minutes had our breakfast on the table, the coffee steaming in front of Thor Larsen who meanwhile had not uttered a word to me.

Then, instead of going away, Leif began speaking to the Captain in Norwegian. I gathered it was about the thieving, the vanished tooth, 'Mlangeni, and postponing action until the weekend. It made Thor Larsen very impatient and he interrupted many times, but in the main listened carefully because, as I said before, Leif always acted as spokesman for the men.

"And you, Eyes," he turned to me at the end. "Fügelsang tells you too believe this black stoker innocent. I tell you, Eyes, I trust your eyes in everything but not with this black stoker. Always you blind how black a man he is inside."

"No, sir, you're wrong," I spoke up with spirit. "I'm not blind. I trust him because I know his people. They will kill and

186

murder when they are hurt, sir, but steal, never. Have you in
all the years he has worked for you ever found anything missing?
Why should he suddenly begin now?"

That last point had a marked effect on the Captain. He had
it in him to be moved by loyalty, having perhaps had too little
of it himself from men and life.

He watched me intently, his expression softening somewhat,
turned to Leif and said in his decisive, irrevocable way: "All
right, Fügelsang, I wait till Saturday night." When I went out
later to see Leif in his galley, he commented: "It's a strange
coincidence about that tooth, Pete. I can't believe Foyn is
behind that tooth's disappearance. Money yes, but a paper-
weight, no. You're certain 'Mlangeni was at his fire all day?"

"Of course," I answered quickly, wondering the while if I
was really as certain as I sounded, for nothing I knew could
have tempted 'Mlangeni more than that tooth.

There followed one of the longest weeks that I had yet known
at sea. The atmosphere in the ship would have been intolerable
had we not had one of our busiest periods and been hard at
work. The only two people in the ship who really seemed to be
enjoying themselves were Ruud and Foyn, who whenever
possible were together, the winchman often in laughter at
Foyn's sly remarks. Gorgeous too hated the suspicion in the
ship as keenly as I did. But he was luckier than I, since he was
free of the secret cause I had for doubting 'Mlangeni. He and
Leif were like rocks in their faith in 'Mlangeni,and that helped
me considerably.

I was almost relieved when Saturday afternoon came and we
tied up at the head of the line right alongside the main quay.

"Pete!" Leif called out as I was about to go below. "I'd like
you to come down with us all to the forecastle for a moment.
We're having a meeting you should attend. And don't worry.
I told you, I have a plan."

He added this last bit to reassure me.

We found the whole crew below, bosun and all, standing
beside their bunks, solemn and taut as if at a funeral. The
moment Leif stepped in, 'Papa' bosun addressed him briefly
in Norwegian.

"I am going to speak to you in English," Leif began then, in his most deliberate way, "because not all of us understand Norwegian. 'Papa' bosun has ordered me to take over and explain why we are here."

Briefly he went over the history of the petty thieving as I have already described it, and ended up by asking if every man there had counted his cash. Before they could reply Foyn spoke up, politely but with deadly intent.

"Mr. Fügelsang, that is not the whole story. You've left out the most important part, you've not mentioned what I've seen these past weeks—"

I knew he was going to tell about 'Mlangeni and straight away rouse the gathering against our stoker.

Leif knew it too and silenced him at once. "Foyn," he told him sternly, "you are not to interrupt. You'll get your turn to speak soon enough. Now have you all counted your money and have any of you found yourselves short?"

Every man there declared what he possessed and the amount that he was short, which added up to £2 17s. od. Only 'Mlangeni stood there upright and silent.

"What about you, 'Mlangeni," Leif asked.

"I have not thought to look," 'Mlangeni replied in a manner that would have shamed anyone that had not been subtly conditioned for suspicion.

"Please look at once, now," Leif told him, his tone less detached than before.

Everyone watched in silence while 'Mlangeni produced his unlocked tin chest, placed it on his bunk, opened it and took out of it some soiled bank-notes rolled round some loose coin.

Slowly he counted it up and then announced quietly, "I have five pounds seven shillings and fourpence. No, it is all here."

At that, first Foyn and then Ruud looked meaningfully at one another and the rest of the crew silently followed their example.

"Well!" Leif announced, now solemn as a judge. "The bosun and I have decided there is only one thing to do in the circumstances. We are going to search everyone's gear here, openly, with you all to witness it."

I saw Foyn go pale with shock, whisper something to Ruud

and almost in one voice, the two of them protested: "We refuse and so should everyone—we know who's guilty—"

"Another word from you, Foyn," Leif retorted, "and I'll ask the Captain to take over."

Foyn obviously did not like this although I knew Leif was bluffing and had no intention of going to the Captain.

Without giving Foyn another chance to argue, Leif addressed the rest of the crew: "It's only fair to all of us. Until this matter is cleared up one of us will be under suspicion. Already the atmosphere and distrust is worse than I have ever encountered in any Norwegian ship. So, to show how serious this is, we'll first inspect 'Papa' bosun's gear and pockets."

After that no one could object.

'Papa' bosun promptly laid his gear on his bunk and spread his cash on top of it.

As I watched the bosun's gear being searched minutely I was thankful 'Mlangeni's bundle was under my bunk. Finally the bosun had to hold up his arms above his head for Leif to feel his pockets. Everything of course was just as the bosun had declared. Then Leif instructed the bosun to search him and again the result was favourable.

"Now, 'Mlangeni," Leif announced with no trace of mistrust in his tone: "We will, if you do not mind, search you next."

The search if anything was more thorough than the previous two had been, so thorough in fact that I saw the rush of heat to 'Mlangeni's cheeks beneath his black face. But again the result was favourable and nothing was found.

At that quite a new kind of look appeared on the faces of the silent, solemn crew.

So it went on with a heightening sense of drama, until only Ruud and Foyn were left.

Nils Ruud, considering his initial protest, submitted to the search calmly enough and when he too was proved honest in his declaration looked round smugly.

But Foyn was as restless as a wild animal caught in a net.

"I will not be searched," he shouted almost at Leif. "I have never been so insulted and I'll leave a ship where a man is treated like a criminal!"

But he could not avoid inspection since public opinion had turned completely against him.

It did not take Leif and 'Papa' bosun long to produce from the bottom of Foyn's duffle bag, tied up in a kerchief, one of the biggest collections of silver coins the *Kurt Hansen* had ever seen. And that was the last we saw of Foyn, who was dismissed from the ship that very night by the Captain.

Before we finally dispersed,'Mlangeni turned to me and said scornfully in Zulu: "Tell them if you like, 'Nkosan, we say in Icoco that for a 'With-ears-that-hear-not' man, the hissing of a mamba will sound like the song of a bird: and also tell that Stirrer-up-of-strife-in-the-house that even if he lives to be a great grandfather, he will never have a shadow."

With that he walked out of the forecastle.

"What did he say, Pete?" A dozen or more voices came at me. I merely told them: "He knows you all suspected him and has been deeply hurt and offended."

I must add that I never saw a group of honest men look more ashamed of themselves.

As I too left and went to the saloon to face the Captain, I couldn't help wondering what had happened to the paperweight. What I was to think about that?"

Profoundly perturbed, I came to the saloon. Thor Larsen was sitting at the head of the table deep in thought. To my utter amazement, for once no tantalus of gin was on the table in front of him.

"Oh, it's you, Eyes," he exclaimed, looking rather unhappily at me.

Quickly I told him what had just happened in the forecastle. Among the many obvious reactions he had I need only mention the relevant one.

"But, Eyes, that does not explain tooth, not? I still will have to question black stoker about sperm tooth, for you not find him in Foyn's gear, not? He is only one, apart from Foyn, who had chance to take him—except you, Eyes, and you could never do such things, not? You'd better to go now and call that stoker at once."

I knew from his voice that there was no evading the issue any

longer. It all was going to end badly. The tooth was gone, and
whether 'Mlangeni had taken it or not he would be so offended
by what was about to happen that there and then he would leave
the ship. In fact, unless I used all I knew of tact and diplomacy,
we would be lucky if he did not assault the Captain and land
himself in gaol.

Desperate, deeply dismayed, I turned to go but the Captain
called me back.

"Eyes," he ordered me. "Give me first my schnapps and a
glass. I have one god-damn thirst."

I went and picked up the heavy mahogany tantalus from its
place under the bracket of books against the ship's side and
placed it and a glass in front of him.

Some instinct made me stand there and watch him unlock
it. He had some difficulty in getting the great gin decanter out,
it appeared to be jammed in tightly with the two others. He got
it out at last and instead of at once pouring out a glass, he remained staring at the place where it had stood as if hypnotised.

"You still there, Eyes," he called out in a strange voice.
"Good! You to come, quick!"

I hurried to his side.

He pointed at the tantalus and said: "Look."

There, jammed up against the other decanter right at the
bottom, was the missing sperm tooth.

"God!" Larsen said at last, looking at me and obviously
relieved: "You know what, my Eyes? Thor Larsen himself was
thief. He steal from himself, not? You fetch that black stoker
here at once. You hear, quick!"

I cannot describe the delight with which I brought 'Mlangeni,
puzzled and still on his dignity, into the saloon.

"Langenay," the Captain said to him, "you one damn good
stoker. You best stoker in fleet. No, you best stoker I ever know,
so I wish for to give you small present."

With that he handed 'Mlangeni thirteen packets of cigarillos,
in fact at that time his entire stock, as I happened to know. It
was typical of him that in this as in all else he knew no limit.

Nothing in that eventful day helped so much to restore
'Mlangeni to his native sense of honour and dignity among his

fellow men. And, I am happy to add, right up to the end of the season the crew went out of their way to make amends. At the end of the season there was not one of the crew, not even Nils Ruud, who did not give 'Mlangeni a farewell present.

Only one more thing remains to be said, about all this. Half-way between this season and the next, I woke up one night in a camp in the bush far away in the interior. I heard first a lion roar, and then the sound like a pistol shot of an elephant near by stripping a piece of bark from a tree. The elephant made me think of Thor Larsen: and hard on that I saw him again staring at the missing tooth at the bottom of his tantalus of gin. A strange idea came to me then from my sleep. I thought I would like to design a coat of arms for Thor Larsen. I would do it in four quarters: first a sea with stylised wavelets; then a black elephant; below it a sperm whale and harpoon; and underneath all the motto "I steal from myself."

CHAPTER ELEVEN

'One-Bullet' and 'Sway-Back'

I CAME then, at last, to that Saturday evening at the beginning of my fourth whaling season, at the moment in the empty squeaking *Kurt Hansen* when I was stowing my gear underneath my bunk in Thor Larsen's cabin, feeling strangely and indefinitely apprehensive. I had just shut the heavy mahogany drawer on my clothes and straightened myself when I heard someone board the deck above me. Someone to keep me company and perhaps explain everything, I thought with relief as heavy footsteps sounded overhead.

I was through the plush curtains of the cabin doorway, out of the saloon and up the companion-way as fast as I had ever been. 'Mlangeni, already changed into his sea-going clothes, was just making himself comfortable beside the warm hatch.

"Oh, Man of Icoco!" I called out, delighted to find him there again so massively real, with a long dark sunset shadow on the yellow wood of the deck beside him. "I see you and I greet you."

He rose immediately, swung round to return my greeting in kind, but, warm and friendly as it was, it perturbed me. Some subtle element that normally would have been present was withheld, and its absence suggested to me that our 'Man-in-the-Sun' was a preoccupied if not troubled person.

I think my dismay was instantly communicated to him, for in that protective manner he had always adopted towards me, he said reassuringly: "Sit here, 'Nkosan, please, and bring me your news."

He moved over to the far edge of the hatch brushing the cover beside him politely with the broad palm of his great hand. Genuine as the invitation was, the sound of his voice was still not as full as it would normally have been. Yet I knew I could not ask him directly what was the cause. I would have to come

G

round to it the African way, which was difficult for me seeing that apprehension had quickened in me.

"Have you seen the Captain yet?" I asked him. "And d'you know where he's gone? And why the *Kurt Hansen* was deserted when I boarded her some twenty minutes ago?"

"The little-killer-of-great-fish, is he not in his place below then?" 'Mlangeni answered, his big black eyes full of surprise. "He was there with another 'Nyanga, when I went ashore to buy tobacco!"

I did not miss the use of the word "another", since it reminded me that Thor Larsen was, in 'Mlangeni's view, a witch-doctor too. I remembered how, three years before, Jack, the butler, on my first meeting with Thor Larsen, had warned me that the Captain had the eyes of a witch-doctor. That moment suddenly seemed like a pin-point of light at the end of a long tunnel.

"Another 'Nyanga, 'Mlangeni! What d'you mean? Did the Captain have a visitor then?"

"Yes," 'Mlangeni told me, Thor Larsen had had a visitor on board, a strange, tall, spare old man, with a dark-grey beard, pointed like the blade of an assegai, and the eyes of a witch-doctor with the light in them of all the dreams in which the 'Nyanga forever walks like a man in his sleep.

There was no doubt from the tone of his voice that he had found the visitation highly portentous. He paused and I had to prod him into speech.

"This visitor, 'Mlangeni, how did he come to the *Kurt Hansen*? D'you know who he is?"

'Mlangeni shook his head and went on to tell me all he knew of the episode. He had joined the ship at about noon that morning to find the Captain, Leif and Gorgeous on board.

"And how were they?" I asked, happy that I was certain of seeing them soon.

"Well, 'Nkosan, well," 'Mlangeni answered, and added not surprisingly, since they had all gone straight from our last season to another in the Antarctic and must have only just returned. "But weary like men who have walked too far and too long from home."

However, 'Mlangeni continued, when he had exchanged greetings with Leif and Gorgeous, stowed his gear and changed his clothes, it was agreed between them that he should stay on watch in the *Kurt Hansen* while they went ashore for the petty shopping necessary after so long a time at sea. He made himself comfortable on deck, and was smoking the last cigarette when he saw the other 'Nyanga.

As I knew, he went on, there were always, at weekends, scores of visitors and sightseers in the harbour, walking up and down the quayside and eyeing the ships. He, 'Mlangeni, was too used to such people to bother his eyes with them. But suddenly he had been compelled to look up. He was certain I would not be surprised at that because I knew what Iziyanga* were: they had the power to direct one's sight from far greater distances than the few feet which separated the *Kurt Hansen*'s low deck from the dock. He was made to look straight into the eyes of this man he had described to me.

These eyes, 'Mlangeni said, were singularly clear, of a blue so pale that they were like the sky at Icoco seen through a white haze of summer: yet so bright that they shone in the shadow of a large wide-brimmed khaki hat with a strip of puff-adder skin round the base of its crown.

Their eyes had met and he had looked steadily at 'Mlangeni, as if he had always known him. 'Mlangeni forced himself to look away, and when he dared to glance at the quay again he saw that the stranger had turned sideways to the *Kurt Hansen* and was walking with long, easy steps right down the line of the whalers, examining each group as he went by them.

'Mlangeni hoped that he had seen the last of the man and that he was merely curious. But to his amazement, when the stranger got to the end of the line of whalers, he turned round and came back again, his eyes intent as before. Clearly he was no ordinary sightseer and his special concern was with one or more of our ships. He passed up and down the entire line thus three times and on each occasion gave 'Mlangeni a brilliant concentrated stare.

'Mlangeni liked this not at all. Afraid that at any moment

* Plural of 'Nyanga: witchdoctor.

now the man might speak to him, he was thinking of going below when to his astonishment the Captain, impetuous and hatless, appeared on deck and made straight for the side of the ship to look over at the man on shore.

The man had halted and turned once more to face the *Kurt Hansen*. 'Mlangeni was certain he had willed the Captain on deck, for he looked at him steadily as if he had known Thor Larsen, too, before. Thor Larsen responded in kind, and 'Mlangeni was not taken aback when suddenly they came out of their trance and Thor Larsen said a rough "good day", to which the stranger silently raised his hat.

'Mlangeni commented: " 'Nkosan, it was clear to see the stranger had walked far and long where the sun is even hotter than here, for half-way between his eyes and his grey hair the skin of his forehead was as white as milk; but all the rest of his face was dark as Leif's coffee.

"Perhaps you wish to step on board, not?" 'Mlangeni mimicked the Captain's tone so well that I couldn't help smiling.

"Thenk you, mister." 'Mlangeni reproduced the man's answer so clearly that I knew he could only have been Afrikaans, or, as 'Mlangeni would have had it, "a Dutchman".

At once the stranger had come on board, shaken hands firmly with Thor Larsen, before being taken off to be shown all over the bridge, wheelhouse and deck.

'Mlangeni shook his head over this unusual behaviour of the Captain. Besides, 'Mlangeni had the impression that the Dutchman hardly knew any English and understood nothing or little of the Captain's highly individualistic use of it. None the less they seemed to need no words for understanding since at the end of their tour the Captain had taken the stranger below. There they had been all afternoon, indeed they had seemed so settled that the conscientious 'Mlangeni had thought there could be no harm in slipping ashore to buy some tobacco. But he had not liked the meeting at all.

"When the Iziyanga begin to gather, 'Nkosan," he concluded ominously, "the shadow of great trouble is come upon us all."

"But what shadow, 'Mlangeni?" I asked. "You mean something else happened today of which you haven't yet spoken?"

"No, 'Nkosan," he shook his head. "Not today."

He hesitated while he looked over the quay, up to the burning sunset ridge upon which the fashionable houses of Port Natal stood tier upon tier, white-faced and red-roofed, already muffled in purple against the falling night. "No, 'Nkosan, not of today, not here but before I came. I stand before you not I. My body and my heart are stirred up like water with mud. I have become a house of dreams."

Poor 'Mlangeni. There was no doubt he was deeply troubled and,like all his people,unable to keep it secret for long from those he believed to be friends. Now I had only to ask to be told that he had not been long home in his kraal at Icoco when he began to be worried.

First, a great black mamba had moved into his wife's hut. The mamba had large, glittering, alert eyes and a yellow scar on his side in the same place as the long scar his great-great-grandfather had received fighting under Chaka as a young man. He had no doubt it was the spirit of his great-great-grandfather come to visit them for some abnormal purpose. They had vacated the hut and daily put milk at the entrance to feed the mamba. They had observed it lying in the sun, curled up like a great metal bangle, but occasionally uncoiling itself to lift its head high, sitting on its tail, while it surveyed the scene as if it owned it. But one had only to look at it closely, 'Mlangeni said, to see it was saying: "Even here at the centre of your own kraal and in the clear light of the sun, watch as I am watching."

It had stayed with them a full round of the moon and then suddenly vanished,not by day, because they would have seen it, but by night. That was the strangest of all things about this strange visitation for, as I knew, mambas never moved at night; their great-great-grandfather therefore could only have moved by night if he wanted to indicate that there was danger about by day.

"But what danger?" I interrupted.

He shook his head and said he wished he knew. There were many other persons who wished they knew. Was not the worst of all troubles, the trouble for which there was no name? He asked the question of the sky, its blue stained with red—as the

sea with the blood of the whale—before he went on to say that almost all the men he met were not as they were, particularly not the men home from towns like Port Natal. They laughed no longer as they used to laugh and their eyes had darkened.

Also there was the cattle. He had never known the cattle so restless at night. There were no lion or leopard about, yet they would low all night long in strange sounds as if questioning the promptings of the spirits of the Amageba,* who as every child knew communed with them. This was so not only at Icoco but all over the land: and it troubled the hearts of all men.

Finally he and Jack, his "brother" and my friend the butler, had gone to consult the greatest seer in the country just before they had had to return to Port Natal.

He was no comfort to them. This seer, 'Mlangeni emphasised, could read the future as I read books. He had made his reputation when still a boy, herding cattle. One night, many years ago, guarding cattle alone, the voice of his dead grandfather had told him to look up at the sky. He obeyed at once. In the clear winter sky over Icoco among the brilliant stars—and no one could have known how great and bright stars could be until he had seen the stars of Icoco in winter—he saw two small and five great stars suddenly break away from the multitude, reverse their course and move against the universe from west to east. A while later they were followed by other lesser stars. The boy reported it to his father, his father to the chief, the chief to their king, and his principal seer. If true, the king's seer had pronounced, it could only mean trouble such as the world had never seen, because in all the long record of portents in his possession there had never been such a revolt in heaven against nature. But the probability was that it was just a young boy's imagination.

As the weeks passed and no trouble came, people began to laugh at the young boy and to tease him for being a teller of tales. Then one day, the magistrate and seven policemen from the provincial capital paid them a rare and unexpected visit. He told them that a great war had broken out in the world and

* Ancient name of the ancient Zulus.

that he had come in the name of their king from across the great water to call on grown men to help in the war.

Questioned by the wise old men with metal rings around their heads, the magistrate revealed that the war had broken out the very night the boy had seen the five stars leave their courses and move from west to east. And what was more, 'Mlangeni said, his voice falling to a whisper with awe, the magistrate explained the war was mainly between five great nations and two smaller nations whose names he had never heard.

Now on this present occasion the same seer had seen again a multitude of small, insignificant stars leave their courses and move from east to west until, one by one, they shot from the sky to vanish into the dark. Two of the brightest among them remained pushing on towards the east and the sun, but at the last moment they too shot out of the sky simultaneously, leaving black streaks to mark their end. The seer could not tell what it meant except that it foretold great trouble for many ordinary men: and the trouble might be marked by the coming together of two extraordinary men. He uttered this last sentence with such a strange tone of immediacy that I had a feeling he had already identified his two extraordinary men.

I was about to question him further when he exclaimed urgently, "Hush, my 'Nkosan. Here comes the little-killer-of-great-fish."

I looked up. Thor Larsen was striding towards his ship with that strange balancing walk of his. He was already dressed in his Sunday best, and his square figure, dark against the evening glow, was coming towards us fast as if engaged in some anthropoidal walking race.

He saw me before he reached the gang-plank and called out loudly, the rasp in his voice harsher for frustration, "There you are, Eyes! Damn time too! Just when I Thor Larsen need you, you come back late. Why?"

It is true my train had been some three hours late, which was not unusual on so long a journey from the interior. It had happened before and occasioned no comment. Why had it suddenly become so important?

I was to know almost at once. Although more reconciled to

'Mlangeni ever since the episode of the sperm tooth, Thor Larsen had continued his strange dislike of seeing us together. He still could not resist finding reasons for separating us. This Saturday evening was no exception. I hardly had time to explain my delayed arrival before, ignoring 'Mlangeni, he ordered me to follow him below.

In the saloon he made at once for his tantalus, lifted it easily and quickly on to the table and poured the glass waiting for it half full of schnapps.

"You sit here, Eyes, and listen."

The gesture was as peremptory as the words, his spirit as always being in a hurry. He was silent only long enough to swallow his gin in five long mouthfuls and to pour another great measure into the glass. But it was long enough for me to tell how the season in the Antarctic had stressed and re-stressed the writing of strain and tension, of constant seeking and killing, in and between the lines of his dark seemingly moon-pocked face.

A quick sum of mental arithmetic told me that it was the beginning of the eleventh year since the Captain had last had a break from whaling, during which time he had packed twenty full seasons, going continuously from one killing to the other. Yet his deep eyes, searching my own over the tumbler shining like a fortune-teller's crystal that he held in both broad hands in front of his wide chest, had the same expression in them as on the day when I had first met him. For them there had been neither time nor season; only one dark, forever empty "now".

However, suddenly the glow of excitement showed in them and he announced: "Today, Eyes, I met a hunter of elephants. Today, for two hours, he sat where you sit trying to talk. Only now I come back from walking with him to tram. Only we not understand much. Why you not here to translate for us? Why, Eyes, why?"

Putting the tumbler down, he searched in his waistcoat pocket, drew out a piece of paper and threw it on the plush tablecloth, saying: "Look! This is name of the hunter of elephants. For two hours, Eyes, he talk and talk and talk, I think, about elephants, whales, the Bible, Job and again elephants. Only I know not clearly how and what."

He slapped a hand to his forehead as if to relieve it of its daze.

I hastened to pick up the paper and saw printed on it in tentative careful block letters: "Herklaas de la Buschagne, 'Ailsa Craig' Private Hotel, Promenade, Port Natal."

Had I tried, I could not have suppressed my astonishment. 'Herklaas' was the Afrikaans from the original 'Hercules'. De la Buschagne was one of the many Huguenot surnames to be found among my countrymen and had been known to me ever since I could remember. He had long been a legend among us up-country as one of our greatest living white hunters.

Thor Larsen, of course, immediately observed my astonishment and exclaimed: "Ah, you know him, my Eyes. This hunter, you know him?"

"I know of him, sir," I corrected, and went on to explain, adding: "He is as famous among the Africans of the interior as among my own people. They all call him 'One-Bullet'."

One-Bullet! The Captain got the meaning at once. "Ah! So he never needs more than one bullet to kill."

The thought depressed him for a while, I think because he remembered how often it took more than one harpoon to kill a whale. Then he said: "But elephant is so much smaller than whale, not, Eyes? And earth does not heave and lift like *Kurt Hansen* at sea, not, Eyes? Sometimes take two, three harpoons for kill. But if ever harpoon come near one-harpoon gunner, I Thor Larsen am such a man."

He celebrated so gratifying a conclusion with a huge swig of gin and then told me the story of the stranger. Like 'Mlangeni, he had been immediately interested in the sight of the man, convinced that there must be something special about a man who was interested in the whaling fleet, if not the *Kurt Hansen*.

To be convinced was to act, and he had gone up on deck to discover what the stranger was after. After this followed Thor Larsen's bewildering account of what had passed for conversation between them. Three things alone remained certain in my mind at the end of the Captain's explosive description of their talk. The stranger had referred Thor Larsen to certain chapters and passages in the book of Job. He wanted Thor Larsen to give him the chance to hunt whales. The Captain had told him

about me and promised to send me to his lodgings as soon as possible to arrange another meeting between them so that they could, with my help, understand one another better.

"So now, my Eyes," Thor Larsen concluded with his hatred of the inconclusive, "you to go at once to this address and tell him I want him here eleven o'clock tomorrow."

Characteristically, it was an order, and I could not help smiling to myself at the thought of what the reaction of 'One-Bullet' de la Buschagne might be if I were tactless enough to render it to the letter.

So, soon after my arrival on board and against my inclination, I was on my way to the promenade to do the Captain's bidding.

I had no difficulty in locating the boarding house, or private hotel as these establishments were euphemistically called. It was a grey three-storied building, with a deep L-shaped verandah, its red tin roof supported on massive pillars at the corners and at either side of the narrow steps leading up from the street. A thick balustrade ran all along its edge, while some hundreds of yards away the long swell of the Indian Ocean broke ceaselessly against the rigid concrete promenade that the citizens of Port Natal had built across the curved fringe of the wide foreshore. The windows of "Ailsa Craig" were small, deep-set and covered with lace, as if someone had fallen out of love with the sun and light. From the dark front door, down a dimly lit passage, came a smell of fried fish and Indian curry to spoil the salt sea air outside. It was obvious to me that the people in the "Ailsa Craig" would be summoned to instant meals by an imperious bell and had already, judging by the stale smell, finished their Saturday supper.

I looked over the men and women on the verandah for someone resembling the stranger 'Mlangeni had described to me but saw none. I had to go inside and, after some trouble, found an Indian waiter who told me to go up a green linoleum-covered staircase, turn left and go down a corridor, at the end of which I would come to room fifteen where Mr. de la Buschagne would be.

I did as directed and went down the bleak corridor to the

sound of "Bye-bye, Blackbird" being played loudly on a gramophone from one of the rooms.

The music stopped and the sound of the sea I loved filled the silence to overflowing.

I stood hesitant in front of a door painted a dirty brown with the number fifteen in khaki figures upon it.

"What on earth possesses you," I thought marvelling at my hesitation. "You've let 'Mlangeni influence you too much."

But I did not relish the meeting and had to force myself, so that I knocked on the door far louder than was necessary or perhaps polite.

Almost at once the door was opened with speed and decision and de la Buschagne, tall and spare, stood before me, as authentically and unmistakably of Afrikaans Africa as biltong. Two unusually brilliant eyes were looking me over while from long narrow lips between neat moustache and well-trimmed pointed grey beard, came one clipped Afrikaans word: "Ja?"

I explained nervously that I was from the *Kurt Hansen*.

That was enough for Herklaas de la Buschagne to interrupt me, step aside, and invite me to enter the room, calling me Cousin in the courteous old-fashioned Afrikaans way as he did so.

The room was what these rooms usually are, furnished sparingly with the cheapest furniture, glossy with excessive varnish to hide the lack of grain in the wood. What was unusual in it was a large stink-wood ox-wagon chest, placed across one corner of the green painted wall, and obviously de la Buschagne's portmanteau. A bandolier full of cartridges lay on it and a gun in a brown leather cover stood behind it in the corner. One look at the cartridges and shape of the cover made me certain it was a nine millimetre Mauser and obviously the owner's favourite weapon, since he had been unable to be parted from it even in Port Natal where he could never use it.

I had barely taken all this in when at the open doorway of the room giving on to a balcony appeared a girl. Behind her and beyond the balcony, stiff as if in corsets, rose the walls of more private hotels, their small curtained windows translucent with amber, transmitting just light enough to show the space between

the windows filled with drainpipes and iron fire escapes. Such a poor view was in itself proof enough that the room in which I stood was one of the cheapest in the "Ailsa Craig" and, combined with the ugly furniture, imparted a Cinderella quality to the impression that the beauty of the girl made on me.

She was not tall but slender, and in the dress she wore, falling to her ankles in the up-country fashion, she looked taller than she was. The dress was of blue linen, slightly waisted, three-quarter sleeves, edged with silk of an astringent green, and a high collar of the same material was pinned to the smooth throat of a long elegant neck by a dark ruby brooch. Her head was shapely; her hair, thick and yellow, fell to her waist in one long thick plait, tied with a green ribbon. Her eyes were large, slightly slanted, and as full of light as her father's, but contemplative, as of a person whose young life had been spent alone, so that she had become accustomed to think thoughts instead of speaking them. The bones beneath the smooth skin were surely drawn, and the oval face was an exciting compound of positive assertion and subtle implication.

As she stepped into the centre of the room to stand under the white electric light overhead, I saw that she, too, must have lived long in places far hotter than Port Natal, for the sun's reflection had left the slightest darkening on her clear skin, like the fine dusting of pollen shaken by the wind.

"My daughter, Laetitia," de la Buschagne said to me, his tone strictly factual. Then he added: "Lets, the Cousin has come from the Captain of the whaling ship that I've told you of."

I thought at that the look in her eyes suddenly became somewhat disapproving. But she gave me a young hand and in a clear voice greeted me with a polite: "How do you do, Cousin?"

"How do you do, little Cousin?" I replied and saw at once that the term, perhaps because the diminutive in Afrikaans is so often used for endearment, had been a mistake.

"Won't you sit down, Cousin," she said coolly and pointed to an empty chair.

I declined politely, saying that I had to get back to the ship at once. I had really only come to bring an invitation from Thor Larsen for Uncle Herklaas (as I called him in deference to

the polite form of the old-fashioned Afrikaans that he had used), to visit him in the *Kurt Hansen* at eleven the next morning.

For the first time since I had met him some sign of feeling showed in de la Buschagne's face, though his voice was taut as ever.

"Thank your Captain, Cousin, and tell him I'll be there," he replied.

"But Vader!"* the girl protested with some dismay. "Vader can't be there at eleven. We shall still be in church by then, as Vader will remember we promised the predicant we would be!"

From the way she addressed her father in the third person, a habit I was to find she never varied, I knew how great was his hold over her and I guessed that perhaps she was also afraid of him.

"If the calf should fall in the pit on a Sunday, daughter," he told her, "Our Lord himself gave us permission to haul it out." He turned to me and repeated: "Tell your Captain I shall be there at eleven."

At this Laetitia looked so dismayed that I took it upon myself to say, with some daring, since Thor Larsen would be most annoyed if he discovered I had proposed an alteration in his command: "I'm certain, Uncle, that if it would be more convenient for you to come somewhat later, the Captain wouldn't mind. He never leaves the *Kurt Hansen* on Sundays until four in the afternoon."

Looking at me with some annoyance, de la Buschagne proclaimed instantly: "No, Cousin. I shall do as your Captain asked. I'll be there at eleven."

There was a rebuke in his voice of "your Captain" which left me unmoved, so gratified was I by the change in the look his daughter gave me. She was obviously touched by my attempt to help her. This was confirmed a moment later when, already in the passage below on my way out, I heard quick light footsteps on the staircase behind me, turned round, and saw her hastening towards me.

"Please, Cousin, I have no time to explain," she begged, putting her hand on my arm and whispering, her face close to

* Afrikaans for Father.

mine. "Please do not let my father go to sea in that ship. Tell your Captain not to take him. Please."

She pressed my arm gently, and without waiting for an answer turned swiftly about to go back up the staircase as fast as she had come down it, and on the whole I was glad she did not wait for my answer.

I could only have told her, if I had been honest, that nothing would make Thor Larsen change his mind about taking her father to sea should he wish to do so, as already I was convinced he did. I doubted even if I had had either the courage or conviction to argue the issue with my Captain, despite a lively desire to help the girl. It would be a brave as well as, perhaps, a foolish man who would try to make Thor Larsen deny the very quality which made him so powerful. Instinct as well as a lively sense of fairness rejected such a course.

The only hope was for the girl to try to change her father's mind but I saw no prospect of that either. I suspected that two such minds as her father's and Thor Larsen's united on any issue could only be changed by some act of God. The thought overawed me. But then, urging myself to a more reasonable attitude, I concluded that the girl was making too much of the whole thing, for what harm could there possibly be in her father taking a trip out to sea in a whaler?

When I told him the news later on, even 'Mlangeni's obvious disapproval of the fact that de la Buschagne was coming to visit the Captain the next day, far from making me reappraise my attitude, oddly irritated me. Perhaps I should have known then that something in me was protesting overmuch.

I was on deck with Leif and 'Mlangeni on that limpid Sunday morning when de la Buschagne arrived. Our Norwegian crew dressed in their rough navy-blue serge had not long gone ashore to church. Gorgeous had just vanished round the corner of a warehouse, a suitcase of new records in hand, on his way to a whole day of music before his dedicated audiences in his apartment. Thor Larsen, already on deck several times pretending to examine his ship but clearly on the look-out for his guest, had just gone below again.

Then, on the stroke of eleven, we saw de la Buschagne round-

ing the corner of a warehouse, its outline trembling in the bright winter sun like a rock under silver water. He was walking fast, with a long easy and resolute step.

The moment he saw him, 'Mlangeni made a noise of disapproval, excused himself with a " 'Nkosan, I've work to do," and hurried below.

De la Buschagne had not long turned the corner when his daughter appeared, walking with an ease and grace that were a delight to watch. I imagined that the fact that she walked some distance behind him was evidence of the disagreement between them. But that, though it still existed, was not the explanation. I discovered later that during her long years alone with her father in the bushveld and jungles of Africa she had always been made to follow him out of regard for her safety, as well as the necessity for the man with the gun always to walk at the head of his line. I was right, however, in concluding that her presence there could only mean that she still hoped to influence her father's purpose with my Captain.

They made straight for the *Kurt Hansen*'s gang-plank and, though in their best up-country clothes, they looked an old-fashioned if not archaic sight.

That her father had eyes for nothing but the *Kurt Hansen* did not surprise me. He after all had been there before. But I was amazed that she could appear so uninterested in the line of ships which never failed to excite me, for she followed in her father's wake with her eyes on the ground.

De la Buschagne started up the gang-plank to come on board.

"Good morning, Uncle," I called out politely.

"Day, Cousin," was the perfunctory response.

At that moment the Captain appeared on deck. He was just in time to see the girl put a foot on the gang-plank.

Ignoring his visitor for the moment, a roar broke from him. "Back, you woman there!" he shouted. "I'll have no woman in *Kurt Hansen*. Who told you come on board, not?"

He turned as if by instinct to look first at me, then to de la Buschagne and then back to the girl, now standing still on the edge of the plank and trembling.

"Back! You hear? I, Thor Larsen, say back!" he shouted again, almost out of control.

I expected de la Buschagne to explain that it was his daughter and to protest against the Captain's brutal way of addressing her. Instead, he merely looked over his shoulder and spoke to her. I heard and understood every word of his clipped Afrikaans.

"I told you, daughter, this was no place for a woman, let alone a young one like you. It's man's talk we are about to have and you had better go back to the hotel to wait for me."

The phrase "man's talk" was a common and, to me, an irritating one in my African world, implying, as it did, an inferiority of the opposite sex. I was not surprised, therefore, that it caused de la Buschagne's daughter to obey, turn about, her head half-bowed, and so withdraw ashore.

I knew also, of course, that many sailors of my day were superstitious about allowing women in their ships because they thought it would bring them bad luck. "Look, Eyes," Svend Johansen had once told me in this regard. "A ship is a woman. If you let another woman on board the two will fight one another for the men in her. Sooner or later they make men in ship mad." Gorgeous also had told me that Thor Larsen was more superstitious than most on this regard. Even so, I had not thought him capable of such lack of manners to a mere girl.

I remembered the strange and tender concern for her father that I had heard in her voice the night before. Something in me gave way. As de la Buschagne stepped on deck, I dashed past him for the gangway.

"Where you going, Eyes? I want you!" Thor Larsen shouted as I went by him.

"That was his daughter you've been shouting at, even if he appears to have forgotten it," I snapped back at him, noticing the surprise on his expression at my first rebellion.

"Eyes! I say, Eyes!" he shouted fiercely, seeing me disappear down the ship's side without any other effort at explanation.

I ignored his cry and ran after the girl whose slender back was now turned to the ship. Reaching her, I took her by the arm and stopped her saying: "Hullo, little Cousin! How are you?"

"Oh, it's you, Cousin," she answered and, turning, looked straight at me.

Her eyes were bright with unshed tears of despair as I thought. But I was wrong. They were tears of anger.

As I tried to soften the impact of Thor Larsen's behaviour by telling her it was an unwritten law that no woman was ever allowed in the *Kurt Hansen* and that the Captain, of course, had to set the example, concluding "I promise you, little Cousin, he was shouting at himself rather than at you. He's an awfully decent fellow, really" she interrupted me.

"If he's so decent," she responded with spirit, "he ought to know better. I've never met so rude a man before"—she used the Afrikaans word "onbeskof", which is stronger than rude. "I've never been spoken to like that by anyone and I won't allow it. I'll have it out with father at once—"

She broke off, perhaps realising what little influence she could have on her father in this matter. All I know is that the tears of anger became tears of distress and rolled bright down her cheek.

"Look, little Cousin?" I said pressing her arm hard. "Don't take it so badly. Sailors all sound a rough lot but they're quite decent really. But they don't see much of women, you know. The Captain'd be awfully upset if he knew he'd hurt you. He was merely giving you an order just as he gives us orders. Come along with me and I'll show you what to do until your father comes back."

The Captain's shout interrupted us. "Eyes, you to come here at once!"

"Presently," I called back with a courage that, when I thought it all over later, made me shiver at the risk I had run of estranging Thor Larsen for ever. "Later!" I turned my attention to the girl again. "Come with me please, little Cousin."

Still holding her arm, I began walking her to the purple Royal Mail ship just ahead of us.

She came reluctantly. "Cousin, you'd better go back or that terrible little man will be angrier than ever. I've caused enough trouble—"

"Just come with me," I told her firmly, and after a moment she began to step out more willingly at my side.

I had in the years behind me made friends of most of the people working regularly in the dock area. I knew all the watchmen employed by the rich Royal Mail Steamship Company to relieve their crews of guard duty while their ships were in port. The watchman on duty on this particular Sunday was a favourite of mine, a retired old Army pensioner, and I had no hesitation in walking the girl up the wide gangway on to the mail ship's gleaming deck, introducing her to him and asking him as a special favour to let her see all over the ship and if necessary wait on one of the benches on deck in the sun until I could fetch her again.

"You'll find this ship more welcoming than the *Kurt Hansen*," I told her with a grin. I turned to the watchman. "They like women in these great passenger ships, don't they?"

He, clearly impressed by the girl's beauty, responded: "Pleased to meet you, Missie, and happy to have you on board."

Relieved, I hastened back on board the *Kurt Hansen* where the Captain, de la Buschagne beside him, stood rigid and silent, staring at me in a way that frightened me. I stepped fast past Leif, who was looking at me with a new interest, and straight up to Thor Larsen.

I spoke to him with both the courage and cunning of fear: "I've made your guest's daughter comfortable in the mail ship, sir, as I thought you'd wish me to. They're used to women in those ships."

Thor Larsen glared at me. Heretically, the thought came to me that perhaps we'd be a better ship if we did allow women on board.

Then suddenly, in his unpredictable way, comprehension came to him.

"Damn you, Eyes," he told me, his eyes betraying his curse. "Damn you—you not my Eyes for nothing! Come! We three go below!"

I followed Thor Larsen and his guest below. To my surprise Leif came behind, his hand warm on my shoulder, to ask the Captain whether he would like some coffee and cake for his guest?

Soon the three of us were alone in the tiny saloon. Thor

Larsen sat at the head of our small triangular table, his tantalus of spirit, tumbler of gin, and his sperm tooth in front of him, his intense eyes determinedly fixed on his guest. I sat on the bench nearest to him and beside me on my right 'One-Bullet' de la Buschagne, so tall that, even sitting down, his head nearly touched the metal ceiling. He had taken a yellow calabash pipe out of his pocket, stuffed it full of tobacco from a small cotton bag which he wore looped around the ends of black braces underneath his ample jacket. The tobacco was dark and so springy that when lit he had to clamp it down with a metal cap fitted to the pipe to prevent it from curling over the bright yellow bowl. His wide hat lay on the table within reach, and to this day I remember how my eyes would go time and again from its puff-adder band curled round the hat, the strangely futuristic pattern of the diamond markings of the snake as vivid as if it were there alive, to the lone sperm tooth showing up in the deep plush of the cloth in front of the Captain like the tip of an iceberg on a velvet sea. They became more and more heraldic as if they were the seals under which two warriors fought an ancient fight.

For two hours we sat there thus, with me interpreting and the air in the saloon turning so blue with smoke from calabash pipe and cigarillos that I could hardly see the gold lettering on the Lloyd's Manual of Shipping in the bracket opposite me. Only once were we interrupted when Leif, without speaking a word, brought in a huge pot of coffee, two cups and a plate of cake for our guest and me. He would have left as silently had not a request from the stranger made me stop Leif to ask him for some salt.

"Salt?" He queried the request, clearly mystified.

I looked at de la Buschagne for verification.

He nodded and added: "Always take salt in coffee and like it black. Never take sugar into the bush with me. It's heavy to carry and useless stuff. In any case the Kaffirs always steal it before you can use it."

All this had to be translated for Thor Larsen and served only to increase his respect of his guest as a man of unique character like himself.

Slight as the incident was, it was a sign of how de la Buschagne, like Thor Larsen, had formed tastes and character down to the minutest detail not so much out of tradition but each out of his own experience of life.

Something of what de la Buschagne's own life had been came out during the conversation that followed.

It began by Thor Larsen wanting to know what he had meant the day before with all these references to the book of Job? Thor Larsen thought he had got the drift of most of their talk: but what had Job to do with it all?

De la Buschagne took the pipe out of his mouth whenever he answered and, elbow resting on the table, held it out steadily in front of him, the mouth-piece almost level with his eyes, which constantly moved from it to Thor Larsen's attentive face and back again to the stem.

He had mentioned Job to the Captain, de la Buschagne asked me to explain, because on the very night of the day he had first seen that elephant of which he had spoken to the Captain, he had opened his Bible at random in camp to read a chapter of it after the evening meal to his daughter as their unvaried custom was, and found his eyes at once on the lines: "Canst thou draw out Leviathan with a hook?"

Yes, yes, Thor Larsen nodded vigorously as he interrupted in his impetuous way, he had understood the lines and had confirmed their content by looking them up in the ship's Bible afterwards.

The guest replied that he had understood the Captain's response, for how could a man be the Captain of a whaler without having "drawn out Leviathan with a hook" many times?

"Yes, yes!" exclaimed Thor Larsen, but what had Job or Leviathan or both to do with the elephant?

The answer was of such import to de la Buschagne that he paused too long for Thor Larsen's liking, who interrupted again at random.

"Ask him, Eyes, how many elephant he kill?"

The question appeared so remote from what was in de la Buschagne's mind that he answered it casually, as if brushing it from his thought like a mere fly from his forehead. "Sixteen

hundred and three . . . perhaps four. I have never been absolutely sure of that last one."

"Sixteen hundred and three!" Thor Larsen exclaimed, astonished. For the moment he was also downcast, as I well knew, because he could not have killed anything like that number of whales. But irrepressible, he brightened again, for I heard him muttering to himself: "But then elephant much smaller than whale."

At that he turned to me, aggressive in his regained confidence: "Ask him, Eyes, what biggest elephant he ever shot? What weight? What tusks? What height? What every damn thing else, not?"

"Rarely more than six ton. But I did shoot one once between seven and eight," de la Buschagne answered reluctantly, as if these questions were irrelevant to his thought. "Close on thirteen feet high at the shoulder: the right tusk, ninety-seven pounds three ounces; the left, ninety-one pounds eleven ounces. All together one hundred and eighty-eight pounds fourteen ounces."

My Captain broke in to answer triumphantly: "Tell him, Eyes, even if he shoot sixteen hundred and four elephant and they all weigh eight tons each, he only shoot a hundred and sixty and two-fifths whales of eighty ton each, and I kill more whales than that!"

Trying hard not to grin at the idea of what two-fifths of a whale might be, I told our guest all this. For the first time he gave the Captain a long, hard, critical look as if he were wondering whether he had been wrong in holding him in such respect.

"Does the man think I'm trying to compete with him, Cousin?" he asked me, proudly on his dignity. "Ask him then how many whales he has killed?"

I translated the last part of his question only.

"Oh, many, many more. I know not exactly how many." Unaware of the tension in his guest, Thor Larsen evaded a precise answer.

That was one of the strange things about the Captain. He must have known the number of whales he had killed because of his exact records, but he would never, not even to me who had

often asked him, say exactly how many whales he had killed, nor indeed let anyone look at his records. Was it because all whales were one to him? Or because he had a conscience in the matter, after all? Or was it because, with his vast appetite for hunting whales, any number, however great, must appear insignificant? I never knew the real answer but the middle explanation was never as convincing a possibility to me as the others.

"I see," de la Buschagne remarked in the voice of a man who naturally tends to make mole-hills out of mountains. "I wonder whether he realises that every elephant I shot could have killed me had I missed or just wounded it? Were his whales ever so dangerous?"

I would have preferred not to translate any of this and get back to the original trend of the conversation. But neither man would have been content had I done so. I therefore gave my Captain a bowdlerised version of de la Buschagne's retort.

It was enough to reach Thor Larsen's heart. Fundamentally fair and helped by his own still unexplained interest in elephants, he admitted somewhat crestfallen: "He is right, Eyes. Hunting whales today not so dangerous. But," his eyes flashed again, "there's a danger enough always for small ships, in high seas and ice and wind. But please to come back to elephant and Job."

That suited de la Buschagne too, for he immediately fell back into the flat, deliberate tone normal to him, and resumed where he had left off. He had been going to say that, big as was the biggest elephant he had ever shot and just described to us, the elephant that he had come across on the day on which he'd read the text from Job round the camp fire, was even bigger.

At this I could hardly repress a whistle of astonishment. The elephant already described to us was so much more than any I had ever heard of that I was near to doubting him. Had it not been for his reputation and his obvious love of cold fact, I would have given him the lie. When he now spoke of an elephant still bigger, I was unconvinced.

The man was instantly aware of my reaction. It was really rather alarming having to sit there as a go-between for two such

sharp, observant, intuitive and immensely experienced men. In any case they were both men already predisposed to assume themselves falsely or at best inadequately interpreted.

"Yes, Cousin," I was informed sternly. "This elephant is the biggest in the whole of Africa."

Thor Larsen took this in avidly and exclaimed eagerly, "Ach, I see. The Caesar of elephants! I knew it. You know him as I well know the Caesar of sperm when I meet him!"

I translated all this, adding an explanation of what the Captain meant by Caesar, as I knew it would otherwise have puzzled the Afrikaaner. He nodded his head vigorously.

Completely restored in his initial conviction that he and the Captain were uniquely outsize by nature, he went on to say that this Caesar of elephants was a lone bull elephant, and he knew that it was the biggest in Africa because he recognised it from the descriptions of the animal that white men and black men from far and wide had given him. Even if he had not seen it with his own eyes, he would have recognised the bull from his spoor.

As a young hunter, it had been his ambition to shoot it. Scores of hunters had tried and failed. Their excuse was always that the elephant was indefatigable and too intelligent and fast for any man ever to catch up with it. Unlike other elephants, it seemed to have no favourite stamping ground, no regular habits or routes, that one could use for its undoing. Like the wind, it came and went from all directions travelling up and down and across the length and width of the land as no other elephant had ever been known to do.

"Ah, a true Caesar indeed!" Thor Larsen exclaimed, his interest soaring and his spirit full of fellow feeling for his companion. "All of the Seven Seas is one for the real Caesar. He travels them all like the winds of change and storm. Thor Larsen know, for all my life I seek him too." He paused and then conceded with a certain reluctant generosity, "This Africa of yours too is great enough to be land-sea, not? But if no man ever catch up with elephant, where his description come from?"

Hunters, de la Buschagne admitted, had never seen the elephant. That was the strange thing about it, he stressed, a

215

certain superstitious awe for the first time inflecting his voice. The elephant seemed always to know whenever there were armed men after it.

"That will not surprise you, Cousin, perhaps?" De la Buschagne spoke directly to me as if he wanted me to help bring home to the Captain's understanding a difficult point. "You must know since you too live in the interior. Animals often seem to be perfectly aware whether man is armed or not armed; whether he is after them or not."

I nodded. "They even seem to know the difference when one is carrying a gun for protection and not for hunting. I remember Oom Piet le Roux told me this too."

"Piet le Roux!" His exclamation of surprise interrupted me. Intense interest appeared in his cool blue eyes as he looked at me. "You knew him?"

"Yes," I told de la Buschagne first and then Thor Larsen. "Oom Piet always told me that out in the bush the intentions of man inevitably communicated itself to the day and its natural children. It did not matter, he said, how secret man kept his design, or lack of design, on animals, nature always knew which it was and broadcast it accordingly."

"Just like the whale: above all the sperm!" Thor Larsen took up the point at once. "But then how you ever kill animals in Africa if this so?"

"Oom Piet used to say," I answered, "that animals, like men, become 'inattentive to life's messages'."

That was so, de la Buschagne agreed. He was certain this elephant owed its long life to its capacity for vigilance and readiness to read and accept the messages of nature. The result was that no hunter, as far as he knew, had ever seen him until the day some months ago, when he, Herklaas de la Buschagne, had had the honour of at last finding him.

Yet old men, he continued, unarmed and alone in the bush between one village of bee-hive huts and the next, women working in the fields, children herding their goats, fat-tailed sheep, and humped and brindled cattle, had seen the elephant over and over again. All their descriptions agreed that it was the biggest and the blackest elephant there had ever been.

There were some old men who believed that it was the spirit of that great bull elephant slain in the beginning of things by the founder of the great Amangtakwena nation of the interior.

De la Buschagne broke off, quick to notice the excitement this reference to my beloved 'Takwena had produced in me, to say, "You evidently know the story, Cousin."

"I know it well," I said. "I know how before this killing the 'Takwena say that all things—stars, earth, sea, animals, men, plants, were all persons and at one. Then the great hero Umdinizuwayo came, stole a coal of fire from the great thunder-bird, and all except men rushed away from him and his fire to set themselves up in the separate places that they occupy today. I know how afterwards the morning star appealed to Umdini-zuwayo to take up his spear and bow and go into the heavens where a giant bull elephant, at war against the new fire, was trampling out the stars. He found it in the middle of the Milky Way and killed it. Where it fell, to this day, there is the black hole in the Milky Way marking the gap that his killing left in the universe." I added, almost to myself, "Even now I never shoot an elephant without a black hole appearing in the bright day in front of my eyes. At one moment there is so much life: then suddenly there is nothing."

Both Thor Larsen and his guest fidgeted a bit at this, rather like Gorgeous after one of Leif's discourses.

"So you've shot elephant already, Cousin!" said de la Buschagne, surprised.

"Yes," Thor Larsen, grasping at this, announced proudly. "He is elephant hunter too but—" he added this quickly in case he might be belittling his guest by the comparison, "only a learner hunter. But please to go on."

De la Buschagne went on quickly to say that this elephant made so great an impression on everyone who saw it that they felt compelled to try to name it. Though nicknames given to the elephant were various, one most generally used was "Sway-Back".

We had to consider, he continued, that the animal stood high on long legs which were as unusually slender as their pads were uncommonly broad. It had immense, curved tusks, possessed a

217

very high forehead, a long large trunk with a pink tip forever turning and curling, catching and analysing the whiffs of smell that came to it from afar and brought it news of the life out of reach of its sharpest vision. Its ears were enormous and never still, moving incessantly to fan its great body both against the heat of the sun and the fiery furnace of life within.

A wild fanatic glare I had not seen before now flashed in de la Buschagne's eyes, and an unimagined passion gave him an eloquence I would never have suspected. I began to have an inkling of the cause of 'Mlangeni's disquiet about the man.

Yes, he went on, he was convinced that if one could put one's ear to the flank of the wild African elephant one would hear the flames roaring inside it. So much was this elephant life on the boil that you could hear its stomach rumbling in the bush hundreds of yards away.

"Pity I not hear whale stomach rumbling or I too shoot over a thousand of him," Larsen exclaimed, determined not to lose advantage now that he had had to concede that his guest's vocation was more dangerous than his own.

De la Buschagne went on as if he had not heard the Captain's interruption, saying that, remarkable as all the features of this remarkable elephant were, the most remarkable thing about him was his walk. He walked with an immense long supple stride and as he walked, he had the strange rolling motion—here he paused to look up from his pipe's stem to the Captain—that he had been told was characteristic of the sailor, and indeed not unlike the Captain's own manner of walking.

Had de la Buschagne deliberately set out to flatter his host, he could not have succeeded more. Thor Larsen came near to being shy with the pleasure that the comparison gave him. He held his head like a war-horse that, after many a winter, had just heard military music again.

So high, de la Buschagne continued, was the elephant's great black back that, watching it move above the sparkling bush, not only did the bush seem to sway with it but also the earth beneath the watcher's feet felt as if it too were rocking. Once a man had seen the elephant and experienced just this effect, one realised that Sway-Back was the only possible name for

him. Until then one could not help underrating the significance of the elephant's name—as he himself had done until the other day.

To realise what that meant, he would like to reiterate to the Captain that for forty years now on and off he had been on that animal's spoor. Here was, he stressed, an unusual fact in the relationship between hunter and hunted that had to be understood. The lives of all the other lovely, vivid, jewel-bright animals of Africa were frighteningly brief, passing before the eyes of the hunter like shooting stars through the night. But the elephant was the only animal in Africa whose life-span was longer, perhaps, than that of the hunter. The life of the elephant, therefore, was long enough for him and his hunters to have a continuity of relationship. That had been so with him and Sway-Back: and of course he, de la Buschagne, had not gone yet.

He could hardly remember a time when he had not known about Sway-Back, first as an unusually wild, reckless young bull for whom everyone predicted a violent, untimely end, but slowly changing over the years into an animal that was held in awe if not reverence. He had said earlier he would have known it from its spoor alone. He did not want the Captain to think that he was pretending to be as good a tracker as the best African hunters who could tell the spoor of any animal from all others of its kind. But he himself was good enough to tell the exceptional from the average, and he had mentioned his recognition of Sway-Back's spoor because it was the best way of showing how long he had known him and how often he had followed him.

At this point the look in de la Buschagne's eyes was most impressive. Much of the reserve and criticism I had felt for the man were themselves rebuked, and I myself was made aware of my youth and inexperience as never before. I knew just enough of the interior and hunting to realise how great and dedicated in his strange way Herklaas de la Buschagne must have been. This new respect I am certain communicated itself through a change in my manner of interpretation to my Captain, who was listening now to de la Buschagne like a child to its first fairy tale.

219

Yet, he went on, he was nearly thirty before he made his first serious attempt to hunt Sway-Back, although he had already known almost all there was to know about him years earlier. Nearly forty years ago he had come across Sway-Back's spoor at about nine in the morning and recognised it instantly. He wished he could convey how impressive an experience this recognition was. Somehow the innermost quality of the animals of Africa was described in their spoor on the earth. For instance, the pug marks of the lion spoke clearly of power and also, subtly, the bite of sharp claws into the red earth belied by the soft, round imprint of the purple pad imposed behind them. The great hoof of the buffalo lay in the track as if carved with iron, and the savage hole punched behind it by the afterclaw in its heels was the dagger with which it finished off its enemies.

But how different was the spoor of the elephant, shaped like a graph tracing the course of the earth round the sun that de la Buschagne once had seen depicted on the blackboard of his school. It was a world on its own, directed at no one, without menace or warning. At the same time it spoke gravely of great power of being, for within the horizon of its foot the ground had been subjected to such pressure that it had disintegrated into the finest powder and shone like silk wherever the elephant had stepped.

So there he was, forty years ago, deep in the bush, the dew still on the grass, a halo of yellow pollen above it where his feet and those of his bearers had shaken it, looking once more as he had already done so many times before at the greatest elephant spoor in the world shining like satin in the dark red earth of a clearing, while one by one around him the fever-birds began their exhortations of praise. The spoor was fresher than he had ever seen it, and as he knelt down beside it to examine it closely, the exclamations of astonishment from his bearers told him that they had recognised it too.

The spoor could only have been minutes old, and a voice from within that he had not heard before spoke to him saying: "This is the chance you've been waiting for all these years! Follow him, quick!"

He was, he would like the Captain please to understand, not

a man of impulse. He was a man of sense and reason. He made his living by hunting and had never been interested in shooting for world records, as the English were so prone to be. But this new voice was so powerful that he obeyed it. When some five minutes later he found the olive dung steaming beside the shining spoor he was certain the voice had been right. A week later when he had not yet caught up with the elephant, was short of food, and his hungry and exhausted bearers were threatening to desert, he thought how wrong the voice had been too.

He gave up and returned to his normal business, determined never to be fooled by it again. But the next time he came across Sway-Back's spoor, and the next and the next, year in and year out for forty fiery seasons, the voice gathering in authority would set him off after the elephant, with its imperious "Now!" only to leave him disillusioned days, sometimes weeks, later with a bleak "Not yet".

Here Thor Larsen, with an upsurge of sympathy that I had never seen in him before, interrupted.

"Tell him, Eyes," he commanded me, "I, Thor Larsen, also know this damn 'Now' which is also 'Not yet'. This voice which speaks two meanings with one tongue! But Thor Larsen damn certain one day other way round. 'Not yet' become one damn big 'Now', not?"

I was not at all certain what my Captain meant by all this but de la Buschagne seemed to know, for he nodded, thanked Thor Larsen and said quietly the "Not yet" had already become his "Now", as he would soon show us.

Strangest of all, he continued, on the rare occasions when he refused to obey this voice, he found that his own proved ways of hunting would fail him. He would not weary us with repetition but the point was that he would have to return, sooner or later, to the spoor of Sway-Back, follow it to the point of exhaustion and utter disillusionment, in order to put himself right with his luck. It was as if defeat and failure in the greater were inextricably bound up with success and triumph in the lesser pursuit of his life.

So it had gone on until a few months ago. He was then engaged in what was his last hunting expedition. He was

determined at the end of it to retire for good, buy a farm out of
the money he had set by and make a proper home for his
daughter. She had been born in the bush and, except for a few
years at a Mission school while his wife was still alive, had lived
his hunter's life with him. When his wife had died five years
before, she had instantly left school at the age of twelve and,
young as she was, had come to look after him. Now, although
physically strong enough to continue hunting, he felt it was
not right to make her live without companionship of her own
kind.

De la Buschagne mentioned this all in perfunctory fashion,
while my Captain just looked back at him as if he were glad he
had not got himself into the position where women could inter-
fere with his whaling.

I myself had a different reaction. Considering the emotion
and even eloquence which de la Buschagne had allowed himself
about his elephant, I was incensed by this austere way of referring to his daughter. This brought my original reservation alive
in me so keenly that I was afraid they would both notice it.
But both were now only too eager to get on with the story to be
interested in my reactions.

So, there he was then, near the end of his last hunter's journey
in one of his favourite areas in the great bushveld beyond Fort
Herald. It had been perhaps his most successful expedition ever
and he had no reason to be discontented except that, as the end
came nearer, a profound and melancholy discontent possessed
him. An urge to give himself just one more hunting season
tempted him as he had never been tempted before. But he had
pledged himself that this would be the end and, whatever else
he had done wrong in his life, he had never broken a pledge.
The temptation clearly was from the devil and so strong that it
kept him awake at nights and drove him to pray for deliverance
from it.

The night before this fateful day had been particularly hard
for him. He had been exceptionally restless for hours. The stars
were so sharp and quick that even lying under his mosquito net
with shut eyes they felt like needles ceaselessly probing his eyelids until his temples ached. Bush-babies and baboons were

whimpering and moaning all night long like children in the grip of their first fear. The leopard's cough for once, even in its native dark, was strangely discreet. From star-rise until an hour before first light a lion roared continuously not in defiance or triumph but as warning to something. Even the bush-bucks' bark for once sounded blurred with apprehension. As for the hyenas and the jackals, never had he heard them wail and whimper so. Even his daughter, who slept always with the innocence of a tired child, had startled him by crying out in some nightmare of her sleep.

He had tried every device known to him for inducing sleep: prayed; sung hymns to himself; finally gone over in his mind every elephant hunt he had ever undertaken. Yet he was still awake near morning. Suddenly the whole bush went quiet and a heavy silence fell around him. So dramatic was it, in fact, that he held his breath.

A dead branch somewhere on the ground near by broke with the sound of a rifle shot. Immediately the bush noises flared up again high to the night. Obviously some great beast was about, so close that he tumbled out of his mosquito net, and dashed for the fire which had sunk low onto its scarlet cushion of coals. As fast as he could, he threw dry wood on it and soon had the flames crackling and flickering high in the centre of the camp. He stood there for perhaps half an hour listening intently, but no repetition of that abrupt violent sound reached him. Yet he was convinced that somewhere in the bush, even if he could not hear it, something overwhelming was taking up position.

At first light he was up and, cup of coffee in hand and his nine millimetre Mauser on his left shoulder, he had gone as was his invariable practice to examine the ground near by for spoor: to read, as he put it, the latest text in the night's Bible.

The dawn that day, he said, was a particularly beautiful one, and it filled him with sadness that he would soon be living a life where he would have to be looking at it through a window or from the shelter of some stoep. When it had blossomed from a sky of rose into the mounting blue of greater Africa, he perceived that well-known satin spoor shining in the red earth within the radius of Sway-Back's expansive foot. Carefully

examining each imprint, he followed the spoor and found that Sway-Back in a bare hundred yards had made a full circle of the camp, to stop where he had begun. There he had obviously stood for a very long time watching the camp before turning about and walking back in the direction he had come. Immediately behind the place where he had turned lay a long dead branch of purple wood. It had snapped clean under the weight of Sway-Back's foot to make that rifle-shot of a sound, which had brought de la Buschagne out of his mosquito net. It had been already clear to him from the spoor that Sway-Back had turned about slowly and reluctantly, in a preoccupied manner. Yes, he reiterated as he saw the surprised, questioning look on my Captain's face, preoccupied was the word. His reactions to the study of the spoor had convinced him that for hours Sway-Back had circled the camp, standing there silent in the dark, thinking as he had never thought before.

It was a mistake not to recognise that all animals had some mind of their own. The hunter who did not take the animal mind into consideration was never a great hunter. The most formidable intellectuals among animals were the individuals who either lived life out alone, like Sway-Back, or formed their own little units of life around them, like the great apes, baboons and cats. Apes perhaps were intellectually the most adroit of all, but with this limitation—that their lives were short and their intelligence dominated by the most apprehensive imagination to be found among animals and one almost entirely devoted to survival. They had a pronounced sense of mischief, but no gaiety or sense of play. In Africa they were the supreme example of the animal living out of fear by their wits.

How different the cats, particularly the lion. It had perhaps the greatest natural intelligence of all, rendered more formidable by the fact that it was free from fear: consequently there was no animal in the bush who loved play, enjoyed the sun and found life as good as did the lion. There were, however, two great limitations to the lion's intelligence: much of it had to go into the study of killing and it had no time therefore to mature because, like that of the apes, the lion's life was short. The elephant had none of these limitations. It had a great natural

intelligence, was totally without fear, possessed no instinct or need to kill except in self-defence, lived long and was able to match its thinking with its experience. Also it was the greatest traveller among African animals. A favourite African saying was "He who travels much, doubts many things." So with the elephant and as a result of all these qualities he had developed the most methodical and logical mind. He had evolved not just habits and customs, but what de la Buschagne was inclined to call a tradition of life. The elephant behaved indeed as if he had a kind of system of reflection. Even when forced to kill, however violent and nimble his first charge might be, the elephant would complete the destruction of his enemies according to a well-thought out plan. He was the one animal in Africa capable not merely of fighting a quick battle but of conducting a whole campaign.

Knowing all this, de la Buschagne had returned to his camp that morning deep in thought, not knowing what interpretation to give events. In fact, after putting down his empty cup of coffee he had gone back and followed Sway-Back's spoor into the bush for another reading. He discovered that Sway-Back, made cautious by his error in stepping on that dead branch, had silently done a second round at greater distance from the camp. This all was so out of character, as the elephant was most adroit at evading contact on the first intimation of any hunter, that de la Buschagne was puzzled as he had never been before.

Then three possible explanations came to him. First, the pace of the spoor showed clearly that Sway-Back was getting old. Secondly, his reluctance to move on indicated that, feeling himself to be old, he had come, as elephants did who lived long enough, to make his stand and live out his last years in the environs where he had been born. Finally, Sway-Back's interest in the camp, incredible as it may seem, showed that he had recognised de la Buschagne's presence.

At this Thor Larsen's excitement, which had long since been on the boil, boiled over.

He wanted to know if this was the legendary elephant's burial ground to which Sway-Back had returned and—

De la Buschagne stopped him there, shook his head and said

he knew the legend and had all his life looked for proof of it in the dark continent but he had never found any. All he could say was that he had a feeling that elephants returned to the scene of their beginnings when they felt that the circle of their lives was closing.

This clearly disappointed the Captain but did not silence him. He wanted to know then how, on so black a night at so great a distance, Sway-Back could have recognised de la Buschagne? He had gathered from what I had told him that as a species the elephant's sight was poor. He then added by way of instinctive placation that "the whale's, even sperm's, sight not good either."

De la Buschagne reprimanded me with a look which implied that only my youth and inexperience could excuse so shallow and brash an over-simplification of a complex issue. The flash of fanatical obsession with elephants in general and Sway-Back in particular was brilliant again in his eyes as he said sternly that the elephant's eyes were quite good enough for their purpose. What need had the elephant of eyes like those of the animals of the open plains that could pick up the flash of the sun on the point of a gun a mile away? In the bush, in which the elephant lived, his eyes were quite efficient enough as he, who had faced a thousand elephant charges, had cause to know. What the elephant needed in his world of circumscribed vision were good smell and good hearing, and in those he was superbly equipped.

To my relief, his eyes left me as he turned to the Captain, saying with great deliberation that Sway-Back, of course, had recognised him by his smell. The moment the long sensitive trunk had recognised it, that methodical brain brought out from the great archives of his memory all the other occasions on which, spread over forty years, a particular man, determined to kill him, had clung to his track like the sunset shadow to his own swaying form.

De la Buschagne was certain that, pondering all this out there alone in the dark under the quick analytical stars of the blackest night that he had ever experienced, Sway-Back not only had recognised him but had come to the conclusion that he and

whoever owned that scent were inexorably linked together and ultimately destined to meet face to face.

Sway-Back, he was convinced, was no longer going to avoid him. He was, come what may, going to live out his last days there on his native ground. He, the man, could avoid or meet him as he chose. But Sway-Back himself was no longer going to take part in the chase.

De la Buschagne said that the realisation that at last he had his chance of shooting perhaps the most formidable elephant the world had ever known, made the hair at the back of his head rise. But almost as soon as he realised it it was spoilt for him by that instinctive voice which had set him on Sway-Back's spoor forty years before. Would not the Captain too, he asked, in a similar situation, have expected such a voice to echo, "Now"? Instead, however, the voice astonished him with a "Not yet" as imperative as had been its original "Now".

Well, like Sway-Back, he too was getting old and about to return to the scene of his beginnings. The burning random years had taught him the futility of going against the voice: he was not prepared to argue with it at so late a day.

So he set about pursuing a normal hunter's day as if nothing unusual had happened. Yet he had not been hunting long before he knew that he was shooting badly. First he missed an easy shot at a buffalo; then shot so badly at another easy target that he wounded the buffalo and had to do what all hunters disliked most, go after it in thick bush. The wounded buffalo got well behind him and stalked its tracker in turn so cunningly that only one of the quickest and luckiest shots of his career, fired on a fast round-about turn, delivered him from certain death. Such incidents convinced him that the day was out of pattern and that he, in some manner, had gone against the natural order of things. Perhaps he should have another look at Sway-Back's spoor and more would come of it?

As he asked himself these questions, the day stood at high noon, the sun directly overhead. His bearers, having disembowelled the huge buffalo, had left the skinning and cutting up for later, and as was their custom were resting in what passed for shade in that world of light and fire. He too should have

joined them or, having decided not to do so, should have taken one of them along with him, for in such country it was better not to walk alone. Yet defying all his own carefully established precedents, he went alone to look for Sway-Back's spoor.

The bush at that hour was silent, of course, except for the mopani beetles. They were to the high noon and the sun what crickets after rain were to midnight and the moon. With quicksilver voices they sang a hymn to the sun that flashed like a mirror with light and shimmered like that passion of sickness called fever mounting to a climax in man's own hissing blood. He loved it as did all the birds, animals, insects and plants of Africa and normally would have allowed it to be for him, for them, a cradle-song of afternoon sleep. So strong and old was his association of rest with the beetle music and the hour that he felt like a man walking in a dream of deepest sleep. This should not surprise the Captain if he knew, as de la Buschagne did, that for its aboriginal children noon and not midnight was the hour in Africa when graves opened and ghosts walked.

He turned to me for confirmation as he had done once or twice before, not only I fancy because I knew, as he did, something of the African mind, but also because he thought my youth would have preserved me against cynicism.

I agreed quickly that my native Africa believed that too. I then added for good measure that I had read somewhere that the ancient Chinese had a saying to the effect: "At noon midnight is born."

That was sense to de la Buschagne because he made the point at once that the sky at noon in Africa was often so blue that it became a kind of black. People spoke of midnight blue; but he thought often of Africa's noonday black. It was that colour on this fateful day, and the slumber of nature around him was more profound than any he had ever experienced. If sleep at night was natural, sleep at so brilliant and seething an hour was supernatural. For instance, he walked by a black mamba coiled on the edge of the narrow track like the spring of a great clock. His foot had come down not a yard from the head of this most vigilant of snakes. Yet so deep was its sleep that not a quiver went through it, and to his relief he had had no cause to

awaken this world of noonday slumber with a shot from his gun.

So he continued slowly through a silence composed of that simmering shimmer of silver sound without movement of air or life of any kind. Even the sun above seemed to stand still for a rest on the summit of its compelling sweep, and the shadows contracted to a tight blurred blot around the base of trees and shrubs. He called them shadows purely for want of a better word, because so brilliant was the day, so great and intense the reflection of light from the patches of scarlet earth, the leaves of trees scintillating like fish scales in the sea of the sky, and the barley-sugar trunks of mopani trees aglow and translucent as segments of amber, that shade was in reality only a tinted sunlight. Never on the darkest night had he known so eerie a moment as this hour when the great wheel of the sun was poised for its roll down the steep slope of the day into abysmal night.

Despite his training, he found himself constantly looking over his shoulder feeling himself to be followed, and not concentrating enough on the ground ahead. Yet it was as well he did so, because there came a moment when, turning to look over his right shoulder, something to the east of him caught his eyes. He stopped and with the utmost care turned slowly to face east, his rifle ready.

A bare twenty yards away, he saw the high, broad forehead of an elephant, an enormous pair of ears moving slowly and ceaselessly like fans held in invisible hands in the bush below. Since the animal stood at a slight angle to him he could see also the dark line of a vast back. Prepared as he was by all he had heard over forty years of the proportions of this elephant, even the little that he could see of it surpassed any picture he had been able to imagine. It was Sway-Back, of course, and with recognition of the elephant, his rifle was at his shoulder and his finger on the trigger, since knowing the animal's reputation he expected it either to whirl about and make off at high speed, or charge. But the great head, still and immovable as some giant bust from the Valley of the Kings carved by a sculptor of Rameses the Great out of black granite, and the long dark back,

remained still and immovable. Only the immense ears rhythmically fanned the melted platinum air.

Sway-Back, too, was fast asleep.

Had he moved at all, even just to shift his weight from one foot to another, de la Buschagne was certain he would have shot for, quite apart from his forty years' longing to get this elephant and his tusks, he could not take any risks or chances with an animal of Sway-Back's reputation. But Sway-Back just remained fast asleep.

Nothing, it seemed, could have proved so conclusively how right de la Buschagne's reading of Sway-Back's spoor and behaviour had been. Sway-Back had made his final pact, his last peace treaty with life. No more evasion, no more travail or travel. Whatever was to come, he was back home where he had begun, to accept all. Sleep, the daily surrender to the will of life, the greatest act of trust possible to its doubting and questing children, was there to demonstrate the completeness of Sway-Back's acceptance. And what a sleep it was! Indeed so much of life was there asleep in the gun-metal being of this, the greatest animal on earth, so deep and so heavy was he with it, that de la Buschagne felt he was looking at the still, immovable centre of a vortex in the stream of existence, drawing all around it from far and wide, down, down, down, like flotsam and jetsam in the maelstrom of a deep sea, to a depth of dreaming never before attained.

He found himself so hypnotised by this colossal example of sleep that even his own eyelids dropped, his gun wavered and his head felt like lead about to drop on his chest. For the first time he experienced what African hunters had often told him, that animals protected themselves by inducing sleep in their hunters; and the greater and more dangerous the animal, the more powerful the temptation to sleep in the hunter. This, they had stressed, was the moment of extreme peril for the hunter as it invariably preceded the charge of the hunted. The thought brought de la Buschagne wide awake with such a start that his finger nearly pressed the trigger of his gun. But Sway-Back had not moved. He still stood there, the greatest monument to sleep ever erected, and so trusting and so innocent that de la

Buschagne might as well have been asked to shoot a sleeping child. Then suddenly he understood. His forty years' quest might be over and his reward was there for the asking; yet he could not take it. The "Not yet" and the "Now" were one.

De la Buschagne was evangelically solemn as he said this, looking from me to my Captain and back again like some kind of a nomad who has suddenly found revelation in the realisation that the wasteland of his spirit and the desert around him are one. Hunted and hunter, he said, seemed to have arrived at the same conclusion. In some way that he could not explain, Herklaas de la Buschagne and Sway-Back were one in spirit. For him to kill Sway-Back would have been a kind of suicide.

And as his mind came out of this long forty-year-old tunnel and he regarded Sway-Back for the first time in his life with eyes free from design of any kind, a most extraordinary thing happened. He would ask my Captain to remember that he could see only the head, ears and part of the back of Sway-Back but the trunk, flanks and legs were hidden by the bush. Against this extraction of the gigantic whole, the bright, molten platinum air was lapping like wavelets of burning water and made what was visible of Sway-Back into the outline of a great sleeping fish, the enormous ears transformed into fins, fanning the livid water to keep the head in the main current of life. The more he looked, the more vivid this impression became. No matter how hard his mind worked to declare it all an absurd illusion, for he was not a fanciful man, to him at that moment Sway-Back looked like a colossal fish. Then, stranger still— for he would ask the Captain to remember that where he stood in the heart of Africa he was a thousand miles from the nearest sea and he, de la Buschagne himself, had not yet ever seen the sea—it occurred to him that Sway-Back was presented to him like that because he had been hunting the wrong quarry. He should have been seeking not the greatest animal on earth but the greatest animal life had ever produced. And that, he knew, was the whale.

De la Buschagne paused. I noticed that his grip on his yellow pipe had tightened so that the black stem, the familiar focus of his brilliant eyes, was trembling like a tuning-fork with the last

reverberations of the true pitch struck from it. He had, both the Captain and I knew, reached the climax of his purpose that Sunday morning in the *Kurt Hansen*. But we had both become so involved with his own drama that neither of us would have interrupted, however long the pause.

In fact I was holding my breath. I had never come so near to liking this strange, taut, driven old man, as when he told us of his moment of realisation that he could not shoot Sway-Back. There was a quality of greatness in such renunciation in so dedicated a hunter. Ideally I would have liked Herklaas de la Buschagne to end his story there. But I realised that there was more to come, and I was fearful of it and once more wary of the man. The sharp, high-pitched squeak of strained steel from the *Kurt Hansen* lifting herself uneasily to the movement of the water beneath sounded like the voice of a bat at nightfall. In fact the movement of my beloved ship, the day on fire against the port-hole and the pattern of white light latticed with bars of shadow of the ripples of sea-water trembling on the low metal ceiling of the saloon, made an impact on my imagination as if I had myself just seen Sway-Back and he had sent my senses reeling with that hypnotic movement of his. The Captain, however, obviously did not share my reserve. If ever there was a man's face hungry for more, his was it.

De la Buschagne paused: then slowly he resumed his tale, his voice now tightly under control. How long he had stood there he did not know. Judging by the displacement of the pale shadows of the bush around him, it was long. Yet to him it seemed only seconds before he tucked his gun under his left arm and turned. Before he left, on an impulse which we sitting here in comfort fifteen hundred miles away in such different circumstances would probably judge to have been as absurd as it was unnecessary, he took off his hat to Sway-Back. He bowed deeply, hat in hand, to Sway-Back, feeling that he was saying an unique hail and farewell to him for ever. Only then did he swing about to go away as silently as he could in order not to break up the greatest sleep he had ever encountered.

He stopped embarrassed, certain that if not I, then Larsen, would have judged his behaviour preposterous. Actually I had

never liked anything more in the man than this last gesture. My Captain's reaction I thought to be more complex. Perhaps he was asking himself whether, in similar circumstances, he would have been able to act in a similar way? But I am certain that he found nothing absurd in de la Buschagne's behaviour.

Indeed one look at our faces was enough to reassure our guest, and immediately he went on to say he had left the scene so obsessed with this new image of a great fish swimming, as it were, in the vast sea of his imagining that he could do no more hunting that day.

What on earth could it all mean? He had no inkling until that night, after the evening meal in his camp, when he opened the great Bible, on the front pages of which were the names of all the de la Buschagne men and their children from the first Herklaas who had fled from la Rochelle at the time of the Revocation of the Edict of Nantes in 1685 to make his home in Africa. There on the opened page, by the light of his camp fire, he had read the provocative sentence: "Canst thou draw out Leviathan with a hook?"

He knew then that Sway-Back, assuming the startling shape of a great fish, had posed a question which could not be ignored.

He had never yet met a question of any importance in his not uneventful life which he had not answered with action. Here, his whole life informed him, was a question that called for deeds. And this question was related to others. He hoped the Captain had looked them up in the book of Job as he had suggested. Questions like "Hast thou entered into the springs of the sea? Or hast thou walked in search of the depth? Have the gates of death been opened unto thee? Or hast thou seen the doors of the shadow of death?"

All the predicants with whom he had discussed the book of Job had always held these questions were asked of Job to make him realise how great and inscrutable were the ways of God and how powerless and insignificant was man without Him. He, de la Buschagne, had been bold enough to differ with them. His reading of life was that the great unknown, the seemingly impossible, were created to provoke man into greater effort to

know and to master more. As he understood them, the words were uttered as a reproach to Job for living contentedly in rich well-being and not striving to extend his knowledge and mastery of the unknown forces of life. This really was the reason for Job's afflictions. The manifest unfairness of God to so loyal a servant as Job was, de la Buschagne believed, a deliberate act of provocation to stir Job into revolt against his own unawareness.

The predicants all reprimanded him severely for such "presumption"—he used the word with a certain desiccated sarcasm. His daughter, much as she honoured and obeyed him, was inclined to agree with them.

Here Thor Larsen could restrain himself no longer. This over-simplified interpretation of Job and the unfortunate use of the word "rich" was exactly cut to the measure of his own mind. He had already been nodding his head vigorously in agreement. It now only needed the mention of a mere girl to make him interrupt.

Forgetting how recent and how scant was his reading of that great enigmatic book of Job, he declared: "You damn right! Parsons, like all rich men and woman, all damn fools. I know because me too, always they criticise. No to listen to them, not?"

Nevertheless de la Buschagne *had* listened to them carefully, and taken all that they had said into serious consideration. But he had neither agreed with them nor changed his mind. That was why he was sitting there and talking to the Captain. He was convinced it was God's will that, before his end, he should also have the experience of what it meant to "draw Leviathan out with a hook".

He paused and instinctively drew his breath before he turned to me, in direct supplication for any help I could give him.

"Ask him, please, Cousin," he implored, "if he will take me in his ship and give me the chance to shoot just one whale. I have not many years more to live—"

He broke off and fumbled in the great pockets of his ample coat, not noticing that Thor Larsen must have long since anticipated this unusual request, so little was he surprised.

"Tell him, Cousin," he went on before the Captain could reply, "I'm willing to pay well for the privilege. I am not rich but I have enough to live on in comfort and can spare this."

With that he produced four bags, like the one in which he carried his tobacco, two from each pocket, undid the noose and poured their contents on one heap on the table. It was the biggest pile of gold sovereigns I had ever seen, each coin the deep marigold yellow of our rich soft, African metal and the whole charged with sullen fire.

Thor Larsen, who had been about to speak, stopped himself, to stare astonished at the gold. He can never have seen more gold in such a heap in the *Kurt Hansen*'s saloon. Soon his astonishment gave way to a certain distaste, for he quickly looked away from the gold to his sperm-tooth paper-weight.

I myself had a distinct reaction of my own. I think gold is a lovely metal but I have always been somewhat shocked by it as money. Copper and brass, and silver, yes, they appear ready-made for exchange. But gold has such beauty in its metal that it seems to lift it above commercial exchange. Judas's betrayal for thirty pieces of silver is more shocking than it would have been had it been done for gold. Gold would have brought an extra dimension of temptation into the matter, tending to make betrayal more understandable. Accordingly the pile of gold aglow on the saloon table between the three of us shocked as much as it surprised me.

I lifted my eyes from it to the Captain. In a moment oddly Faustian, there was something strangely Mephistophelean about him too. And how loudly the steel in the *Kurt Hansen* squeaked!

Thor Larsen was the first to break the silence.

He waved his broad hand in a gesture of dismissal at the gold and turned to me. "Tell him, Eyes," his gruff voice ordered me, "I no want his gold, not? Tell him, Eyes. Quick!"

I told de la Buschagne this.

His eyes darkened with disappointment, as if assuming that his mission was about to fail. He started drawing the gold towards him but I felt certain that he was searching fast for an alternative. He would not be the man who had remained

undismayed by forty years of failure on Sway-Back's spoor if he accepted defeat there and then.

"Tell him quick, Eyes," Thor Larsen hastened to add, as the first coins clinked in the bottom of the bag. "It's good to put gold away, not? I give him the whale but not for gold. He give me something else."

I could feel deeply that now my Captain in his turn was nervous. In our small saloon there was not just one climax of a personal process of long standing to be reckoned with but two.

"Something else, Cousin?" de la Buschagne's eyes came off his gold, a new expression of eagerness on his face. "Tell him he can have anything I have. But what would he like from me?"

Thor Larsen, aware, I believe, of the enormity of the price he was about to exact from his guest, made a grimace out of an unfamiliar smile intended to ingratiate.

He laughed too loudly as he said, "Tell him, Eyes . . ." He paused again while he and de la Buschagne eyed each other like two wrestlers about to engage. "Tell him," he resumed, his voice reduced almost to a whisper: "I give one damn big whale if he promise to give me Sway-Back."

I was prepared to see the dialogue between the two hunters end abruptly there and then. After the moving account de la Buschagne had just rendered, I could not see how he could let my Captain "have Sway-Back". It would be an act of betrayal of which so austere and upright a spirit would be incapable. In fact I expected an immediate rejection.

However, to my amazement I heard de la Buschagne exclaim involuntarily: "Has he been after the wrong quarry too?"

"What's that, Eyes? Quick!"

Thor Larsen, alarmed that his bargain had proved unacceptable, wanted to know the worst at once as was his custom.

However, before I could tell him the Afrikaaner stopped me: "Just tell him I am considering, Cousin."

"Tell him to consider this too," Thor Larsen ordered me, relieved. "Tell him I give him Caesar for Sway-Back."

Nor did he stop there. Encouraged by the gravity with which de la Buschagne was pondering his proposal, he went on to enlarge on the reasons why he offered not the whale of the greatest

size but one which, in his opinion, was peerless and the whaler's most precious quarry. "And, Eyes," Thor Larsen concluded, "tell him remember this about sperm: he may not be heaviest whale. Heaviest is blue whale and heaviest blue whale always is female not male. But in sperm, bull always bigger than cow. *He* not *she* master of the sea!"

As I told de la Buschagne all these things about the sperm that the Captain had told me so many times, his interest increased until finally it was transformed into a brilliant lust.

Even Thor Larsen sat back, clearly convinced that with this last observation he had dangled the most attractive bait in front of his guest's strange appetite. Yet even so he watched de la Buschagne anxiously.

He did not have to wait long, however, for suddenly de la Buschagne, having pocketed the last bag of gold, leant forward and held out his hand. Thor Larsen's own rushed out to meet it. They shook hands vigorously and long, while the guest affirmed: "One Caesar for Sway-Back. I promise. But tell him, Cousin, he is getting the best of the deal."

I did as I was told, sadder at heart than I could explain. I had been the go-between in an act of elemental betrayal, and I was filled with a strange desire to rush out of the *Kurt Hansen* for ever. In fact I don't know how I got through the next half-hour interpreting for those two men. There was something obscene about it. Our saloon, that respectable fisherman's parlour, was transformed into a kind of counting-house where things were put up for sale that no human being had the right to sell.

Yet I got through it, and when de la Buschagne got up to go at one o'clock it was all arranged that I would call on him at the "Ailsa Craig" as soon as possible and give him the Captain's detailed proposals for his venture into whaling. I believe Thor Larsen would have offered to take him out with us that very night, were it not his first excursion into the whaling grounds that year. Professional in the highest degree, he declared firmly he wanted to see first what whales were about so as not to waste his guest's time.

All that agreed, I dashed out ahead of the pair following behind me. I did so in order to call on de la Buschagne's

237

daughter and break the news to her, which I was convinced I would do more gently than her father. I knew how greatly distressed she would be by it.

She was just coming out of the main entrance to the first-class quarters of the mail ship when I appeared on deck. Her eyes were large with excitement.

Before I could say anything, she had me by the arm saying, "Oh, Cousin: that was wonderful, I can't thank you enough. I've never seen anything so lovely. It was like a fairy tale. I'd love to travel everywhere in so beautiful a ship!"

I was happy that I could share her enthusiasm to the full. I too was still fresh enough to such ships. At one with her in her delight, and she still holding my arm, I led her down the broad ladder on to the quay and began to walk her slowly towards the *Kurt Hansen* because I was in no hurry to end the experience.

She was just describing some details of the ship when she saw her father and Thor Larsen standing side by side at the head of the *Kurt Hansen*'s gang-plank.

She broke off, dismayed, and her grip on my arm tightened. "Oh, Cousin, what has happened? What have they decided?"

I looked into her wide, green-blue eyes. They were full of fear. Indeed, before I could answer her, she spoke: "You needn't tell me. Father is going with that dreadful little man of yours, is he not?"

"Yes," I answered quietly.

"What are they getting out of all this?" she asked with passion. "What price is father paying your Captain? Don't tell me that little man is doing it just for love of a stranger he never met before?"

I would have liked to tell her she was doing Thor Larsen an injustice. But I had no time as her father, his mission complete, was now anxious to go and was impatiently beckoning his daughter to him.

All I had time to say was: "They've swapped a whale for an elephant."

Despite her father's imperious signal, she stopped dead in her tracks and asked in a voice sharp as a knife: "Swopped a whale

238

for an elephant, Cousin? You speak as if they've been trading stamps! Pray, any elephant? Or one particular one?"

"Sway-Back, I fear," I answered bluntly, taken aback by her tone.

"I feared so too," she answered. Suddenly a different emotion overcame her and her eyes filled with tears. "Oh, Cousin, how perfectly dreadful!" she exclaimed. "May God forgive him, for he doesn't know what he's doing."

With that she went forward, a look of an extraordinarily mature resolution upon her, to come to a halt at the foot of the gang-plank.

Without looking at Captain Larsen she said, "Here I am, Vader."

De la Buschagne didn't answer. He just shook Thor Larsen once more vigorously by the hand, then walked down the gang-plank and as he passed his daughter said curtly, without even turning his head: "Come along, Laetitia."

So incensed was I at his casual manner that I wanted to run after them and hit him. But I stood there humiliated in the powerlessness of the young. My feelings were not improved by the fact that, as Laetitia was about to round the corner of a warehouse in the wake of her father, she turned round as if half expecting to find me following her. Seeing that I had not, she looked in my direction and raised her hand in farewell.

My evening session with Leif, Gorgeous and 'Mlangeni did nothing to help remove the disagreeable feeling that the morning's events had left in me. Gorgeous said nothing at all when I told them what had happened in the saloon between the three of us. He couldn't really follow the detail of the dialogue but I knew that he instinctively disliked its conclusion. Leif listened intently. He interrupted only once and that was when I described de la Buschagne's unorthodox interpretation of Job.

"He certainly has a point there," he declared. "But he seems to have forgotten the devil that exists in argument. Doesn't he know yet how dangerous it can be just to make one's own point and nothing more?"

I was not quite certain what he meant. All the same I shook my head and went on with my account to the end.

"D'you really mean, Pete," he said, "that the Captain and this old man really agreed to exchange one lone sperm for this remarkable elephant?"

"I do," I answered distressed.

"Who do they think they are to play give and take with life's greatest creatures? They're not theirs to barter. Those two men aren't gods. Have they forgotten that they too are flesh and blood? I doubt that any good can come out of this."

'Mlangeni, his massive head bowed, muttered sombrely, " 'Nkosan, tell them that at Icoco we have the saying: 'One kraal cannot follow more than one 'Nyanga without coming to harm.' "

I told them, and on that note we dispersed to go below for some rest before leaving Port Natal, as was Thor Larsen's custom in the early hour of the morning.

I was to begin my fourth whaling season in the *Kurt Hansen.*

CHAPTER TWELVE

Storm without Wind

WE HAD had such exceptional luck right from the beginning of our first week's whaling that it looked as if Providence were out to cancel the misgivings which Leif, Gorgeous, 'Mlangeni and I had shared in varying degrees. Besides, being lucky meant we all had to work unusually hard and were too tired in our brief moments of leisure for much self-examination. Then Thor Larsen himself had never been in a better mood. The new members of his crew were as sceptical of the formidable reputation he had among whaling men as they were of the reservations that a few of the *Kurt Hansen*'s company had about him.

Young as I myself was, I was only too ready to let all this diminish the acute apprehension with which I had begun the season. I was not yet aware of what I now know to be an elementary heresy of the canon of life itself: that success in the daily business of living is proof of Providence's support of that particular way of life. I should perhaps have had a deeper look into the story of Job when I went to check the passages which had played so significant a role in the exchanges between Thor Larsen and Herklaas de la Buschagne. Had I done so I might have discovered what a sombre warning that book was against so superficial a reading of this deeply enigmatic matter of luck. I might have seen it for what it is—an attack on our all too common presumptuousness, showing that Providence or God or whatever we choose to call the ultimate transcendental reality may well inflict great misfortune even on those whom it loves best and who serve it most. I might then have been more on guard and less inclined to assume that because the *Kurt Hansen* was daily breaking whaling records our lives in it were on the right course.

Above all I might have been more analytical of the Captain's

new mood and seen how excessive it was. It may well be that our lives need excess, indeed can only achieve proportion and symmetry through the movement of profoundly asymmetrical hearts. At the same time it is true that excess presupposes a kind of unawareness and carries within it the seed of ultimate correction; a form of confrontation, if not fateful retribution, by some dark aspect of itself which has been denied its share of light.

Today I could console myself with the argument that, even had I been fully aware, I would have been unable to influence events, seeing what an impervious character the Captain possessed. But had I, for instance, looked into the immediate cause of the excess, as I could have done by following the spoor of my initial misgiving and then taken my conclusions to Leif, who can say that that wise man could not have changed our Captain's mind and made him withdraw his invitation to take Herklaas de la Buschagne whaling?

After all, Thor Larsen was not dependent on de la Buschagne for elephant hunting. For three years now he had had an invitation from my family to come hunting with them, and I had rejoined the *Kurt Hansen* this time with a pressing injunction from my father to bring home at the end of the season "the man who had been so good to me". All that was necessary was for Thor Larsen to renounce Sway-Back. That really was the heart of the matter. He had not earned the right, as Leif had already implied, to shoot Sway-Back while in a sense de la Buschagne had. But de la Buschagne had no licence from life to harpoon the Caesar for which Thor Larsen had served so arduous and long an apprenticeship. No one could have been better equipped to restore these two excesses to their native proportions than Leif. In fact, of our company, he and 'Mlangeni were the only two whose misgivings kept them indifferent to our success at sea.

I had never known 'Mlangeni so preoccupied and so silent by his fire. As for Leif, in the days that followed he showed by the way he cross-examined me about de la Buschagne and got me to report daily on my conversations with the Captain, how his mind remained exercised over the affair. Moreover my error was not merely one of omission. I found myself actively arguing

the point not only with Leif but also against what remained of misgiving in myself. Surely, I would say to him, we were being unreasonable and hyper-critical about our Captain? Did it really matter whether he or de la Buschagne killed another whale when so many other people would do the killing if they did not? The same applied to elephants; and after all, what was it that we feared?

I still remember Gorgeous's "Hear, hear! Pete!" when I first spoke up on these lines.

But neither 'Mlangeni nor Leif was to be persuaded. 'Mlangeni looked at me sombrely and made me go red with embarrassment by speaking to me for the first time with something of reproval: "Trickster that you are, 'Nkosan! Would you, too, be a little star out of course?"

Leif, quick to suspect from 'Mlangeni's tone that there was a weight of meaning in this exchange, made it impossible for me not to translate exactly what he had said. As a result the whole story of 'Mlangeni's uneasiness, from the appearance of the great mamba at Icoco to the seer's vision of the defection of the stars, came out.

Gorgeous dealt with it characteristically by shrugging his shoulders and vanishing below.

Leif however took it all very seriously—as seriously as I had done before I allowed the matter to become an argument inside myself. That was one of the ironies of it all. If anyone should have continued on Leif's and 'Mlangeni's side in the matter, I should have done. That I did not should have shown me how far away I was from my own natural centre, and arguing against them should have warned me how extensive was my own underground of doubt.

Leif, I suspect, knew all this, for he was throughout at his gentlest with me and let me off more lightly than did 'Mlangeni. He told me: "You have a point there but it's only a point, Pete. I have in mind no particular consequences for us all from this. I just do not like the thing for what it is within itself and that is enough for me. If I tried to look farther than that I am certain I would see less."

But what should have warned me most, perhaps, was the

243

fact that, like 'Mlangeni, suddenly I became, to use his phrase, "a house of dreams". Normally I slept too soundly to know whether I had dreamt or not. Yet now not a night passed in which I was not woken up by dreams. Now I dreamed nearly every night and often I woke full of horror.

One morning even the Captain, preoccupied as he was, asked me several times, "You not well, my Eyes, not?"

To which I protested quickly with fierce emphasis and an over-eager smile: "I've never felt better in my life."

But we were all people who were, as Leif often remarked, too busy to live: or, to put it another way, too busy to give ourselves over fully to the processes of our imagination. Yet, to be fair, we were all, right from the beginning of this Thursday, too afflicted with real intrusions to be able to give self-awareness a chance.

The process began with a breakdown in the *Kurt Hansen*'s engine room. I had only just emerged from one of my nightmares and was still lying awake in the dark, listening to the Captain snoring in the bunk opposite mine, when the beat of the ship's engines suddenly slowed down to considerably less than its former rate. And even at that slackened pace, knowing the sounds of the reliable ship as well as I did, it sounded to me as if the engines were straining. Whether it was just my young upstart devotion to normal explanations, I argued also against this evidence of my senses. I told myself that nothing could possibly be wrong and that the reduction in speed must be due to the fact that we were close to Port Natal and preparing to wait in the great roadstead for first light, as we always did when we had quarry for the slipway of a factory which worked only by day.

I could have persuaded myself accordingly and gone to sleep again had it not been for Thor Larsen. Professional, even in his sleep, he picked up the change of the engine's pitch at once. His snoring stopped and at the same moment I heard the rustle of woollen blankets thrown from his bunk. The light switch abruptly clicked on. Thor Larsen was already standing in his long woollen underwear beside his bunk looking unbelievingly at his watch.

"Something damn wrong, Eyes," he growled when I sat up quickly in my bunk. "What for to slow down when Port Natal still hour steaming away? What for engine make so sick noise. Listen, Eyes."

I listened, knowing now that he was right. While speaking he had been pulling on his sea-going clothes as fast as he could. I began to follow his example but had hardly shed my pyjamas before, growling to himself, he vanished through the curtains.

Not a quarter of an hour later, he joined 'Papa' bosun and me on the bridge. All his good spirits had gone. He might have been the man we knew on Sunday night, after his last glass of gin, heading out to sea, instead of the successful harpooner going home with three great prizes lashed to his ship's side.

Neither of us dared question him. We just stood there, the laboured pitch of the ship's engines setting the planking shaking under our feet. At long last he announced in Norwegian to the bosun that the *Kurt Hansen* was to go straight from the slipway to the quay and that it was possible the crew might have the day off.

"But you, Eyes," he turned to me, "you to stay in ship. What for, I speak later, not?"

The reason was revealed to me in the afternoon. The whaling company's chief engineer had been summoned by then, spent an hour below with our engineer, and gone back to his office, to send his second in command and half a dozen mechanics on board. Some of the propeller-shaft fixing had loosened in our engine-room base. Leif informed me that the chief engineer had angered Thor Larsen greatly by insinuating that he had asked too much of his ship and handled it badly.

Both Leif and I, for once, were together on Thor Larsen's side in the matter. Our Captain was too good and experienced a sailor to have done anything of the sort. We put the chief engineer's remark down in general to the strange jealousy that exists in all ships between bridge and engine room; and in particular to envy of Thor Larsen's skill at getting more out of his ship legitimately than any engineer thought possible or found comfortable. But that was all beside the main point. What mattered was that the damage would take at least until Saturday, if not Sunday evening, to repair and that we were lucky not

to be put in dry dock for longer. There was no question of any more whaling that week and the crew were duly given leave to go ashore.

When I broke the news to my friends, Gorgeous was delighted. He was one of the first ashore to make as much of this windfall as possible. 'Mlangeni looked hard at me as if he were expecting some sort of admission of error from me. When I did not speak, he shrugged his broad shoulders and asked of himself and the day as much as of me: "Do people still not know then that it takes only one steer to lead a herd of thousand astray?"

"What did he say?" Leif asked.

"He was implying for the umpteenth time that troubles never come singly," I answered, now thoroughly rattled by what I thought was 'Mlangeni's obstinacy in making the worst of everything. "And he wonders why I won't recognise the fact. He's just like some broody old vulture among us."

"But Pete!" Leif remonstrated, astonished by such an unusual display of irritability in my manner. "One could just as easily criticise you for refusing to recognise that a comfortable belief in everything being for the best doesn't somehow prevent the worst from happening."

"There you go again—really it's too much," I exclaimed, turning my back on the pair of them and, without waiting to see how they'd taken it, went below.

For a moment I thought I had gone from the frying-pan into the fire. Thor Larsen was sitting immovable in his place at the head of the table, staring at the steel wall of the saloon in front of him. His game book, shut beside him, indicated that the entry of his latest kill was complete; the state of the decanter and wet empty tumbler showed he had already been drinking. From behind he looked as if he was back in the prison of "nothingness" that was his home when there was no whaling to be done.

My instinct was to take a book and my bathing things and leave the ship at once. I had not yet learnt the futility of trying to get rid of my problems by changing the location in which they were inflicted on me. I was too inexperienced to appreciate their unfailing capacity for following one around. I was there-

fore about to slip quietly through the plush curtains into the cabin to collect my things when, without turning, the Captain spoke.

"Ah, there you are, my Eyes." How he knew I was there seemed most mysterious to me. Even more amazingly his voice was cheerful and warm. "I want you to fetch Elephant Hunter, now! Quick! Hear?"

He turned his head and shoulders sharply to look at me as if convinced that there was nothing more certain in human beings than their inability to get the simplest of orders straight. His eyes were astonishingly clear and after a long, searching look they warmed with anticipation.

He spoke again, almost teasing me: "Not to stand staring, my Eyes, but quick to go at once, not?"

I was delighted to find him in so positive a mood and also glad to have something definite to do. I was half-way to the "Ailsa Craig" before I thought of the full significance of the change in him. For change of a startling kind it was. Normally, even with his schnapps to help him, just the regular weekend break in whaling was as much as he could bear. Now he had his break more than doubled, his ship crippled, and he himself insulted by his owner's engineers as well. Yet not a trace remained of the depression which seemed to threaten us in the early hours of the morning when he came up from the engine room to join 'Papa' bosun and me on the bridge.

Why? The question forced itself on me, and the answer when it came moved me deeply since it showed me, as nothing else had yet done, how deprived his life had been, how bleak a price he had paid for such all out dedication to his calling.

Now, for the first time in his life he could look forward to something beyond whaling. He had Sway-Back. I knew the answer from a certain child-like expression poignant in his time-creased, wind-stained face. I knew that look well, because I had seen it so often on the faces of new boys at school when after the long grim months of their initiation they realised that at last their first vacation was near. The strange unexplained interest in elephants had suddenly found a point and possibly of expression in Sway-Back. The sense of wonder, man conceived as a

hunter on the spoor of infinite mystery from which the searching heart derives its meaning had been reinforced by Sway-Back. Caesar, casting a phosphorescent glow in the darkness of his spirit, was no longer alone but had company in the burning bush of Africa.

I think it was this realisation that impressed me though it did not cure me of misgiving. The Captain might well be doing something wrong, as Leif and 'Mlangeni believed. Perhaps no one should step outside his proper shape as the Captain and de la Buschagne were preparing to do, even if Thor Larsen had earned the right to make his own mistakes. I was not to be shaken in this conclusion and it became the anchor on which I swung in the storm to come.

How genuine it was I knew from my reaction to the sight of de la Buschagne's tall, gaunt figure standing on the corner of the verandah of the "Ailsa Craig" where he could watch the junction of the promenade with the main street which ran along the side of the hotel. Even from afar I had the impression of taut alertness, so quick were the movements of his head from side to side. No person or vehicle passed him without being inspected by his pale blue eyes, as if he were a custom's officer on a strange frontier searching travellers for contraband. On that crowded verandah, with people all around him, untidy, dishevelled, slack and relaxed in their chairs, he was the only one on his feet, meticulously dressed. A few days before, seeing him thus, all the alarm bells in me would have been set ringing. But now, as a result of the conclusion which I have just mentioned, I went relatively unperturbed to our meeting.

The moment he saw me he turned swiftly about and came to the verandah steps to meet me. Because of the unusual eagerness with which he shook my hand and the way he took my mission for granted, I believe he had been on the watch for me ever since we had last parted.

He gave me no chance even to explain why I had come. "Day, Cousin," he announced. "I am all packed up and ready. I'll just tell that coolie to get my things and we'll go."

I disliked instantly his use of the word "coolie", for the over-worked Indian porter, just visible, stood listlessly beside the

narrow desk in the dark hallway behind him. De la Buschagne had been there long enough to have learnt the man's name. It was just another example of our colonial aversion to making our relationships with our coloured countrymen specific. Making them specific would have meant humanizing them, but we preferred to limit our recognition of them to convenient categories. There was, however, more to it than just prejudice in de la Buschagne's attitude. He had, almost to the point of arrogance, the inability of the utterly dedicated to achieve personal relationships of any kind. He tended to value people not for what they were, but for the extent to which they could serve his dedication. Even I, who was young and of the same people, remained an unspecified Cousin to him, though he knew well the name by which I went in the *Kurt Hansen*.

"We're not going to sea just yet," I answered. "We're in harbour for repairs. The Captain has merely sent me to ask if you would be good enough to join him in his ship."

"Repairs, Cousin?" Disappointment filled his pale blue eyes. Yet as a man who had had often to endure frustration of his most cherished desires, he wanted to know the worst immediately. "Does it mean that your Captain will have to call our expedition off?"

"Not at all, Uncle!" I told him quickly. "We hope to be ready for sea again by Sunday, at the latest. The Captain would just like to see you again."

"I'll come at once then," he answered, relieved, pulling his hat on his head and ready immediately to walk off the verandah.

"But your daughter, Uncle?" I assumed that, since he did not know Larsen well, he could not possibly realise that he would most likely be gone for hours. "Should you not . . ."

I got no further, and stopped confused and uncertain, expecting the reproof I saw on his face to come out in short, sharp words. But he just stood there in silence looking hard at me, knowing, I am certain, with all the experience and cunning of the old that the weapon of silence is deadly against the young.

I began to stammer out an explanation: "Captain Larsen, Uncle, I'm certain is expecting . . . rather he's hoping—you'll spend some hours with him—I thought—at least, I wasn't sure

—I mean to say I'm sorry I didn't make that clear at the beginning—"

"I see," he interrupted me curtly. "But there's no need to be concerned about my daughter."

He turned his back resolutely on the hotel and quickly went down the verandah steps onto the crowded pavement.

There was something so compulsive about his air of authority that I would have followed him meekly if a sense of unfairness had not been joined by indignation at this casual disregard of a daughter whom he must have known was already in a state of anxiety about him.

Impulsively I hastened to the desk in the dim hall of the hotel. "Please," I asked the Indian porter, "tell Mr. de la Buschagne's daughter, when she comes in, that her father has gone to the whaling ship in the harbour and will be away some hours."

The porter smiled at me and said: "I'll tell her right away, master. She's only just gone upstairs."

I thanked him and hurried outside to join de la Buschagne. He was standing on the pavement, waiting. I fully expected him to ask what had delayed me. But he was immediately back on the track of his main preoccupation.

"Come, Cousin," he told me briskly. "We mustn't keep your Captain waiting."

Without consulting me, he beckoned to a ricksha-man in the stand opposite the hotel. The man had immediately spotted de la Buschagne as a stranger to Port Natal and therefore a potential customer for any of its novelty. When I arrived on the pavement, he was already importuning de la Buschagne by blowing a series of urgent blasts on a football whistle held firmly between his teeth. Blowing it, he leapt to fantastic heights between the slender shafts of his ricksha. It was a common enough sight in Port Natal and yet I had never become used to it. So strange indeed was the complex of feelings aroused that I had determined never to use a ricksha and until this moment never had done so.

Even the way these ricksha-pullers were dressed seemed utterly unrelated to our brash, busy, colourless and European

day. This man's head-dress, for instance, was made of tall feathers dyed green, blue, red, yellow and black in colour. From it protruded the horns of a great steer, so polished that they shone like warm Baltic amber in the sun. His broad shoulders and chest were covered with a canvas tunic, falling to his knees and worked over with beads of the same uncompromising colours arranged in precise geometric patterns. His arms were bare but the wrists flashing and jingling with bracelets of copper, steel and outsize brass curtain rings. His legs below the knee were painted white, but his ankles again were bright and shining with more circlets of metal and bone. As he blew his glittering whistle, his teeth would show a dazzle of white against his black skin, and whenever he came down from the peak of one of his great leaps, the glass and metal jewellery upon him resounded like some percussion of antique music. His jewellery did not sit upon him like decoration imposed from without, but seemed as natural as painted feathers are on a bird of paradise. Even the spokes of the wheels of his ricksha were hidden behind cardboard disks bright with harlequin colour, and the passenger seat was covered with leopard skins. He looked like some messenger from the court of time, and indeed his vehicle might have come straight from Bacchus to fetch us to some harvest festival of great summer. Instead it was the cheapest form of transport available in a modern city. Today I wonder at the iron limitations of our awareness that prevent us from seeing how great the heart, and how heroic the spirit, that can make carnival of so mean a trade.

De la Buschagne had hardly begun his imperious gesture before the ricksha-man dashed across the promenade towards us. Throwing the shafts down, he jumped nimbly over them, unslung from his wrist the straps of a fly-whisk made of a gnu's tail, and deftly brushed the skin on the seat with it.

"Father of fathers," he addressed de la Buschagne with the exaggerated names of praise a sense of occasion in him demanded, in a voice that could be heard all over the front. "Chief of chiefs! Bull followed by a thousand heifers! Elephant darkening this place of a hundred thousand fires with your shadow! King of kings, behold your wagon!"

He stood on one side and de la Buschagne stepped magisterially into the ricksha as if he had done that sort of thing all his life.

"Tell him where to go, Cousin, and to be quick," he called to me over his shoulder.

I did as I was told, politely. I was deeply incensed because now I found myself trapped into using a ricksha for the first time in my life. I resented the knack de la Buschagne seemed to possess of throwing me into battle against myself.

I did not know then that the battle of the universe is made specific for us in the small and has to be fought out not only in heroic issues, but in a trivial series of choices during our daily round. Had I recognised this then, I might have had the heart to dissociate myself from de la Buschagne; instead, I conformed, and even the ricksha-man helped me on the road to self-betrayal by being so pleased at hearing himself addressed in his own language.

I shifted uneasily into position beside de la Buschagne, before expressing my resentment obliquely by remarking: "You may not know it, Uncle, but ricksha-pullers don't live long."

"Really? Why?" he replied in a tight, matter of fact way.

"Because they strain their hearts pulling such heavy loads as us about Port Natal all day." I spoke sharply. "Because day after day they pull us about until the sweat runs like water off them. Then for hours they have to stand about in wet clothes waiting for another heavy load. As a result they develop weak chests and either die like flies in winter of pneumonia, or get consumption."

"How do you know all this?" de la Buschagne asked, unconvinced.

"The whole of Port Natal knows it," I retorted, bitter now over my own feelings of complicity in the matter. "Everybody talks about it but nobody does anything to stop it. They go on using rickshas just the same and making money out of the licences and taxes they impose on these poor devils."

But de la Buschagne might not have heard a word of my outburst. "People!" he exclaimed with scorn. "They'd say anything, Cousin. If you ask me, this "Ou Nasie"* is a good deal

* Paternalistic Afrikaans term for Africans.

tougher than you think. Look, this fellow is enjoying it no end!" Then, dismissing the matter, he added: "But tell me about your ship."

Indeed our ricksha-puller was giving a convincing imitation of someone who felt himself to be inordinately privileged and happy in his work. He soon managed to work up into a run taking, despite his load, the stride of a lone, long-distance runner. Every now and then he would leap high into the air, calling out a battle cry as he did so before coming down with the growl of a warrior giving his enemies their *coup de grâce*. Every time this happened the shafts of the ricksha flew up, and de la Buschagne and I were thrown so far back that we were made to clutch the sides of the vehicle for safety. In the process our heads jerked and our bodies shook like those of puppets manipulated by the dark archaic runner in front of us. We resembled caricatures of human beings in motion. There was no doubt that all the manifest honour of the occasion was with the ricksha-man; the mockery was ours. My own face felt hot with a mixture of self-consciousness and guilt. But de la Buschagne looked indifferent to the world and utterly content in the knowledge that he was covering the distance to the *Kurt Hansen* faster this way than he could have walked it.

I longed to point out the signs of increasing strain in our ricksha-puller, the sweat running down his legs, the dark wet stains spreading all over his glittering tunic, his laboured breathing. Above all I wanted de la Buschagne to realise how the man never slackened his pace, giving nothing but the utmost of his capacity. But de la Buschagne gave me no chance. He asked so many questions about the *Kurt Hansen*, her mishap, work, crew and Captain, that I had not answered them all by the time we pulled up sharply at the *Kurt Hansen*'s side.

Thor Larsen was standing at the head of the gang-plank waiting for his visitor. I think our method of arrival pleased him greatly because of his Norse associations with ricksha-men which he had revealed to me that placid Sunday afternoon when we first met those long three years before. I suspect he found a certain rough poetic fitness about it and was inclined to accept it as a good omen.

He called out: "Good, my Eyes, good! You take Viking transport to Viking ship, not?"

He laughed aloud and then addressed de la Buschagne in a voice as anxious to please as ever I had heard him use. "To step on board please, Mr. Hunter, my friend!"

De la Buschagne had already taken out a leather purse with the intention of paying the ricksha-man. In fact he was un-latching its flap with a deliberation which convinced me that he was going to bargain hard over the price.

But Thor Larsen stopped him with a loud, "No, no, Mr. Hunter. Eyes to pay now. Thor Larsen pay after! You my guest, not? Please to step on board now."

De la Buschagne seemed only too ready to do as he was told, for without protest he went on board and disappeared below with my Captain.

I was left alone with the man for a moment. He stood between the shafts of his ricksha, unsteady with exhaustion, his chest heaving. Yet his eyes, big, dark and clouded with fatigue, were steady on mine, without demand or expectation in them.

I was moved by his silence and found myself thinking of a Sindakwena saying: "The journey makes the stranger at dawn a neighbour beside the fire at night." I added a thought of my own: "And he who shortens his life for another should be a brother forever."

Suddenly everything in general and this episode in particular felt so wrong, and I felt so helpless to do anything about it, that I had to force myself to some sort of control.

I looked at the panting, sweaty man and I longed for a new kind of coin that would enable him to buy back the wastage of vivid flesh and blood, the portion of his scant ration of time and reality that he had just used up on de la Buschagne and me. But all I could do was to empty my pockets into the two black hands held out so politely towards me. Paying money can be the easiest evasion of a human debt, yet, had he not been so exhausted, I believe he would have danced his gratitude over such an unexpected weight of silver in his hands. All he could do was to call out a profound "Auck, my 'Nkosan. Auck!" Then he called out that untranslatable "Kenon!" of his people.

Twice more he repeated the sound, looking up at the blue winter sky as if that were the direction from which his reward had come. Then he looked straight at me and announced: "Where you go, 'Nkosan, I go."

I shook my head sadly, thanked him and said, "I fear our road together ends here."

Nevertheless, he has travelled space and time with me ever since.

"But the 'Nyanga?" he asked, startling me back into immediate reality by calling de la Buschagne a "witch-doctor" as frankly as 'Mlangeni had done. "Surely the 'Nyanga will have need of someone to take him back to his hotel?"

"He may be many hours," I told him.

"I'll wait for the 'Nyanga, 'Nkosan," he answered swiftly and pointed to the empty ricksha stand by the harbour gates.

He was already in position there sitting by his ricksha when I looked back just before ducking through the entrance to the *Kurt Hansen*'s saloon. I think he was expecting that for, tired as he was, he jumped up and raised his hand high above his head in a kind of heraldic salute. I knew that nothing would now make him break the pact thus passed between us.

CHAPTER THIRTEEN

The Bee Swarm

Down in the saloon, the necessity of devoting myself to the task of interpreting for Thor Larsen and de la Buschagne soon forced me out of my world of private turmoil and argument. The talk, and it was excellent, was talk about whaling and hunting. Each man was passionately interested in the experience of the other, and their appetites grew hugely on the information they fed to each other. There were moments when they sounded like a pair of early Jesuit zealots meeting after a lifetime of service in separate halves of the pagan world to compare the results of their labours. It would take an extra sharp squeak of the *Kurt Hansen*'s metal straining to the range of the Indian Ocean swell always searching the harbour defences in depth, or a muffled clang from the tools of the engineers working overtime in our damaged engine room, to break those spells.

What impressed me most was that neither man ever spoke outside his own experience. I became almost jealous of their experience because their talk made me aware of how little I had yet had of life. All the same it was astonishing how this envy was mitigated by the way the Captain included me in his plans. That happened when they were discussing the Fort Herald area in which Sway-Back had come to make his peace with life.

I interrupted the Captain then to say that we could easily take him to Fort Herald from my home, hunting all the way as we went, because it was so near.

"Near? What you mean, near, Eyes?" he asked.

"About five hundred miles as the crow flies," I answered.

He looked amazed, then banged on the table and laughed with satisfaction: "You call five hundred miles near! Ah, my Eyes, your Africa is land-sea, and you speak like land-sailor. You and Mr. Hunter, my friend here, land-sailors, not?"

Grinning like a mischievous schoolboy, he looked from de la

Buschagne to me to make sure we had appreciated the ultimate compliment he felt he had just paid us and Africa.

"All right, Eyes. At end of season. You take me to this place. And you, Mr. Hunter, my friend, please to meet us there. And then, my Eyes, your account in whale book closed. Debt, forever kaput, not? I give you personal receipt, not?"

By that time it was just half past nine on the saloon clock and obviously long after de la Buschagne's normal bed-time: during his life the sun had been his only valid timepiece and the dawn his sole alarm. Seeing the hour he was astonished, stood up and, promising to return the next day at the same time, prepared to go.

Thor Larsen I believe would have liked to go on with the session all night, but out of his increased respect for de la Buschagne he made no attempt to detain him. He came to his feet as if spring-propelled, went first through the curtains and so up on deck.

He was waiting for us, dark and indistinct by the rail at the side of the gang-plank, to say goodbye. And again he had to have his idea of pleasantry, for, as he shook de la Buschagne's hand, he called him "Mister Land-Whaler, my friend!"

The rasping laugh which followed this remark echoed back across the empty dock-side from the long blank wall of the warehouse opposite the *Kurt Hansen*. The night was deep and so black that stars no bigger than the point of a needle were distinct in it. Yet I had the illusion that the Captain's gust of laughter made them flicker like lamplight caught by a draught. At the same time the tip of that tall night, like a tree of fruit deliberately shaken, reluctantly dropped a great solemn orange star on to the sky over the ocean. I watched it burning out with incredible swiftness. My Captain and de la Buschagne however were so busy shaking each other's hands that they had not noticed it.

Then beyond their shadows, past the corner of the silent warehouse, hard by the harbour gates whose metal glistened as with dew under a street lamp, I noticed the ricksha stand. It was empty. I could not have been more astonished. Something, I knew immediately, was wrong.

De la Buschagne, whom I had informed long since that the ricksha would indubitably wait for him, noticed it at the same moment.

He called out: "I thought you told me, Cousin, there would be a ricksha waiting for me?"

"I did, Uncle," I answered, dismayed by the ready reproach implied in his tone not only against me but the ricksha-man as well. "Perhaps he's waiting further down the street. I'll come with you and look for him."

But it was no use. One glance up and down the long street, its tram-lines glinting bleakly under the street lights was enough to show us he had gone.

"Ag, these Kaffirs," de la Buschagne exclaimed, transferring the greatest weight of his disapproval to the ricksha-man. "A person can never depend on them."

"You could depend on this one," I said emphatically, remembering the look in the man's eyes and his salute. "There's something wrong or he would be here as he promised."

My tone was a mistake. It convinced de la Buschagne that I was just indulging the facility of the young for exaggeration.

He asked in the wryest of tones, "Wrong! Why?"

"Look," I told him plainly. "If you knew this place as well as I do, you'd know that at this hour there's not one but dozens of rickshas plying up and down the streets. There's not a single one in sight for half a mile or more. It's never happened before. Something *is* wrong."

"I see, Cousin," he answered, and paused. "I expect we had better walk then."

The "we" didn't improve matters as far as I was concerned. But I knew that I couldn't refuse to see him home since the Captain would have expected it of me.

I set off the shortest way possible to the "Ailsa Craig", the two of us walking fast and silently, side by side. The branch streets were unusually quiet and, of course, also empty of rickshas. I would have pointed the fact out to him had I not suddenly began to wonder what my chances were of us finding his daughter on the hotel verandah. The mere possibility diminished my resentment at having to show him the short cut home.

However, when we finally arrived opposite the "Ailsa Craig" corner where the main street of Port Natal and the broad promenade met, and there was not a ricksha in sight, I could not resist drawing de la Buschagne's attention to it.

Reluctantly he admitted: "Perhaps you're right after all, Cousin."

At that moment I caught a glimpse of de la Buschagne's daughter standing on the strategic corner of the hotel verandah, surveying the two thoroughfares—rather as I did the ocean from my fore-top for whales, I thought.

She saw us almost as soon as I saw her. To my disappointment she immediately turned away and quickly made for the back of the deep verandah where I could just descry her graceful figure hastening by the entrance and vanishing through it without a backward glance: all, I suspected, because she feared her father would be angered if he saw she had been waiting up anxiously for his return.

Despite my disappointment, I was glad for her sake that de la Buschagne had not seen her. His eyes were still examining the promenade hopefully for just one ricksha, to prove me wrong.

Seeing none, he remarked: "It certainly does begin to look strange. Still, you can never tell with this old nation." And at that he held out his hand to me and said curtly: "Night, Cousin. No need to cross the street. Same time tomorrow."

My usefulness at an end, I was dismissed and free to return to the *Kurt Hansen*. This time I did not hasten but walked slowly back my favourite way along the sea front. The great night, the quick stars, the sound of the sea and the long white manes of these great Indian horses streaking out of the darkness quickly cancelled all that was petty, complaining and frustrated in me. Indeed, I felt like myself again until I came to cross the long narrow spit of land which separated the front from the harbour of Port Natal.

There I had to walk between long, high concrete barracks built to house the thousands of black men working in the docks. I had done this scores of times before and at this hour had always found the barracks silent since their occupants rose early and worked long and hard all day. But on this occasion the dark,

pressing hard against the walls and unlit windows, vibrated with sound. I expected the sound to vanish at any moment but as I passed the building I was met by the noise of thousands of men talking strangely and urgently together in the dark. I stood still to listen more carefully. At once I noticed that,although pitched low, they were angry voices. Indeed they were voices of a common mood forcing itself into the minds of all sorts and conditions of men, like a single swarm of bees about to abandon the warmth of their separate hives and join in an attack within the precincts of their colony. I could not detach one single word from the general vibration but the message of fury was plain enough to make me fear.

I love and I trust my aboriginal, my own native Africa, except when its spirit swarms. Europe has learned over the centuries to build some defences against the dark collective impulses which from time to time throw themselves against the individual mind of man like those tidal waves raised by some unseen up-heaval at the bottom of the sea, setting out on a round of des-truction upon the unsuspecting foreshores of the world. Seeing how often the best defences so far contrived in Europe have been overwhelmed, my fear for my comparatively defenceless black countrymen can easily be imagined. I saw, as if by some flare of my imagination, those vivid black individuals each clothed bright in his own immediacy of life, gone insect swarm-ing, as this humming, buzzing sound in the barracks suggested.

I felt utterly sick at heart. To this day I find one of the most disheartening experiences in life that of the individual surren-dering his own private shape to a general collectivity. But at this moment I thought particularly of my ricksha-puller and his kind, for I was sure they too had swarmed, seeing that on their daily round of the widespread city they were cullers and purveyors of rumour, gossip, news and messages for an indigenous population which had no other means of obtaining information.

I stood there long, all this going through my mind,and vainly trying to lift something specific from that angry buzzing sound. In the end I had to go back to the *Kurt Hansen*, comforted only by the thought that whatever trouble the sound portended it

did not involve my beloved little ship. Yet even such slight comfort was soon to be shaken.

I was walking as quietly as possible towards the saloon entrance across a deck I thought to be deserted when in the stern on my right I saw the dark shape of a man outlined against the distant city glow. It was 'Mlangeni, who should long since have been asleep.

Indistinct as he was, there was something so forlorn about his attitude that I could not ignore him. Besides, my conscience had been nagging me all evening for having been quite so irritable with him earlier on. Touched with remorse, I walked over to him.

He must have heard me coming yet he remained immovable, leaning over the rail, facing the heights above the harbour, the night standing there high and opaque on its toes between him and the ring of rocks called Icoco.

I put my hand on his shoulder. "Why are you still up, Man of Icoco?" I asked.

"I am just up," he answered, his voice low and flat without its usual music.

"What is it that you are thinking?" I tried again.

"I am without thought, 'Nkosan."

"Look, 'Mlangeni," I asked vehemently to beat back the rush of helplessness in me. "I know you're troubled. What more is there to the trouble?"

"It has no name yet, 'Nkosan. Its name is still to come."

He paused and it was as if the silence between us were so great that I could hear the stars crackle and the night itself tremble as it stood upright and stiff with apprehension. Could he, perhaps, be listening in to the bee-swarming sound of his countrymen in the barracks beyond the docks?

The thought seemed fantastic. Yet I would have put it to him had he not spoken: "Men have strayed into the path where they meet only things without shape!"

"Oh, 'Mlangeni," I exclaimed. "Please don't trouble yourself so. Let me help. Tell me what it is so that I can try to help."

"I would, my 'Nkosan," he answered at last with emotion at my concern. "I would, but I am not I. I have stood here since

you and that other 'Nyanga went ashore, waiting for 'Mlangeni to come back and talk to 'Mlangeni. But 'Mlangeni has not come back. Perhaps we should look for him in our sleep."

I had a bad night. Tired as I was, I was awake long before the daylight came to hem the curtain between my bunk and the saloon. Normally I would have got up then but I found myself reluctant to face the day ahead. I would have lain there until the Captain, who was still snoring in the bunk opposite mine, made his move had I not then heard clearly in the morning stillness 'Mlangeni calling from the deck to someone on shore. In the three years I had known him this had never happened before: such a thing would have been beneath the dignity of a man who studied the secrets of the sea.

At once I was out of my bunk, through the curtains in the saloon and kneeling on the bench alongside the triangular table, my ear to the open porthole. It was useless to look out as the porthole was well below the level of the quay, and I would only have seen the latticed reflection of sea ripples on the oozing wall.

"You say our brothers call us. Why?" 'Mlangeni was asking someone on the quayside making no attempt at secrecy since he knew no Europeans spoke his tongue.

"Because today we have to kill and perhaps to die!" came the loud response, followed by a chorus of voices rushing above me past the ship like a great gust of wind down the length of the docks until it vanished in a whisper: "Yes! Oh yes! At last we shall kill."

It was one of the oldest calls to battle in Africa.

I listened no more although I could hear the general sound of the exchanges between 'Mlangeni and men on the quay continue. I was back in the cabin dressing silently and as fast as I could. Without washing or brushing my hair, I went through the curtains and rushed on deck.

'Mlangeni by then had ceased talking to men on the shore. He was standing silently in the stern where I had found him the night before, his back to me, just listening to the calls of his countrymen being relayed from one gang of black workers to another from end to end of the great dockyard and beyond.

The sun was just about to rise, the sky was without cloud or

wind. There was not a ship, warehouse, crane or shape in the vast harbour that did not have a halo of light around it. And beyond, the heights of the city, with their white-walled, red-roofed houses, great gardens lit with the flame of spathodia, bauhennia and giant magnolia and a purple sky bowed tenderly over it, all had a beauty, a freshness like the look of innocence of the young just coming out of their sleep. If ever there were a day made to encourage increase in life I would have thought that morning was one. Yet, as I went to join 'Mlangeni, I would hear from far and wide men openly calling not for life but death, crying out aloud to one another:

"Our brothers call us! Today we must kill or die!"

One of the strangest things of that pure morning of fateful paradox was that in the midst of all this shouting and calling to battle I saw white European watchmen, the crane drivers, the overseers of black stevedores, the water policemen, the tug-boat officers, tally-clerks, and pilots pouring into the dockyard area as if this were just another routine day no different from a thousand others in the undramatic serial of their lives. They did not seem to notice this unusual call constantly going out from one end of the harbour to the other ensuring that every black worker received and understood its message.

As for myself, had I been inclined to doubt the evidence of my own ears, one look at 'Mlangeni's face would have been enough to shake me out of any complacency and show me how deadly a threat was built into the foundation of the day. When I greeted him, he responded automatically, without looking at me.

I had to take him by the arm, pull him from the stern rail and say: "No, 'Mlangeni. The trouble of which we spoke has a name and shape now. What is it and why?"

He turned slowly. His dark eyes, like windows at sunset, were aflame with the reflection of a setting light. They did not see either me as an individual or that bright beautiful day around us. They were looking instead deep at some vision aflame in his blood, all his senses focused on a past beyond human discernment. But the past is a magnet drawing men towards it, whatever their private will or desire, for impersonal rearrangement in a tragic order of its own cast-iron and pre-selected field.

263

"You've heard, 'Nkosan," he told me, "as I have heard."

"I have heard. But why this summons to kill?"

He looked at me hard and long and then from me up at the funnel, the foremast, the crow's-nest, down to the bridge and across to the ship's upturned bow, where the harpoon gun wrapped in canvas pointed like a forefinger at our suspended purpose at sea. All was shining with light as with dew.

I think in the process a memory of all he had experienced in the ship and the way in which it had set him apart from the life of his countrymen on shore must have been evoked in him. The sense of that difference as well as, I hoped, a recollection of what we had all shared in the *Kurt Hansen*'s tight European world, came momentarily between him and that vision on fire in his blood.

He shook his great head and said: " 'Nkosan, last night at eight-fifteen an Indian trader in the market cheated, as they all always do, a young Umfaan* out of his change. When the boy protested they killed him."

"But how do you know all this is true?" I asked in sheer unbelief.

He replied at great length telling me how scores of his countrymen had witnessed the murder and reported it to the white police, who had refused to act.

I argued with him long and patiently. I ran ashore even to buy a newspaper, hurried back and showed him that there was no report of such a killing in it as there would have been had it really occurred.

He remained utterly unconvinced, saying that the ricksha-puller who had brought the news to the men with whom he had just spoken was a reliable man of good repute and honest tongue. He told me even the ricksha-puller's name, and that of the kraal he came from in southern Zululand, to show how meticulous the report must be. There could be no doubt: murder had been done and cried out for revenge.

As he talked I had no doubt Port Natal was facing one of the most terrible threats in its history. I myself knew only too well

* Zulu Boy.

the bitter feelings all black men shared about the Indians, and their firm conviction that their own primitive trust and naiveté was used constantly by the sophisticated orientals to trick them. I knew how baffled they were that the white men in power could use Indians as middlemen in their dealings with Africans, since white men despised the Indians openly as no other coloured race in Port Natal.

With such a state of mind of so long a standing, the truth of the report of the Zulu boy's murder was really, in a sense, irrelevant. Enough crime to justify revenge had already been committed in the eyes of 'Mlangeni's countrymen. If not this murder that they so firmly believed in that morning, something else as plausible would have bubbled up in their minds to justify the action for which all those sonorous voices were calling as 'Mlangeni and I talked on deck.

It was my first encounter with one of the most mysterious phenomena of history. History is not just a progression of ascertainable cause and effect. It is not a result of what actually happens in life or what is true in demonstrable fact, but rather of what men imagine to have been true or to have happened. It moves without rhythm or logic, and after long periods of apparent stagnation leaps suddenly, melodramatically and often disastrously into great unknown areas of life. Indeed, it would be interesting to approach history as if one were about to investigate some kind of electricity of the human spirit. The reported murder of the Zulu boy was like that Old Testament cloud no bigger than a man's hand, on the horizon of that bright morning. Before long the storm it portended would break, and the sombre charge of electricity which had slowly accumulated in the Zulu heart and mind over the long years of their unnatural life and submissiveness to foreign ways, would leap like forked lightning at Port Natal. Something must be done and done quickly to prevent it: but what?

My own immediate concern was for 'Mlangeni.

"Promise me," I pleaded with him, "that whatever happens you will not go ashore today."

He stood up. Tall as I was for my age, he looked down at me, a good six inches taller.

1*   265

With the simplicity of the irrevocable he said: "My brothers call me and I hear!"

Thoroughly frightened for him, I rushed below to search out Leif in his galley. I told him all I knew and feared as fast as I could. Whatever doubts Leif might have had of my judgement in other matters, he trusted me implicitly in things concerning 'Mlangeni and his countrymen.

" 'Mlangeni has already refused you, Pete," he told me gravely. "We'd better go to the Captain."

Thor Larsen was already in the saloon dealing with the hangover of the night before, by drinking schnapps. At Leif's request I told him my story again from beginning to end.

He listened without interruption. "And what you think, Eyes, these black people do today?"

"There will be a massacre of Indians, if not Europeans, before the day is out, sir, unless something is done quickly." I spoke up sharply with impatience thinking of 'Mlangeni, whom I feared at any moment now might be dashing ashore. "But couldn't you please do something about 'Mlangeni, first?"

"What to do with black stoker, later, Eyes," he reproved me. "What to do about this danger you speak of on shore, more important, not? But what to do? I think police already do something?"

I thought of all those impervious white faces I had already seen clocking in for work in the dock area. If they, working with Zulus every day, were so unaware, I could not see the police being more alert, and told my Captain so.

"Then to speak to the police and tell them, not?"

"Yes, sir!" I hastened to agree. "But please, 'Mlangeni first, or he'll be gone. It won't take long."

"All right, Eyes. All right!" Thor Larsen spoke almost angrily because he could not help finding my concern for 'Mlangeni out of proportion and beyond his understanding. "You, Eyes! Run and call engineer here."

In the few minutes it took me to fetch our engineer and bring him into the saloon, Leif, I could tell, had used his influence to make certain that Thor Larsen really understood my story. The Captain at once started talking to the engineer in Norwegian,

ordering him to find work for 'Mlangeni in the engine room at once and keep him at it until further orders, and not to let him out of his sight or on deck for a moment.

The Captain arranged all this with an ease, speed and authority for which I could have embraced him.

"To go with engineer now, Eyes," he told me. "Then to come back here after, not?"

"Thank you, yes!" I responded, following our portly, staid engineer out of the saloon and up on deck so fast that I trod on his heels once or twice. I thought we were too late and my heart seemed to stop. 'Mlangeni was not there.

I looked up and down the long quay and across to the harbour gates and took heart from the fact that he was not to be seen there either.

"I think he's gone below, sir," I told the engineer. "I'll go and call him," and I went so fast down the forecastle ladder that I nearly fell at the bottom.

'Mlangeni, to my relief, was sitting on his bunk, his tin chest open in front of him. He was busy tying at the back of his neck the ends of two thin leather strips sewn like apron-strings on to a rat's skin. I knew instantly how justified my fears had been, for an old 'Takwena warrior had once confided in me that in war there was no better charm than a rat's skin, because rats were so expert at dodging missiles and darting for natural cover. 'Mlangeni clearly had begun his preparations for battle.

" 'Mlangeni," I told him breathlessly, "your engineer wants you!"

For the first time since I had known him, he looked at me with angry reproach. Harsh with resentment he said: "Would you try to trick me on a day such as this?"

I looked him straight in the eyes and said in a voice I did not recognise as my own: "Yes, 'Mlangeni, my brother, on such a day I would not hesitate to trick you if it would help. Yet it is as I have said. I come from the engineer and he comes from the Captain to summon you."

So sullenly did he continue looking at me that I thought for a moment he would refuse. But the long years of his life at sea were too strong for his new bee-swarm self. Had he been with others

of his own kind the result no doubt would have been different. But he was alone in a tight white world and forced to be himself by himself.

After a while he looked away, stood up, slammed the lid of his chest down so that it crashed to, kicked it violently under his bunk and without a glance at me walked to the ladder and climbed on deck. He was already preceding the engineer through the engine-room entrance when I stepped into the sunlight again. For the moment he was safe, but what of the rest of the day?

I stood there for a second looking at the harbour and the city. The long level light of the sun had lifted the town and heights sparkling above the purple shadows ebbing like a neap tide on the earth below. I had never seen the place look more beautiful. The contrast of such beauty with the ugly apprehension within me was difficult to bear.

Ostensibly life in the harbour had fallen into its normal pattern. The calls to battle had died away and everywhere black stevedores and coalmen were hard at work. But usually these men all sang as they worked: one man leading each gang of labourers, the rest responding in chorus. It was one of the most attractive things about Port Natal; there was always natural music made by men as they worked beside the sea. On this immaculate morning they worked in silence.

I looked at the white men in charge of the gangs working near the *Kurt Hansen*, at the crane drivers in their high cages, so well placed to observe the entire scene, thinking they, too, must have noticed it. But I saw not a sign that they found anything strange about the day. More fearful than ever, I went below.

Leif meanwhile had fetched me my appetising breakfast. He was sitting beside it, facing Thor Larsen, and clearly had gone on talking to him to some purpose.

"Ah, good, there you are, my Eyes," Thor Larsen exclaimed, unusually gentle and forthcoming for him. "First to eat and then to talk, not?" I must have looked a bit dismayed at this for he said: "Yes, Eyes, to eat. On such days most necessary always first eat, not?"

So while I tried to eat, with Leif sitting there calmly, in case

he was needed, the Captain spoke at length to me. He tried to convince me that with all the shouting and calls to battle which had started at dawn, the police must know of it and would already be investigating and taking precautionary measures.

His conclusion was too much for me. I pushed my plate away from me and jumped up, determined at once to prove Thor Larsen right or wrong.

"No, no, Eyes! To sit down and eat, at once, not?" Thor Larsen ordered me severely.

"Please sir, I can't," I pleaded. "Let me just run ashore and ask the water policeman at the gate what he knows about this. I'll be back in a tick to report to you."

I think for all the desperation in my tone Thor Larsen would have insisted on my staying if Leif had not intervened.

"I'd let him go: he may well bring back the news that you are right."

"All right, Eyes," Thor Larsen consented reluctantly. "To go quick and come back here."

The water policeman was sitting in his hut near the gates, eating sandwiches and drinking thick red Indian tea out of a Hong Kong flask for breakfast. He had the morning newspaper open on his knees and was studying the latest reports on form in the racing columns. It was all enough to show me that, for him, this day was no different from a thousand others before it.

We knew each other well by sight, in fact he had known me for so long that, in spite of all the inches I had added to my height and shoulders, he still had the paternalistic habit of calling me 'sonny'.

"Hullo, there, sonny," he greeted me. "Why so bright and early? Off to town already?"

I shook my head and asked him if he'd noticed anything unusual about the docks?

"Can't say I have," he answered faintly surprised. "Should I have done?"

I told him what I knew as calmly as I could. He listened patiently at first but later started munching his breakfast again.

"That all, sonny?" he told me with a full mouth when I finished. "Then there's nothing to worry about. These black

fellows are just like children. They must have their games of make-believe. Why, they've been shouting and calling out things to one another while working all day long ever since I've known them. Singing too—"

"They're not singing now."

For the first time his complacency was shaken. Perhaps his senses had already been telling him for some while that the docks had been abnormally quiet.

"Ja. You're right there. It is a bit quieter than usual round here," he admitted.

He frowned and stirred as if to reach for his telephone. Hope began to rise higher in me. But suddenly he relapsed into his routine self and reached instead for a sandwich observing: "But that's not really so strange, when you come to think of it. They have moods. These black fellows are just like children. Now if you'd as much experience as I—"

"Inspector, d'you speak Zulu?" I asked.

"Zulu?" he repeated, taken aback. "Can't say I do. But that doesn't—"

"I speak Zulu as well as I speak English," I spoke vehemently. Time was short. "And I promise you there's no make-believe about the call to battle I heard today. And this silence is not just moodiness. Please telephone your office and warn them. This is terribly serious."

Telling him what to do was a mistake. Also my persistence pushed him out of his level humour.

"Look, sonny," he told me. "I'm a great deal older than you. You needn't tell me my duty. I'll keep a watch on things and do what's necessary. So don't worry." He went back to his paper and breakfast.

The interview was over.

I hastened back to the *Kurt Hansen*. Thor Larsen and Leif were still in the saloon. Leif was talking to him as I entered, and judging by the few words I heard he had been persuading Thor Larsen to listen to me.

"Well, what, Eyes?" the Captain asked.

"It was as I thought, sir," I told him word for word what had passed between the policeman and me.

Even Leif was surprised at my report, but the Captain un-expectedly was outraged.

"Damn, Eyes," he shouted. "Policeman damn fool. Other police not such fools!"

"I'm afraid they may be, sir," I protested, too despondent to point out that what we were up against was the unawareness of a whole city.

"Well I, Thor Larsen, I soon make that right," he answered, his intense grey eyes fierce with resolution. "You to finish break-fast at once. I go telephone owner's representative. I make him speak to police . . ."

"But he won't," I called out dismayed. "And for heaven's sake don't mention me, sir—"

Larsen silenced me at once.

"I know all," he snapped. "But when I speak, he act. Always that's so, not?"

He was like a house on fire with confidence. If it were only a question of a contest between him and me and my old host I was ready to believe we would win. But there was so much more to it than that. I would have tried to express something of this had not Leif spoken.

"The Captain's right, Pete," he said. "It's the best way. Indeed what other could you suggest? The police must take notice."

"Of course. Thor Larsen right," the Captain proclaimed loudly, getting up just as I was beginning to admit that there was indeed no better way. "I go telephone."

He was a good deal longer than we'd expected and walked back into the saloon with a look of battle on his face, and a flush of pink underneath his sallow skin that was not caused by gin.

He poured himself another glass of schnapps, thrust the stopper back into the decanter, and ordered me fiercely: "To get ready, Eyes. Soon car comes."

Half an hour later Thor Larsen in his navy-blue serge and I in my best suit met Andrew Watson's portentous black car, drawn up opposite the *Kurt Hansen*'s gang-plank. The chauffeur stood cap in hand, holding the back door open for us, exactly as

I had seen him do three years before. But he had the same look on his face that 'Mlangeni had had, showing that the mood which had so frightened me down in the harbour also existed on the heights above the city. It was a terrifying example of how efficiently and fast this dark bee-swarming purpose could spread itself out among a people.

On the way to Watson's office up town, we had examples of how both mood and purpose were consolidating themselves of their own volition and preparing for the moment of sinister resolution. For instance, unlike the night before the streets were now full of rickshas. All the ricksha-pullers we passed were going about their business with a heightened sense of purpose and a quickened tempo. The leaps between the shafts of their rickshas were higher, their cries louder and more challenging; the stamping of their feet in the waiting stands where they solicited their traffic, was like that of men of one of the Chaka's impi about to set out on a raid. But what struck me even more were the calls exchanged by those ricksha-men when, loaded with passengers, they passed one another in the streets. It was always the same cry. One would cry, "Four o'clock," and the other respond: "Yes, my brother, four o'clock."

It was the first time in all the years I had been in Port Natal that I had heard strange black men in the streets "brothering" one another openly thus in the streets. It could only mean that from wherever they came, despite differences of families, clans, tribes and geography, they now felt themselves to be one in the powerful secret masonry that the call to vengeance had formed in their spirit.

Even Thor Larsen noticed the change.

We had been sitting silently side by side considering what tactics we should use against my old host when suddenly he said: "Those ricksha-men, mad, Eyes! Not? What for they jump and shout so much?"

I told him what I thought. They were making certain everyone knew that at four o'clock in the afternoon, the time when factories closed and public work in winter ceased, they would all join to go into battle.

"But how battle, Eyes? They have no guns!"

"They have knives and sticks and stones, sir," I told him. "They can fight. Just look at that, sir."

I broke off to point at what appeared almost as a deliberate illustration of what I was telling him. We were halted at a cross-street. On the corner an old Indian peddlar was waiting, his body bowed with the weight of fruit and vegetables he was carrying slung from the ends of a bamboo pole balanced on his shoulders. A young Zulu, in a house-boy's uniform, suddenly dashed out of the crowd on the pavement, hit the old man across the head with the hunting stick that they all carried and ran away as fast as he could.

I thought the policeman on traffic duty would go after him because he saw it as clearly as we did. I expected that the Europeans around would rush to hold the Zulu boy, because the blow had been so brutal that the frail old Indian had fallen down on to the pavement, his fruit scattered far and wide, some rolling into the traffic. Instead the Europeans laughed as if it were all a boyish prank. The traffic policeman smiled. The old man sat up dazed and feebly feeling his head.

"By God, that damn strange!" Thor Larsen exclaimed, as we drove on. "You right, Eyes. Something damn strange about this place today."

I looked back to see the old Indian still struggling unaided to get to his feet. I told my Captain that this was the African's instinctive way of seeing how far he could go without the Europeans interfering. The news of this house-boy's probe into our defences of law and order would soon be known all over the city and its suburbs. Next time perhaps someone else would practise something a little more serious on some unsuspecting Indian.

I remembered then what I had read in the history of the many uprisings of the people in my country and in other countries too. The main positive defence at the beginning was to keep the Africans apart, to prevent them from massing. The greater the number, the greater the danger; for numbers, in such a mood, was like a powerful hashish to them. They got emotionally and mentally drunk and congealed into a demoniac oneness. When this happened only violence could break up the

solidity. I begged Thor Larsen, when he spoke to my old host, not to forget to ask him to impress upon the police how imperative it was not to let the Africans mass that day, and immediately to break up any gathering, however small.

But my Captain's confidence in his influence over the owner's representative was soon to be shaken. Andrew Watson started by keeping us waiting for a quarter of an hour. This for me was a clear indication of what value he set on our report of the great emergency and also, perhaps, of his disapproval of my connection with the affair. I watched Thor Larsen becoming more and more impatient, refusing to be seated, and walking up and down the large office as if it were the *Kurt Hansen*'s bridge, until I feared he might storm through the inner door into the private office.

When we were summoned into his office by Watson himself, Thor Larsen was so angry that I thought he would give him several rough chunks of his home-made mind. But the owner's representative, who had probably provoked all this for his own secret intent, saw with pleasure how well he had succeeded and made a great show of welcoming us.

Thor Larsen cut him short to comment aggressively, "I come for emergency, Boss. You tell him, Eyes."

Thor Larsen was pointing at me, and for the first time the man had to take notice of me. He glared surprised, I believe, because so much had I grown that he could no longer look down on me physically as he had done when we last met. But as I looked into his pale, pink-veined eyes I knew that, as far as his feelings about me were concerned, he had not changed.

"Eyes?" he questioned in the midst of fussing over the Captain. "Please step in, my dear Captain—and sit down. What does that mean?"

"Pete then," Thor Larsen snapped, throwing himself into a leather armchair.

"Pete?" The man exclaimed again, determined to play the role of a judge who was not prepared to know anything of his own accord but only according to the evidence laid before him.

"The Captain means me, sir," I hastened to explain because

274

the Captain at any moment now would explode and wreck all chances of our getting a proper hearing.

"I see. Eyes and Pete, so these are the names you sail under these days?"

His choice of smile and tone of voice deliberately made "names" the equivalent of "false colours". Were our purpose there not so serious I would have walked out of that office there and then. As it was, I was trying to control myself when Thor Larsen spoke up. "Boss, you listen to Eyes, quick. I told you on telephone this damn serious!"

He listened then to my story, his patience obviously strained to the uttermost. It was difficult to tell my tale to such a man in so locked a mood, but I told it and finished in detail, to the end, not forgetting to mention the attack on the old Indian we had witnessed on the way.

"If there's anything in this at all," he announced when I'd finished, "I'm certain the police will know about it and do what's necessary. But I must say it all sounds pretty exaggerated to me."

"Ja. That's what I thought, too, Boss," Thor Larsen remarked sarcastically. "Just you try police and find out, not?"

"I'll tell you what I'll do." Our host looked at Thor Larsen as if doing him a great favour. "I'll speak to the Commissioner of Police at the Club at lunch. He's an awfully good chap and is there every day."

"That could be too late," I said sharply.

"Why?" he asked, without looking at me. "You yourself have told us four o'clock is the critical hour. That still leaves plenty of time."

"The thing should be broken up now," I answered. "It's important that the Africans should not be allowed to mass."

He brusquely silenced me, reiterating that the police would know what to do.

"Eyes is right. Lunch too late. Speak police now, quick."

My Captain, who in principle always mistrusted any post-ponement of action, spoke emphatically.

"I'm sorry, Captain," came the cool reply. "I'm not going to worry a busy man and make a fool of myself into the bargain.

As I've promised, I'll tell him all you've told me at lunch. You really must trust me to know my city and people better than you do; after all, you are a comparative stranger here. Now if you'll excuse me, I have a great deal to do."

I believe Thor Larsen wouldn't have given up even then, had not this last bit about his being a "stranger" struck him as accurate.

Even so, he gave in with bad grace, saying in his roughest voice: "Hope to God you not find too late, Boss."

Larsen then stood up abruptly and, unaccustomed to defeat, ordered me "Come, Eyes," and walked to the door without any effort at leave-taking.

I hadn't expected much from our interview, but this was altogether too much. Despite my Captain's order, I was unable to move and stared at Watson with such unbelief that he exclaimed, nettled, "Well, you've heard your Captain's order."

His voice was the same that he'd used three seasons back when he'd broken in on me sitting with his butler and servants at the bottom of his garden. Somehow the memory served me. If I could do nothing in general, perhaps I could do something in particular, as I had tried to do for my friend 'Mlangeni.

I pleaded, "Please sir, Jack, your butler—would you see that he's not allowed out on the streets today?"

He looked me over from head to foot as he repeated, "You're keeping your Captain waiting."

As if he had not noticed Thor Larsen's gracelessness, he called past me into his secretary's office where my Captain was already at the outer door. "Thank you so much, Captain, for your trouble. Good day now, and I'll see you on Sunday."

Thor Larsen didn't bother to respond. In fact he was silent all the way to the *Kurt Hansen* except for an occasional "Damn!" that broke out of him like gusts out of a squally day.

He left the car and dashed up the gangway of his ship like a man coming home. I stood irresolute by the car watching him vanish into the saloon entrance. I thought for a moment I would appeal to the chauffeur to go to Jack and beg him and all the servants to stay at home all day. But one look at his face

told me how useless that would be. So I just thanked him and followed my Captain on board—but not into the saloon.

First, I went into the engine room to see 'Mlangeni. The repairs must have gone much better than expected because I found him preparing for a fire again in the ship's boilers. He was covered in sweat as he dug his shovel into the coal to pile it on the wood. When I spoke to him he didn't stop working but said with a remoteness that hurt far more than my old host's dismissal, "Do you not think that today already you have spoken too much?"

I left him to go back to the saloon. Thor Larsen oddly enough was standing by the porthole looking at the slimy wall of the quay and, for once, not drinking.

I believe he had been waiting for me because he immediately came to sit in his chair at the head of the table, ordered me to sit down as well and said with a certain hesitation which I had never suspected in him: "You know, Eyes, one time, when I young as you first time we meet, I too in fore-top with another whaler. Great storm coming. Sky yellow, water brown, big swell. God knows how from where because no wind, I see Caesar blow, far, far, far away. I tell whaler beside me. He not see, he not believe. Again Caesar, he blow. Again I say: 'Look big sperm, he blows.' Again no one believe. Five times that happen, all no good. You know old whalers say, I say too, great sperm always come in tooth of great storm. That evening when great storm comes, everyone believe young Thor Larsen. But believe too late . . . Today you see Caesar blowing plenty. But no one believe. Perhaps, four o'clock, storm comes. Then everyone believe—"

This home-spun effort of the Captain to comfort me moved me very much, but unfortunately just then he was cut short by the appearance of both the company's chief engineer and our own appearing in the saloon. I say unfortunately because I had a feeling that, with the Captain in this mood, we might have talked really intimately together for the first time, and so I would have come to understand him better and perhaps help break that seal on his terrible loneliness.

The engineers had come because they thought the repairs were

complete, but they would like to take the *Kurt Hansen* for a trial run out to sea to give the work they had done a thorough test. In fact our engineer had already taken the liberty, in the Captain's absence, of preparing to raise steam in the ship. He could be ready in an hour. Nothing could have pleased my Captain better, nor me. I felt that 'Mlangeni, about whom I was still deeply uneasy, fearing that when the time came at four o'clock he would break out of the ship and join his countrymen ashore, would now be safe out at sea.

Then I thought suddenly of de la Buschagne and his daughter. The arrangement was that he should call back on Thor Larsen in the afternoon. He must be told. Also he should be warned of the danger that threatened the town and told to keep himself and his daughter indoors. I interrupted the technical discussion between the engineers and Thor Larsen to suggest that in the circumstances I should go and tell de la Buschagne that his visit was postponed.

"Ah, good, Eyes. You go at once." The vigorous nod of his head showed how thoroughly he approved of my proposal.

I went ashore then and out of the harbour past the quayside policeman who, the moment he saw me, became re-absorbed in the racing columns of his paper.

Out in the streets the very air felt to me as it must have done on the last day in Pompeii before Vesuvius erupted. The streets were full of signs of abnormality which, though trivial in themselves, made up the great imponderable electricity of a catastrophic discharge. For instance, all the Indian hawkers had vanished from streets usually so crowded with them. They anyway had heard the alarm. The Indian shopkeepers, instead of standing in the entrances of their premises, soliciting custom, were well inside behind the counters. Zulu messenger boys, all armed with sticks, were running about their errands. Whenever they passed an Indian shop they pranced up and down in front of it as if about to smash the windows or charge inside, before they ran on chanting. So great everywhere was the feeling of menace that I was quite relieved to walk up the steps of the "Ailsa Craig". It looked an impregnable keep of normality, its verandah crowded with comfortable people having "elevenses".

The Indian porter told me that de la Buschagne was out, but his daughter was in. So I waited for her in a small lounge crowded with tables and chairs and smelling so much of fresh smoke and stale beer that I was grateful I was not kept waiting long.

She came in quickly before the porter could announce her, for obviously anything to do with the *Kurt Hansen* was a source of potential alarm. Her lovely young face, which so far I had found as mobile and responsive to her thoughts and feelings as a pool in a wood to sun and brush of wind, was now strangely set with apprehension.

She held her hand out to me quickly and I took it, finding it cold for so warm a morning.

She asked me, "What is it, Cousin? I fear father is out."

"Nothing much," I hastened to reassure her. "Only to say my Captain regrets that he can't receive your father in the ship this afternoon. We have to go to sea unexpectedly." I went on to explain why in unnecessary detail, because I was enjoying being with her. I think she was aware of my reaction and pleased for reasons of her own to have the chance of talking to me alone.

When I had finished my elaborate explanation she said, "Is that all? I'm glad." Then added quickly: "I suppose, Cousin, there's no hope of dissuading your terrible little Captain from taking father whaling with him?"

I shook my head at her eager face and saw her wide blue eyes contract with the tension.

I protested, "He's not a 'terrible little Captain', Cousin. You wouldn't say that if you knew him. And if your father wants to go with him, why should he say no? I think you should stop your father from going, rather than blame my Captain."

"Stop father!" Even the suggestion was enough to amaze her. "You don't know father. But anyway, Cousin, forgive me, please. I'm being less than fair to you. Thank you for coming." She held out her hand to me as if that were the end.

I took it, telling her "There's nothing to forgive. But there is something else that I must tell you, far more serious."

"Is it about father?" she interrupted me, over-anxious again. As I shook my head quickly she asked suddenly, "Could we talk

about it walking on the sea front? I've not been out all day and father won't let me walk alone."

Soon, side by side, we were walking along the sea front, past cafés, amusement stalls, bathing pools, aquarium and a great snake park, out on to the firm sands in the direction of the dunes where I always spent my Sundays when in harbour. The sea was sparkling calm and without a ripple, its sound like a rustle of silk in our ears, and the sunlight a flicker of flame around her yellow head.

As we walked I told her the whole story from the moment I had heard the bee-swarm sound the night before.

When I'd finished she said simply, "That explains why the Indians in the hotel have been so peculiar all day." Then she turned to me suddenly, almost in tears, adding, "Oh, Cousin, I wish we'd never come to this dreadful city. I'd give anything to be out of it, even if it meant going back to the bush."

I wished I had words to comfort her but I had none; and there was no comfort in me either. I could only put my free hand on the one she had round my arm and press it.

She looked out to sea and went on as if to herself. "How terrible that on such a lovely day people can plan such dreadful things against each other. Oh, Cousin, sometimes I think beauty is the bravest thing on earth. It goes on day after day, in spite of all the ugliness men bring to it. Will it never stop?"

Again I had nothing to say and had to leave it to the sea and the sun and the beauty of the day to answer her. We turned silently about and walked back to her hotel without speaking.

Then a glance at my wrist-watch, a gift to myself out of my last season's bonus, showed me that I had to hurry back to my ship.

As we said goodbye on the hotel steps, I asked her, "Promise me you and your father will not go out of this hotel from lunch time on?"

"Promise!" she said and smiled at me which, considering what she was feeling, I thought to be very spirited.

I got back to the *Kurt Hansen* just as she was getting ready to cast off. We were well out in the middle of the harbour before I heard the sirens in the city announce the lunch-time break in

work. When they went again at two o'clock we had done a round of the great bay at half speed. So successful had that trial run been that the engineers asked Thor Larsen to take the ship out to sea. Out there for nearly two hours in the gleaming roadstead of Port Natal, the *Kurt Hansen* was put through all possible variations of her paces, until the engineers declared she would be fit for sea by the morning after some minor adjustments which they would finish in the night. Good as the result was, it disappointed the Captain, who had secretly hoped that he'd be able to snatch one day's whaling out of his last days in Port Natal by going to sea that same night. Leaving port at dawn on a Saturday gave him no time, since by an unwritten law of the fleet he would be expected to be back in the evening to give his crew their weekend in port. Any whaler which tried to work on a Sunday would have had a mutiny on her hands from her God-fearing and superstitious crew.

Meanwhile, I had been most grateful for this unexpected interlude. It not only made 'Mlangeni safe, but kept me occupied and interested, and I don't know how, without such objective help, I'd have endured the fear seething inside me.

But the moment the ship turned about and I saw how accurately Gorgeous had aimed her nose for the entrance of the narrow harbour mouth, fear rose uppermost in me again. My watch showed it to be just on four o'clock. With the ship's glasses slung over my shoulder I climbed swiftly up to my position in the fore-top. I had just unslung the glasses and was busy focusing them when I heard the sound of the sirens calling out the end of a winter day's work in the harbour. Quickly I turned the glasses to the land and searched the harbour front. From that height in that light and with the *Kurt Hansen* close in, about to cross the bar at the harbour mouth, I saw the whole of the great docks from end to end in amazing detail. And at once I knew how right I had been to fear.

There were three main gates from the city into the enclosed harbour area but at least half a dozen minor ones, used by the thousands of black people working at the docks for getting to and from their barracks. Instead of trickling through all of these gates and entrances as they normally did, I saw that the various

gangs already released from work were all running as fast as they could towards the main gate on the broad streets leading towards the Indian quarter of the city. What is more, they must have brought, hidden under their coats when they came to work in the morning, their sticks and carving knives; every man I could see had either one or both of these in hand. Although dressed in the rags of their European environment, they ran as warriors of Africa, their sticks held like the yellow hafts of assegais in their hands and knives glittering in the sun. Already the open space at the great gates was filling up with prancing men brandishing their weapons, their blackness rapidly spreading out all over the vacant sunlit area like a pool of spilt ink on yellow parchment. As I watched, the head of the crowd began to push in a thick stream through the gates. Beyond it, the broad busy street was packed and shining with the cars of businessmen going to their homes on the heights above the town. A policeman was directing the traffic at the crossing just opposite the gates. Not the least amazing thing about the un-believable day was that when this great tide of prancing black men, stamping, brandishing, feinting and shadow stabbing, came into the main street among the traffic, the policeman held up one hand in a long white glove to halt the cars, and with the other waved the Africans across the road. I suppose he could not have done anything else except carry on as if nothing un-usual was happening. Had he tried to stop that human tide he would have been pushed out of the way or killed. I don't know how long he stood there thus as stiff and mechanical as a railway signal, for our movement in-shore made him sink out of sight behind the great warehouse of the harbour. But when I last looked, the tide of angry men was still flowing thick, high and wide through the gates and growing in the vacant marshalling area inside the harbour.

At the same time across the water I heard, rising high into the air, like a dark satanic Hallelujah, the battle singing of the Amazulu. I had heard it many times before as a form of enter-tainment. But hearing it high up in the crow's-nest, surging across the shining, silent harbour water that evening, and sung to its own inner deadly purpose, it was something quite new.

The sound seemed to come not out of thousands of throats but from far down in the stomachs of men burning with ancient fires. It was like a great tidal wave from some remote submarine eruption coming up over the rim of a tranquil ocean, to rear and curve over that passive, sparkling, transparent afternoon before crashing down blackly on the long golden foreshore of the level light between me and the city and quenching it forever.

The nearer we drew to the quay, of course, the louder the sound of this song became, until nothing else could be heard in the harbour except this constant syncopated reiteration of brother calling to brother to join in a great washing of Amazulu spears. During the brief pauses between one repetition and another I could now hear, from far and wide on all sides of the city, the same song being sung, as if all were joined in the same vortex of music plucking.

Ahead of me I saw the great dockyard now was strangely empty. The streets were totally without pedestrians. Still I remained in the fore-top listening to the battle music converging on the Indian quarter and ebbing away from me. Finally I could only just hear it through the alchemical gold of the evening air. When it seemed on the point of vanishing altogether, I heard the first brutally sharp salvo of rifle fire. The singing stopped. Far away as I was, I then heard the great call rising from the base of thousands of throats to "go in and kill!" Finally the sound of shooting took over entirely.

Below me, I saw 'Mlangeni rush on deck like a horse that has thrown its rider, and rush to the side. The noise of the shooting and the distance of the ship from the quay showed him that he was far too late. He fell down on the deck and beat it with his fists and his head, again and again. I was about to scramble down to join him when I saw Leif appear, kneel down beside him and speak to him. At first 'Mlangeni seemed not to hear. Then he became quite still and presently got up and allowed Leif to take him by the hand and lead him through the entrance to the saloon. High as I was, I saw that his cheeks were wet and shining with tears.

We docked finally at half past five, the sun going down with a calm clarity that looked like indifference in the face of what

I imagined had happened on shore. I left my fore-top and climbed down into the purple shadows heavy on the deck. The moment the gang-plank was thrown ashore, I was across it and running to the gates. They were, I could see, locked but I hoped to get news of what had happened from my acquaintance the water policeman. He had gone and a new man that I did not know was on duty, white-faced, tense, armed with rifle and pistol. The moment he saw me he came out of his hut to order me back to the ship.

Thinking it unwise to face 'Mlangeni just yet, I hung about on deck until it was dark, hearing the sound of shooting growing much less but still breaking out spasmodically all over the city. When it was quite dark I thought I saw a sharp red glow within the general gleam of the city, rising above the dark line of the warehouses. Immediately, like a monkey, I went up the rigging into the fore-top. A score or more of fires had broken out all over the town, indeed some were flaring even from the heights above the city.

When I could endure the cold in the fore-top no longer, although the fires were burning higher than ever, I went down and decided that, come what may, I must go into the saloon to get warm, for I was as chilled within as without.

Thor Larsen and Leif were at table talking almost in whispers. They signed to me to be quiet and told me they had just drugged 'Mlangeni with morphia from our medicine chest and put him to sleep in my bunk.

When they'd told me this, Leif stood up and said: "I'll get you some food, Pete. You've hardly eaten all day."

I didn't feel like eating and my face plainly said so, but he went out all the same.

Then something in me gave way. The imagination and foresight that these two men had shown in the way they handled 'Mlangeni, and now their gentleness with me, was in such a contrast to all that had happened that day not only to me but to all life, that I just put my head on the table and cried as I had not done since I was a child.

Thor Larsen, distressed, got up and began pacing the saloon, saying again and again: "Not to mind, my Eyes. Not to mind.

Everyone believe now, great storm has come. Not to mind. Storm soon over."

It was not over by morning.

But the situation was sufficiently under control for the harbour gates to be opened and some traffic to move in the streets, though no labour came into the docks to work at first light as was normal. I'd been up at dawn and dressed before my Captain and 'Mlangeni stirred, so I had noticed all this from the cold, dark deck.

I went ashore and walked to the harbour gates, half-expecting a water policeman again to stop me. It was my old acquaintance now who was on duty, fully armed, sitting reading his newspaper intently, and for the first time it was not the racing news. I could tell from the banner headlines spread in the largest and thickest black type across the pages how great and sombre was the news.

When he saw me at the entrance to his hut he looked up exclaiming: "God! What a mess!"

I asked if I could cross the street to the tobacconist's to buy a paper for myself.

"Help yourself." He waved his hand at the street as he spoke. "But if I were you I wouldn't go up any farther. It isn't safe yet. The side streets are full of all sorts of battle-drunk Zulus creeping back to their barracks."

I thanked him, hastened to buy a newspaper and was back in the saloon just as 'Mlangeni, dazed and not knowing precisely where he was, came through the curtains. Seeing me, he stopped and glared at me.

Some instinct made me go to him, take him by the hand and pull him towards the table. He came unwillingly.

"Please stay with me, 'Mlangeni, and I'll tell you what's happened," I begged him.

It was the best thing I could have done, since more than anything else he wanted knowledge of the day before. I could tell that from the hungry look he gave the newspaper I spread out on the table.

I read out the whole tragic story to him. Though the detail here does not matter, I did not deny him the smallest trifle.

Over a thousand Indians, many of them women and children, had been killed by his countrymen, over a thousand of his countrymen had been shot by the police. The fighting in the main city was over but still going on in the bush around Port Natal.

Soldiers, sailors, territorials, all had had to be called in to help the police before the Zulu attack on the Indian guards was broken. The death roll was expected to be high. The damage to property ran into millions of pounds. The cause of the riot, of course, was the rumour 'Mlangeni had repeated to me, which according to the paper was untrue. The amazing thing, apparently, was the speed with which the rumour spread. Half an hour after the alleged murder took place it was being repeated in places within a radius of twenty-five miles. The news was accompanied by an editorial calling for an enquiry into the failure of the police to foresee the riot and take preventive action.

As I read, I knew that the facts of the story would explain to him my concern for his personal safety. Long before I ended he was reconciled to me in his heart, but not to himself.

Finally he cried out in anguish: " 'Nkosan, what shall I answer when they ask at Icoco: 'And where were you,' Mlangeni, the day of the washing of the spears when your brothers called you?' "

"Tell them the truth, 'Mlangeni," I told him. "You were at sea under the orders of your great Captain."

I do not know how much that comforted him, particularly when, late that afternoon, Thor Larsen, back from a visit to the owner's office, told us that Jack, Nkomi-dhl'ilale, 'Mlangeni's "brother", was among those shot in the Indian quarter.

"Auck, how many times more shall we have to string the beads* before all is told?" 'Mlangeni asked of the sky, before turning away from us and going to the *Kurt Hansen*'s stern to be alone.

Up to that moment we all had been confined to the *Kurt Hansen*, but Thor Larsen now announced that the crew could resume the normal weekend routine.

* One of the similes of mourning: tears being beads strung tight on a single thread of sorrow.

Making me follow him down into the saloon, he seated me at the table and spoke to me sternly. "Look, my Eyes," he told me. "Not to feel sorry any more for black stoker or for yourself. Not? Everyone know you were right and sorry instead. Storm over now. New voyage to begin, not? I want for you to go to hunter. Tell him I want him in *Kurt Hansen* tomorrow night. Nine o'clock. Tomorrow we start looking for Caesar for him."

If he were right in his constantly reiterated belief that the great Caesars were found only in the teeth of great storms, then we would merely be going from a storm on land to a storm on sea. Yet I was grateful for the errand because all day long I had wondered, not without anxiety, how Laetitia de la Buschagne and her father had come through the past twenty-four hours.

Unfortunately I was not to see her. When I arrived at the hotel they were in their rooms and, in answer to my knock, only de la Buschagne came to the door. Rifle in hand, he stood there upright as ever, and it was as if the whole of our pioneering past in Africa were suddenly personified in him.

He did not ask me in because, he said, his daughter was resting after a sleepless night, which considering the circumstances was understandable.

He himself, I thought, had never looked better. It was as if the feeling of emergency, the sense of danger, and the fighting had profoundly stimulated him. More talkative than I had ever found him, he told me that people had laughed at him for bringing his gun with him to Port Natal. He had, of course, never been without it for years and no one would be laughing at him now. After receiving my warning from his daughter he had taken his gun out of its cover, loaded it and slung his bandolier of ammunition across his shoulder. Then when the singing and the shooting started he had gone down below and installed himself, rifle and all, in the porter's chair beside the desk. There he had been all night and all day until half an hour ago. But now, he too was rather tired and preparing to go early to bed.

When I told him my errand he remarked, "All the more reason for me to have a good night then, Cousin. Tell your Captain I'll be there at nine sharp tomorrow, thank you, and good evening."

Taking it for granted I understood why he did not ask me in, he shut the door firmly and promptly turned the key.

Disappointed, I went below and walked out of the hotel. A group of white people were standing talking with unusual animation beside the verandah steps. It seemed a sign of the demoralization and profound shock suffered by the Indians that the Indian staff of the hotel had not yet collected their evening delivery of milk, for a dozen bottles of milk still stood forlornly white in the shadows against the dark wall of the verandah behind them. On the other side of the road a tall, well-dressed Zulu, obviously educated, in the European sense, was just walking by with a bowed head. As I appeared on the verandah steps the Europeans laughed out aloud at something funny one of them had said.

Even to me there was something misplaced about the sound considering what sort of a day it had been. But to the Zulu it was too much. He suddenly charged across the street not knowing exactly what he was going to do. But when he saw the milk bottles he made straight for them and kicked them violently to pieces. Then shoving his hands in his pockets, he gave the white men, now gaping with unbelief, a look of defiant hatred and stamped off, raging, into the night.

"The Captain is not right," I thought as I made for the *Kurt Hansen*. "The storm on the streets may be over but it has only just begun in the hearts of man."

At dawn the next morning I was walking along the promenade to spend my Sunday as usual beside the sea. As I saw the bright colours of the rising day aflame on the windows of the hotels along the promenade, I thought of de la Buschagne's daughter and wondered if there was anything I could do to help her? One simple thing presented itself to me then so clearly that it gave me courage enough to go at once to the "Ailsa Craig". The dazed Indian porter was just coming in for duty at the desk and, when I asked, gave me a pencil, envelope and paper. I wrote a little note asking de la Buschagne's daughter if she would like to come for a walk with me at three in the afternoon, as there was something I would like to discuss with her. I gave the porter a shilling and asked him if

he thought he could find a moment to give it to her when she was alone.

He assured me he could, and so I went on to spend my morning as usual beside the sea.

But today everything was different: all that lovely long crystal morning I found myself missing the sound of singing from behind the dunes. Jack's messianic voice going up in the stillness was absent. So too was the sight of the little column of searching black souls in their rough blue smocks going solemnly across the yellow sands for reconciliation and communion with "their great neglected father the sea". There were not even race horses pounding the glistening sand nor Indian fishermen in their black boats riding the mother-of-pearl surf. The morning became melancholy and empty, and I was glad to pack up at half past two, to get my answer from Laetitia at the "Ailsa Craig".

I got there early and was relieved and overjoyed to see her at a table by the entrance, obviously waiting for me. She was dressed exactly as the first time I had ever seen her and yet looked rather older. Perhaps the stress of the past few days, the sleeplessness and the anxiety had brought out unusual shadows under her eyes and made them seem even bigger and more shining than before.

The moment she saw me, she jumped up, held her hand to me and said, "How nice of you, Cousin. I have been longing for another walk."

She made no mention of her father but I had the impression that he was out.

We spoke first, of course, of the terrible two days behind us. The detail of what we said does not matter. All that mattered was the sympathy we discovered and exchanged for one another's plight. When I told her about 'Mlangeni and the death of Jack, she held hard on to my arm and wept for them.

From there we went on to discuss the days ahead of us which, I saw at once, she feared as much as ever, though, when I asked her, she could not say why. It was just a deep feeling, like physical pain. I did all I could to reassure her by telling her how safe and highly organized an occupation whaling was, but

she was not convinced. I hastened to add then that I had thought of a way out of some of the uncertainty she would suffer in her father's absence. For that reason I was taking her to the signals station of Port Natal to introduce her to the two men who manned it.

These were two retired British naval yeomen of signals. I knew them as Mr. White and Mr. Clarke but they were invariably known as 'Knocker' and 'Nobby' to each other. 'Knocker' White was a Cockney from London, had a cleft palate, and spoke English with a Cockney accent; 'Nobby' Clarke was a Plymouth man and had a rich West Country burr to his voice. They had given me the freedom of their station and I had spent many an afternoon with them drinking endless cups of Indian tea and being initiated into their immense experience and knowledge of ships and the sea.

I told her all this in detail and described these warm-hearted men at length, because I noticed how far out of herself my account was taking her. I even made her laugh by imitating Mr. White's voice, cleft palate and all. These two men, I told her, knew every whaler by sight and recorded all their movements in and out of harbour minutely in their log-books. They would be the first to see the *Kurt Hansen* returning to harbour, the first to tell whether she was coming in with harpooned whales for the slipway to the factory, or for lying up in her berth at the main quay. That was important, because as a rule we would be in and out several times before docking for the weekend some time on Saturday afternoon. I am certain they would be delighted to telephone news of the *Kurt Hansen*'s movements to her at the hotel and even, if she liked the idea, give her access at any time to their station.

She liked the idea so much that she thanked me warmly exclaiming, "Oh, Cousin, you've been very good to me."

Since it was Sunday we found Mr. White and Mr. Clarke in their best uniforms, their 1914–18 war ribbons bright against the dark navy-blue, having a lively game of conjecture with each other over the ships showing up fast after one another, as they tended to do on a Sunday in order to have an early call on the pilot's services on the Monday.

They called de la Buschagne's daughter "Missie", made a great fuss of her (obviously greatly taken by her beauty), produced one of those extraordinary fruit cakes that the English love, a great assortment of biscuits, and made several pots of tea as red as the Limpopo in flood. Then they insisted on her looking at the ships through their telescope, and recited the names of their ports of origin, departure and destination to her: Tilbury, Newport News, Valparaiso, Auckland, Yokohama, Saigon, Sydney, Genoa, Surabaya, Copenhagen, Mandalay and Southampton. Finally, they assured her that every movement of the *Kurt Hansen* would be reported to her by telephone and that,whenever she liked, the signal station was open for her use. As Mr. White would have it: "You can make this your front parlour by the sea, Missie, whenever you like."

The warm goodbyes could not have made that part of my day happier or more successful. The feeling left me only momentarily when, wishing me goodbye on the hotel verandah, she said: "Take care of yourself, Cousin, and him too if you can, for he'll need it."

CHAPTER FOURTEEN

Homeward Bound

.

I WENT back to my ship as the sun went down in a far better frame of mind than when I had left in the morning at the first sign of its light. I even ate a supper which astonished and delighted Leif and was on deck at nine with the Captain, to watch de la Buschagne come on board, his nine millimetre Mauser slung on a shoulder and one hand holding the strap to keep it in position; in the other he carried a cheap little suitcase. Thor Larsen must have noticed the gun, and though I believe it was the first time he had ever carried an armed passenger, he did not comment on it but welcomed de la Buschagne warmly on board and took him off at once to take my place in the cabin below. I could not tell whether de la Buschagne even saw me or not, for he did not greet me. He had eyes only for the Captain, and there was a light in them which made me suspect that for the first time in his life he was not only excited but exalted, carrying himself like some Old Testament seer about to receive a new revelation of the God he served.

He was up and dressed as soon as the Captain and I were and in the wheelhouse to see Gorgeous deftly guide the *Kurt Hansen* out to a regular sea. He proved himself a good sailor, and was not sea-sick. When I climbed up the fore-top at first light, installed myself for the day in the crow's-nest and started to look about me, the first thing I saw below on deck was de la Buschagne staring up at me. He had taken off his wide-brimmed hat because the *Kurt Hansen*'s speed created a brisk wind, and was holding it in his hand. He was dressed in his hunting clothes, a khaki whip-cord bush jacket and trousers and heelless shoes that, I was to discover, he had made out of leather he had cured and tanned himself. He looked strikingly incongruous on the *Kurt Hansen*'s deck, with a whaling crew all round him getting the

ship ready for action. But on his face I saw the same exalted and expectant look of the evening before.

He was soon joined by Thor Larsen and taken off to the bow to watch the harpoon gun being stripped, and to inspect its mechanism. Thor Larsen went again and again through a pantomime of swinging, aiming, and firing it so realistically that I was almost surprised not to hear the gun boom. When he was certain de la Buschagne understood, he made him grip the gun and go through the motions himself. I was amazed then how instantly our visitor seemed to belong and become one of us, so certain were his actions and so authoritative his stance behind the gun. Thor Larsen himself was obviously surprised and impressed, because I saw him slap de la Buschagne approvingly on the shoulder and take him down below for breakfast.

They had hardly gone when 'Mlangeni appeared and seated himself on deck, legs wide apart and his broad back against the hatch. He did not at once look up and wave at me as he had always done but sat there, head bowed, picking half-heartedly at the plate in front of him. Finally he looked up and waved at me. Grateful as I was, I knew that, despite the sun and the healing blue of the day, he was feeling black and dishonoured inside. When de la Buschagne reappeared and, although startled to see a black man on deck, would have spoken to him, 'Mlangeni made it impossible by keeping his eyes on his plate. As soon as he had finished his food he gathered up his plate and mug, went to the *Kurt Hansen*'s side, and spat into the sea as his dead "brother" Jack had once years before exhorted me to do on leaving Thor Larsen's presence.

Not long after I spotted our first whale. It was a great blue one and it took Thor Larsen until four in the afternoon to harpoon her and get her alongside the ship. He had made de la Buschagne sit on the gun platform just where the ladder from the deck joined it, because the platform was too small to carry another man who had not yet got his sea-legs and could easily, therefore, get in the Captain's way. But it was a place where de la Buschagne, tall as he was, could sit down and follow every detail of the real hunt and kill. When the gun boomed, however, it was too much for him. In an instant he was on his feet,

watching the yellow line snaking at the back of the whale to hit truly home. At that he waved his hat triumphantly in the air and called out something in Thor Larsen's ears.

Certain that his quarry was properly hooked, he turned to de la Buschagne. I thought they were about to embrace but he took his guest's outstretched hand in both his, and then made him stand beside the gun while he reloaded it. Even when that was done they stood there, side by side, until the whale after one last great "flurry" lay alongside, sulphur bottom up, in a crimson shroud of its own blood.

So big was the whale, so late the day, and so empty the placid sea where I had searched in vain for another blow, that Thor Larsen turned about for Port Natal with the intention of dropping his quarry at first light and being out at sea again before the daylight. All the same I stayed in the fore-top as was our custom until sundown, looking round about me for any intelligence that might help us the following day.

As the sun went down I went below to join Leif, Gorgeous and 'Mlangeni for a gramophone session on the foreward hatch. As I was about to sit down with them, de la Buschagne came by on his way below, calabash pipe in hand, smoking.

"This is better than shooting elephant, isn't it, Cousin?" he called out, the light of the chase in his eyes.

"Perhaps," was all I could say, so distasteful was his attitude to me.

Gorgeous had put on the gramophone first Strauss's "Death and Transfiguration", and then Verdi's "Requiem". It was great and tragic music, resolved not in the abolition of the tragic but in its acceptance and, through acceptance, the discovery of meaning in suffering. As I listened, and watched the stars come out and the night deepen, it did me a great deal of good and made the *Kurt Hansen*'s deck a natural temple. Nothing could have served 'Mlangeni better either, for in tears it took the bitterness out of him, made him "string his beads" and accomplish his "necklace of sorrow", to hang around his proud and wounded spirit.

I put out my hand and pressed his arm—and there we were once more four-square against whatever life had ahead for us.

So reassuring was the feeling that I had no desire to go to the saloon and end it by facing de la Buschagne. When the music was over I went to supper with Leif in his galley and didn't go to my couch in the saloon until it was late.

I felt somewhat ashamed then of my judgement of de la Buschagne because, as I went quietly past the clear way of the saloon, the lights were full on and de la Buschagne was kneeling on the floor, his grey head buried in the Captain's chair, his hands clasped devoutly before him, his black Bible open on the saloon table, saying his prayers. I stood there for a moment and he sighed deeply, stood up, and saw me.

Briefly we looked in silence at each other before he said quietly in Afrikaans, "Cousin, good night, sleep tight." On that note he went through the curtains to his place in my bunk in the Captain's cabin.

Twice more, on the Tuesday and the Wednesday, we had an almost exact repetition of our experience on Monday, on each occasion taking an outsize blue whale to its last home in the owner's factory. After the third, Thor Larsen announced that in his opinion de la Buschagne was now sufficiently prepared to have a shot at the very first Caesar that came along. He did this unaware of the unanimous disapproval of his decision among his crew. After all, to them whaling was a straight-forward business and every whale caught made a financial difference to them because of the liberal system of bonuses paid for each catch by the owners. For that reason the harpooner among them was always the best and most experienced gunner, and by no means always the Captain. The news that Thor Larsen was allowing this incongruous stranger to try and shoot a sperm, still the most valuable of all whaler's quarries, struck them as utterly irresponsible and unworthy. They were all convinced that de la Buschagne, who had never been at sea until a few days before and certainly never fired a harpoon gun, would miss and—as they all put it—"miss at our expense".

Leif and I did what we could to counter the sudden discord by telling them of de la Buschagne's unique career as a hunter and great reputation as a natural shot. They scorned the argument, remained unconvinced, dissatisfied and irritated with

295

their Captain, though too frightened of him openly to protest. Suddenly we became an unhappy ship, charged with sullen electricity. I had never before seen our Norwegians so moody. Often I saw them stand up from their work as Thor Larsen and his guest, now inseparable, went past, giving them a dark look which one would have believed impossible from such blue eyes.

But the Captain, so intuitive in all else, was strangely impervious to the change of mood in his ship. He was so absorbed in de la Buschagne that, seeing them together, for all their differences in appearance, race and vocation, they looked like a pair of fateful Siamese twins. I think they themselves felt that their lives had been joined together by fate and only some mystery of chance and circumstance could put their union asunder. That knowledge gave them an exaggerated sense of privilege denied to ordinary men, and a feeling of being above the common law of life which seemed, to me, at its most intense that Thursday morning when at dawn we dropped our third giant blue whale at the slipway.

It was an odd morning for a winter in Port Natal, being unusually warm and close. I myself, in the fore-top just for the fun of seeing the *Kurt Hansen* into the harbour, had not at all liked the way the sun came up over the sea. There was neither cloud in the sky nor wind, yet out in the east, where the sun was burning, there was something in the atmosphere which blurred its winter clarity, seeming to slow down its movement, making it rise heavily and turning it yellow as the yolk of a broken egg.

When I came down on deck I found everyone complaining of the airlessness and warmth of the morning. As in a hurry we were just about to cast off, a messenger came running down from the factory as fast as he could, waving a white paper at the ship. It was a message from the owner's representative. The most alarming weather reports from ships and meteorological stations were pouring into the port office. The glass was falling in a melodramatic way. There was no doubt that a cyclone of unusual force was moving in from Madagascar and Mauritius. For the first time in known history it was feared a cyclone might hit Port Natal itself, and Thor Larsen was strongly urged not to

put to sea. Far from being alarmed at the news, the Captain was delighted.

Had he not been right about that feeling in his bones that a reckoning with Caesar was close at hand? Sperm always came in the teeth of storms, the greater the storm the greater the sperm, and here—he waved the note on company paper he had just received like a flag for battle at de la Buschagne and me—was confirmation that one of the greatest storms in history was near. Of course, he would not dream of missing such an opportunity. We would just go straight out to sea and find our Caesar.

"One moment, Cousin," de la Buschagne called to me as I turned to go back to my post and Thor Larsen walked across the deck to go to his bridge. "Why does the Captain say great sperm come with storms?"

"There's no exact why," I told him. "He thinks it's just so, in the mysterious way of the sea. He once told me that in stormy weather the great squids on which the sperm feeds are forced out of hiding in the valleys where they live at the bottom of the sea, and come up for air. It is easier then for the sperm to attack and eat them."

He would have liked me, I know, to stay and answer more questions but at that moment there was a roar from the Captain, already on the bridge, for de la Buschagne to join him.

Soon we slipped away smartly from the factory side and turned about deftly into the main channel of the Bay, only to be held up by two large cargo ships, deep in the water with freight, coming in to dock. First I was astonished and then uneasy when I recognized them as ships I had seen leaving port just before we entered it at dawn that morning. They could have turned about only because their agents, as a result of the latest weather reports, had recalled them. They were ships of about ten thousand gross each, one of the Clan, the other of the Harrison line, both reputable companies of great experience. I knew they would not have turned their ships back without good reason in these desperate post-war days of cut-throat competition at sea. I comforted myself with the thought that all sailors, not excluding Mr. White and Mr. Clarke, had always said that

in a great storm they would prefer to be in a whaler than any other ship, particularly ships deep with cargo. But this comfort did not last long, for as we came down the final channel to cross the bar, I saw from all sides that the whalers of our fleet were making for the harbour.

My first thought was that our fleet had been unusually lucky and come in all together with record catches. But my glasses soon showed them to be empty-handed. Their falling barometers and the good sense of their Captains must have been the incentive that sent them thus running for shelter.

But even this did not bother our Captain, once he had re-assured himself that they were without exception empty-handed. I could see him pointing out one after the other to de la Buschagne, laughing because they were without catches whereas he had just dropped so rich a one. When one of them, not believing that even the *Kurt Hansen* could be so foolhardy, closed in on us and bellowed through a megaphone at the bridge to ask whether Thor Larsen had looked at his barometer, he just laughed all the more, telling them they could run back to mother earth, but he was going out for sperm.

The moment we were out in the roadstead Thor Larsen set a course almost due east, as far as I could judge, on a bearing pointed half-way between the southernmost tip of Madagascar and Mauritius, the quarter in fact in which the cyclone was most likely to be spinning. From there on the day began to change rapidly. The sky lost its blue, became a milky white, then sulphur yellow and finally a murky brown with strange streaks of orange in it. The atmosphere became so heavy even in the fore-top and so solid in front of my eyes that I found myself trying to move it by brushing it constantly with a kind of reflex action of my hands from the front of my eyes. By noon the sun was so veiled and morose that I could look it reprovingly in the face with my naked eyes.

The sea itself was completely smooth, like some kind of silk, and the weight of air ironed out the great Indian Ocean swell almost level with the brown, dull surface, until it had hardly any spirit left to rise. At noon we saw several blue-whale blows, and hard on them in seven different places seven giant torpedo

bodies leaping, like salmon, high into the air and coming down with a splash that raised fountains of pure white water. It was rare, and almost miraculous, to watch a hundred tons or more of warm flesh and blood take to the air as easily as sparkling sprats, hang there gun-metal bright for a moment before falling back into the sulky sea. But the sight was also sobering because I realised that even the whales were finding it too oppressive below, and coming up for more and more air. Then I pointed and shouted: "There! There! They blow!"

Usually there was an immediate response from the helm to my shout as the *Kurt Hansen* swung at once like a greyhound rounding on a hare, towards the direction in which I pointed. But this time she kept steadily on her course. I thought the atmosphere was so heavy and thick that my shout had not reached the bridge and shouted again as loudly as I possibly could. I drew only a loud bellow from the Captain on the bridge and,turning to look down,saw he was beckoning me impatiently.

Almost dazed with unbelief at such an unusual reaction, I hurried below. I could see at once that every one about on deck was as mystified as I was.

"What whales blow, Eyes? Blue or sperm, quick?" Thor Larsen asked me, his intense grey eyes as full of fire as I had ever seen them.

"Blue, sir," I told him, then went on to say that I had not only seen them blow, but seven of them leaping high out of the brown water like salmon.

"Ah, trying shake sea-bee and barnacles from sulphur bottoms," he commented, highly satisfied. "Good sign. Always bellies itch more when storm coming. Like old men with their rheumatism, not?"

He laughed at that as I stood there unable to comment.

He searched his mind for words for his next thought as he often did. "Look, Eyes," he told me finally, grinning, as if he was well aware of the enormity of the gamble he was taking and excited by all he was wagering against reason, experience, and traditional practice. "Today Thor Larsen not interested in blue whale or any other damn whale. Only sperm. Great sperm soon to come and you not to shout until sperm blows, not?"

I nodded, too amazed to speak and too much aware of how such conduct would provoke a crew already irritated and highly critical of their Captain.

"Good, my Eyes." He put his hand on my shoulder and pressed it as warmly as he had ever done. "Always I not forget you good, damn good. And today you find Caesar for me and Mr. Hunter, my friend? Then to go, quick, my Eyes!"

There was such an Elizabethan finality and something so valedictory in his tone and action that I was moved by it, as well as by the warm unexpected tribute which went with it.

I went from the bridge and across the deck without looking at anyone, ignoring even a loud whisper from Nils Ruud, who was standing at his winch, obstinate in his disapproval of his Captain and anxious to feed it with the latest news. I went up the ladder and had just settled myself into position when the whole sky began to groan, creak and squeak as if the imponderable lead of the atmosphere were too much and about to force the heavens to crack. At the same time the *Kurt Hansen* gave a sudden little jump up and sideways, like some living thing that had nearly trodden on a snake on the road. Perceptibly surprised, her impudent nose went into the air, a shiver went through her which I felt even in the crow's-nest, and she came down again into the water with an audible complaint from the metal. I saw then the strangest movement of sea-water that I had ever seen: a series of what seemed little more than great ripples rolling towards us out of the east in a long unbroken line from north to south. Even the greatest of the Indian Ocean swells that I had so far experienced had never shown such continuity and perfect coordination of movement. Then the ripples without altering direction or purpose would divide into shorter segments, curving and breaking independently of one another. But these ripples presented a united front as they rolled towards us over a brown sea, with a dull metallic glint on top and a line of black shadow in their wake. They could mean only one thing: they were the silent, swift-footed scouts of a greater disturbance so dense, single and compact that it had hit the ocean like a great rock hurled into it by an Odyssean blow. I had no doubt that we had crossed the far frontier of one of those storms

300

I've already described when I saw my first sperm three seasons before.

I looked astern, and between the *Kurt Hansen* and the sun I could just make out the mist of pearl of some blue whale dissolving in the dense air. Out there it looked so calm, bright, and normal that when I resumed searching the ocean ahead and saw how fast the sky was losing lustre without a single cloud to account for it, I had an overwhelming conviction that we were heading in the wrong direction. Strangely, there was no wind to explain either the great ripples or that strange moaning sound in the sky. The air remained heavy and without movement and yet all the time the ripples rapidly grew into swells which increased in stature until the *Kurt Hansen*, going all out, was riding them high and sliding fast down their smooth sides to pick great sprays of white in their sombre valleys. Meanwhile the wailing, like Valkyries massing somewhere beyond the sullen sun to bemoan their losses in a battle for Valhalla, grew louder in my ears, making me feel extraordinarily lonely and exposed in my tub high in the air. When right ahead low on the horizon in the east the sky went a strange distorted black and became visibly tormented and in violent movement, as if I were watching the prancing shadows thrown up by a great ring of dancing devils, the feeling soon became something akin to a nameless fear. And by then the new swell rolling down on us out of the east had grown truly great and terrible. We hit it with such increasing force that the explosion of the impact scattered spray right up to the mast head. I thought the Captain would at any moment reduce speed if not turn about. But one glance at the bridge where he stood with de la Buschagne beside him, both looking more than ever like partners in a singular fate, showed me that he had no such intention and was enjoying himself hugely.

Far away to the south-east against the band of shifting shadow on the horizon, the curtain of the day had a black hem fluttering in the draught of a weird whistling. It was there that I saw the unmistakable, sharply angled, white blow of a sperm. It came out of the dark sea with such purpose, speed and power that it passed before my wondering eyes like a shooting star at

twilight, before gathering itself into a ball of mist, light as thistledown, and slowly vanishing. It was the greatest blow by sperm I had ever seen, and even as I shouted and pointed, the thought "Caesar, at last!" flashed into my mind.

The response of the *Kurt Hansen* was immediate. She swung from east-north-east to south-east as fast as she had ever done and steadied herself on the quarter at which I was still pointing. Only then did I turn to look at the bridge expecting the Captain to summon me for a detailed report but he signalled back that it was unnecessary.

I warmed at this sign of his confidence and, in order to show him that I was convinced we were at last after the real quarry, gave him a "thumbs-up" sign which drew a grin and another approving wave from him. I was about to resume my watch on Caesar when away to the north-east I saw twelve more sperm blowing. I felt in duty bound to call out and direct my Captain's attention to them. But as I expected he was not interested in them and signalled me to concentrate on the first blow. All the same, the news obviously pleased him greatly, for it seemed confirmation of what he had always firmly contended; that sperm not only kept close company with storms but also travelled in schools, with the exception, of course, of the Caesar who preferred to "go it alone" and hold the rest of his kind at their distance.

Fifteen minutes later, almost exactly in the same place, Caesar announced himself with another series of great blows. It needed only the slightest of corrections from Gorgeous at the wheel to send us pounding down on to the spot like a racehorse coming into the straight. By then I was myself so absorbed in the excitement of so unusual a hunt that I hardly noticed how the *Kurt Hansen*, on her new course, was catching the huge swell still mounting steadily sideways. She was pitching deep into dark valleys of water, but as she pitched, rolling so far over that instinctively I gripped the sides of my tub in case I fell out into the water. There I could see not one black tri-sail of a shark but a dozen or more like those of a convoy of death keeping station on its flagship. I could tell from the movements and stance of the crew at action-stations that they too had been drawn out of

all irritation and doubt into their Captain's mood. Thor Larsen possessed a dark genius for making all men who served with him, whether they liked it or not, into an extension of his own will.

The next time Caesar blew, he was barely three-quarters of a mile away and still almost in exactly the same place. This was so unusual that my direction was challenged from the bridge and a deck-hand sent running to question me. He had great difficulty getting up the rope ladder, so fast and deep was the ship pitching and heeling. When he reached me he made no effort to climb over the top but hung there rather precariously while I reassured him and gave him precise details of Caesar's position and extraordinary behaviour. There was still no wind, just this immovable, heavy air of which I have spoken, but such a moaning and groaning was going on that we had difficulty in hearing each other.

All the time we talked I kept on looking at the place where Caesar was blowing. We had just finished when I saw his wonderful, fluked, butterfly tail appear on the crest of the great black swell barely a quarter of a mile away. He sounded steeply and seemed to me to be in a great hurry. Yet I suspected that with all that moaning of the universe and those walls of black sea-water, like mounds of some archaic fortifications, between him and us it was not the sound of the *Kurt Hansen*'s racing approach that alarmed him. He had private reasons of his own for diving as fast as he had done and in the same area. Out of all that Thor Larsen had told me about sperm and his eternal battle with the giant squid, "the monster of evil" as the Captain had years ago called it, the conviction came to me that one of the greatest sperm bulls in history was behaving in such a manner because in some deep-sea valley below us he had located evil of unimagined proportions, perhaps tempted out of its submarine fortifications by the storm just over the rim of the horizon, and this was Caesar now engaged in the most formidable encounter of his long lone life.

So great was my faith in this conclusion that I told the deck-hand, "Tell the Captain that when we reach the exact spot where the sperm sounded I'll raise my hand." I hesitated, appalled for a moment by my own temerity, but my firm

conviction drove me on to add, "Tell him I suggest we stop there and wait. He'll be up soon and not far away, judging by his strange behaviour. Tell him this is a whale like no other we have ever hunted!"

Even so, I was relieved when I saw the Captain signal that he had not only understood but approved my message. I saw him almost at once then ring for half speed to the engine room, hand over to 'Papa' bosun and Gorgeous, and go down on deck followed by de la Buschagne. I was amazed how well the latter walked the heaving deck and climbed on to the harpoon platform which now, with the ship's reduced speed, was no longer shipping either water or spray. Even so the ship was dipping so deeply into the swell that the water rose to within a foot or two of the bow's brim. I knew it was going to be one of the most difficult shots in whaling history even if we got the chance to harpoon at all. But what was going to be even more difficult in that sea of mountains would be playing the whale and getting it lashed alongside. I dismissed the thought as quickly as I could because that way was exposed the madness of what Thor Larsen was trying to do. Instead I drew comfort from the sight of the Captain's confident stand by the harpoon gun, his testing it and aiming it this way and that, as at ease as if doing no more than giving a demonstration in the great tranquil harbour behind us.

I had a return of misgiving, as I am certain all the crew had, when he handed over the butt of the gun to de la Buschagne. But even that lightened when I saw this singular old man, his bush shirt lightly flapping in the air of the *Kurt Hansen*'s reduced speed, his hat deeply pulled down about his ears, the glowering light like yellow oil on the snakeskin band about its crown, incongruous-looking as ever yet repeating the Captain's exact movements without hesitation as if he had done nothing else since boyhood.

They had barely established themselves in the bows when we hit the whale's immense slick, satin on the swell, and as arranged I had to signal to the bridge to stop engines. We lay there for some seven minutes with no vibration from the engines to remind us that the *Kurt Hansen* had power of her own. She lay there like the powerless plaything of those monumental swells.

With the moaning of the air unabated and the shadow-show of dancing devils on the horizon growing higher and wilder, it felt as if we were utterly abandoned. Even the sharks had gone, and although I looked everywhere I could see no signs of their fins. Between the moaning of the sky I heard the rustle, swish and whistle of the heavy smooth swell brushing and rebrushing urgently against the *Kurt Hansen*'s sides.

Then suddenly, almost straight ahead, less than a hundred yards away and right on the summit of a long black range of water, the blow came again. It came from behind a swell with such force that despite the moaning in the air I could hear it hiss like a volcanic geyser. My shout was still ringing in my ears when I saw a range of swell following the first but rising to such a frightening height that despite the sullen light it grew translucent as it rose upward. Rising with it, deep inside the amber water I saw from end to end the body of a great bull sperm, head up, tail down, stretched out like a fish in aspic. Hard on this there was a swirl of water as the swell reached its peak and a ruff of foam, the colour of coffee and milk, unfolded all along the velvet crest in which imperial Caesar lay blowing again a great but muffled blow.

This time every one in the ship saw its blow and the *Kurt Hansen*, already leaping forward at full speed from my first shout, was fast closing the narrow gap between Caesar and ourselves. But so quickly was the swell rushing, like a wave of crude oil, towards us and blocking the view below, that I doubt if anyone saw what I saw. I saw Caesar's great square battering head, his jaws slightly parted and the corner of his long mouth upturned as if in a grin of triumph. His dreadnought head seemed covered, as I thought, with giant sea-weed from the jungle in the ocean valley from which he had just come. But when instantly I put the ship's glasses on him I saw that they were long writhing tentacles trying to get a hold, or purchase, on that platinum crown of Caesar's. They failed, and during the seconds when I had Caesar in the focus of the glasses I saw them being sucked like some kind of deep-sea spaghetti into his mouth. I had no doubt that we had found Caesar in his moment of victory devouring a great cephalopod of evil for his

high tea. That accounted for the strange muffled blow: and also for the fact that he lay there wallowing in front of us singularly preoccupied and unobservant like a ship of war, battle over, with engines stopped.

Thor Larsen had taken in the situation immediately and I could see him stand at de la Buschagne's left shoulder with uplifted hand ready to give the signal to fire. De la Buschagne, legs well apart and, because of his great height, somewhat crouched, had swung the harpoon on the place where Caesar had just slid down the slope of the swell rolling towards us. As the swell took us, lifting us rapidly until it held us aloft on its crest, there was Caesar rising on the slope of the next great wave, busy completing his swallow. Again I was astonished how naturally and expertly the harpoon gun in de la Buschagne's hands followed Caesar's movement. Just before Caesar came to the crest of another lull of black water, Thor Larsen dropped his raised arm and shouted so loud that I heard it in the fore-top. "Take him!"

The gun boomed and there followed that exciting serpent-like flight, mamba-swift, of harpoon head and yellow rope through the air and above the swelling mound of water. As always, it looked as if the harpoon had been aimed too high, but at the last moment it fell quickly. Just as Caesar was lifted high into the air like a conqueror by his own element, the harpoon struck him in the middle of his long battle-worthy body. Unfortunately it hit too low to break his spine, but considering the conditions it was miraculously well aimed. There was an explosion like a bomb against Caesar's side just as he started to slide over the steep crest of the wave and immediately vanished into the sea behind. I had never seen the slack in the rope of the harpoon run out quicker. Before Nils Ruud could unwind his winch the buffer spring at the end of the *Kurt Hansen*'s derrick was stretched taut and dangerously quivering. Caesar, fatally wounded, had not dived straight ahead in line with the ship's course but gone off at high speed at a right angle to it, moving with such power that for the moment the *Kurt Hansen* was being pulled slowly broadside to the swell, labouring with her head held well down.

But what horrified me most was that, when the war-head within the harpoon exploded and showed us all how well Caesar had been hit, de la Buschagne, exalted and triumphant, turned his back on his quarry in the sea and put both his hands on Thor Larsen's shoulders shouting: "I got him, I got him, my friend!"

I was as astonished as I was dismayed by this action, for I would have thought he would have been prevented from making so foolish a move by his hunter's training. One of the most elementary rules is that one does not turn one's back on one's quarry until one has walked up to it, gun at the ready, and made certain it is dead. The greater and more dangerous the quarry the more imperative the rule. The Captain, too, was for a moment tricked out of his professional self, and delighted to put both his broad harpooner's hands on de la Buschagne's shoulders.

They stood there together, a pair of prodigal brothers, in the bows, unaware that as the *Kurt Hansen* dipped low a wall of eager black water was rising above them. Normally the *Kurt Hansen* would have risen to take it like a chamois but with Caesar desperate with death, pulling it deeply down and also athwart the weather, the buffer-spring of the derrick (which could take a strain of twenty tons or more) snapped, releasing a sound like the vibrations of some outsize tuning-fork loud on the morning air.

At once the ship lurched awkwardly, stumbled in its stride, head half on to the wall of water. I saw both Thor Larsen and de la Buschagne thrown off balance, fling their hands out wildly for support from the harpoon gun. They missed, and the sea came green over the bow washing deeply over the deck so that Nils Ruud only saved himself by embracing the levers of his winch.

When the *Kurt Hansen*, shuddering, shook itself free of the sea again, Thor Larsen and de la Buschagne had vanished. I looked about and astern of the *Kurt Hansen* but there was no sign of them. Then, aloft between me and the yellow afternoon sun on the summit of a swell rolling majestically towards the far-off coast of Africa, I distinctly saw de la Buschagne's hat with its snakeskin band, floating away from us.

Without hope I shouted at the bridge and pointed. But there was no one on the bridge except Gorgeous skilfully doing the best he could against the sea and Caesar. 'Papa' bosun had left it already, carrying in his hand the axe which was always kept for emergencies in a bracket against the wall behind the wheel. Going as fast as his frame and the heaving sea would let him, he went to join Nils Ruud where the harpoon cable was at last beginning to unwind, smoking, from the winch's drums. Already another swell was bearing down on us. Whalers say that the sea grades its waves in ascending scales of seven. This swell must have been the seventh, and I had a feeling of doom as I watched it coming towards us, with such an easy and oily approach. It was utterly impossible for us even to think of turning about to search for the Captain and de la Buschagne. Thank Heaven 'Papa' bosun was as strong as he was determined. He raised his axe swiftly, brought it down fiercely at least four times because the manilla cable was about to meet the eye of the hawser of steel which was coiled around the rest of the drum. Then, mercifully, the cut cable vanished from the deck and shot with the speed of a bullet through the hole in the gun platform, still dripping with sea-water.

Immediately the *Kurt Hansen*, down by the bow and listing heavily to port, bobbed upright, her old resilient self, just in time to take the giant swell without shipping too much water. Before the next onslaught Gorgeous had her facing the sea, nose dead on. With her speed reduced to a quarter she began to ride the swell as easily as a duck some troubled water. For the moment we were out of danger, but one glance ahead showed me how far we still had to go before we were safe. I was deeply amazed to observe since I had last watched the eastern horizon how high and wide the whirling, fluttering, ragged shadows dancing there had risen. Now, as far as I could see in front of us there was nothing but range upon ascending range of black-brown mountains of water with great valleys of shadows in between, like the foothills of some oceanic Himalayas. So bad was the prospect, in fact, that I knew I had to leave my fore-top immediately if I was ever to get down that day. There was no duty now to keep me there, and no sooner did I realise this than

I climbed out with great difficulty, if not hazard, and made my way slowly below. 'Papa' bosun was back on the bridge with Gorgeous, and I went straight up to tell him how things ahead looked from on top. He just nodded and spoke to Gorgeous in Norwegian.

On the peak of the last wave 'Papa' bosun rang for full speed ahead, Gorgeous brought the wheel full round and the first in the next ascending order of seven waves had not yet taken us when the *Kurt Hansen*'s upturned nose started swinging around. The fourth wave in the series took us half astern; the last, with us running straight before it, lifted us and seemed to carry us up and on as easily as a surfboard towards Port Natal and straight into the setting sun. Somehow I knew then that the *Kurt Hansen* and we who were left in her were out of danger, so easily did she ride, thrust and parry the great seas driving after her.

But what of Thor Larsen and de la Buschagne? There could be no question of searching the sea for them in those conditions. And if they had been alive, swimming or floating in the waters, I would have spotted them before I came down.

Sick and sad at heart, I went below to the saloon. Leif was waiting for me. For a long while we did not talk, but he sat there with me and because I was shivering he took out Thor Larsen's tantalus, poured some rum from a decanter into a mug of boiling coffee and made me drink it. Only then did we talk the platitudes of the great recurring finalities of life like birth, love and death, forever old and yet forever new. They have, these platitudes of tragedy, all the force of the original, as if they had never occurred to mankind before.

When at last Leif left me to go to his galley because he said the crew, cold and stricken at heart too with tragedy, would need the hottest and best supper he could give them, I sat there staring into space. I realised then that I had never known how much I could miss the Captain. Thinking thus, I saw first his lone sperm-tooth paper-weight standing on the plush of the saloon tablecloth. Beyond it, in the corner underneath the bracket containing Thor Larsen's manuals and game books, was de la Buschagne's gun garlanded with his bandolier. I

choked back my feelings,and an instinct that I could not refuse made me pick up the paper-weight and the gun and bandolier and go up on deck with them.

It was dark outside. The stars and Milky Way were visible, but in the haze spread around the storm like pollen their light was blurred and oddly yellow. The moaning sound had gone from the sky but the black air was loud with the swish and hiss of mountainous water thrusting by us. The *Kurt Hansen* was riding the sea superbly and leaving its gallant mark in a trail of phosphorescent steam behind her. There were no lights except a glow at the mast-head from our riding-lamp and another fainter one over the compass in the bridge. I went to the side of the ship then,and after a moment of awesome hesitation tossed de la Buschagne's gun and bandolier into the sea, feeling that they belonged there. I was about to toss Thor Larsen's tooth after them when some disproportion in the act stopped me. We had had already enough of disproportion. Our Captain now had Caesar to keep him company and that should be enough.

Alone I stood there for a long time, feeling calmer both for what I had done and for what I had not done. Though still heavy with grief almost beyond endurance, and despite the strange windless storm raging around me, I recovered some of the old feeling of belonging that I had experienced on my first night out at sea in the *Kurt Hansen*. It was as if I were no longer trying to be what 'Mlangeni had suggested at the beginning of the season, "a little star out of course". Rather was I coming back through this tragedy into the progression of time and order of day, night and seasons. How long I was there I do not know, but when I went into the saloon Leif was waiting to give me my supper. I told him what I had done before I sat down.

"Good, Pete," he told me simply, patting my shoulder.

"But this," I said, taking the sperm tooth out of my pocket: "I wanted to send this after him as well but I couldn't."

He nodded his head in understanding and I went on: "I thought I'd give this to 'Mlangeni. I thought it would somehow make Thor Larsen and 'Mlangeni right with each other. Things were never as they should have been between them."

"I agree," Leif said. "Thor Larsen has no living relatives.

I believe you and that strange old man who died with him this evening were the nearest to him that he ever had. So do what you will with it."

Later in the evening Leif brought Gorgeous, just relieved at the wheel, and 'Mlangeni to join me for more coffee and rum in the saloon. We talked little, but just being together seemed to break up the load of what had happened into four separate parts, thus making it easier to shoulder. Sometime towards midnight we mentioned the future. I think Gorgeous did so first, stammering a bit after the strain of all he had been through. No one knew better than I how wild, wide, high and abandoned had been the water coming against us, and how expertly Gorgeous first had rid us of Caesar, and then turned dangerously about to run with the sea. He said now that he had done with whaling and would not renew his contract. He'd give up his flat in Port Natal and go to Europe, at last, to listen to truly great music before it was too late.

"I would," Leif agreed. "You've long owed it to yourself."

Gorgeous answered with rare self-knowledge, "This time I don't think I'll go back on myself." He turned to 'Mlangeni. "But I'll miss you and your teasing, Langenay, old friend."

"Auck, 'Nkosan Gorgeous," 'Mlangeni replied, " 'Mlangeni will always be there at Icoco, to keep this one true thought alive for you."

"At Icoco, 'Mlangeni?" I asked.

"Yes, my 'Nkosan," 'Mlangeni replied, his deep voice full with feeling. "I shall ask at once for permission to go back to the Amageba. I have been here too long already."

I was moved by his use of the word "Amageba". It is the ancient name of the Amazulu for themselves and means the shadows left by the departed sun which rest on the mountain tops in the west. It expressed in a single image everything that was best in 'Mlangeni's heart and mind.

"Then when you go, 'Mlangeni, please take this with you." I took Thor Larsen's sperm tooth out of my pocket and put it in his hand.

He stared at it unbelievingly before asking, "All this for me, 'Nkosan?"

311

"Yes," I told him. "Leif agrees with me that our Captain would have wanted you to keep it to show the Amageba. It's a memorial of all you've done, and of all the fires you've lit and kept bright all these long years on the great water."

"Auck, 'Nkosan," 'Mlangeni said and bowed his great head.

"And you, Leif?" I asked quickly. "What will you do?"

"I shall carry on as before, Pete," he answered slowly. "I have some years to go before I'll be free of all my responsibilities."

"No, Leif," Gorgeous protested. "I'd chuck it. You've done more than your bit. You deserve a break."

"The break for some of us is doing what's nearest at hand," Leif answered steadily.

Steaming at half speed,we made the roadstead of Port Natal at noon the next day. We had it to ourselves and lay there riding the biggest swell the people of the city had ever seen. The spray from the surf between us and the land rose so high and thick that I felt, still with the sense of death strongly in me, as though it were the seventh veil of the ultimate mystery. We lay there all day. Towards sunset,with the veil of spray between us and the city smoking with rainbow colour, 'Papa' bosun was tempted to run for the harbour longing, as we all were, to unload the *Kurt Hansen* of the heavy news she carried, and reluctant also to have another black night outside the harbour to join the dark inside us all. However, he wisely decided that nimble as the *Kurt Hansen* was, we should not run across the bar before the swell had abated somewhat.

All that long afternoon in spite of the spray I could with my glasses pick out the "Ailsa Craig" on the sea front and wondered, heavy at heart, about de la Buschagne's daughter. How was I to break the news to her and what was to become of her? I was certain that Mr. White and Mr. Clarke would at once have reported to her our arrival in the roadstead, for they'd have known how the cyclone alert, published with banner heads in all the papers, would have alarmed her.

I was to learn afterwards that that was exactly what had happened. Mr. Clarke, focusing his glasses on us and methodically examining the *Kurt Hansen* as she stood in the roadstead

had noticed the damage to the forrard derrick, but supposing it to be nothing much had made no mention of it when telephoning "Missie".

She had hurried down at once to the signals station, frightened, at first, by the thunder of the sea and the way the enormous swell tossed us high and then sucked us low but overjoyed to see the *Kurt Hansen* still intact. In the end the two signalmen had reassured her completely with their genuine belief in the superb seaworthiness of whalers, while they brewed her several pots of tea and fed her with English biscuits. When night fell,she had gone back happily to her hotel.

At sunrise we saw that the black storm-cone on the signals mast had been lowered, for the swell had gone down considerably in the night. Moreover all the jaundice of the cyclone had spun away from Port Natal and vanished from the sky in the east where the air was blue, fresh and innocent. We made our run for the harbour, Gorgeous timing his approach perfectly, taking us in dead on centre of the channel. By nine we were docked at the quay to see the anxious owner's representative, warned of our approach by the signals station, and also the Port Captain, watching our mooring operations. The gangplank was hardly ashore before they were on it and crossing on board. 'Papa' bosun, with Leif to interpret for him, was there to receive them while I stood well away on the far side of the deck. I could not hear what was said but it was not much and they went below to the saloon almost immediately.

They had not been there long before Leif reappeared, called me to him and said: "You're wanted, Pete."

There was a warning note in his voice, though I couldn't imagine why. But I had never been able to find any reason in Andrew Watson's attitude to me.

I found the Port Captain installed at the head of the table, Watson at his side, then 'Papa' bosun, and a place opposite them left for Leif and myself.

"This is the boy I told you about," Watson, without looking at me, told the Port Captain as I sat down.

I had then my first good look at the Port Captain. His name was Harry England and he looked to me as English as de la

Buschagne had looked a Boer. He was not tall but very broad-shouldered, had thick fair hair going grey at the temples, a pleasant long face with a somewhat determined jaw, firm mouth, very blue eyes, observant and quick, and a pair of thick bushy brows above them. His face was both red and deeply tanned by wind and sun. He carried three rows of war ribbons on his navy-blue jacket, among which were the D.S.O., D.S.C. and Croix-de-Guerre. The buttons of his uniform shone like gold, his starched collar was without a blemish and everything about him suggested that he was a fastidious, frank and immensely experienced person.

He looked me straight in the eye and said: "I understand you were aloft in the fore-top when this tragedy occurred, and therefore best placed to see what happened. Could you please tell us in sequence how you saw it from beginning?"

I told them my story, from the moment when I had been told by Thor Larsen to ignore any other blows except those of a sperm right to the moment when de la Buschagne made the fatal mistake of turning his back on the sea and both he and the Captain were lost overboard.

He didn't interrupt me or ask any questions. At the end he merely turned to Watson to say: "Well, I think that's all plain sailing. I've nothing to ask. This young man has told his story extremely well to my way of thinking, but perhaps you—"

"Yes, I have," the man interrupted brusquely as he looked at me for the first time. If anything he seemed to dislike me more than ever.

"You say," he told me, "that you had never seen so wild and dangerous a sea as you were heading for?"

"Yes, sir," I answered, "But—" I intended to add that I was a relatively inexperienced sailor.

"Yes or no will do from you," he snapped.

I saw the Port Captain's bushy eyebrows rise with surprise and his frank blue eyes focused sharply on my questioner's face as if he were seeing the prosperous, popular whaler-owner's representative in a new light.

"When you spotted the sperm whale, could anyone else below

have done so as well?" Watson continued, as aggressive in tone as ever.

"No, they couldn't, sir," I answered.

"Therefore, if you had not chosen to call attention to that blow, none need ever have been the wiser?"

I saw the Port Captain's face cloud with disapproval at the whole trend of the questions but he restrained himself and said nothing.

I began to protest. "But our Captain, sir, had—"

"I don't want any arguments from you. The fact is that if you had not been so irresponsible as to report this blow in conditions that you yourself have confessed you knew to be highly danger-ous, this tragedy would not have happened?"

I was spared answering him. Harry England, with the fairness which was perhaps the one great passion of an otherwise un-impassioned nature, became really angry. "I don't understand you or your question at all, sir," he said, his voice cool as it is in those who know how to use their anger legitimately and not to be used by it. "This young man was not in command of the ship. He was under orders, obeying orders, and merely doing his duty as he had to."

"Duty, my foot!" came the reply. "I've known this boy far longer than you have and he's always been irresponsible and a source of great trouble from the beginning."

"That's not true, sir," Leif had turned to the Port Captain and was speaking up quietly without apparent emotion. "He's been with us for four seasons now and never caused any trouble at all. On the contrary he has been one of the best, hardest-working and most liked members of this ship's crew. Our dead Captain trusted him as he did no one else."

"Well, the Captain did wrong to trust this fellow in the end, as he'll no doubt know by now," the owner's representative replied rather brutally with a cynical laugh. "Duty or no duty, this lad will never be allowed in any of this Company's ships again."

"And that," Harry England told him politely, "will be your Company's loss. But in any case this young man is not on trial. He has told us all he can and we can now go on to hear the rest. Thank you very much."

He not only held his hand out to me but got up and walked to the entrance with me, saying: "You've nothing to blame yourself for. You've done well. Remember always, taking and giving, giving and taking orders as you did that day at sea, is the lot of a man. Good luck to you."

I went on deck and, because my hours in the *Kurt Hansen* were now numbered, since I had decided long since that I would leave whaling for good, I thought I'd climb up to my beloved fore-top for one last look around.

It was a lovely morning. I could still hear the unusually loud swell on the breakwater beyond, but it was clearly diminishing because even as I watched I saw a line of signals being run up to the head of the tall mast on the bluff, giving a ship standing up over the horizon her order of permission to approach and enter. The lighthouse behind in the clear air was white and trembling, and the dark evergreen of Zululand was sparkling with sunfire. The water of the bay was a silver-smooth looking-glass made especially for the serene face of the madonna-blue sky. The smoke from scores of funnels and factory chimneys grew blue and tall like palms of a distant desert mirage in the tranquil air; on the heights beyond, the flowering trees and shrubs sparkled, shone and flickered as if all were eager, young and innocent, and death still only some far away event. I went over every detail of the scene as if looking on it all for the last time. At the same time I wondered how all this bright pageant of nature and human enterprise before me could show no sign that something had gone from it for ever and that it would never know our Captain and de la Buschagne again.

As I thought thus, I had an odd vision of a world of pale shadow and fierce sunlight in the burning bush beyond Fort Herald in the far interior of Africa. I saw Sway-Back, secure now against human betrayal, standing fast asleep and dreaming of the hunter who had renounced death as a means of mastering him even after the long, harsh decades spent on his spoor: and as he dreamed all the ghosts of Africa walked around him. At the same time the strange matter of luck recurred to me, suggesting that the answer to it lay somewhere in that vision of Sway-Back. Perhaps even the deaths of the Captain and his

friend, both tools and instruments of the tragic fate through which they had come together for an end to which they were born, could be called luck. And perhaps sometime, somewhere, despite all appearances against it, that luck could prove to have been good since it seemed to make the future whole?

I came out of this introspection which flashed like a shooting star through the darkness of my mind, to look at the heights above the harbour still leaping with morning fire. Never had I seen the blue over the interior of Africa stand up so high and wide, like an archangel with wings outstretched in welcome, beckoning me home from the sea. I heard human voices and, looking down, saw the owner's representative and the Port Captain below me saying goodbye to the *Kurt Hansen*'s crew and then going ashore and driving away in the former's large car.

I went down to the saloon, thinking I would now get my things together, say my goodbyes and close this chapter of my young life as quickly as possible before seeking out de la Buschagne's daughter.

Finding the saloon deserted, I could not resist sitting down at the table to give it all a last, long glance. Looking round it, my eye caught sight of Thor Larsen's game book on the bracket against the wall. I got up, took it out, and lay it open on the table in front of me. I read the last entries of the three great blue whales we had caught that week written carefully, painfully and yet also confidently, sprawling in Thor Larsen's thrusting harpooner's hand, the ink of the writing astonishingly fresh. I took up the dead Captain's pen and wrote something below his last entry. It is significant that suffering revives something so old and abiding that it compels thought into archaic forms. I wrote, "Killed perhaps the greatest bull sperm of the seas," and also added below it, "Here endeth the last and final chapter of the life of Thor Larsen, sea captain and great harpooner of whales."

I had hardly finished my writing when I heard 'Mlangeni's voice on deck. Perhaps we all need suffering before we can understand what creation suffers continuously and forever on behalf of life on earth. I could tell from the way 'Mlangeni's beautiful Zulu voice now came as it were from the pit of his

stomach, that out of his own experience he was wide open to the suffering of someone else.

" 'Nkosanana, Little Princess," he was saying gently, "prepare to string the beads."

I jumped up. De la Buschagne's daughter, her anxiety no longer to be endured since our ship had been signalled in at the main quay at nine and she had had as yet no sign of her father, had obviously come to find out the reason for it.

I rushed on deck. She was standing on the quay by the gangplank, not daring to set foot on it because of the way Thor Larsen had ordered her off that Sunday morning. She was looking at 'Mlangeni, not understanding his words but alarmed by his tone, her eyes dark and her beautiful face full of concern.

When she saw me, however, she smiled and called out gladly, "Ah, there you are, Cousin. I'm so glad. D'you think I could just have a word with father?"

"Come on board, little Cousin," I answered quietly.

The smile left her and looking puzzled she said hesitantly, "But Cousin, I can't. I'm not allowed—"

"Today you can, little Cousin," I interrupted her. "Please come on board."

She came up the gang-plank then with a look which I shall never forget. It was the look of a woman knowing that she is about to receive confirmation of what she has all along known and feared despite the reasons, arguments, logic and denials brought to bear against her.

When we were both seated alone in the saloon I told her, "Your father and my Captain are both dead."

She did not cry at once as I had expected. Perhaps she had known, foreseen and in a sense fore-suffered it all for far too long. Quietly she begged me to tell her all. Only when I came to the moment when her father, in his moment of triumph, had vanished overboard with my Captain, did she put her head between her arms and cry. I went on with my tale, and she stopped crying only when I told her how I had thrown her father's gun and ammunition into the sea that same night. Lifting her head she said: "I'm so glad, Cousin. That was right."

She cried a while longer before taking out a handkerchief to

wipe her eyes. Then she asked uncertainly, "I wonder what I should do now?"

I remember that the silence that followed her question was filled with the metal in the *Kurt Hansen* squeaking from the surge of the great swell outside, the loud call of the gulls and the warning wail of a ship siren signalling she was going full speed ahead down the main channel out to sea.

I answered, "You are coming with me."

She began to protest. "But, Cousin, how—" She stopped suddenly.

It was then that I was sensible of a conviction and an authority which can only come to us when we have encountered and experienced death in life, and out of that experience have realised that chance and circumstance which when they have us in their grip appear so haphazard, yet,when looked at through the focus of an end such as that of de la Buschagne and Thor Larsen, can be seen to have been working with amazing and mathematical precision. All the evidence of how fine a slide-rule and how great a sextant so-called chance had used was plain to me now in the hair-fine way that it had had navigated the lives of two people of such different races, origins, ages and calling as de la Buschagne and Thor Larsen, so as to bring them together to meet for their predestined end. I did not doubt that something of the same precision had brought de la Buschagne's daughter and myself together at that moment in the *Kurt Hansen*'s tiny saloon. This gave me courage to see through the fog and uncertainty of life which clouded me at that moment.

I took her hand in mine and asked, "How long will it take you to pack?"

"An hour at the most," she answered, too surprised to argue.

"Give it an hour and a half then, little Cousin," I told her firmly. "Then I'll call to take you home."